MORE PRAISE FOR COTTON SMITH!

BEHOLD A RED HORSE

"A fine read for a cold winter's evening."

—*Roundup Magazine*

"From his vivid descriptions of a prairie night, to his hoof-pounding action scenes, Cotton Smith captures the look and feel of the real West."

—Mike Blakely, Spur Award–winning author
of *Summer of Pearls*

PRAY FOR TEXAS

"Outstanding! A must read! Lively characters in an unforgettable setting. Cotton Smith is one of the best new authors out there."

—*ReadWest*

"Plenty of pulsating action for fans of the traditional Westerns, not to mention plot twists and a wonderful collection of characters."

—*Roundup Magazine*

"It is impossible to read *Pray For Texas* and not come away changed."

—Loren D. Estleman, Spur Award–winning author
of *Black Powder, White Smoke*

DARK TRAIL TO DODGE

"Hard-eyed characters and six-gun action. Smith knows cattle drives and cowboy lore."

—*Publishers Weekly*

"A wealth of realistic details that will have readers tasting trail grit in their morning coffee . . . [with] this well-crafted enjoyable Western."

—*Booklist*

"One of the Top 25 books of the American West."

—*ReadWest*

"An entertaining, believable and fast-paced tale."

—*Dallas Morning News*

BACK FROM THE DEAD

A haze of smoke blanketed the saloon, interrupted by gunfire from the rear, seeking the moving Bass Manko. Throughout the room, fourteen other men were huddled, or lying flat, hoping to avoid stray bullets. All except the same drunken, standing cowboy who was now a dirty statue against the far wall. He watched the two gunmen who had entered the saloon from the back door like they were part of some theatrical play. The bearded man held a Winchester; a new handgun was shoved into his waistband. The second gunman with a pockmarked face and stringy hair extending from a derby hat was half kneeling, trying to locate Bass.

Neither had any idea of where Cade Branson might be. The two gunmen assumed Gilmore had killed him and he was lying somewhere beyond the front corner of the bar where they couldn't see. Smugly, they were now after only one man.

Suddenly, from a new position—behind the bar— Cade stood and fired at the bearded cowboy, only twenty feet away. . . .

Other *Leisure* books by Cotton Smith:

SONS OF THUNDER
SPIRIT RIDER
BROTHERS OF THE GUN
BEHOLD A RED HORSE
PRAY FOR TEXAS
DARK TRAIL TO DODGE

COTTON SMITH

WINTER KILL

LEISURE BOOKS NEW YORK CITY

To Don D'Auria
and my friends at Dorchester Publishing.

LEISURE BOOKS ®

August 2004

Published by

Dorchester Publishing Co., Inc.
200 Madison Avenue
New York, NY 10016

ISBN 0-8439-5113-3

The name "Leisure Books" and the stylized "L" with design are trademarks of Dorchester Publishing Co., Inc.

Printed in the United States of America.

Visit us on the web at www.dorchesterpub.com.

WINTER KILL

Chapter One

"By God, I'm gonna hang Bass Manko. Nobody steals my beef an' gits away with it. Nobody." Titus Branson screamed into an autumn sun that could only belong to Texas.

His slump-shouldered frame was a bullwhip in the saddle, snapping back and forth in rage. The wide brim of the rancher's weather-weakened hat shivered with the ragged cough trailing his vehement outburst. He shifted the phlegm in his lungs and wheezed.

His horse's ears whipped back to determine if it were at fault for the outburst. With Titus Branson, it was always someone's fault. Except his.

Wincing visibly, his oldest son, John, had just reported he had sent three men to town after Bass Manko as his father had ordered. They were missing a hundred head that should have been in the northern pasture on the other side of the low ridge. The Bransons owned or claimed grazing range no one could ride across in one day. The Bar 6 was the region's biggest spread, by far. This was the first time since the early days anyone had tried to steal their beef.

Rustling was tearing at the lifeblood of some of the area's small ranches. They complained of losing great numbers of cattle. Three had already sold out and left. But nobody paid much attention to their whining. Their problems were chalked up to Mexican raiders from across the border—or bad management. Titus was certain it was the latter since the Bar 6 had experienced no losses other than natural ones—until now.

John's sweating horse was an indication of his urgency to deliver the news about carrying out his father's orders. A nervous twitch at his mouth anticipated his father's fault-finding reaction.

"Why didn't ya git him when ya had the chance? Where were ya, John, when I needed ya?" Deep wrinkles swarmed around Titus's narrowing eyes. He coughed again. Deeper this time. The back of his right hand half-heartedly covered his mouth.

"Sorry, Paw."

"Sorry don't git crap. How long ago did ya send 'em?"

"W-Well, right after you told me to. Hour, maybe." John looked up at the sun to gauge the time passage. "Could be an hour an' a half."

"Who'd ya send?"

"Pete . . . an' Moss . . . an'—"

"Did ya send Gilmore, like I tolt ya?" Titus leaned forward in the saddle. His hard face was reddened by too much sun, whiskey and hate.

"Yes." John blinked away his guilt at sending the huge ruffian, known in the region for his brawling. Ed Gilmore, one of their riders, had killed two men in fistfights and maimed another for life. But, for the most part, he had been a dependable hand and was loyal to Titus Branson to a fault.

For the first time, Titus smiled. "Good. Big Ed'll handle that grinny sonvabitch. Prob'ly a'fer we git thar." He rubbed his chest to rid it of his swelling hatred. "Bet he were right happy to do it, weren't he?" He rubbed his unshaven chin. "Did ya tell him I wanted 'nuff left to hang?"

"Yes, Paw."

Beside the freshly liquored, unshaven cattleman Titus's middle son, Dish, laughed wickedly, loud and guttural. He licked his always-chapped and split lips and shook his head. Finally, he would get rid of his rival for Susannah Harding's favor. Dish Branson favored his hard-nosed father in temperament but his rugged face looked like left-over family pieces had been shoved together, giving him a lantern jaw and small beady eyes. But thinking alike was enough to make Dish the favorite son. Rarely did Titus criticize him anymore since Dish told him off four years ago, in no uncertain terms. Titus loved it.

Of course, the youngest son, Cade, never paid any attention to what his father said, good or bad, and hadn't since he was old enough to understand.

He rode toward them from the other direction. He wore a patched long coat over an old shirt, a gray woolen vest and a faded kerchief tied loosely around his neck. His once-white hat with the wide brim curled up in front was pushed down on his forehead, a leather string tie-down knotted and dangling below his chin. The eagle feather, attached to the brim tie and popping in the breeze, gave him the look of a Comanche warrior coming from the reservation.

Like most days, Cade was the only Branson wearing a handgun. Dish and Titus rode with only saddle rifles; John carried no weapon. Cade, though, loved the feel of a pistol in his fist. It was Dish who had first showed him how to use one when Cade was seven. The only man in the region who could handle a pistol better was Bass Manko.

The gun was part of him, carried in a tilted holster, near the left side of his belt buckle. Handle forward for a border draw across his body with a leather tie-down thong holding the hammer in place until the gun was needed. It was no cowman's pistol for shooting rattlesnakes or a runaway horse. Cade's Smith & Wesson revolver had a cutaway-front trigger guard for speed and the sight had been filed off for a faster release from his holster. It was a gunfighter's weapon and his reputation with it was already known.

There was the widely repeated story of him coming up alone on three drifters trying to steal family cattle. It was the only documented attempt at rustling in the last three years. His killing one and wounding the other two was becoming the stuff of legend in the region. However, he refused to let his father hang them, insisting on taking the two would-be rustlers to the town marshal. Dish and his father were about the only people who never spoke of the courageous act. Even John liked to tell it.

Ignoring the advance of his youngest son, Titus pointed at his oldest, the most frequent target of verbal abuse and the only one who would accept it. "Dammit, John, every time you're in charge out hyar somethin' bad happens. Two years back, ya let that wind whip 'em into a stampede and we had to chase 'em fer miles. Lost ten head that day." His lungs stormed into another prolonged round of hacking and gasping, leaving blood on his lips.

"Now, ya up an' lose a hun'nert. Damn, boy, what were ya thinkin'?"

"What's going on? We all set for cow gatherin'?" Cade asked, reining alongside his father and two older brothers.

Silently, the other three Bransons admired the smooth way he handled the green horse, a barely broken buckskin.

Dish grinned but the smile didn't reach his eyes. "Bass Manko dun ran off some of our beef. We're gonna git the bastard an' hang 'im. He's prob'ly bin doin' all the rustlin' 'round hyar."

"There's no way Bass did that—or any rustling," Cade responded in a flat, but firm, voice, shoving his chin forward to reinforce his statement. "You know it as well as I do, Dish." The youngest of the Branson brothers, and the most defiant, squinted to hold back some of the late-afternoon Texas sun. "So do you, Paw. Instead of blaming somebody, why don't we track where they went? That'll tell us what really happened. Let's start the damn roundup now and get it over with. We can bring up the chuck wagon tomorrow like we planned and let the other ranchers join us whenever."

If Titus Branson heard, it didn't appear so. He was busy pulling a small flask from his pocket under his trail-worn chaps, coughing several times to clear his throat. Snorting his rejection of Cade's response, Dish swung the other way to look at his older brother, John.

"Answer yur li'l brother, John. Put 'im in his place. Paw's too drunk for windyin'." As he spoke, he silently noted he was far enough away to avoid Cade's fist.

John Branson's tense shoulders rose and fell, followed by a twitch at the corner of his mouth. He pushed his curl-brimmed hat back on his head and laid his tanned hands on top of the saddle horn.

"Well, Cade, I saw a rider who looked a lot like Bass near there this morning," John finally said, shrugging his shoulders. Self-consciously, he pointed in the direction of the far ridge. "When I rode over there later, all those cows were gone."

"What do you mean 'looked a lot like Bass'?"

"Well, he was wearing a black hat and riding a fancy black horse."

"How close were you?"

"I was clearing that ridge. He was down in the pasture. With the cattle."

"So you see a rider half a mile away—with a black hat and a black horse—and you're going to hang a man for that?" Cade's gaze cut into John's face. "What kind of nonsense is that? Don't we have enough work to do without going off on some fool's errand?"

"Well, that's a good question." John rubbed his mouth and eyes to erase Cade's intensity. "What do you think, Paw?" The corner of John's mouth twitched again. "I guess it could've been somebody else. I didn't really see Bass's face. It was Dish who—"

"Didn't ya heard me the first time, boy? Gawd-dammit, listen. I said we're ridin' to town an' hangin' that sorry-assed bastard. He kin steal other folks' beef—but not our'n." Titus took a long swig from the flask and shoved it back into his pants pocket. His swallow of the biting liquid brought out gritted yellow teeth and a grunt of satisfaction. Razor-thin eyebrows bubbled upward against his protruding forehead.

His wife's death years back, combined with years of whiskey, had shriveled Titus Branson into a bitter man. Consumption was accelerating his physical leanness as well. But there was nothing new about his cruelty. Everything that went wrong had to be dragged out, every detail examined and blamed on someone. The next time he thought of a past mistake, the same process would occur. Over and over. Of course, in his mind nothing that went wrong was ever his fault. Ever.

If it was his mistake, his twisted mind would blame someone or something for him having to do what he did. He firmly believed his large ranch would have been even larger but so many things had always been lined up against him. Now, fall roundup was only days away. A time to brand and count and ready the herd for winter. A time to complain once more about what could have been.

"Damn, what is it about ya, John?" Titus continued, yanking down the front brim of his worried Stetson, more concerned for the moment about his oldest son's behavior than answering the challenge of his youngest son or even going after Bass Manko. "I remember the time ya let the chuck wagon catch on fire. An' when ya was eight, ya rode that good mare an' she came up lame. Damn, boy, can't ya do nothin' right?"

He could recall any mistake, any wrongdoing, any imagined slight ever made that affected him and rattle them off like a recipe whenever he wanted to make a point, especially to his family. And his oldest son, John Titus Branson, usually got the brunt of it. John had learned it didn't help to argue. That just made things worse. Nothing was ever forgiven or forgotten when it came to Titus Branson. Nothing.

"Ya never 'member to put grease in the buckets neither. It's a wonder we got any wagons that can move at all. Heaven help ya, boy, when I'm gone. Thar'll be no one to ke'p ya from destroyin' ever'thin'." Titus's endless complaining was like the wind to Dish and Cade, but to John it was God declaring him unworthy. "I suppose you dun forgot to bring a brandin' iron too. Did ya? Answer me."

"I-I didn't think we'd be doing any branding until day after tomorrow. That's what you said."

"Oh, that's fine. Real goddamn fine. What if we dun come across'd some young'uns that need iron now? Huh?"

Cade had heard enough. "If we do, I'll ride back and get

the damn thing while John ropes it. But that's about as likely as snow this afternoon. The cows are way back in the brush. That's why they call it a roundup." His voice was a knife. "But at least it makes more sense than chasing after Bass for something he didn't do."

Titus swung in his saddle toward Cade and was surprised at the look he received. He couldn't figure this son out. Cade didn't even look like him; he looked like his mother, Titus's late wife—but like she had been with someone else. That couldn't be. Not Martha Ann. Even if she did hate him. God bless her soul.

"I'll jes' keep that in mind, Cade." It was supposed to sound tough but there was a faint sense of uncertainty at how his words would be accepted.

"You do that."

Cade's glare made the older man turn away, coughing.

Like his mother, Cade was inclined to take sides with those who needed it the most. The odds never mattered. Both were easy to misread because of it. Stray dogs were always in the house, to Titus's constant dislike. Around the county, Dish was thought to be the toughest but anyone who had seen Cade in action questioned that claim. Both had broken noses, a result of the other's fist. No one could remember seeing John in a brawl of any kind.

If Dish was summer thunder, Cade was winter lightning—and John was a spring mist that couldn't make up its mind whether to rain or not. It was Cade Branson, not Dish, who had won last year's county bare-knuckle championship. Dish hadn't entered; he was too busy working cattle. Or so he said.

A stray breeze tried to alert everyone that autumn was coming. But the season was already known and its tasks well understood. Soon the Bransons and their riders—in unison with cowboys from the region's other ranches—would be pushing reluctant cattle out of the brush, ravines and over hills for branding and sorting, before winter took control. Across the plains, small fires would soon dot the land, along with an occasional chuck wagon, as sweating men from the various ranches held hot iron to any animals, young or old, missed during the spring gathering or which were late-born, and castrated the young bull calves.

Herds were separated for next spring's trail drives and by brand. A joint gathering was less costly in men and supplies. Made sorting the various animals by their correct brand easier too. Titus Branson liked the idea of all the ranches being together because he was suspicious of everyone—even in the years when there were no indications of rustling from his herds. In the last year, most of the smaller ranches had been crying about losing cattle to rustlers but the Bar 6 hadn't had any problem. That's all that mattered to Titus. He didn't care that three ranches had been sold to new owners either. He hadn't met any of them and didn't care to. That was Dish's responsibility. Right now he blamed John for not being diligent enough and told him he should have had Cade involved. That was as close as he would get to recognizing Cade's courageous stand against cow thieves.

Under Cade's hat with the front brim pushed up against the crown, a tanned angular face rarely gave away any emotion—a chiseled face that was easy to look at, unlike Dish's. A tiny band of freckles had yet to disappear from his Roman nose, making him appear somewhat boyish. Intense blue eyes cut through to a man's soul but rarely let anyone see inside him.

His casual voice belied his tenseness. "You know, our herds are really spread out this year. There's no tellin' where those lost beeves are—until we start cuttin' brush." Cade made a zig-zag motion with his right hand.

With dark hair brushing against his hard shoulders, Cade definitely favored their mother in looks and attitude. Yet there was a glimpse of something, or someone else, there too. Dish used to tease his brother that he was actually an Indian and the family had adopted him.

"They wouldn't have gone that far in less than a day, Cade. Not by themselves. There's plenty of grass and water," John said dismounting and glancing at Cade, then Titus. Laying the stirrup fender over the saddle seat, he began to tighten his cinch. Fiddling with his horse's tack was a frequent task for him. He was always reminding his brothers of the need to recognize that their horses lost weight when ridden hard. Both were annoyed by his reminders; both could ride rings around him on a poor day.

"It's a hangin' we're goin' to, Cade, then we'll start the roundup. Ya gonna bring the rope, little brother?" Dish leered at his brother and wiped his mouth with his shirt sleeve. "Or do ya wanna use mine? Course you couldn't catch Bass wi' a rope if he were a'sittin' in our kitchen." He snorted a laugh. Everyone knew Dish was the best roper around and Cade was one of the worst.

Titus's snarl became a chuckle, then a cough. "You should kick his ass fer sayin' that, Cade."

Chapter Two

"I've already done that."

Cade's words slapped the air hard. Dish's tongue walked across his dry lips; he tried to laugh but it came out more of a choking sound. Parched saddle leather creaked like it needed soaping and a circle of dust flittered from his batwing chaps as he shifted his weight to face his younger brother. His gaze flitted toward the gun on Cade's hip, then bounced away like it was hot.

"Ya wanna try kickin' my ass—right now?" Dish snarled.

He was two inches taller and thirty pounds heavier than Cade. Dish Branson was difficult to deny, always pushing, always after whatever he wanted. Confidence gained from rarely being stopped from achieving his objective, whatever it was, made him even meaner. His eyes met Cade's and the mental assault began. But there was something else in Dish's eyes. Respect. Or was it fear?

From their physical appearance, no one seeing Dish and Cade for the first time would guess they were brothers. Yet both had the same fierce glint in their eyes and the same up-turned corner of their mouths, like they had a private joke on the world. They were the sons of a cruel cattleman who cursed everyone and everything for his problems and an intense, caring mother who had often talked to herself and held her dreams close to her heart. Many who knew the couple figured she died young having to put up with Titus Branson.

"Gawd-dammit, boys, save sum o' that fer Bass Manko," Titus commanded, but it was clear he enjoyed watching his boys fight, especially if he thought Dish would win.

His late wife's favorite son had been Cade and everyone knew it. Even Titus. And that made his affinity toward Dish even stronger. Because of her insistence, Cade spoke Spanish, and even passable Comanche. Titus thought it was a terrible waste of time to learn "Injun." Almost sinful. Most of them were locked up on reservations. Neither his wife nor his youngest son had paid any attention.

Dish's real name was "Richard." His father shortened it to "Dick" as a baby, Cade pronounced it "Dish" and that stuck. The two brothers had never been close, though. When they were young, Dish enjoyed beating on Cade whenever he got the chance. It always aggravated Dish that his younger brother never showed any emotion or attempted to fight back no matter how vicious the attacks were. John tried to keep them separated on those occasions but was rarely successful. Dish always found a way to get around him and beat on Cade mercilessly.

Until one day. Cade was fourteen, Dish, seventeen. No one in the Branson family ever forgot that day—or talked about it around either son. Dish Branson came home with a broken nose, cracked ribs and a badly bruised face. The only thing he said was, "Cade did it." It was the last time the older brother attempted to fight his younger sibling.

"Come on, Dish . . . Cade. Please," John said as he stepped back into the saddle. His face was a frown. It was as close as he could come to challenging his father's wishes, implied or otherwise. His legs stutterstepped in the stirrups.

Definitely, John was the brother who didn't quite fit with the other two. He had inherited his mother's soft face and gentleness but Cade had her distinctive looks and intensity. Yet both had their mother's smooth tan complexion; Dish was ruddy like his father. But John's tall whip frame was a mirror of his father's and of Dish's. So the difference wasn't physical at all; it was his tentative manner that made him seem like an outsider. Simply enough, he was wound tighter than a bandage around cracked ribs from being a cruel father's first son.

"Sure, sure. I was jes' jawin' on 'im a little," Dish said but his glare told Cade he meant every word of it. "We kin settle this later, if needs be. Ri't now, we got us a hangin' to tend to. That thar's a hangin' wind I feel." He chuckled.

He glared at his younger brother but only long enough to realize Cade's intensity was more than he wanted.

"You wouldn't be saying something like that if Maw was alive," Cade said.

"Come on, we're still doin' stupid stuff that Maw wanted, like leavin' our boots out on the porch," Dish said, rubbing his coarse fingers along the top of his lariat tied next to the saddlehorn. "She's gone now. So we don't need to be a'doin' sech."

Cade's eyes flashed and sought Dish's but the older Branson was studying his lariat. "No. We will keep leavin' our boots on the porch, like she asked. It's a nice tribute to her memory. An' it keeps dirt out of the house. That's why she had us do it."

"I'll walk through the house with mud a'trailin' me, if 'n I please." Dish looked up.

"You'll do it once."

John stopped the growing agitation between his two brothers with a question. "Dish, when you get a chance, take a look at the chuck wagon—in case we're missing something. Ah, you too, Cade."

Before Dish could respond, Titus coughed disappointment that his oldest son hadn't already had the wagon's contents checked, then rattled off a string of things that should be there. "Do ya got rope, guns, tobaccy? How 'bout lanterns and kerosene? Yah got baking soda . . . eh vinegar, lard, matches, calomel? How 'bout them stake ropes for the horse string?" His list was exhausting, as he asked about bandages, needles, axle grease, salt, lard, castor oil, baskets of grain for the horses, cooking equipment, cans of tomatoes, peaches, branding irons, kindling, salted pork, sacks of beans, sour dough and sugar.

When he stopped to cough, John acknowledged all those things were there.

"Well, what 'bout an extry wheel in case we break one?" Titus asked with a glint in his eyes.

"No, sir, I didn't bring one."

Dish laughed. "Hell, if we break a wheel, we can go git one at the ranch. Forgit it, Paw. Ain't nobody more thorough than John. He's probably got us a gal or two in the wagon to keep us warm at night." Dish laughed at his joke.

John frowned. "Oh, I wouldn't do anything like that, Dish."

"I were kiddin', John."

"Oh."

Changing the subject, Cade patted the neck of his horse without lowering his gaze. "Seems to me it would make more sense to ride over where John thinks we lost our beef and take a look-see, instead of windying about what is or isn't in that damn wagon." He cocked his head and glared at his father. "Chances are we'll find 'em if we spread out and look hard enough." Usually it was hard to read what was going on in Cade's mind but not now.

Dish flinched, started to say something, thought better of it, and swallowed. His hard eyes drifted toward the Comanche warrior choker around Cade's neck. "I see yur still wearin' that Injun magic thing Maw dun gave ya. When are ya gonna take that off, anyway? You're a white man, ain't ya? Or do ya figger yellin' a little Comanch' at our beeves will git 'em rounded up?" Dish glanced at Titus, who was watching a calf wander toward them.

Twenty feet away, the young animal's mother eyed the foursome suspiciously. When Titus saw the cow wore Emmett Johnson's brand, he swore and waved his coiled lariat at the calf to make it run back. He grunted his satisfaction but another outburst of coughing cut it short.

Cade's first response to his brother's teasing was to touch the necklace at his neck, a gift from his mother on his fourteenth birthday. At that time, she told him it had belonged to her father and was, indeed, Comanche. Rows of small elk bone were carved with symbols of winter and highlighted with white, light-blue and silver beads—a design no one had ever seen before. Martha Ann Branson said it had been handmade by her uncle who once lived with the Indians. She told him to wear it proudly. Unlike the wall built between himself and his father, Cade could never resist any request she made of him. He had never taken it off, nor forgotten his last promise to her a few years later. It was a secret he didn't discuss with anyone. Not even his best friend, Bass Manko.

His second response was in Comanche. *"Keta nu kuya a-ku-tu."*

"Whad'd ya say? Dammit, are ya swearin' at me? Ya better not be swearin' at me in Injun. Or is that Mex?" Dish's face matched the crimson of his father's.

"I said . . . 'don't be afraid of me' in Comanche. I am your brother, remember?"

"Don' be . . . what the hell? I ain't afraid o' you, you little sonvabitch." Dish swung wildly at Cade, who didn't move but said something else in Comanche and smiled.

"Hell, quit all that pawin' and bellerin' and let's git ta goin'. We kin ride down thar on the way to town," Titus growled and spurred his horse. The three brothers didn't catch up for twenty yards.

The four horsemen galloped across a green Texas valley blossoming with a lake of brown cattle and clusters of blue and white wildflowers that didn't realize summer was over. Rolling hills held the pasture in place with the help of a fat stream. Sentries of blackjack, post oak and juniper were hunkered in groups beside the precious water as far as the eye could see.

None of the Branson men spoke as they rode, each wandering to a private place in his thoughts. John was trying to decide if he should tell Cade that three of their men were already headed for town to find and hold Bass Manko until they got there. He decided it wasn't his authority to do so. It was his father's. Still, it bothered him that Cade didn't know. Bass Manko was his best friend.

Seeing this part of the waterway was an ever-festering boil for Titus. The major part of the stream—where it widened to the east—was on range that had been controlled by another rancher, Tobias Rice. Now his widow owned it. A snarl wandered across Titus's mouth; he had misread its importance years before. He blamed his late wife for not letting him take that land for his own, before Rice did. He hated him for it. His Bar 6 ranch could easily be twice as big if they controlled that much water.

Dish slapped the reins against his horse's flank to make it keep pace with Cade's dappled gray horse and to give action to the eagerness he felt. No one knew he had paid a cowhand from the Half-Moon 5, a small ranch to the south, to move those hundred cattle to a watering hole that was actually part of Rice's grazing land. He was paid extra to ride a black horse and wear a black hat. Just like Bass Manko. Dish told him it was a joke he was playing on his brothers. He grinned again and told himself that the wild man deserved to hang; he was probably guilty of all kinds of crimes in the area.

After all, Bass was a whore's son; no one knew who his father was although there were a number of good possibilities, including Titus Branson. She had died when Bass was twelve and he blamed the town for it. His quickness with a gun earned him occasional jobs with ranchers wanting to keep rustlers away. Most of the time, though, he made a few dollars singing in saloons. His clear voice and fine guitar strumming were a popular favorite in the region.

Cade was often with him, leaving John and Dish to help their father with ranch chores. Dish bristled when he thought of it. How would his young brother react when he learned Big Ed Gilmore and two other Bar 6 hands would be grabbing Bass before they even got close to town? Dish thought the longer this news was kept from Cade the better. It would make it easier for Cade to understand this was a family matter. It would also be sweet to watch Cade's reaction when he told him. Too late to save his friend.

Locked-away heat passed through Dish's body as his mind released the memory of catching Bass with Susannah behind her folks' horse barn when they were kids. He had nearly killed Bass with his fists; only Susannah's pleading stopped him. That and a timely attack by Cade who happened to hear the scuffle and rode in to see what was happening. Dish often wondered why his brother was there but never asked. He could still see her standing there, sunlight caressing her tearful face, as she held her unbuttoned blouse together. Dish grinned as he recognized today as the last day he would have to worry about Susannah Harding caring about Bass Manko.

Cade's mind was whirling with the need to find the cattle. Surely his friend wouldn't do such a thing. Bass was wild, yes, but not crazy—and he wouldn't do anything like this. John was wrong, that was all. Cattle could drift anywhere and usually did. In the corner of his thoughts, he couldn't help wondering if Dish had something to do with this whole thing.

Although he and Dish were usually clashing over something, they all three did share one thing in common—or had, at least. Susannah Harding, Marshal Emmett Harding's daughter. Titus would probably burst into pieces if he knew. Even now, she lay on Cade's mind like an eternal rose petal. Dish didn't know of his brother's feelings or it would have triggered a massive fight for certain. After all, Dish had loved her since the first day she attended the one-room school and just knew they would be married some day. She was three years younger, like Cade and Bass Manko. Of course, every boy in the county was in love with her back then. She had a teasing smile that would make the toughest boy weak and tongue-tied. Later on, God gave her a body that was a tease all by itself.

Dish had already asked her to marry him six times and each time she refused. As far as Cade knew, his brother never realized he had a thing for her once, too. It never went beyond a few kisses. When Cade found out his best friend, Bass Manko, really loved her, that was enough to stop seeing her. Dish's obsession for her had nothing to do with it. In most cases, if Dish wanted something, that would have been just the reason Cade needed to go after it.

Skirting across a line of lumpy hills, they headed for the ridge that masked their northern pasture. A proud Texas sun pulled simmering heat waves from the earth to create blurred silhouettes against the horizon. Overhead a red hawk watched them, sailing on the unseen billows of heat. Like a song, the hooves of their horses made soft pushing sounds in the long grass, interrupted by loud clacks on the sun-baked red clay, then back to soft patters, as the ground changed back and forth beneath them.

Immediately ahead was a defiant ridge of gray rock, topped with dried-out buffalo grass and a forlorn bush with three scraggily branches. A gray-brown jewel atop a long finger of raised land, stretching out and linking with a sea of green in the distance. The land in this part of Texas seemed to split itself between dark hills, brown prairie and rich grazing land. They cleared the top of the ridge and John pointed in the direction of a flat open spoon of pasture. It was empty except for three slow-moving steers. He said something none of the others could make out but they assumed this was where the cattle should have been.

Without waiting, Cade kicked his gray, heading straight down the incline and quickly disappearing among the line of trees holding the far side of the pasture in place. Dish watched him go and rubbed his nose without thinking about it. Cade had broken it a few years ago and severely beaten him. That was the first time Dish could recall Cade ever really hitting him. Dish hoped it was the last. He had never seen anyone so fierce in his life.

At one point in the fight, Dish had tried to pull off Cade's choker necklace and that had ignited something inside Cade beyond reason. It was the day Dish knew he could no longer fight his younger brother and win. More than that, he now actually feared his younger brother and hated himself—and his brother—for the weakness. When he told Cade about Gilmore and the others, Dish figured he should not be too close.

John followed his youngest brother, looking back at Titus and Dish, who showed no inclination to search the trees. John reined his horse to a stop at the base of the ridge. He would wait too. After fifteen minutes, Cade reappeared and loped toward the three Bransons, waiting impatiently at the base of the hill line.

"Looks to me like someone drove a bunch toward the Rice's." Cade reported. "Maybe I'll have a look over that way."

Dish gritted his teeth and patted the Winchester stock protruding from its saddle sheath under his right leg. "No. We bin foolin' around long enough. Bass is usually in the Four Aces this time o' the day, ain't he, Cade? Singin' songs an' the like. We'll find 'im thar."

"Are you going to tell Marshal Harding about this?" Cade asked.

"Why in the hell would we bother talkin' to that broken-down tin star?" Dish fumed. "He ain't worth nuthin' but lockin' up drunks—an' too old to do a good job o' that. What do ya want from that ol' Welshman?"

"Justice."

"Justice, my ass. The only justice for Bass Manko is the end of a rope."

"I won't let you do that." Cade's response was hard.

"What the hell ya mean ya won't?" Titus Branson snarled at his youngest son, swinging in the saddle toward Cade. Titus's whiskey-flamed face was dark crimson. A string of phlegm-laced coughs followed and he squeezed his eyes shut to stop the pain.

"Paw, ya know Cade an' Bass are buddies. They's always doin' somethin'—while me an' John are workin'."

Shaking away the spell, Titus's red eyes sought his youngest son's. "T-This hyar's about blood, Cade. I want ya with us. I want ya pullin' on that rope." Titus's voice was as soft as any of the three brothers could remember. "Are ya denyin' your paw?"

Cade stared back. Only the slightest twinge of his upper lip gave away the anger building within him. Dish grinned and wiped his mouth with his hand. No one spoke and the earth came closer to watch. John took a deep breath and said quietly, "Come along, Cade. I know it hurts but it's something that has to be done."

Cade glanced at his older brother and, for an instant, pitied him. It was as if he had never seen John before. What a sad excuse for a man he had become and it was all their father's fault.

"Hell, by the time we git thar, Gilmore an' the boys'll have 'im drawn an' quartered, anyways." Dish watched his younger brother as he presented this new aspect of the situation. He gauged the distance between them and was satisfied. "John sent 'em towards town . . . an hour back. Why do ya think we ain't bin in no hurry?"

"Longer ago than that, I think," John added, solemnly. "Probably more like two."

"What? You sent Gilmore? What the hell were you thinking?" The words spurted out as Cade kicked his horse into a gallop. "Go to hell, all of you."

Stunned, the three Bransons watched him ride away. Titus Branson reached for his rifle and dragged it from the sheath. Dish frowned and John mouthed, "No." As Titus levered and brought the gun to his shoulder, Dish pulled the rifle down so the bullet exploded into the earth near Titus's horse's front hooves. All three animals jumped. Titus's horse reared and threw him. John's horse spun in a circle. Only Dish kept his horse from doing anything more than prancing a little. In his hands was his own Winchester, levered and ready.

From the ground, Titus Branson shook his head to clear it from the jolt and the whiskey rattling in his brain. His hand went for the rifle laying a few feet from him.

"How you figger on usin' that?" Dish's question jarred like a fist. "Ya gonna try usin' it on me now?" His rifle was pointed at his father's chest.

"Whatcha doin', aimin' that thing at me fer?" Titus looked up at Dish and coughed, his hand frozen halfway toward the gun. Blood settled in the corner of his mouth.

Glancing toward the disappearing Cade, Dish eased his rifle into a cradled position within his arms and returned his attention to his father. Brushing himself off, Titus was now standing. "Might've cracked my ribs, dammit, Dish. Why'd ya do that?" He erupted into a wracking expulsion of mucus.

"Reckon I didn't like the idee o' a father shootin' his son," Dish said, letting what passed for a grin return to his face. "Heard tell o' that durin' the War." He licked his lips to refresh them.

"Oh, I wasn't gonna shoot 'em. Jes' let 'em know I was mad."

"He knows. Let him go, Paw. He'll be back," Dish said, surprising himself at his leniency. In his heart he knew the real reason was he didn't want anything to get in the way of hanging Bass Manko. He could almost see Susannah rushing into his arms.

"Wal, are you two gonna quit on me too?" Titus growled. He hadn't moved toward his fallen rifle, however.

John quickly responded, "No, sir, we're ready." His entire body jerked with the emotion.

"Wal, ya ain't too ready. Ya ain't carryin' nuthin' to shoot with." Titus shook his head in disgust. "Ya figger Bass is gonna sur-render to a purty please?"

"My Winchester's in the chuck wagon. At the ranch."

"Dammit, boy, don't ya beat all."

Dish laughed again. "Come on. We don' want Gilmore to have all the fun. We'll git John's gun an' head on in. I'll bet Manko's bin a'rustlin' our beef for a long time. We dun lost fifty head last fall, remember?"

In the back of his mind, he wondered if Cade would try to find his friend and warn him. He shook his head to rid himself of the thought. Surely, his brother wouldn't do anything so foolish. Dish knew Cade and Bass were friends but this was a family matter. The youngest Branson had made it clear he wasn't interested in being a rancher. Once he talked about becoming a gun store clerk and once, a lawyer. It seemed to Dish that Cade went out of his way to flaunt his dislike of their father and he hated him even more for it. In his heart, Dish knew he was his father's favored son and had quietly decided to live up to the responsibility.

With his rifle in his hand, Titus's response was to spur his horse. Dish passed him, laughing. John faithfully eased his horse alongside his father. He seemed to be the only son who realized their parent was dying and was greatly saddened by the recognition. Should he say something to his father? Should he try to comfort him? Titus glanced over with reddened eyes filled with vile and spittle slipping from the edge of his curled mouth. John lost his nerve and watched Dish whip his horse toward their ranch. How he wished he were more like Dish—or Cade.

Chapter Three

" 'Well I had myself a dream the other night,
When everything was still.
I dreamed that I saw my girl Susannah,
She was coming around the hill.
Now, the buckwheat cake was in her mouth,
A tear was in her eye.
I said, that I came from Dixie land,
Susannah, don't you break down and cry.
I said, Oh Susannah,
Now don't you cry for me.
'Cause I came from Alabama with my banjo on my
knee.' "

Bass Manko's blond hair brushed against his shoulders as
he raised his head to reinforce the end of the song. His fingers strummed chords of conclusion. The dingy saloon was
half-filled. Men's conversations made a garbled, yet pleas-

ant, sound mixed with a little applause and one loud request to sing it again.

He liked the sensations of a good saloon; they made him feel alive. It was time for a break and a free whiskey—a perk of the job. After his drink, he would move to a table before returning to his singing and order a steak, or whatever the cook in the back was offering. Bass's face was dominated by large fawn eyes and an ability to smile as he talked.

Happy-go-lucky, he met every morning like it was a long-lost relative. And likely as not, a song would pop from his smiling mouth. More than one woman had succumbed to his confident, easy-going manner. Or was it those wonderful eyes? Or that seductive voice when he sang? Including Susannah Harding.

He stood and laid his guitar on the chair scooted into the corner of the room. A black, wide-brimmed hat that had long ago given up any resemblance to shape lay on the floor near the chair. Ignoring the hat, he adjusted the black gun-belt, lined with silver studs. A matching holster held a silver-plated, ivory-handled pistol, butt forward. He walked easily toward the bar. His large-roweled Mexican spurs talked as he moved and the wide-bottomed Spanish pants swayed to the rhythm. Black leather cuffs, also lined with studs, were worn over the loose-fitting sleeves of his blue bib shirt.

He was two inches taller and twenty pounds heavier than his best friend, Cade Branson. But no one who knew them would bet against the Branson brother in a fist fight. A gunfight would be a different matter altogether. Actually, their friendship had grown from a fight after school. Dish Branson had interfered, stepping in to beat up the younger Manko but Cade wouldn't let him. That act spawned a closeness that carried the two young men through every manner of adventure and escapade. Although their appearances were quite different, both were athletic and quick.

Bass eased next to the long, uneven bar and waited for the disinterested bartender to bring him a glass of whiskey—from the good bottle kept underneath. Saloon owner's orders. Hot liquid bit at his throat and he swallowed to ease the sting.

A man in a three-piece suit slid beside him. "I'd sure like to hear *I'll Take You Home Again, Kathleen*. No hurry, of course. Finish your drink. Here, let me buy you one."

"You know, that's one of my favorites too. I'll sure do it."

"Thanks, Bass, I appreciate that," the man said, leaving a gold coin by Bass's elbow and returning to the table where he was playing poker. "It's also my lucky song."

Chuckling, Bass pushed the coin into his pocket, past the silver-studded gunbelt. He hummed a chorus of *I'll Take You Home, Kathleen* to himself and took another swallow of his drink, listening to the man tell the others at the table that he was about to get real lucky.

A redheaded waitress, older than she wanted to appear, passed beside him, letting her fingers dance along his shoulder and tug lightly on his hair. Her elongated face looked as if a giant invisible hand had grabbed her chin and stretched it.

"What gal wouldn't love to have locks like these?" she purred, pausing for him to react.

He turned toward her, grinning as usual. Her red dress did its best to show off her freckled body.

"Well now, honey, I reckon most boys wouldn't care a hoot whether you were yellow-haired or bald. There's too many other things to appreciate."

Her smile invited him to a closer inspection at his convenience as she walked on to give her order to the bartender. Bass watched her, sipped his drink and returned to the song.

" '*Oh, I will take you back, Kathleen*
To where your heart will feel no pain
And when the fields are fresh and green
I'll take you to your home again.' "

Bass sensed the presence of the big man behind him.

"Hey you sonvabitch. You bin rustlin' our beef."

The growling, whiskey-enhanced challenge came from a large, wide-shouldered man with barrel arms and a thick chest shoved into a too-small, striped shirt. His wide suspenders had seen too much trail. Bristly eyebrows rammed against each other over a bulging forehead. Black eyes couldn't wait to enjoy the destruction coming. A high-crowned hat made him appear even bigger.

It was Big Ed Gilmore, sent by John Branson.

Two companions laughed from their position against the closest wall, where they had slipped in unnoticed. They were anticipating Gilmore's next conquest. The likelihood of a Branson bonus was uppermost in their minds, if Bass Manko was dead before the family arrived. After all, how tough could a saloon singer be? Both Branson cowboys were proud of the revolvers shoved into their waistbands above their chaps. Both were enriched by the whiskey they had enjoyed on the way in, from a hidden flask the big cowboy kept in his saddlebags.

The threat jerked the entire saloon into a hush. The dealer at the closest table advised the participants to keep playing. A German farmer shouted something no one understood. An annoyed businessman yelled, "Take it outside!" A fat cowboy hollered, "Snap 'im in two, Ed! That's Big Ed Gilmore. Saw him kill a fella with a bear hug. Dun broke his back, yessir. Damn awful to watch."

Without turning around, Bass said, "You're an idiot or a liar. Or both."

The heavy-muscled Gilmore reached for his shoulder but Bass had already moved. The Branson cowboy was stunned by a hard knee to his groin as Bass completed his spin. Nauseating pain froze the big man's entire body. He doubled over to keep the agony from destroying him. As part of his spin, Bass drew his ivory-handled pistol and jabbed its barrel into the bigger man's gasping mouth. All motion was a single blur.

Gilmore was proud of his physical skills of punishment. He had expected Bass to keep talking, then move naturally to his right when the cowboy grabbed his shoulder. This anticipated move would have placed Bass directly in the powerful man's murderous grasp. The same situation had been created in the same way with four other men. Two had died an agonizingly cruel death; one would never leave his bed again; and one had gotten away with only broken ribs.

Bass looked into the pained man's face. Bass's smile was constant, masking the threat in his eyes. "Now, which is it? Are you an idiot—or are you a liar? I think you're both, big boy. If you move, I'll put your head on that back wall. Ugly mess. I wouldn't do it. Your choice, though."

From the corner of his vision, Bass saw Gilmore's companions exchange hurried communication, standing against the outside wall. The taller man, who looked like a bearded goose in a cowhide vest, said something to the stocky cowboy beside him. The taller man's eyebrows jumped with each word.

With childlike exaggeration, the shorter man with the half-smoked cheroot cupped his hands in the upper rims of his shotgun chaps, his right hand inches from the butt of his gun. He was excited about the prospect of acting like a gunfighter. No one moved in the saloon, except the same dealer who calmly shuffled and began dealing cards. Everyone was watching Bass as he yanked his pistol from Gilmore's jaws.

"Better tell your ugly friends to stand real still. You die first," Bass warned softly.

With the groin shock wave taking control of his stomach, the big cowboy slowly raised his huge arms and yelled, "He's got iron! Don't do nothin' stupid. He'll kill me. K-Kavanaugh! M-Moss!"

"Now, back up, unbuckle that gunbelt and the one holding up your pants. Let your gunbelt—and your pants—hit the floor," Bass said, as he shifted the pistol to his left hand and yanked Gilmore's pistol from its holster.

"What? My pants? Are you—"

"Crazy? Who wants to know?" interrupted Bass. "Some folks around here think so. But that's just because I like killin' fools like you. Humor me, big boy. I don't take well to anyone so ugly touchin' me."

Turning Gilmore's pistol in the direction of the other two Branson cowboys, Bass fired almost casually. As he did, the gun in his left hand pushed into the big man's stomach. Against the wall, the compact man yelped as the blast slammed him against the wall and his shirt sleeve, above his leather cuffs, blossomed with blood. His teeth slammed together, chomping off his cheroot. The loose piece bounced off his chest to the floor. His pistol flipped into the air like a wounded duck.

The saloon shouted its awareness of the problem and men scurried for cover. A tall Frenchman dropped to his knees and prayed loudly in French; the same annoyed businessman muttered for someone to go for the marshal but no one made any attempt to do so. A waitress screamed and dropped a tray of drinks onto the lap of a man who hadn't yet decided to move. Everywhere, men dove for cover, except for an inebriated cowboy watching from the middle of the room.

"You know, I wouldn't ever try to pull a gun on a man I didn't know," Bass spat. "It's a good way to die ugly." He turned back to Gilmore and pushed his revolver barrel under the big man's chin. "Better have your six-gun checked, fat boy. Pulls to the right a little. I was aiming at his head." Bass laughed out loud at his joke. "That's a joke, fat boy, I didn't hear you laugh. I want to hear you laugh. Now." He moved Gilmore's chin upward with his gun barrel.

Gilmore groaned and tried to laugh. It came out like an animal in pain.

Anyone who knew Bass Manko knew he spoke in short bursts of energy and words. Certain expressions were used often, then discarded. Currently, "Mighty fine," "Ugly" and "Who wants to know?" were his favorites.

"Who the hell sent you ugly bastards? Who'd be fool 'nuff to hire the likes of you three?" Bass snarled his questions. "Answer me, fat boy. I still wanna know if you're an idiot or a liar, or both."

The big cowboy looked like he was going to be sick. Waves of nauseating pain swirled through him. One of Bass's revolvers was cocked and lodged firmly against his belly. Any movement could discharge the weapon, even if he was able to land a serious blow. Standing against the wall, the remaining Branson rider was equally frozen. Their wounded companion sat on the floor, squeezing his bloody arm. A cold stare of rage, mixed with fear, was directed at Bass.

"W-We ride fer the Bar 6. John Branson sent us," Gilmore finally managed to explain.

"The Bar 6? John sent you? Cade's brother? What did Cade say about it?"

"D-Dunno. Didn't see him. H-Honest. T'weren't our idee."

"Now I know you both. Who the hell said I was stealin' your cattle?"

"A-Ah, John, I g-guess. Well, the old man t-tolt him to s-send us a'fer ya. Hold ya fer hangin'. They's a'comin'. with the rope." Gilmore tried to smile but the pain turned it into more of a grimace.

Behind the bar, the big-eared bartender was slowly dropping his hands under the bar. Slipping inside the door, Cade Branson growled a command that hit the already tense room like a left jab. "Bartender, you'd better come up with a glass of beer." In Cade's hand was a readied revolver.

A slightly green bartender raised his hands like they had touched a hot stove. The bearded cowboy spun his head toward the new voice. From the floor, the wounded man squirmed to look; his pained eyes shimmered with hope in seeing one of the Bransons. Gilmore turned to see who it was, shaking his head in disappointment as soon as he realized it was Cade, not Dish. At the back of the saloon, three townsmen slipped hurriedly out the back door.

"Well, howdy, Cade, wondered when you'd get here." Bass's evergreen smile widened and his fawn-like eyes flashed. "These boys say they were sent by John. Somethin' about misplaced beef."

"Came as fast as I could. Paw, John an' Dish are headed this way, I reckon. They were when I left, anyway. You need to get out of here."

"I ain't afraid of John. Or your paw. Or Dish. An' I sure ain't troubled by this bunch. Besides, I didn't steal none of your paw's beef. Have ya eaten?"

"I didn't say you were—an' I know you didn't rustle any cattle. Anybody's," Cade responded. He paused and added, "Not since breakfast, anyway."

The teasing brought a wider grin to Bass's face. "Who's counting? You go on. I'll be fine. Mighty fine."

"If you're staying, I'm staying."

Bass's smile grew even wider, flashing white even teeth. "Sure, who wants to know?"

For a moment, it seemed like they had forgotten about the three Branson riders. But Cade glanced in their direction and growled, "You three are done. You can draw your pay at the ranch."

"Are you sure you're missing beef? Anybody check to see that they didn't just wander off?" Bass grinned again and waved his guns in the direction of the three stunned cowhands. "Cattle like to do that, you know, especially before fall roundup. With idiots like these watchin' them, they could be in China. Or Kansas City, for God's sake."

"What do you know about it? When did you ever work a roundup?" Cade teased. He took another step into the saloon and studied the room, observing without comment that the tables were empty of men now hiding beneath them.

"Just because I don't want to spend my life nurse-maidin' some stupid cows doesn't mean I don't know what goes on." Bass responded, then realized his friend was kidding.

Laughing, Bass turned his attention again to Gilmore, whose pants and gunbelt lay in a lumpy pile around his boots. The big man was holding his groin with both hands, moaning softly. "Is this big boy with his pants down your paw's idea of somebody I should be afraid of?"

"Why are his pants down?"

"Who wants to know? I told him to do that." Bass jabbed Gilmore's chin again with his pistol.

"John said he saw someone who looked like you moving some of our beef. That's all I know. Hell, that's all Paw and Dish know."

"Well, John wouldn't lie." Bass's face saddened and he looked beyond Gilmore at the lone Branson man standing against the wall. The man looked like he was going to vomit.

"No, but he wouldn't stand against Paw either," Cade observed, looking at the same man, then back again to Bass. "Come to think of it, he's not the cattleman Dish is either. Poor John. He's the most wound-tight man I've ever seen. Couldn't make a decision if his life depended on it. That's Paw's fault. The son-of-a-bitch."

"Would Dish take on your paw?"

"I don't know, Bass, I don't know. Maybe," Cade said. He touched the choker around his neck with his free hand. "But he doesn't like you."

"Because of Susannah—or doesn't he like my ears?" Bass chuckled at his own joke and put his hands, holding both guns, behind his ears to make them stand out.

"Mostly Susannah but Dish is a lot like Paw. He gets up in the morning looking for something to be mad about."

At first, Bass thought his friend was joking when he burst into the saloon to tell him. Now he realized Cade had turned his back on his family to save his life. Bass thanked him warmly in his blurting manner of speaking that was sometimes hard to follow, like trying to wash your hands under a spurting water pump. Cade never had a problem with the abruptness. Although occasionally Bass would switch subjects so quickly that it took awhile to catch up. And if he became attracted to a word or a phrase, it would pop up everywhere in his conversation until another caught his fancy.

"You gotta go back, Cade. That's your family. You can't stand against your family."

There were times when it seemed like Bass was actually two different men; one was gentle and caring, almost child-like, the other, hard, reckless and quite cruel. When he thought about it, Cade wondered if the real Bass Manko was the latter or just an acquired style to keep people from getting too close. In the end, though, it didn't really matter.

"No, thanks. I belong right here."

"Mighty fine, we'll just wait for your kin to arrive then. I've got witnesses aplenty." Bass waved in the direction of the saloon. "Hell, half the men here know I was here all day."

Bass told Gilmore to move back with his friends and he tottered across the floor, encumbered by his downed pants and gunbelt, holding his groin.

"You still didn't answer why his pants are down," Cade said, his gaze covering the Branson men.

"Well, I could've killed him, I guess. Damn ugly, he is. Seemed like the gentler thing to do at the time. But you can go ahead and kill him, if you want. He's one of yours. Or was. Doubt if anybody would miss somethin' as dirt ugly as all that. Even Dish."

Shaking his head, Cade commanded, "Drop your gun-belts on the floor—and your pants. You don't want your big friend here to have all the fun."

The standing cowboy hesitated, his eyes seeking courage from Gilmore. Bass Manko's pistol boomed again. A hole exploded in the middle of the floor, spewing splinters in all directions. The wounded cowboy jumped up, holding his arm, his eyes wide. He spat the remaining portion of his cheroot toward the floor and stared at it.

"Why'd you do that, dammit. We . . . we dun nothin'," the bearded cowboy yelled.

"That's why. My friend told you to do something and you didn't. Do it or I'll shoot again," Bass snapped and a wicked grin followed. "And not at that damn floor either."

A flurry followed as both cowboys rushed to complete the order. Halfway through unbuttoning his pants, the chunky man vomited on himself. The bearded cowboy turned his head in disgust but continued to hold him.

"Just because he's hurt doesn't mean he can't join your little dance," Cade said. "Help him with his gunbelt and his pants."

Bass bit his lip to keep from laughing as the would-be gunman tried to unbuckle his wounded friend's belt and take down his pants without getting any residue on his hands. Gilmore stood, watching with dull eyes, his hands now at his sides.

"It's better than bleedin', boys," Bass observed. "Let the big boy do it, he's real good at takin' his pants down. Kinda likes it, being so ugly an' all."

Gilmore looked over at Bass; his eyes glared hatred and his fists opened and closed at his side. "We'll meet again, Cade. We'll see about us being fired. You'll have to answer to Dish—and me."

Chapter Four

"I don't want to see you when I get back to the ranch," Cade Branson said. He uncocked his pistol, spun it in his hand and holstered the weapon.

"What's that supposed to mean?" Gilmore turned toward Cade.

Cade's eyes flickered. "We don't want assholes on our place. Draw what's owed you an' ride. Don't be riding any Bar 6 horse either."

Laughter rippled through the saloon and Gilmore whirled to meet it. His snarling attention brought an immediate end to the response.

"Get outta here," Bass barked. "I'm real tired of seein' so much ugly. Now."

Only a slight hesitation preceded the three hobbling toward the saloon door, their pants flopping against their boots, gunbelts leaving a trail behind them as the weapons fell away from the crumpled clothing. Cade opened the door for them to pass.

Gilmore stopped in front of him, towering over Cade. "Next time will be my turn, little man."

"Really." Cade's mouth cocked into a half-smile. "I take it you're as stupid as you are big."

Through him came an exhilaration, like a young boy stepping out into a snowfall for the first time. It happened before every fight he had ever had.

A massive frown rippled over Gilmore's forehead and his right arm swung. No one could agree about what happened next. Saloon patrons had almost as many different versions as there were customers. One thing they all agreed on was that Ed Gilmore started it and Cade Branson ended it. No one had seen that happen before.

Gilmore's massive right fist came at Cade's head with the fury of an angry night train.

Anticipating the attempt, young Branson coolly parried it with his left forearm, pushing the vicious blow into air. Cade's own right fist exploded into the bigger man's stomach, followed by a left jab that drove even deeper. Both hit the big cowboy so hard everyone heard the impact and Gilmore's breath leaving. He grabbed his stomach to hold back the spreading agony, gasping for air that wouldn't return. Gilmore's friends couldn't believe what they were seeing. But Cade Branson had been raised on fighting and this big man was nothing compared to Dish or even some of his neighboring competitors. Strong but slow, Gilmore relied as much on fear as strength to overcome his adversaries. He'd never fought someone who knew how to fight. He'd never fought someone who wasn't afraid of him. He'd never fought someone like Cade Branson.

From the bar, Bass reminded the bearded cowboy and the wounded man to keep back as Cade landed lightning-fast blows to Gilmore's face and stomach. Gilmore staggered and swung another right fist that hit Cade in the shoulder so hard he lost his own breath for an instant. Cade recognized the bigger man had a definite advantage in an extended fight when his sheer size would wear down Cade's strength. He also knew the man was capable of breaking his neck or his back if he ever grabbed him.

That concern drove Cade further and he hit Gilmore with a combination of jabs and crosses that left the bigger man wobbly with his arms half-raised. Then came Cade's uppercut, delivered from his waist, shattering the man's jaw. On that, most in the saloon could agree later. The distinctive cracking sound was obvious. A tooth flew into the air and bounced on the dusty floor. Blood spurted down Gilmore's chin and he collapsed, his head thudding against the doorframe.

Heaving, Cade started to yank Gilmore to his feet. Cade's fists were bloody and raw. Bass stepped away from the bar. "That's enough, Cade. He's finished. Let him be." He waved his pistol in the direction of the bearded cowboy and his shorter companion holding his bloody arm. "Alright, you two, get your ugly friend and drag him outta here. We've seen all we want."

Cade looked up at Bass, not immediately recognizing either his friend or what was happening. Frustration and anger were demanding more. He lifted the nearly unconscious Gilmore to his feet with his left hand and cocked his fist to deliver another blow.

"No, Cade. He's done."

In mid-strike, Cade stopped and released the bloody cowboy. Gilmore fell against his two friends, nearly toppling both of them. Cade turned away without looking back. Regaining his balance, the bearded cowboy ignored the wounded man moaning about his arm aching and tried to pull Gilmore to his feet but couldn't begin to lift him. Gilmore's battered body was dead weight. Outside the saloon, town clerks watched, interested more in whiskey than the fight.

The shorter man wearing a striped woolen vest over a frayed white shirt finally asked, "Would you get that sorry fool out of the way? You're keeping us from drinking."

Laughing, the other clerk added, "Aren't you boys a bit chilly?"

Bass agreed. "I told you to drag all that ugly away—an' let those fellas pass."

He holstered his pistol and walked over to Cade, standing to the side and beginning to withdraw from his fighting trance. Bass put his arm on Cade's shoulder and tossed Gilmore's revolver onto the pile of discarded weapons and gunbelts.

"We'd better get somethin' on those hands, Cadie, before they swell up like ugly pumpkins." Bass's smile was warm. "Hellva way to come for a visit with your friend, eh? Mighty fine."

Cade nodded. The two friends sauntered outside to watch the little group struggling with their embarrassment. People watched from windows or across the street, enjoying the sight of the would-be toughs in such a silly situation. The bearded cowboy had somehow managed to get Gilmore on his feet and was half-dragging, half-carrying him now. Their wounded comrade was left to wobble behind them. Several times, the three men looked back to see if Bass and Cade were still watching. Each time, the two friends motioned for them to keep moving.

Gradually, the bustling town returned to normal. Busy people came and went from stores offering every manner of goods and wares. The main street was lively with a wagon-maker, a blacksmith, two liveries, a sawmill, two hotels, a grain supply store, numerous saloons, two known whorehouses, one quite grand, and a combined stage station, postal and telegraph office. Bass and Cade stood, taking in the daily activity and letting their attention wane from the three cowhands. Cade felt like he had been fighting all day.

Freight wagons loaded with cotton bales and other produce grunted past them. The drivers pointed at the wobbling cowhands and roared. A squad of arrogant Union soldiers rode past Bass and Cade, suspiciously eyeing their weapons. A few hundred yards from the far outskirts of the primary cluster of buildings they could see a new school house with only half of the roof finished.

Two Irish immigrants crossed directly in front of them, talking and waving their arms in energetic conversation and barely cognizant of the two riders. In a loud, snarling voice, Bass observed that the Irish had also settled in San Antonio. He had a particular dislike for the Irish but Cade didn't know why. Bass commented that the remote area of town was, "full of brawlin' an' partyin' and rundown houses. They call it Irish Flats."

"They're good, hard-workin' folks, it seems to me, Bass."

Bass gave him one of those looks that said Cade hadn't experienced much of life yet. "Just wait, my friend. I'll remember you said that."

"Why don't you ruffians just get out of town and let good people alone." The statement was directed at Bass and Cade. It was a feminine voice. Both men turned directly into the snapping brown eyes of a saucy young woman with a turned-up nose and high rosy cheek bones, wearing the clothes of an ordinary cowhand.

Cade Branson couldn't think of anything to say to Susannah Harding. He'd never seen a woman so captivating without making any attempt to be, or apparently without any awareness of her impact on men. Her long brown hair was pulled back into a tight bun, mostly hidden by a misshapen hat. Her simple shirt was hardpressed to cover proud breasts; her face glowed with a hard-work freshness he could only remember seeing once before.

In contrast to Cade, Bass immediately grinned, bowed and asked, "Afternoon to you, miss. Were you addressing the ruffians or us good folks?"

She laughed. "What are you two doing anyway?" She looked every inch a rancher—and every inch a woman. "Was that your doing? Why did they have their pants down? Dad won't like that."

Suddenly aware of his own silence, Cade blushed slightly and turned back to see what had happened to the three cowboys. They were out of sight. His arms and hands ached from the fistfight and his shoulder reminded him of Gilmore's ability to destroy. It seemed like he had been in town for days, not minutes. He was half-listening to Bass explain the situation to her.

"Cade, are you all right?"

He suddenly realized she was talking to him. His blush darkened and he stammered, "Oh, yeah, I'm fine."

"Surely your father—and your brothers—don't think Bass had anything to do with stealing your cattle. Father said most people think Mexicans are the problem."

Cade wasn't certain how to respond. Bass did it for him. "Oh, it's nothing, honey. We'll get it all straightened out. Say, what are you doing in town? Did your paw make you a deputy?"

"Came in to get supplies. He and Seth are over at the general store. Roper's around here too, somewhere." Her smile at Bass was the most wonderful thing Cade thought he had ever seen. He blinked to disconnect the feeling.

She smiled again, first at Bass, then at Cade. "I'd better let you go. Father's expecting me to help him. He's not very good at deciding on quantities, you know."

"Sure, sure. Any excuse to leave us." Bass touched her arm, bringing her gaze back to him.

"You know better than that, Bass Manko." Her long eyelashes flirted with him, then turned their attention on Cade. "So do you, Cade Branson."

With that, she walked away, her range-worn denims rustling a brisk cadence. Both friends watched her walk, mesmerized by the take-charge authority in her voice and manner, and her simple beauty.

"Buy you a drink . . . ruffian?" Bass laughed, slapping Cade on the back as they re-entered the saloon.

Several cheers greeted them as they strolled inside. At the bar, they slipped beside an elderly man with stringy white hair sipping beer. Squinting gray eyes surrounded by deep spider webs of wrinkles studied them carefully. A permanently tanned face with an equally white upper forehead and rough-hewn hands spoke of a farmer's life. His mouth sagged at the corners but an iron jaw didn't lack for discipline. An ill-fitting suit appeared to be his "going-to-town"—and Sunday meeting—clothes. The right shoulder seam was unraveling but it seemed to fit the man. But there was an aristocratic European air about him, in spite of his dress.

A halting, raspy voice, adorned with scattered German phrases, soon gave away his heritage. "*Ja*, better you to be watching for Herr Gilmore. You made him to look *schlecht*. Ah, bad. *Ja*, you did so. He vill have to kill you for this." He took another swig, emptying the schooner, slammed it down on the bar and burped twice. "If I to be you, I vould to ride on. *Sehr* fast. *Ja.*"

"We do thank you, sir, for the advice," Cade answered, rubbing his hands together to relieve the soreness gathering there. "But I reckon we'll stay. Got kin comin'."

Bass waved at the big-eared bartender and he quickly came over. "Whiskey for us. Another beer for the gentleman here. An' somethin' my friend can soak his hands in."

"Y-Yessir. Right away."

"*Danke*, that becomes nice of you." The man re-examined Cade and Bass. "Now I to be thinking you was fighters for the Confederate States of America. *Ja?*"

Slightly surprised to hear the formal name instead of "Stars n' Bars," both nodded and said, "Hood" at the same time. Taking a hint from the older man's formality, Cade added, "Hood's Texas Brigade. General John Bell Hood, sir."

"*Das gut.* I figured you be Southron fighters, from the way you take on the fighting." The clear implication was that the two young men weren't farmers. He glanced in both directions. "You should not be telling that to everyone. Most Germans around this town vere Union. *Oooch, nein* me. I thought States should decide for themselves on the slavery. And most things. Not that I vas for the keepin' of folks, mind you. *Nein. Nein. Oooch*, terrible thing to do—to any on this land."

Bass smiled. "I'm Bass . . . Manko. This is Cade Branson. What's your name?"

"*Mein* name *ist* Joe Creek."

"Joe Creek?"

"Sure, an it is to be really Josef Criquette. *Mein vater* was French-German. *Mein mutter*, she be all German. But no-

body can to say *mein* name. So Joe Creek it to be. Good
'nuff."

"Glad to know you, Josef Criquette." Bass grinned after
his proper pronounciation of the old man's name.

"I take it you weren't born . . . around here," Bass said.
"Did you come over from . . . Germany?"

"*Ja*. Me and *mein bruder*, Axel . . . we be comin' to United
States of America. From the city of Baden in the old country. Sixteen and twelve, us vere. Axel, he vas older than
me." Criquette paused, looked away and swallowed. "Axel,
he dead five years. *Gott* . . . bless his soul."

"I'm sorry about that."

"*Danke schoen*." After a snort to hold back an emotion
that wanted out, Criquette shifted his body toward them
with his left arm leaning on the top of the bar. "I be likin'
your singing. *Ja*. Yah don't be knowin' any German songs,
do yah?"

"No, afraid I don't. Maybe you can teach me one."

Criquette smiled wanly. Bass stood next to him, Cade on
the other side. Bass, as usual, was eager to engage in conversation. Cade was mentally somewhere else and not interested in their conversation. Joe Criquette continued to tell
Bass that he and his wife and their six children farmed to
the southwest of town. His family was in the general store
doing their monthly trading. He proudly added that his wife
made the best sausages in the whole region. Without being
asked, he said he didn't care for the German Club, the gathering place for many wealthy Germans. Too snotty for him,
he said, and punctuated the observation with a German
phrase Bass could only guess was an off-color description of
what he thought of those who went there.

The bartender brought a bottle and two glasses. Both

hands shook slightly as he presented them. "On the house. I'll be right back with a bowl of water—and the beer, all right?"

Cade nodded. A step behind the bartender's exit, a small salesman in a brown, ill-fitting suit and toothy smile came up to greet them. He eased himself between Cade and Bass as if he were a long-lost friend. "My name's William H. Sullivan. Friends call me . . . William. Ah, I'm a drummer. Fine soft goods, you know. I represent the best there is in these entire United States of America. Lancaster Linen Company. I'd be right proud to buy you two a drink. Those toughs sure tangled with the wrong men this time." The salesman chuckled nervously. "Shoot, I thought you were just a singer of songs. Boy, was I wrong."

Bass grinned and shook Sullivan's hand. "Rather be singin' myself. Couldn't be helped though." Cade merely observed that they already had drinks and poured whiskey into the two glasses. He opened and closed his hands rapidly to ward off the advancing stiffness.

The bartender returned and ceremoniously set the beer down in front of the old farmer, hoping for an opportunity to say that it too was free. The only response was from Bass who asked where Cade's water was. Immediately, the bartender left to complete his task, happy to be away from these two men who had taken control of his tiny world, seemingly without even trying. Criquette glanced over at the salesman, nodded indifferently and grasped the new beer.

"*Prost!*" The old German held up his glass in a toast.

"Here's to ya!" Bass countered and touched the farmer's glass with his own. Cade held up his glass in tribute, downed most of the whiskey and coughed. Criquette mumbled something in German no one could understand and took a long gulp, letting some of it settle on his wrinkled upper lip.

Pausing to straighten his tie and wait for Bass's attention, the little salesman launched into an authoritative-sounding recital. "Well, that big fella's quite the brawler, I hear. Talk is that he's killed men before—broke their backs. Five or six, I believe." He looked away as if examining a mental file and then continued, "Hard to tell about the other two. Savage pistol-fighters, I imagine."

The nervous bartender returned with a stoneware bowl half-filled with water and a towel draped over his arm. "I put some salt in it for you." The bartender glanced at Cade. "It's supposed to keep down any swelling."

"Good 'nuff. That oughta do it." Bass grinned. "Stick 'em both in there, pardner. Before they're ugly pumpkins."

"Easy for you to say," Cade managed a thin grin. He placed his right hand in the bowl and tossed down the rest of his drink with his left before slipping the other hand into the water.

"Here, let's add some of this. That'll help." Bass poured some of the whiskey into the bowl, grinning. "You can drink it afterward."

Glancing at Cade's hands soaking, the little salesman waved authoritatively at the bartender but the big-eared man ignored the signal. "Say, you sing real fine. Reminds me of a fella I heard in St. Louis once. Beautiful voice. Irish tenor, he was."

Cade glanced at Bass, knowing his friend wouldn't like the comparison to an Irish tenor. Bass hid his dislike with a swig of his whiskey.

"Hadn't been in this place before," Sullivan continued, savoring the sound of his voice. "Let's see, I've been calling

on Jason Herald—he owns the Herald General Store—
about two years now. More like two and a half. Well, almost
two and two-thirds, really. Good business an' getting better.
This city's really growing again. My home's in Iowa. Say, I
didn't get your names."

Chapter Five

"Didn't give 'em," Bass said with a smile. "Bass Manko. This is Cade Branson. An' this is our friend, Josef Criquette."

"Good to know you, all of you gentlemen."

"*Mein* missus doesn't buy . . . linens. Too much of the cost." Criquette said, more to himself than anyone else.

Sullivan eyed him disdainfully, trying to determine why this farmer was even with these two men of the gun. Cade nodded and told Bass to pour him a drink.

Bass laughed and grabbed the bottle. "Sure, sure, I make a good servant."

"This time put it in the glass."

"Rules, rules, rules. Good 'nuff is good 'nuff."

Criquette chuckled and shrugged, enjoying the banter and Bass's use of his phrase. After half-filling Cade's glass, Bass waved at the bartender and received hurried movement toward him. "Bring us another glass." He turned toward the salesman. "We'll buy you a drink, Mister Sullivan."

"Well, that's mighty nice o' you boys. Mighty nice."

Bass patted the old man on the back. "You ready for another, Joe?"

"You still to be buying?"

"You bet."

"*Das gut.* I still to be drinking."

"Good 'nuff. Bring another beer too." Bass hollered and sipped his own drink.

Under his breath, Cade muttered, "Remember, you've got company comin'."

"How could I forget?"

The card-playing townsman who had requested Bass sing "I'll Take You Home, Kathleen" found enough courage to return to the bar and remind him of his promise.

"Excuse me . . . sir. I'd sure like to hear, you know, that song—when you . . . start playin' again. No hurry, of course," the man said, unable to keep his eyes from dropping to Bass's holstered revolver. He wanted to ask about the town's ordinance against wearing firearms but couldn't bring himself to do so.

Bass responded like the man was a long-lost friend. "Oh, glad you said something. I'll be going back to my guitar in a minute or two. Gonna finish this drink first."

"Oh, sure, sure. Thank you, sir," the man replied and hurried back to the table.

Sullivan began jabbering non-stop about his products, his home in Iowa, his wife and their three daughters. An occasional nod from either Bass or Cade was all that was required to keep the little salesman going strong. Gradually, the little man gave them a few more details about the valley, presented as only a salesman like him would do. What he didn't know, he made up, or so it seemed to the two young men who had grown up in the region.

"Quite an on-going problem with all the cattle thievery.

Makes one wonder how effective the law is around here. But I understand the local marshal is, ah, a bit past doing much." He closed his eyes, opened them and snapped his fingers. "Oh yeah, best thing in this town is the fine-lookin' widow who owns this place. Now she'd be quite a catch." He finished with a wink, an affectation he did often, annoying Cade more each time it occurred. Bass didn't seem to mind.

The bartender brought the extra glass and another beer. Hesitating, he asked Cade if he wanted new water. Cade shook his head negatively and the man hurried away. Bass poured a drink for the little salesman and handed it to him. After a quick sip, Sullivan continued with his assessment of the town. Most of the townspeople were happy with the progress, he observed. A few clashes between Mexicans and whites but nothing serious. He made a comment about the Mexicans and Bass couldn't resist saying Cade's mother was Spanish. That brought an instant flow of backpedaling and complimentary remarks about the Mexican people.

Criquette chuckled and downed the rest of his beer. "Not all *der* rustlers you to be jabbering about are coming from *der* land of Mexico on *da udder* side of *der* river of Rio Grande. Some be close by, me think. Something *falsch* goes. *Ja.*"

Annoyed at the interruption, Sullivan stared at him but the German farmer wasn't paying any attention. The rough-faced old man ran his fingers around the edge of the empty glass but Bass hadn't noticed he was without beer. The happy-go-lucky gunfighter was watching his friend massage his bruised knuckles.

Sullivan noticed Bass's attention and asked, "Does that hurt?"

Without looking up at the salesman, Cade said, "No, I do this every time I go in a bar. It's an old Comanche ritual."

"A-Are you . . . C-Comanche?"

"Haven't decided."

Bass roared and the salesman realized Cade was putting him on and quickly returned to his assessment of the area, starting with a reinforcement of Gilmore's fighting reputation. On the salesman's last trip through the valley, he had heard about Gilmore beating a cowboy to death. No one had objected; Marshal Harding couldn't get any witness to challenge Gilmore's claim that it was self-defense and had to let him go free. Getting no reaction from any of the three listeners, he returned to the subject of the region's economy, with barely a short breath between. Although cattle were far and away the leading source of commerce in the valley, some mining and a few milling operations were well in place. Several ranches were well known for their horses too. And the town's general store "carried the greatest line of soft goods in the entire region."

Bass poured him another drink, growing more and more annoyed that the salesman didn't realize they had grown up in the region and knew far more about it than he did. The little salesman thanked him, drank half of it and continued, warming to his task of sharing "confidential insights."

"Commerce in the whole valley seems mighty good to me. Lot of real hard money rollin' around," Sullivan gushed and tossed down the rest of his second drink. "Gosh, my sales have tripled, I think . . . yes, tripled, in the last two years. People like it here. Beautiful country. Hard country, of course. Primitive but magnificent. Maybe me an' Parmelia should retire down here. I hope to bring her on my next trip." He paused to consider his own comment. "Do you think the stage will be safe? I hear the last one wasn't bothered."

A cold shiver galloped down Cade's back and he glanced toward the saloon door.

"Look out, Bass!" Cade yelled and shoved Sullivan hard. His water bowl flew into the air, spewing water on the little salesman as he caromed off Bass and fell against a table, waving his left arm in the air. Diving to his left, Cade grabbed for his revolver with his wet hand. Like a wild mustang reacting to trouble, Bass shoved the old farmer ahead of him to the floor, pulling his revolver as they flew. Criquette's German curse was cut short as Bass landed on top of him, driving air from the old man's stomach.

At the doorway was Gilmore holding a double-barreled shotgun. Traces of dried blood lined his chin. Pig-like eyes were slits of hatred. Cade fired twice at Gilmore; both bullets punched hard into the big man's stomach. Gilmore's shotgun bellowed and tore into the bar, ripping off a chunk of the border frame. Errant buckshot cut into Sullivan's exposed bicep. He yelped and rolled to the floor, curling up like a baby. He cried out for help, tears wetting his cheeks. He shut his eyes tightly to keep the sudden roaring horror away.

Rolling away from the old man, Bass also fired twice at the staggering cowboy. Without another sound, Gilmore wobbled to his thick knees and fell forward. His face slammed against the floor planks like a dull axe. The little salesman gaped wild-eyed at the back of the large room. Two other gunmen were trying to get a clear shot at his new friends. It was the bearded cowboy with Gilmore and a third man who hadn't been with them before. The stocky cowboy with the shot arm had apparently not joined them in revenge. When the wounded salesman fearfully turned back to see if Bass or Cade were hurt—or worse—he saw Gilmore was already dead.

Cade was nowhere in sight and Bass lay on top of the old man. Crawling for safety behind the bar, the little salesman sobbed uncontrollably. As he rounded the corner of the bar, his eyes met the blank expression of the crouched bartender. Both jumped at the surprise encounter and backed away to their previous locations on the floor.

Bass raised himself from Criquette who lay unmoving, spread-eagled on the floor and gasping for breath. He couldn't tell if the older man had been shot or just had the wind knocked out of him. Bass lifted the old man's shoulder with his left hand and he groaned, "*Ich bin . . . gut*, Herr Manko. There be . . . more *schlecht* men. Bad. Killers. *Ja*, get to moving. *Gehen. Gehen.* Go." Bullets sought Bass's head and grazed his shoulder as he dove toward a table and chairs; Criquette didn't move, trying to find air in the tightened room.

A haze of smoke blanketed the saloon, interrupted by gunfire from the rear, seeking the moving Bass Manko. Throughout the room, fourteen other men were huddled or lying flat, hoping to avoid stray bullets. All except the same drunken, standing cowboy who was now a dirty statue against the far wall. He watched the two gunmen who had entered the saloon from the back door like they were part of some theatrical play. They had sneaked into the saloon at the same time Gilmore came from the front. The bearded man held a Winchester and a new handgun was shoved into his waistband. The second gunman with a pockmarked face and stringy hair extending from a derby hat was half-kneeling, trying to locate Bass.

Neither had any idea of where Cade Branson might be. The two gunmen assumed Gilmore had killed him and he was lying somewhere beyond the front corner of the bar where they couldn't see. Smugly, they were now after only one man.

Suddenly, from a new position behind the bar Cade stood and fired at the bearded cowboy, only twenty feet away. Cade's appearance, to the man's immediate left, surprised him and he swung his Winchester toward Cade too late. Cade's revolver belched three times before he ducked back behind the bar.

Flying backwards, the bearded man landed on top of an empty table and lay there, unmoving. His right arm slid off the table with his Winchester death-gripped in his hand. The pockmarked gunman fired, breaking a bottle of whiskey on the back counter.

Meanwhile, Bass slid behind a table near the center of the room. Two slugs blistered the floor beside him. A third burned his hip. A fourth spit a chunk of wood from a chair, thudding inches from his taut face. The shots were hurried, the result of a too-confident man who suddenly realized the trap wasn't working right and he was the one outnumbered.

Twisting his body into firing position from behind the marginal safety of the table and chairs, Bass fired at the second gunman. With a flip of his left hand, Bass overturned the table. The movement was greeted with a shot into its center. Splinters flew as the slug dug in the blackened wood. The solitary gunman also dropped behind a table and two chairs, trying awkwardly to turn the table over without standing.

A low cursing from behind the bar gave away the bartender's new position. The pockmarked gunman fired at the noise, then delivered two probing shots as Bass drew his second pistol, holstering the empty one. He glanced over his shoulder to assure himself that no one else had entered the saloon behind him. A widening blood circle surrounded Gilmore in the doorway. The little salesman had crawled around the edge of the bar. He was sitting there, holding his arm and praying softly. Laying on the ground in the open, Criquette told him to shut up.

Sounds of someone else praying, mixed with a few frightened gasps, rushed to fill the void of sound between shots. One of Bass's fresh cartridges dropped to the floor and rolled as he tried to shove it into a chamber. A spray of splinters showered his arm from a blast that sought the bouncing travel of the bullet. Finally, it came to rest against the leg of a chair ten feet away. Bass looked at the cartridge, then into the eyes of a scared townsman trying to lie as flat as possible against the far wall. Bass grinned and pulled another cartridge from his belt loops. Another bullet clipped the table leg beside him.

Bass thought Cade was probably edging toward the far end of the bar where the bartender had been or was, to put the gunman in a crossfire. But the gunman had apparently forgotten about Cade or thought he was dead. From the corner of the bar, the young Branson waited patiently, trading places with the terrified bartender. In his hands was the bartender's double-barreled shotgun Cade had taken from the shelf under the bar. At his side was the box of shells. Gulping away vomit that wanted release, the bartender pushed himself against the far inside wall of the bar and crawled to the middle. There he sat crosslegged, holding his hand to his mouth.

Every time the gunman fired, he exposed his right arm from behind the now overturned table. Cade waited until the man fired again, then fired both barrels. The man's pistol sailed into the haze. He panicked. His shirt sleeve was half-crimson. Jerkily, like a newborn calf, he stood and pulled a second gun from his belt with his left hand. The movement was slow. He half-stumbled to his left, wildly seeking cover he didn't see. He fired once, the bullet flying through the open door.

Bass's handgun roared, then roared again. The pockmarked gunman snapped backward strangely, like a marionette yanked by an angry puppeteer. Two black holes appeared over his left shirt pocket, about an inch apart. He tried to level his wobbling gun but his shot drove a hole into the floor at his feet. A third shot from Bass's gun tore into the gunman's temple. He spun completely around, firing another shot of his own into the ceiling. His body crumpled against the back wall. A red streak marked the body's path as it slid down the wood.

The acrid smell of gunsmoke, sweat and fear lay about the tightened room. Customers were still crouched behind every possible hiding place, not yet believing the gunfight was over. In spite of the stifling humidity of the room, Cade was not sweating. Neither was Bass. No one offered to help them stand. Three men hurried through the back door, another through the front, taking advantage of the silence. Against a far wall, the drunken cowboy began to clap his hands.

The gates of the saloon door banged open. Titus and Dish Branson stood, holding cocked Winchesters, their attention fixed on Bass Manko. Two steps behind them was John Branson, carrying his rifle with almost equal determination.

Titus smiled triumphantly. "Now I've got ya, ya cattlerobbin' sonvabitch. Yur gonna hang, by God. Yur gonna hang."

Dish stepped beside him, legs spread apart, his cocked rifle pointed at Bass. Dish's face glowed with satisfaction. The saloon's patrons, in various positions of hiding, were as motionless as an oil painting in the hotel. None of the Bransons had yet seen Cade who was mostly covered by shadow at the far end of the bar.

"No, he's not. You can turn around an' leave. Or you can join this bunch you sent earlier." Cade's challenge made all three Bransons jump in surprise.

Wisps of spidery smoke wandered innocently away from the barrels of Cade's borrowed shotgun. The weapon remained pointed at Titus's chest.

Titus jumped at the sound of Cade's voice. "What? Cade? What're ya doin' hyar? Are ya standin' ag'in yur own?"

"I am, when they come after an innocent man. That makes you nothing but a bunch of outlaws." Cade moved closer, along the back side of the bar. His shotgun was empty but the Bransons didn't know it.

Kneeling on the floor, Bass was pointing his revolver at Dish too. Behind Bass somewhere, he heard a fearful sigh and he grinned a wide, toothy grin.

Dish tried to look confident. He had been supremely so before entering. But silent questions to himself were beginning to assault his composure. Wasn't that shotgun kept under the bar? How wide a pattern would it blast? Would he be hit much if Cade unloaded it at his father? Would Cade shoot? Was Bass's gun empty? Would they dare to shoot? Right in front of witnesses? Why did he always have to be put in the middle when others failed their jobs? Why? Surely Bass and Cade realized they could die too. They were outnumbered. Were they crazy? Or were the two of them that good?

John finally spoke. "Cade, who killed Gilmore and Moss? We met Kavanaugh on the street. He's been shot too."

"Who the hell ya think did it, John?"

Titus's evil laugh erupted into a cough and he spit mucus

and blood. Cade noticed his father's shirt was drenched in sweat, far more than the day or the ride to town demanded. From outside the saloon, there were muffled sounds of people coming toward the fight. Sounds of men running. A few were brave enough to peek around the door frame to see what was happening inside. Others joined their curious observation.

Then came a shout that was a rich growl, a Welsh battle-cry of sorts.

"What in Hell's teeth is going on here?" The voice was a trumpet charge. No one had a gravelly way of speaking quite like Marshal Emmett Harding. The wiry older lawman, of noticeable Welsh descent, stepped quickly past John.

"Step aside, Titus. You too, Dish. Who's been shooting in my town? There's enough of this rubbish."

Surprised and displeased, Titus Branson turned to see the lawman in the doorway, chewing on a wad of tobacco, holding a cocked Winchester. Harding had icy eyes of turquoise set off by a thick graying mustache and arched eyebrows. He stood with his bowlegged legs apart, the gun cradled in his crossed arms, more like a man going hunting than a readied peace officer.

A wrinkled gray suitcoat seemed to match his reputation for being too old for the job. And a buttoned vest couldn't quite hide an older man's paunch. But a clean white collarless shirt, buttoned at the neck, expressed a sense of respect for the authority of his office. Under his coat could be seen the bulge of a shoulder-holstered Colt. His high-crowned Stetson and nearly knee-high, mule-eared boots told where he preferred to be—on a horse, or training one on his small horse ranch outside of town.

Whatever he wore, Harding was a man who no longer expected people to jump when he commanded. Those days were gone forever. The authority that had once radiated from the man's wiry frame had disappeared into a deeply lined face and a slightly bowed back. A limp was a reminder of the hazards of wearing a badge for a long time. No one could recall the awful gunfight he had survived to get that wound. Or cared. It was accepted that he spent most nights at home, except for weekends when cowboys tended to get rowdy. It was accepted but laughed at, behind his back.

Dish Branson snorted his disrespect for the lawman. "This hyar's Branson business. Not yurn. Yo-all kin go on 'bout puttin' drunks in jail. If'n ya kin catch any." He turned toward the door. "Go on home . . . all o' ya. Git along now. Git."

"There is sorry I am, Dish, but I'm not interested in your take of the matter." The old Welshman stepped like a pasture bull past Dish and into the smoke-layered room. For a moment, he appeared like the marshal of ten years earlier. Trying to take charge, Marshal Harding glanced at Cade. "Son, you can be putting that Greener aside now."

"I'll decide that, Marshal. No disrespect."

John Branson stared at Cade's shotgun as if seeing it for the first time. An expression of discomfort melted into concern.

Harding chuckled. "I bet you will, at that, Cade." He waved his arm toward the three cowboys standing in the middle of the room. "What went on here, boys? God's oath, I be needing the truth."

Cade was surprised Harding even remembered his name. He hadn't seen the marshal for some time and whenever he did, at Harding's ranch, the lawman was either working with his horses or reading a book. Bass told him the marshal was partial to novels by English authors and Tennyson poetry. According to Bass, the old man liked the young singing gunfighter. Cade thought his friend was exaggerating or misreading indifference as caring.

John agreed aloud, "Yeah, anyone see this fight?"

Dish stared at his older brother as if the man had just retched on Dish's boots. Bass was now standing, his pistol remaining aimed at Dish's mid-section. Dish didn't remember seeing him get up.

Trying to regain control, Titus waved his rifle for emphasis and restated what Dish had just said. "I said, go on 'bout yur business. Every one o' ya. Them's two o' our hands. Thar on the floor. Daid. Gilmore an' Moss." He coughed and shook his head to stop the wracking.

With disgust painted on his lined face, Marshal Harding looked at Titus. "Dammit to Wales and back, nobody's going anywhere. Not until I say so. Now shut up, Branson, and let me talk to these fine lads."

Muffled laughter sputtered from someone crouching under a table in the middle of the room. Titus started to respond but didn't. Partly from his wheezing and partly out of fear. No one else seemed to be aware, or cared, that his own son held a shotgun on him. He should have known Cade would do something like this.

He muttered, "Ya should'a never tolt Cade 'bout Gilmore comin' ahead."

"Shut up, Paw. I'll handle this." Dish's face was scarlet, his eyes slits of barely controlled rage.

John thought Dish looked even more like their father than usual and he shivered.

Chapter Six

Bass and Cade glanced around the room as the saloon's patrons began to surface from their hiding places. Both young men were interested in hearing what they would say. Bass caught Cade's eyes and grinned; Cade shook his head. A large man in a business suit had accidently been hit in the leg and was being helped to his feet by two friends. He cursed loudly when the pain grabbed his body. Cade wasn't certain if Harding was helping them because of Susannah's interest in Bass or not. He hoped not. He hoped it was just a lawman trying to do his job, even if he was past his prime.

"You can lower those guns. Dish. John. Paw," Cade said, laying his own shotgun on the bar.

The move wasn't as trusting as it appeared. The weapon was empty and he wanted his right hand free. He tried to ignore the ache and stiffness in his hands from the fist fight. Dish said something and Titus lowered his Winchester to his side. Dish mirrored the movement and John was close behind. Bass nodded, spun the revolver easily in his hand and holstered it.

"We seed it all, Marshal," the large-eyed cowboy waved his arms. His eyes were only on Marshal Harding. His friends watched him with their arms crossed as if preparing to assess his testimony.

Pushing his curled-brim hat back to reveal a band of untanned forehead, the cowboy began to tell what he saw. "These three . . . dead ones, hyar, hyar an' thar—they came in from both doors an' they tried to kill these two strangers. Yessir, tryin' to catch 'em unawares, they was."

The cowboy's arms jerked even more wildly as he warmed to the task. He went through the entire encounter, starting with Gilmore's first attempt to beat up Bass. Midway through his recitation, the cowboy stopped and laughed. Almost a girlish giggle at first, then a joyous explosion of guffaws. His two friends knew what was coming and joined in, slapping their knees with joy.

"Marshal, ya should'a seed it," the cowboy said, tears running down his cheeks. "These two made Gilmore an' his bunch drop their pants an' march outside. Lawd a mercy, never seed the like."

The room was silent, except for chuckles that bubbled to the surface throughout the saloon. Outside, a loud voice shouted, "Man, I wish I'd seen that." Then the wounded townsman agreed, "By Gawd, that big sonvabitch Gilmore's been asking for it for a long time. He finally squared up with a man. If needs be, Mister Branson, I'll stand with your son, Cade an' this hyar singer."

"That be the right o' it. We ride for the River S. If'n ya knows ol' man Seymore, ya knows I talk the straight line." The cowboy with a handlebar mustache and red suspenders standing next to the tall wrangler with the big eyes burst out his support. Immediately, he looked to his friends for their approval. Both nodded enthusiastically like the matter was settled.

Marshal Harding spat, missing the spittoon next to the bar boot railing. That was his only response.

Criquette uncurled himself from the floor and slowly stood. He held his hand against his stomach to ease the pain and his words came heavily, marked with the need to grasp air as he spoke. "Herr Marshal . . . these two men came to this drinking house . . . to have the whiskey . . . and share the talk. They *ist mein* friends. *Ja*, they bring *nein* trouble here. *Nein*. Herr Gilmore tried *var* hard to kill them. Herr Gilmore veren't good 'nuff. His friends, who like to be back-shooters, veren't neither."

Running his tongue over cracked lips, he returned to the bar, looking for his left-behind beer. It sat unharmed and Criquette grabbed the glass and took a long swig, disinterested in any more discussion on the topic.

A few feet away, the little salesman, William H. Sullivan, rose gingerly, holding his wounded arm to his chest with his other hand, wincing as he began to speak. "I'm proud to say that I saw the whole thing and agree completely with the assessment already rendered." He straightened his tie with his good hand, then remembered his wound and quickly held his arm again. "Whooie, I'll tell you, I've never seen shooting like that before in my whole life. I wouldn't have missed it for the world—and, believe me, I've seen some in my time."

"So these two young catamounts were just defending themselves after Gilmore and these hoot-owls jumped them like Saxon vandals for no damn reason," Harding repeated the assessment while his gaze took in the combatants and the witnesses.

"Yessir, Marshal, that's it. And they did a right fine job o' finishin' the fight, I'd say." The wide-eared cowboy shook his head to emphasize the statement and his two friends babbled agreement. Around the room came further indications of support.

The cowboy with the handlebar mustache whirled toward the lawman to add his feelings. "That piece o' crap lyin' thar tore up Jimmy Wright—fer nothin'. He were a good friend o' mine an' you let this bastird go, Marshal."

"Aye, ever sad I was of that doing but no choice was I given. Nobody would step up and say what they saw. I couldn't hold him on 'want-to's.' The law needs facts, son."

Somewhere in the room, a whisper disagreed with Harding's claim, indicating it was more about being afraid of Gilmore than any concern about the law. If Harding heard the disparaging remark, he didn't act like it. Murmured agreement tiptoed through the saloon but the cowboy's face was dark crimson, his body trembling from anger. "Don't know 'bout that, Marshal, but these boys dun saved us the trouble o' killin' Gilmore ourselves."

Glancing at the spittoon next to the bar boot railing, Marshal Harding spat a brown stream that slammed against the floor a foot from Titus's boots. It wasn't where he was aiming. The rancher jumped backward.

"Titus, Gilmore works for you—or he did until lead changed things," the lawman said. "What in Hell's teeth are you dallying in here—you an' Dish an' John—with your Winchesters all ready to go?"

Titus coughed to clear his throat and Dish took the momentary delay to respond instead. "Gilmore don' work fer us no more. Fired 'im last week. Heard he were after Bass hyar an' we came to he'p. My brother—Cade, over thar—got hyar in time. Thank Gawd. We was a mite late." He glanced at Cade and his eyes asked for support.

Marshal Harding didn't wait for Cade. With his chaw making his cheek into a fat ball, the tough lawman turned his attention on the Bransons. "Now, Dish, don't be peeing on my boots and be telling me t'is raining. Just what the bloody hell are you, your pappy and big brother doing here? What's this I hear about some of your steers up and missing—and you think it be Bass's work?"

Dish's eyes were hot. How dare this old man challenge him? His fist tightened on the Winchester at his side.

"Dish, you're not that good," Cade's voice was low and threatening. "I'd like to hear that story again too. The first time I thought it was something Bass could make into a song. Real fanciful stuff." His smile was separate from the intensity in his eyes. Dish saw both and took a breath through clenched teeth.

Grinning widely, Bass began to sing. "Come along, boys, let me tell you 'bout a day . . . when cattle were missin' an' Dish came to say . . . it's hangin' I'm for . . . no, it's to save the fine lad . . ."

John joined the outburst of laughter in spite of himself and Dish spun to glare him into silence.

"Marshal Harding. Your work is done here. Let's get this place back to having fun." The icy command came from the back of the crowd jamming around the saloon door.

Out of the curious mass came a woman as stunning as most men would ever view. The gathered townspeople stepped aside for her to pass. A quick glance at Bass was a speech. Cade had seen her several times before when he came to do something with Bass. Her appearance never ceased to rattle his soul. She would make almost any woman look like a little school girl. Except Susannah Harding, he thought.

A fitted, navy-blue pinstripe silk skirt and o-shaped bodice were gathered tightly at her waist. A wide copper belt with insets of silver and gold accented its smallness and the ampleness of her bosom. A white cheissette collar, white gloves and exaggerated full sleeves at her elbows completed the attire. Her daring hemline was four inches off the ground in front and dragged along the floor in the back. It was difficult to tell her age. God had done well to hide it but she was at least ten years older than either young gunfighter. Neither thought about that, however.

Cade stared at her without thought of how rude it might seem. He heard Bass chuckle and say, "Howdy, Missus Rice. It's mighty good to see you."

"Thank you, Mister Manko. I take it you've had more to do here than strum your guitar." This time her voice was moonlight. Soft and soothing.

"Yes, ma'am. It's been a mite busy. Everything's fine now. Thanks to my good friend, Cade."

"Thank you, Cade. Cade Branson, isn't it?" Elizabeth's eyes sought Cade's and she smiled at him sensuously as if he was the only man in the room.

"Yes, ma'am. It is." Cade swallowed away the intimacy of her stare and said, "Sorry about the ruckus. But we didn't start it."

"Well, you certainly know how to make it end."

Laughter gurgled throughout the saloon.

Clicking off her smile, she turned her attention to Harding. His face gave away no indication of what he thought.

"These men clearly did not start this situation, as violent

as it may have been" she declared. "You've heard from up-standing witnesses to that fact."

Elizabeth Rice held two fingers of her left hand with her right in front of her waist. Only the closest observer could notice a slight trembling in her left hand. She looked around at the assembled crowd, motioned with both hands to indicate she was speaking for everyone. Near the front, a woman elbowed her husband next to her and he apologized without asking why she bumped him.

A hint of rose touched Elizabeth Rice's cheeks but it was not from paint. Her eyes were emerald green and sur-rounded by long dark lashes that pulled and pushed a man in a single blink. In a lifetime of looking, a man would rarely be blessed with seeing such a beautiful woman more than two or three times. Thick petticoats rustled as she pre-sented herself. A queen to her subjects.

She wore her wavy dark hair pulled back within a match-ing hat with a curled red ostrich feather. Her eyes glistened with confidence and sought the soul of every man in the room with but a glance and the hint of a private smile. Cri-quette slid toward Cade and whispered that this was Eliza-beth Bingham Rice, rich widow of a wealthy cattleman. Cade smiled—her ranch butted next to theirs but the farmer didn't know that.

In addition to her late husband's ranch, she owned this saloon and one of the fanciest brothels, the Gower House—and had just purchased a neighboring ranch as well. She lived in town, letting her foreman run the cattle operation. The tone of the message was one of respect. Surprising, considering the source. Cade already knew the rest about her, mostly from Bass who had worked for her for over a year, singing in this saloon.

Not taking his eyes from the woman, Cade said, "That's

some kinda lady, Joe. Could make a man do a lot of wrong things—and love every one of them." He shook his head.

"*Vielleicht. Frau* Rice *ist kalt. Kalt.* Ah, cold. Some be saying she killed her husband. *Ja.* He vas owner of der Circle R. Now she be."

"Not a bad way to die."

To the customers in the saloon, Elizabeth's voice was warm honey. "It is good these men have been eliminated, even if it were by a violent act. May their tormented souls rest in peace."

Before anyone else could respond, she turned to Cade and Bass, ignoring the presence of the marshal or the other Bransons. "As the proprietor of this establishment, I apologize, sirs, for this unfortunate incident. Mister Manko, I trust this won't detour you from bringing us more of your fine music."

She folded her arms, noting with satisfaction that she was the center of attention with the men inside the saloon and the crowd pushed against the door out on the sidewalk. Not to mention the two young gunfighters who were studying her face and frame with great interest. She expected as much.

Reaching up to hold the back brim of her hat for a moment, she knew the extension of her arm brought men's eyes to her bosom. "It is always a pleasure to see you, Marshal, sir. Your dedication to duty does honor to our town." Her hand slowly returned to her side, curled fingers passing down her body. "I trust this burst of diligence is an indication we might soon see the end to the cattle thievery throughout our lands."

"Your rustling problems are not the jurisdiction of this marshal. T'is that of the county sheriff—and the Rangers, if you please," Harding replied and spat toward a spittoon

close to a support beam, barely hitting the outside edge of
the container's bottom. "But I have decided to assume that
responsibility since the noble Sheriff Swisher is not well. I
will be present at the roundup."

"Good. Very responsible of you, Marshal." She eyed Dish
Branson fuming angrily at the door. "Mister Branson, let us
hope our roundup goes well. You may have heard the Trenchards just sold. To a man from Houston. Poor Mr. Trenchard couldn't see his way to stay what with all the cattle
taken from his land. More than a fair price he got, though.
Of course, I'm not a cattleman like yourself—but it's good
to invest in the land, don't you think?"

Dish rolled his tongue against his cheek, glad for the distraction. "No, hadn't heard 'bout it. If I had, we would'a
bought it. But I reckon you'll find ranching a mite tougher
than roundin' up purty ladies fer dancin' an' sech." He
chuckled at his joke and elbowed John to respond accordingly.

Instead, John touched the brim of his hat toward Elizabeth.

Dish snorted his contempt at the courtesy.

Her petticoats swinging, Elizabeth spun on her toes to
leave for the stairway leading to her office on the second
floor. Almost like a ballet movement, quite ceremonial in
its impact. The copper belt caught the light and glistened
its importance. Her motion hid a cruel smile of satisfaction.
As if on cue, the saloon burst into activity.

"Hold on a minute, Widow Rice." Marshal Emmett
Harding had a voice that could still ring through a battalion
on march. "These two boys be needing a declaration of
their innocence—from the men that saw it—put to paper-
writing and signed pretty-like. Just so there's no misunder-

standing later. Right? Maybe even Widow Rice would be so kind to put her moniker on the sheet as well."

Elizabeth spun back, her face tight with anger. Harding recoiled slightly from the unexpected hatred in her eyes. Elizabeth's furious look quickly clicked into one of annoyance.

"I don't see why my signature would be necessary," she responded. "I did not witness the activity. As far as I am concerned, there was no crime committed—or are you impugning the word of my patrons?"

"Im-pew-ning?" Harding laughed as he repeated the word slowly, his Welsh sense of rhythm taking over. "Hell's smile, I haven't impugned anybody for nigh onto ten years."

That brought a chuckle from Cade. His right cheek displayed a hidden dimple as his smile cocked to that side. "Yeah, but when you did, I reckon they stayed impugned."

The lawman's throaty laugh was echoed by the three cowhands.

Cade couldn't help but stare at Elizabeth Rice and she smiled, putting a hand on her hip as she stood. He rubbed his chin and his stare finally slid to Titus Branson who was looking around for an easy way to leave. Dish was talking to John about something that made John wince.

"Seems to me we should also get some signatures of any folks who will say Bass Manko was in this saloon all day and couldn't have been near the Branson ranch." Cade motioned toward his friend.

His statement drew smiles from Marshal Harding, as well as Bass and Criquette, a wink from Elizabeth Rice and a painful stare from Titus. The senior Branson held his left hand to his mouth to hold the wracking inside. His eyes studied his youngest son with contempt. Dish finished his words with John and turned back to face Cade. The middle brother's face was a snarl. A few seconds later, the little salesman got the significance of his words, chuckled and shook his head.

"This writing seems like a savvy thing to me," Bass declared. "To make sure ol' Dish here doesn't get a short memory. Would appreciate any folks who would say I was here. Good 'nuff is good 'nuff. But, of course, we wouldn't expect you to sign, Missus Rice." His smile at Elizabeth Rice was his best as his eyes sought hers.

The voluptuous saloon owner returned the intimacy without any indication of being coy and, immediately, ascended the banister again. Pausing against the railing, Elizabeth's face was a mask; no one could possibly guess what she was thinking or feeling.

After laying his rifle on the bar, Harding pulled a stubby pencil and an odd-shaped sheet of paper from his coat pocket and wrote a quick statement of what happened. Four customers stepped up to witness the paper as well, followed by the three River S cowboys. They also signed beneath a second statement lower on the page that attested to Bass being at the saloon all day. Proudly, the wounded cowboy added his "X" at both places.

Criquette strolled over to sign his name, a scrawly presentation, but a complete "Joseph Wilheim Criquette, Farmer" under the statement of self-defense. He quietly told Bass that he couldn't sign the other because he hadn't been there all day, then said he had to leave since he had promised his wife that he would only have one beer. The elderly German warmly invited him to come and see him some time, shook hands with both Bass and Cade and left.

Eager to leave, Titus Branson shoved John toward the entrance. John hesitated and asked, "What about Cade, Paw? Is he coming with us?"

A string of raspy coughs followed. Through bloody teeth, Titus growled, "I don't give a damn what he does. From this day on, he ain't no son o' mine." He coughed again. "Prob'ly never was. That no-good whore of a wife prob'ly was bred by sum goddamn Injun." He walked on, hacking and spitting.

John stood, unable to speak or move. Dish turned toward him and uncharacteristically put a hand on John's shoulder. His face carried the strain of hearing their father's curse.

"Let's go home, John."

Tears welled in the corners of John's eyes. He tried to speak, choked on the emotion at the edge of his throat but tried again. "W-What about Cade? Y-You heard what P-Paw said. I-Isn't he a part of us now? Y-You have to do something, Dish." He swallowed the bubbling anxiety and changed the subject to ease it. "W-What about Gilmore an' Moss? They worked for us."

Dish was staring at the saloon wall. "Maybe she'll want me anyway."

"W-What?"

"Huh? Oh, nuthin'." Dish blinked away his mental distraction. His plan had failed horribly. His mind was whirring with frustration. "We'll leave some money with Mister Crandall for the buryin'—a'fer we ride back." He started to say their father would be next to need funeral services but realized his brother couldn't handle that truth.

"I-Is Cade coming?"

"Ask 'im an' find out. I'm goin'."

"Dish?"

"Yah?"

"I think Cade whipped Ed with his fists." John's countenance changed, a glimpse of pride glistening in his tear-swollen eyes.

"Hell, that thar's as likely as a penguin comin' through this saloon, John. Cade's good but that damn Gilmore was a bull."

"Dish Branson," Marshal Harding snorted loudly as he shoved the signed paper back into his coat pocket.

Spinning around, Dish's eyes glistened with contempt. "What?"

"Be forewarned. I'm letting you and your pappy and your brother off this time. But don't come to my town wearing iron again."

Dish's mouth opened to respond, thought better about it and muttered to himself.

"I didn't get that, Dish," Harding said. There was a slight tremor in his fingers and he clasped them together to end it. Age was the reason, not fear, but he knew how it would appear.

"Nuthin'. I didn't say nuthin'."

"Sure you did, Dish. Collect your face and give me the particulars. Look you, I can take the words. What was it you said?"

Dish's deep breath swelled his chest before he let it ease through his teeth. "I said ya were too old to be wearin' that badge."

"There's a good boy. And?"

"Ya couldn't stop me from doin' anythang."

Marshal Harding balled his tobacco juice and let it fly toward the spittoon against the bar's footrest. He missed badly and the spray splattered along the brass rail and onto the bar itself. His smile curdled at the miss, then his tired eyes returned to Dish.

"Your little brother said it best, Dish—you aren't that good."

Dish glared at Cade, then brought his scowl to Harding's face but the arrogance behind it was already waning. "You're still old to be lawin'. That's why them li'l ranchers is a'fightin' off them Mex rustlers. Ya cain't catch 'em."

John tugged on his brother's shirt. "Come on, Dish. Let's go home."

"Shut up, John. I'll dee-cide when we leave."

"But, Dish, you heard the marshal. He's not responsible for cattle and the land."

"I said shut up. Hardin' ain't no good wharever."

"That's not right, Dish. He's an old man—like Paw."

"That's the probl'm, John. 'Tween Hardin' and that sickly county sheriff, thar ain't no real law 'round." Dish squeezed his rifle in both hands.

"We haven't had any trouble." John glanced at Harding who was now talking with Cade and Bass at the bar.

"Them Mexs don't want to tangle with Bransons."

"They don't want to tangle with Cade."

"Whaddya say?"

"Nothing."

Chapter Seven

Gradually, the saloon returned to drinking and playing cards and the doorway emptied of the curious.

At the edge of the stairway, Elizabeth Rice gestured as if dismissing peasants. "Johnny, a round of drinks on the house. And give Mister Manko and his combative friend whatever they want."

Forcing a smile, Elizabeth turned and went up the stairway, fully aware that most of the men watched her, even with free liquor waiting. Halfway up, she stopped once more and looked back, winked at Bass and announced loudly, "Marshal Harding, I am glad to hear you will be protecting us ranchers from those Mexican outlaws during the roundup. County Sheriff Swisher is ill—and you know there are no Rangers within a week's ride. The town will be fine. It's the ranchers that need your help. On behalf of my fellow ranchers, I thank you."

Dish grinned wolfishly, glanced at the old lawman and left.

"Thank you, Widow Rice. I will tend to that responsibility—even though it is not bloody mine to do," Harding answered rather sheepishly.

Without further comment, she continued up the stairway. Harding shrugged drooped shoulders and ambled over to his Winchester laying on the bar. Both Cade and Bass joined him, thanking the old lawman for interfering.

"Aye, nothing it was, boys. Don't think you two needed much help. That Gilmore fellow, he's been a real bad one for quite a spell." He stared at Cade. "I hear you took him down with the wind in your fists, boy. That would have been something to see. Thought I was going to have to do so myself." He winked.

Bass grinned and slapped Cade on the back. "Don't ever bet against him."

"Now there's a thing. Don't think ever I would."

Cade nodded his appreciation.

"T'is not to be spoken of—this time—about you boys carrying guns in town," Harding said, studying both young men. "T'was a good thing, probably. We'll let that bide. This time." The gimpy lawman bit off a corner of a new tobacco plug and offered the same to Cade. He nodded "no thanks" but Bass accepted the offer with relish and asked if the marshal knew how Elizabeth Rice was doing with her husband's ranch. Harding shrugged. It was clear he didn't think much of a woman owning a ranch—especially a city woman—then he spat at the same now-closer spittoon and, as usual, missed.

"Of course, welcome she'd be on a cold winter night, wouldn't she?" the old lawman drawled and rubbed his chin. "Of course, a lead she-wolf can turn on any wolf that gets in her way."

Something in his comment seemed more than a flippant

one to Bass. He grinned and glanced up at the second floor balcony but Elizabeth had already disappeared into her office.

Cade found himself evaluating Harding on his manner of speaking, a pleasant combination of Welsh rhythm and phrasing, curse words and straight-forward presentation. An ever-present wall of authority separated him from others. Cynicism lay just beneath his words, a view of people and their weaknesses that came from upholding the law for a long time. His love of tobacco and his consistent inaccuracy with spitting made Cade wonder if the man was equally poor with a gun. He had never seen him use a weapon of any kind. Word was he was still the marshal because the town council didn't want to deal with the unpleasantness of firing him.

Of course, the youngest Branson had known Harding since childhood. He had grown up in awe of the lawman, fearing his stern countenance. Then, as a teenager, he began to see Harding in a less flattering light. Even Cade had heard the rumors that time had caught up with the lawman and he would soon have to be replaced. He wondered if Susannah had heard them and how she felt about the criticism of her father.

Smiling widely, the tall cowboy with the big eyes sauntered over to them and said the three hands were going to enjoy some cards before heading out to the roundup starting tomorrow morning. Their boss had approved of their outing, he said, like a small boy explaining hooky from school. They were having a supply wagon filled at the general store and were taking it directly to the initial camp.

Casually, the lawman asked, "You River S boys been having any trouble with rustlers?"

"Naw, them Mex boys been a'missin' us. Leastwise, so

far," the cowboy said, his eyes widening even more. "We think it's real fine you be comin' to the roundup. We sure don't need no shootin' trouble there."

Harding nodded his appreciation and the cowboy hurried away. Cade, Bass and the marshal stood for a moment in silence, watching the cowboy rejoin his two friends.

Harding broke the awkwardness, pointing with a permanently bent forefinger at the torn slash in Bass's pant leg where the bullet had clipped him. "'Tis mean-looking, that burn, Bass. But damn worse you've had, I reckon."

"Yeah, there's been a few that didn't like my singing."

The old lawman smiled in the crooked way of his. "'Twas fixing to get supplies when my Susannah—my youngest, you know—told me of a ruckus down this way. She said you two were doing the warrin'. Said she ran into you lads outside this fine establishment. Figured I'd best wander down this way to see what was going on."

"What did she say?" Bass felt his leg wound to determine its severity and quickly decided it was only cut flesh.

"There is lovely in much of her sayings but that you wouldn't want to hear," Harding laughed. "I'll let that bide."

"Good 'nuff."

Cade wondered if the lawman knew his daughter and Bass were in love. Surely, he'd seen Bass around their small place and figured it out. More intriguing, it was hard to believe such a hard-looking, shriveled man could produce something as lovely as Susannah.

"Excuse me a minute, Marshal Harding, I need to say something to my brother," Cade said, looking at a forelorn John Branson standing next to the doorway, watching them.

"Name's Emmett. Save that 'Marshal' stuff for someone who needs it." The gruff lawman casually picked up his Winchester from the top of the bar, eased the trigger down and leaned the weapon against the bar with the butt on the floor. He looked over his shoulder and saw who was waiting.

"Cade, you be going easy on your kin now. They made a bad mistake today but don't make them pay too high."

The offer of informality surprised Cade. "Thanks . . . Emmett, I appreciate the advice. But I think I'm the one who'll do the paying."

With the old man's thoughtful nod as a send-off, Cade walked straight for John who bit his lower lip.

"I-I'm s-sorry, Cade. W-We s-shouldn't have."

"Not your fault, John. It was Paw's—an' Dish's."

"I-I'm n-not sure h-how P-Paw's gonna . . . take—"

"Don't worry about it," Cade interrupted. "I'll go over to Black Jack's. He'll put me up for a few days."

Black Jack Sante had been a buffalo hunter in its days of glory and now lived by himself in a tiny shack in the shadow of a boxed-in canyon at the edge of the prairie. Both Cade and Bass liked the grizzled veteran and had learned much from listening to him talk about the yesterdays of a land thick with buffalo, Indians and long grass. Black Jack had been the closest thing to family Bass Manko knew, letting the lad stay with him whenever he wished. Both carried pistols he had altered to yield faster performance and wore holsters he had made to do the same.

"B-Black Jack." John repeated the name like it was some faraway land. "Yes, I believe that's for the best. Right now."

"You go on, John. Paw will be needin' you. He looks worse."

John's face tightened. "Oh, I don't think so, Cade. I thought he looked a lot better than a month ago. I've been hoping he would go to Doc Langford but you know Paw."

Cade didn't want to discuss the matter and looked around

for a reason to leave. "John, I need to talk with the fella over there. He was wounded in the gunfight."

"Oh . . . sure. Don't worry about burying Gilmore an' Moss. Dish an' I will stop at Mister Crandall's an' leave cash money for it." John cocked his head to the side, almost like Dish or Cade did on occasion. "We'll get the roundup goin'—on schedule, I'm sure. Better plan to show up, though. Day after tomorrow, at least. Paw'll be mad if you don't." He looked away. "I guess he wouldn't have to know. I don't think Paw will be joining us for the roundup. Dish will be mad, though, if you don't. He won't like the marshal showing either."

Cade gritted his teeth to keep a response from ramming into John's stilted view of things. "Sure, John. You take care."

"I-I don't think . . . Bass took those cattle. I-I never did."

"Neither did I, John." He held out his hand.

John took it eagerly and met Cade's gaze. "I'll be . . . seein' you . . . soon."

Cade watched his oldest brother leave wiping his eyes. At the hitching rack, John looked up and saw Cade standing in the saloon doorway. Unwrapping the reins, he stared down the street at his retreating brother and father, then back to Cade. "Y-You're still my brother, you know."

"I know."

After John rode away, Cade went to William H. Sullivan. Slightly in shock, the wounded salesman leaned against the far end of the bar, nursing his wound. After greeting him, Cade examined the unusually quiet salesman's bloody arm. A clean wound. The bullet only grazed flesh.

"You're all right, Sullivan. Just cut the skin."

"Well, I think I've had enough excitement for one day—

maybe a whole year." Sullivan studied his arm, alarmed that it continued to bleed. "Maybe I'd better go see the doctor. Then catch the next stage . . . home. You think it will be safe?"

Cade tried not to smile. "I'm sure it will."

"Say, does this mean I can say I was in a gunfight?"

"Well, I don't know why not. Just don't use our names when you tell it."

Sullivan thought about the statement, nodded his head in agreement and said goodbye, holding his arm like it was broken as he left the saloon. He stopped beside Bass and the marshal to complete his exit.

Cade returned to the other end of the bar where Marshal Harding and Bass were waiting with a new bottle of whiskey and three glasses. Four Mexicans were lifting the dead bodies to remove them as the bartender shouted directions they apparently didn't understand or didn't care to. Cade glanced at the obnoxious bartender who looked away and immediately began talking more gently. Along the bar, men were lining up for their free whiskey, some clamoring to be served immediately.

"Just remembered something. All your walkin' around reminded me, Cade," Bass said as Cade rejoined them. "I promised a fella a special song. I'd better deliver, then I'd vote for somethin' to eat. What do ya say?"

"'Twould be a pleasure," Harding agreed. "'Tis not often I get to hear fine singing. Home I be most nights, you know."

Bass grinned, "Yeah, I heard that."

Cade thought he was going to sing *Oh Susannah*. A twinge of jealousy slipped into Cade's mind and he pushed it away. This was his best friend. No woman should ever come between them. No woman. Not even one like Susannah Harding. But Cade was pleased when his friend began singing the tender Irish ballad, *I'll Take You Home Again, Kathleen*. He followed that with two of his favorites, *The Old Chisholm Trail*, and the haunting *Female Highwayman*.

As Cade watched Bass perform, the old lawman studied Cade. Harding seemed unsure of how to proceed, then loudly proclaimed, "Ever glad I am to have this chance to speak with you, Cade. Had my eye on you two boys for some time. But your pappy always sets off my powder. Sorry it is. Always it's been, I reckon. Not sure why but it is so. Don't suppose he's jealous of my magnificent ranch, do you?" He chuckled and his eyes sparkled.

The young gunfighter couldn't remember being sized up any more intensely.

Harding spat. This time he managed to hit the spittoon less than a foot from his right boot. Wrinkles ran to stay close to Harding's squinting eyes as he began to share what was on his mind. "But forget that. Cade, has the Bar 6 been troubled by rustlers? Other than this thing today, I mean. Four small cattlemen—Trenchard, Donnell, Gray and Richardson—complained about losing cattle like it was pouring old ladies and canes before they sold out. Hard to do the figuring, if it was for real, their troubles—or just not smart ranching." He gathered tobacco juice and spat again, this time missing the same spittoon by six inches. "Aye, but there are the stories of a Mexican leading the outlaws. He be wearing a black scarf about his face. What is your take of this sadness?"

"How's anybody know what he wears? I thought they struck at night—when riders weren't around."

"Heard that from the Circle R foreman, Jordan Maher."

"Wonder how he knew?"

"Chased 'em once."

"To answer your question, we haven't had any rustling

problems. Heard about some of the others having trouble. Don't know what to think of it." Cade turned away from watching Bass to face the old marshal. "Guess there could be Mexican bandits crossing the Rio. Seems funny they'd only bother them, though."

"Aye, the same answer I came down upon. But there's pickin's a mite closer to the big river, don't you see?" Harding judged the distance to the same spittoon, cocked his head slightly to the right and let a brown stream fly. It hit the side of the container and slid to the floor.

"I heard you lost your deputy awhile back. I knew Henry Endore. I'm real sorry." A frown crawled across Cade's forehead and stayed there.

Harding rubbed his chin, then took a quick gulp of whiskey. His mouth twisted to help the fiery liquid go down. "Aye, and a fine lad he was. A fine one. Found him face down, I did. Five bullets in his young body. Had to be telling his folks, I did. Worst day I've ridden through in a long spell. A day for the Devil to sing."

"What happened? I heard it was rustlers."

"Aye, it was," Harding said, wincing with every word. "He was an outrider with the Richardson herd. To keep it safe." He took a deep breath and let it free slowly. "Aye, and I asked him to do this thing. The herd got through the night. He didn't."

"I reckon Henry knew what he was doing."

Harding stared at his half-empty whiskey glass and refilled it from the bottle. His hand shook and Cade tried not to notice. Harding offered the bottle to Cade who indicated he didn't need any more. The lawman took another gulp and wiped his mouth with the back of his hand, barely wincing as the rye sought his throat.

"I think of sending him all the time. That I do," Harding said through clenched teeth.

Cade tried to move the subject away from the deputy's death. "Well, except for today's blowup, we haven't had any stolen beef. Course, you never really know until roundup's over."

"Strange, isn't it, lad? Just those four small ranchers have been cherry-picked to who-shot-John."

"I don't know what to tell you. Never talked with any of them much. Just to pass the time when I've seen them on the range." Cade pushed his hat back on his forehead and let the stale air seek sweating hair. "Maybe we'll find we've been hit too. But none of our riders are reporting anything like that, though. Not so far, anyway. Maybe we've just been lucky."

"Aye, but I don't think luck is what it's about, son. I think it's your gun," Harding said. "If rustlers there are about, I think they heard about you being gun-savvy and they are just plain going elsewhere. Aye, that's what I think. As sure as a Welshman can sing a fine hymn. No offense."

Cade was beginning to wonder if the crusty lawman was actually probing for something to see if the Bransons were rustlers themselves. "Emmett, I don't see how one—"

"Oh, but good sense it makes, Cade. All about the valley, the story spread of your run-in with the three rustlers back awhile it was. Hell's teeth, that's all a lot of folks were jabbering about for months. Damn, why wouldn't such rustling bastards want to ride clear of you?" Harding said. "Hell, I am scratching around the bone here—and I know better. Hiring you—to be my deputy—is my aim. Both you and Bass. There is sorry I am for taking so long to get to it."

Cade was quiet for a moment. Bass was laying down his

guitar on his chair amid much heavier applause than usual. "Coming from you, that's quite a compliment . . . Emmett but I'd better pass. Guess I'm hoping all this will blow over—between my family and me."

"Aye, figured as much but I had to ask. Sure would be liking to have you with me. I need a man true as the sun comes to the hill. No deputies right now do I be having. Only Roper. He's not really a lawman, you know. Just a friend. Helps around the jail. Sweeping and such. Has a wee trouble keeping the dish level, you know." He took a gulp of his whiskey. "Roundup starts on the morrow and I must be there."

"You really think they'll hit during roundup?"

"Wish I could be knowing such. But all the herds cuddled up from everywhere be mighty tempting targets. Easy to come after during winter too, come to think on it. Still, being there, I must."

Cade ran a finger around the edge of his glass. "I reckon County Sheriff Swisher is all laid up."

Harding grinned a lopsided smile and patted Cade on the shoulder. "That's what his deputy told me—and then said he wouldn't be doing anything either unless the sheriff ordered him. But it's my job to keep this town safe and safe it is not with beef being run off—if they be."

"You sound like you're not certain Trenchard, Richardson and the others really had rustling trouble." Cade cocked his head to the side. "Do you think something else is going on?"

"Just being careful, son. Best way to play cards—and keep the law. I figure being at the roundup's as good a place as any for me. Town'll be quiet as a sleeping yellow chick." The old lawman grinned. "They'll be chirping about me at the roundup. That can't hurt. A comfort of old age, being talked about."

Cade returned the smile. "It just hit me. What do you know about these new owners?"

"Aye, you're heading down the same trail I've been. They've just shown up—at the right time. Like the cut of a new dawn. Interesting to chew on, isn't it?"

"I've met Absalum Sil. He's the new owner of Richardson's place. Looks more like a farmer than a cattleman to me. A damn mean farmer. He doesn't talk like a man from around here."

"Aye, no more than pig's feet look like a crow's." Harding chuckled. "Black Jack told me I'd be taking to you. Nothin' like your pappy or Dish. No offense."

"You know Black Jack?"

"Black Jack and I, we go back a long way. He told me you and Bass were his prize pupils, two of the best he'd ever seen with a six-gun." Harding's eyes laid softly on Cade's face. "He also told me you were one to ride the river with."

"Black Jack's been good to me. Figured to go there before heading . . . home. Need to talk with him a little."

"Well, if it doesn't work out at home, you be welcome to come and stay at my place for as long as you want. No strings attached about wearing a badge. Make you work for your supper, though."

"That's mighty nice of you but I'll be all right. Bass might be interested in becoming your deputy, though. He's better with a gun than I am, anyway."

"I reckon you be underrating yourself, son. Now if this old lawman was to be letting the word out that you were with me, that'd be a day for the King." Harding rolled the tobacco chaw around inside his mouth. "Look, Cade, I may be getting long in the tooth, but I haven't lost my hearing yet. I hear what folks be saying, about me being too old for this job. Sadly, they whisper that old age comes not on its own, you know. But I figure they don't . . ."

He stopped in mid-sentence as Bass rejoined them with a wide smile. "That's enough singin' for awhile. I'm starving." He glanced at Cade, then at Harding. "Don't worry about Cade. He's always bringin' up stuff his mother told him."

"I'd say Cade Branson is a man to ride the river with." Harding spat again at the spittoon. This time he missed by over a foot.

Bass patted Cade's arm and his smile widened further. "I'll drink to that."

Cade's smile was slow but it arrived. "Let's drink to a good roundup—for everyone."

Marshal Harding chortled and nodded his head. All three downed their whiskey in hard gulps. Slamming his empty glass on the bar, the lawman suggested they eat at the hotel instead of the saloon. Better food, he said. If it was agreeable with them, he would like to invite Susannah and his son, Seth, to join them. Roper would likely do so too. Cade and Bass agreed and they left. The bartender waved but they didn't notice.

A long-faced businessman stopped Harding as they left. In a pious tone, he expressed his concern about the marshal being out of town during the roundup. Harding thanked him politely and told him directly that the ranchers needed him more at the moment. The businessman walked away, unconvinced of the rightness of his decision, and immediately ordered a drink from the bar.

As they walked outside, Cade said, "You know, I think I'm going to take my horse over to the livery for a bite of grain and watering before we put on the feedbag ourselves. I damn near ran him into the ground coming here."

Harding started to spit his agreement on the wooden

sidewalk for emphasis, then re-aimed it for the street. "Like to see a man who tends to his horses."

"Bass, why don't you go on with . . . Emmett and I'll catch up. No need for all of us going."

Bass snapped a wide smile. "Good 'nuff. That's the best idea I've heard since the marshal suggested eatin'." He frowned at his friend. "Or are you gonna go lookin' for Dish?"

"No, Dish has left town."

Cade was loosening the reins of his buckskin from the post when he saw Susannah Harding come out of the general store. The marshal waved her over. She smiled, waved back and walked purposefully toward them. Cade returned to his task. She was only a few feet away before he looked up again, not knowing what to expect.

Afternoon sunlight touched her face and a breeze hurried to caress a stray lock of hair that had rebelled from the severe hairdo and lay down her sun-kissed cheek. Bass drank in her unspoiled beauty as she approached. She wasn't as stunning to look at as Elizabeth Bingham Rice but few women were. Cade felt himself drawn to Susannah in a way he knew he shouldn't. She was Bass's woman and he was her man.

"Well, it looks like you two won the war." She glanced at Bass, then Cade.

"Well, it's hard to tell one ruffian from another," Cade said, feeling a rush through his body and surprised that he had said something before Bass did.

His blue eyes fixed on hers and she was the only thing near. She returned the intimacy. A sweet rose blush filled her cheeks. Silence awkwardly pushed its way between them. Her femininity climbed all over his senses. His body tensed and tingled in a way he knew she would not like. He was her friend; Bass was her boyfriend. There was a big difference. She blinked and smiled at her father, then at Bass who smiled and removed his hat.

Rubbing his unshaven chin, Cade was angry at himself for not thinking to remove his hat before. He tore the hat from his head, letting his dark brown hair ruffle against his shoulders, smiling and making a short awkward bow. He almost bent the attached eagle feather against his thigh. His horse nuzzled its impatience against his arm. Annoyed at the animal's interruption, he turned to push the big animal away.

Without noticing the visual exchange between Bass and his daughter, Marshal Harding asked where her brother was. She pointed at the store and looked back at Cade as she did. He rolled and unrolled his hat brim with both hands, trying to think of something to say. "It is a nice day, isn't it? We've been fortunate so far."

Her eyes met his again, then concern filled them. "Oh, I almost forgot! The shots. Those men, did they . . ."

"They tried plenty hard, Miss Harding. It just wasn't . . . good 'nuff," Bass answered, holding his hat in front of him with both hands. She was much younger than the breathtaking Elizabeth Rice, and hardly dressed in fashionable attire, but still easy to look at. His gaze took in her hair, her face, her breasts and her entire frame, all arranged in working ranch clothes more suited for a cowhand than a woman. Especially not one of such beauty.

"Are they . . . ?" The fear in her eyes was real. She didn't seem to notice Bass's appraisal.

"They won't be trying anything again," Bass answered quickly, trying to position himself so it would be awkward for her to look directly at his friend.

"Father, I would've thought you wouldn't let such men into town."

Both Bass and Cade were taken aback by the comment and the personal reference but couldn't think of anything to say in response. The lawman spat and told his daughter that the men had done nothing against the law until they went after Bass and Cade. It was clear from her facial reaction that she didn't agree.

"If your father stopped every man with a reputation from comin' to town, there wouldn't be many in the saloon." Searching her face, Bass bowed slightly, hoping for some indication of her feelings toward him.

She looked up again to meet his gaze. "Oh, you're wounded."

It was the first time in his life Cade wished he'd been hit with a bullet. Bass smiled and reached out to touch her arm. "I was lucky. They weren't. But who's countin'? Your father saved us from a lot of trouble."

Susannah's next remark surprised all of them. "Father, did that awful Rice woman talk with you . . . in there?" Her face was stern and unrelenting with her desire to get an answer.

Marshal Harding responded by spitting and growling, "Let's be getting something to eat. Sound good to you, Sissie?"

"You didn't answer my question, Father."

With a sheepish grin, the old lawman shook his head, more in wonder than anything else. "Yeah, she be wandering in. 'Tis her place, you know. Told me where to get off before you could put the fiddle on the roof. Didn't she, boys?" His gaze sought their involvement—quickly.

"I believe she asked to be remembered to you and your

brother." Bass returned his hat to his head. And, for once, tried hard not to smile. His mouth wrinkled at the corners.

"Ah-huh. I can imagine." Susannah said and looked down at herself involuntarily. "An' I suppose she had you two panting like dogs?"

Marshal Harding frowned. "That's enough, little lady. The Widow Rice has done nothing to you."

Words started to form but she bit her lip, inhaled to relieve the pressure.

"Are you . . . two . . . joining us?"

"Cade and I would like that very much. After he takes care of his horse."

Chapter Eight

Cade Branson muttered an awkward goodbye and slowly began leading his horse down the street. He turned back to see Susannah heading for the store to get her brother.

Marshal Harding was nowhere in sight, probably checking his office to see if his hung-over prisoners were sober enough to be released. He was known for taking the homeless off the street at night and giving them a place to sleep and a meal.

Pulled to Susannah as if she were a magnetic force, Cade saw her talking and smiling with Bass. Cade turned back, angry at himself for looking. Even more angry for not saying that she was as good-looking as Widow Rice. To him, anyway. And she was.

From her second-story office window, Elizabeth Bingham Rice studied them from a slight break in her curtains, but none noticed.

Fifteen minutes later, Cade walked through the hotel lobby and into the adobe-walled restaurant to join the others. Stoneware jars dangling from an overhang beam clinked their welcome. A teenaged Mexican boy squatted inside the foyer, strumming a guitar and singing an old song about wild women. Curled beside him sleeping was a large red dog. A few feet away was a torn sombrero for contributions. Cade had heard the song before and knew enough Spanish to make out the words. Slipping his hand into a vest pocket, he winked as he passed, repeated a line from the song and tossed a coin into the hat. The young singer grinned and sang harmony to Cade's response.

A recently scrubbed earthen floor first caught Cade's attention as he stepped into the restaurant, then he saw Bass, Emmett and Susannah at a table in the far corner, along with her brother and Roper. He'd met both men several times over the years. Acting as hostess, a barefoot girl with large brown eyes greeted him in a mixture of Spanish and English.

From their table in the corner, the old lawman waved enthusiastically. Susannah smiled, then looked down at herself involuntarily. Pointing at the marshal, Cade told the girl in Spanish that he would go there. Nodding, she led him in that direction as if her job depended on it. He nodded at Union soldiers at one table who gave him a stern look as he passed. At Marshal Harding's table, he said, "*Gracias*, señorita," and she gave him a smile at being called a woman that stretched across her brown face. Cade noticed immediately that the old lawman didn't have his usual chaw in his mouth and assumed Susannah had made him get rid of it when they came into the restaurant.

"Did you get that fine animal settled in?" Harding said, loud enough for anyone in the room to hear, whether they wanted to or not. There was something about a Welsh voice that carried.

". . . that fine animal settled in?" came the repeating phrase from the white-haired man at the table.

Cade and Bass were reminded that Roper, a raw-boned man of indeterminate age and slow mind, constantly imitated Marshal Harding, often repeating his sentences as they were said, almost like an echo. The repetition was irritating to them but apparently not noticed by the Hardings. Today, as usual, Roper was dressed like the old lawman, wearing a suitcoat several sizes too large and a buttoned white shirt, mule-eared boots and a dirty hat with a wide brim that sank around his head. The dimwitted man's whole life had become a bluff of sorts, trying to appear like the man he admired most—Marshal Emmett Harding. However, he didn't carry a shoulder holster as the marshal did. Most likely, Cade assumed, because the Hardings wouldn't let him.

What hair Roper did have was curly at the ends, and snow white, covering most of his long ears. Thick eyebrows looked like they were pasted on his circular face. A narrow nose was anchored by a stringy white mustache. His eyes were squinty like he was always staring into the sun. But his face was otherwise free of any signs of aging—no wrinkles, no lines, almost boyish in structure. It was as if the horse kick to his head as a child had stopped the aging process as well as slow his mind. The man was of little use around the jail but the marshal didn't seem to mind. Although not an official deputy, Roper had been with him for most of his adult life and thought of himself as part of the family, and so did the Hardings.

"Cade, you be knowing Roper, don't you?" Marshal Harding said.

"That be right, I am Roper. I take care o' Emmett. I have seen you at our place—with Bass Manko to see Miss Susannah."

"It's good to see you again, Roper." Cade shook his hand and it was like gripping a piece of rough-hewn timber, and just as strong.

Roper was probably a year or two younger than Marshal Harding but recently had taken to "caring for" the old marshal like he was an aged invalid. It infuriated him but Roper didn't seem to realize.

"Well, God bless you, Roper, you can't even take care of yourself," Marshal Harding's twenty-year-old son, Seth, blurted. He was seated next to the older man.

Roper's unwrinkled face squeezed into something like a dried apple and he looked away.

Susannah jumped up and went over to him. "Roper. Roper. Seth didn't mean that. He was just teasing you. We all know you take good care of . . . Emmett, don't we?"

She glared at her father who gradually mumbled, "Aye, Roper, he does be taking good care of me."

"Seth!" Susannah's face was stern.

Embarrassed, her younger brother glanced at Bass and Cade, then back to Roper. His gentle face twitched along the right corner of his mouth and he reached over and put his arm on the older man's bony shoulder. Roper shivered at the touch.

"Roper, come on now, you know I didn't mean that. You're the best. I pray for you every day. I really do. God bless you, Roper." His hands came together as if in prayer and he glanced at Cade and Bass to see if they were properly impressed with his religious attitude. Both young men knew of the young Harding's calling, or at least, his often spoken inclination to become a minister. Much to his father's disdain.

For an instant, it appeared like the old jail helper wasn't listening. He pursed his lips like he was forming an "O."

Turning his head toward the young man, Roper's jack-o-lantern smile of missing teeth told a story of pure love for the Harding children.

"You're the best, Seth. You're the best, Miss Susannah." He paused, rubbed his unshaved chin and grinned again. "You're the best, Emmett."

Returning to her chair, Susannah introduced her brother. "Cade, I believe you've met my brother, Seth." She smiled at her brother. "Seth, Cade is one of the Bransons, you know."

"Of course, I know Seth. How are you?" Still standing, Cade shook Seth's hand.

Seth was nervous, rubbing his right hand on a leather vest before accepting Cade's hand. His features were gentle ones. Cade assumed the young man must favor his late mother in appearance. Brown hair was combed straight back, making his forehead more prominent and making him appear fragile. His thick nose was the only feature that reminded of his father. His simple black suit reminded Cade of a preacher they knew back home. Even though they were close to the same age, he seemed much younger than either Cade or Bass. Cade vaguely recalled him from school. Seth Harding never entered any of the boys' games before and after the teaching, preferring instead to talk with the teacher about some aspect of the day's studies that interested him.

Clearly, the young man wanted his father to consider him worthy of the honor of being his son but something else was there too. Seth Harding carried an air of righteousness, of a self-annointed closeness to God that Cade had seen often in fiery Methodist ministers and stoic Roman Catholic priests. Maybe that's what reminded him of a preacher more than Seth's simple blacksuit. But the young Harding also appeared to have the personality often found in the son of a strong, domineering father. Cade felt sorry for him, thinking immediately of his oldest brother, John. Why would a father do that to his son? he asked himself.

"From what I heard, you two were real angels of retribution in that saloon." Seth cleared his throat, a thin nervous sound. "Of course, nothing of good ever came from such a place, or any of the other wicked places in town I shall not mention."

Bass's eyebrows raised and he appeared amused. Cade shot him a scornful glance. Making fun of a man's son wasn't smart, no matter how silly the young man's piety seemed.

"We didn't have much choice, Seth. It wasn't a big deal," Cade said, trying to keep from staring at Susannah seated between he and Bass.

It was difficult to concentrate. He could smell her soft presence, an intoxicating fragrance of sweet soap and womanly musk and it made his whole body tingle. How strange this day had been, he thought. Who would have guessed he would end up sitting next to her? But Bass's captivating eyes and easy smile sought her attention and more.

"Well, certainly it was. You were God's chosen messengers to bring justice to those evildoers," Seth proclaimed in a stilted manner and cleared his throat again. Cade and Bass were more interested in his sister than anything the young man had to say but both listened politely. "Why, they're talking about you two everywhere in town. I even heard Pastor Dorsey comment on it—and he is truly a man of God, as I hope to be some day."

His eyes were bright with interest, studying every nuance of the two strangers' appearance and hoping they picked up on his comment and would ask him about his calling.

Marshal Harding's expression showed his son's ambition to be a minister was not high on his list.

Roper repeated that he'd heard the two were "hellers with a gun." The lawman told him not to repeat such nonsense; Seth told him not to say "hell." Roper looked puzzled and hurt by the rebukes.

"If you're askin' can we handle ourselves, the answer is good 'nuff. There isn't anybody better with a gun than Cade—unless it's me," Bass said. He glanced at Harding, then smiled at Susannah.

Before anyone else could ask another question, Susannah said, "Do you two often get in fights like that?" Her expression displayed both amusement and concern.

"Susannah," Harding said, continuing his frown toward his daughter. "Where are your manners, girl?"

"That's alright," Bass responded, displaying a mouth of straight white teeth.

"I believe the term is 'pistol-fighter.' Pistol-fighters, that's what they are calling you," Seth interjected and cleared his throat.

Roper said authoritatively, "Pistol-fighters is good with pistols. Uh-huh. Had me one ons't but she didn't pan out. Not fer me anyhow."

Clearing his throat twice, Seth held the edge of the table in front of him with both hands. "Maybe you could help Dad get rid of the rustling out in the valley. It's really gotten bad. Sheriff Swisher isn't able to work the county right now and the responsibility falls to my father. I think several ranchers sold out because of that. I'm hopeful the new owners are God-fearing men and will invite me to conduct prayer meetings during the roundup." Seth's own glance at his father surprised him; Marshal Harding was nodding agreement.

"Some of those new boys don't look like the prayin' type," Bass advised. His eyes sought Susannah's for approval.

Seth straightened in his chair and continued, "That is of no consequence to me. Next spring I hope to leave for the seminary anyway."

"Next spring be a long time from here, boy." Harding's tone was of a man tiring of hearing his son's same request.

Susannah looked at her brother and mouthed, "Not now." Seth frowned but said nothing.

A squat Mexican woman in an off-shoulder peasant blouse and a layered skirt that swished rhythmically presented herself at their table.

"What fine fare have you got today, young lady?" Marshal Harding boomed.

With little interest in the subject, she reported in halting English that they could have steak, beans, tortillas and fried potatoes. They had no eggs but radishes and squash were available. Without asking, the lawman ordered steaks, beans and potatoes for everyone, a plate of tortillas and a pot of hot coffee.

". . . and a pot of hot coffee," Roper repeated.

Eager to continue with his father's apparent blessing, Seth began to tell Cade and Bass about the amount of rustling going on in the region. To him, the problem was one of "tortured souls and unrepentant sinners who only needed to be shown the way of our Lord" and the problem would disappear. Marshal Harding's growling response was cut short by Susannah's disapproving glare. But the lawman couldn't resist. Speaking loud enough to stop his son's recitation, Harding repeated his assertion that the ranchers who complained probably didn't know enough about cattle to make it. But if there were any rustlers, it had to be Mexican bandits running stolen cattle across the Rio Grande into Mexico, where no one dared to go after them. Not even the Army.

He had met all of the new owners, except whoever bought the Trenchard spread. He had heard the news only this morning from the banker. His assessment was that the cattle business was a hard one and observed that it was foolish for a woman like the Widow Rice to think she could be successful. He didn't look at his daughter when he spoke of it, however.

Bass wanted to ask if he had ever seen her socially, but decided it wasn't the right time. When they were alone, he would follow up on his hunch that the marshal had some kind of connection with her at some time. He'd seen it in Harding's eyes at the saloon. He knew the look, even in an older man.

"Right you are, Seth. That's what I need you boys for." Harding slammed the table with his fist. "I need somebody who can put the fear of God in those outlaw bastards. Make them choose another place to ply their treacherous trade."

Swallowing, Seth managed to say, "Father, I wish you wouldn't use that expression. It's blasphemous." His eyes widened and his back straightened in a combination of righteous indignation and fear of how his father would respond to the criticism.

"Seth, you are right." Bass put his elbows on the table and leaned forward. Seth beamed but was uncertain just what he was right about. "I told Em . . . your father . . . that I'd be available to help stop those Mex riders." He patted the gun at his hip and grinned. "Nuff's 'nuff."

Susannah's eyes widened and Cade almost blurted out that he would come too. Instead, he rubbed his sore hands under the table and forced himself to look at the marshal and not Susannah.

Nodding affirmation, Marshal Harding said, "I'd like you to come too, Cade, if things don't work out for you and your family. Sure as the sun comes to the hill, I would." He rubbed his forever-tanned cheek, pressing hard to keep his fingers from trembling. "I'd be singing a fine Welsh tune, loud and to the hills about having guns ready for those Mexican bastards. Aye, that's what I'd do—if you two were to be putting on the star." He grinned. "T'is already forgetting I am that you two were wearing iron in my town. Against the law."

Unnoticed, a flicker of concern shot across Bass's face. "Didn't figure you were into selling your gun, Cade. Even to the law. That's a big step, my friend."

"Dish told me about some new kind of fencing—barbed wire stretched from pole to pole—to cut off pastures. Would that help stop the rustling, Emmett?" Cade responded, not answering Bass's question or looking at him.

Harding shook his head. "Perhaps, but there is sadness in that awful wire. Devil's hatband, they be calling it. King's already using it to keep his land fit and proper. Over Brownsville way. Of course, he be having wood fence too. Been at it longer than most, even your paw or the Richardsons. Shoot fire, he's having folks living on his land, like they do with the fine nobles in Europe, you know. They work for him and he lets them build their houses on his land. 'Tis not God's way." He looked at Seth, his eyes daring his son to comment on his language.

Seth appeared not to have heard, moving his fork a few inches from his plate. Realizing any more comments about his father's lack of religious restraint would only have negative consequences for him personally, Seth folded his arms and was silent.

"I heard it's a real empire," Cade said, stealing a glimpse of Susannah out of the corner of his eye.

"Good word for it that be, empire. That King, he's a real . . . king." Marshal Harding chuckled at his observation.

"So you think having some extra deputies might help clear up this ugly range trouble." Bass folded his arms and smiled at Susannah. "You don't really think those small ranchers had rustling problems, do you? Or do you believe that wild tale about a Mexican in black leadin' his outlaw band around an' about? I heard Richardson and Gray weren't real good at brandin' their own beef."

Harding's chin thrust forward. "Hard to tell, Bass. We are blessed with some of the best damn cow country anyone ever laid good-seeing eyes on. Must look like honey in his thumbs to a rustler, I would think. Plenty of grass. Most years, plenty of water too. Tobias Rice, bless his soul, dammed the main spring years ago but there's still plenty to go around. There is sorry I am that damn barbwire will come." He frowned at the thought, then continued, "Wintering's a mite mean but naught to paw and beller about. A man would have his head in his feathers not to see we've got some of the best damn cow-calf outfits in Texas, boys. Crossbreds more than the great longhorn now. And smart-looking he-stuff that would make any cowman swell up and bust his buttons. Aye, 'tis so."

". . . swell up an' bust his buttons. Aye, 'tis so." Roper rubbed his chin as he spat out the same words.

Cade tried not to look at him; he couldn't help wondering how his father or Dish would react to the marshal's description. Certainly his father thought he had the finest cow operation in the region but he would never admit the others were also good. He also noticed Harding didn't really answer Bass's question about the cause of the ownership turnover.

Marshal Emmett Harding was a tough man who had made his life into one of bringing law and order to this part of Texas prairie. It was a different kind of toughness than that of his father. Much different. Like many longtime lawmen, he still expected his opinions to be treated as laws, but he could no longer make that happen. He looked upon the region as his own, even though his part of it was a tiny horse farm.

Cade couldn't remember when Emmett Harding wasn't a lawman. Stories about him in his younger days were the stuff of campfire yarns. There was a time when he was judge and jury, if necessary—a stern Welshman for certain. But he also was known for paying little attention to cowboys letting off steam by "getting in their cups," as he would say it, as long as they didn't do any damage or hurt anyone. Cade figured the lawman still would make one serious enemy, in spite of the gossip about needing to replace him. He wasn't sure why he felt that way. Certainly not from the man's mannerisms or his expressed thoughts. Harding would make a hard-nosed boss, but he liked the man. To himself, he admitted that the old man would likely favor Bass over him, because of the Welsh's love of good singing. He wondered if Susannah's feelings would also matter.

"Only four ranches haven't turned over—Bar 6, River S, Half-Moon 5 and the Widow Rice's spread. That's quite a lot of change in a year . . . eighteen months," Marshal Harding continued, moving salt and pepper shakers around in his tanned fingers and avoiding Susannah's gaze when he mentioned the saloon owner's name. "I figure those damn Mexicans will find the rest of them soon enough. Sure as

Hell's waiting around the corner for a straying Welshman. That's why I must be making a stand at the roundup. That black-scarved rascal must know his days are numbered."

Repressing a smile, Bass wanted to interrupt, but decided the marshal needed to talk through his view of the situation first. Even if it meant telling things everybody in town already suspected. Bass glanced at Susannah and winked. She frowned slightly, then smiled.

Cade pretended he didn't see the interaction. Not able to resist any longer, Cade glanced at Susannah and she was staring at him. She looked away and he returned to Marshal Harding's recital, knowing his skin was reddening at his collar.

Chapter Nine

"Of course, it could be those cowmen upped and skedaddled because they just couldn't cut the leather when she needed it. Too bad. They ran tail just when it's getting fat, seems to this old Welshman. Hard to believe men like Richardson and Gray, especially, would do that. Tough roosters, they be," Harding continued. "Hell's a'smilin', hard cash money's a mite scarce yet. Better than hen's teeth, though. Aye, a mite better. Maybe they just got a fine bit of gold for their places and decided to move on to a land of sweets and honey." He chuckled and waited for both young men to join in with their own happy responses.

"I used to know that, but it didn't seem worth knowin' so I fergot it," Roper announced for no apparent reason, lifting his chin in a manner that reminded Cade of the old lawman.

Susannah leaned over and whispered in Cade's ear that this was now one of Roper's favorite expressions. He'd heard one of the hands say it and now he used the expression all the time. Cade inhaled her brief closeness, nodding at her words without really hearing them. When he finally realized their significance, he chuckled that it reminded him of Bass. He wasn't certain if her warm smile in response was for him or his friend. The Mexican woman interrupted with a pot of coffee in one hand and a stack of cups in the other. Without a word, she distributed the cups around the table and proceeded to fill each one with the steaming hot liquid. Her task completed, she left.

Setting the shakers aside, Marshal Harding picked up his cup and blew on its surface, looking up at Bass, then at Cade. The tip of the lawman's tongue pushed against the inside of his cheek, pushing it out like a sideways tipi. "Aye, 'tis hard to be the small one. But selling out to strangers be a bit odd, don't you think? Why wouldn't they come to you Bransons first? Did Richardson or Gray or any of them come to you boys for an offer?"

". . . come to you boys for an offer?" Roper echoed the statement, acting as if the thought was his own. He was busying himself pouring spoonfuls of sugar into his coffee; a string of white grains encircled his cup.

"No, I'm pretty sure they didn't. Fact is, Dish talked about the Trenchard spread a few months back, wondering if he might be interested in selling. Butts up to us—on the east, you know."

Harding frowned at Roper before continuing but the addled jailer didn't notice. "Didn't think so. Of course, they might not have wanted to do business with you boys. No offense, but your pappy an' Dish aren't the easiest dogs to share a bone with."

"You wouldn't get any argument from me on that."

Harding nodded. "You'll brand anything missed in the spring and try to get next spring's trail herd separated this fall. Five-wintered stuff, likely it be. Mix in some of your bad animals. You know, bad feet, bad eyes, bad bags and such. Dry cows mostly. Don't hear me wrong now, they'll make fine eating in a fancy New York restaurant. Long as they be fat an' sassy from all that long grass you'll catch along the way. Good as any King can bring, I'll tell you that." He spun his cup around slowly in both hands and took another sip. "I reckon you Branson boys will be putting your trail herd in that fine pasture north of the wood. Good water. Grass'll hold. Down in that fine valley that'll keep the winds off those great beasts. Worst of it anyway. Make it easier come springtime for you. Easy for those damn rustlers, too, even with your boys in line cabins out an' about." He was talking a little too fast now, trying to get all of his thoughts out before they reacted.

Cade was surprised at his knowledge of the Bar 6 operation.

Bass was clearly bored.

After taking a sip of his coffee, Marshal Harding shifted his feet to draw new life into aching joints. He was trying to let Cade—and Bass—know that he understood the region's cattle business well. His gruff words were providing relief from the built-up tension he had created within himself worrying about whether or not to offer just Bass a position as his deputy. Something Black Jack Sante said about Bass had stuck with him.

Bass was a shade better with a gun than Cade, the old buffalo hunter had advised, but the flashy young man hadn't made up his mind about on which side of the law he would stand. Black Jack thought if Bass stayed close to his best friend Cade, he'd be fine. If not, he would ride as an outlaw. The lawman looked around as if searching for an answer hidden behind them. A slight flush darkened his face. He frowned, rubbed his hands together and began to tell them about his own horses raised on his small ranch outside of town. Cade would love his horses. Besides, it was time to quit talking about rustling and ranches. He had shared enough for this day.

"Hell's bright eyes, boys, we got some top horses in our string. There isn't a rancher around that doesn't have a green eye. Even your pappy and Dish, I reckon. No offense. Good ones that's for damn sure. Easy mouths. Good ways too. We got them all, morning horses, all-day horses, ropin' horses, night horses, river horses. Got some top-notch peg horses too. Turn on a button, they will. Pay isn't so good carrying a badge, so selling horses helps a mite, you know."

"Uh-huh, sellin' hosses he'ps a mite," came the expected repetition from Roper.

Harding looked at his weak-minded assistant as if seeing him for the first time. He took a deep breath. "But we can't have rustling around here. If the county law won't do it, it's mine to do. Of course, I've got to find out for certain if these sell-outs were just from beetles in the barnyard—or too many stolen beef." He rubbed his chin, watching Cade for any reaction. Seeing none, he continued, "I don't get around as fast as I used to. An' somebody shot my last deputy." He shook his head. "Goddamn their black-hearted souls. I've got to find those killers too."

"What makes you think two more men would make any difference?" Cade asked. Beneath, he squeezed his hands into fists and opened them, repeating the exercise to ease their stiffness. The lawman was pleased to hear the words "two men."

"Reckon that depends on the two men." Harding's forehead curled into a question again.

"You an' me, Cade. We make the difference." Bass's response was quick. Definitely the marshal wanted Cade, not him. He attempted to hide his disappointment.

"Sure would take a comfort in having you two with me." Harding said. "Pay isn't so great, I know. Town's not real good that way. I can pay thirty a month and meals when you're working—and I'll buy the bullets." His offer came at the heels of his first statement like a cowdog working steers.

"Huh-huh . . . an' I'll buy the bullets." Roper said and began to scratch his groin with both hands. Seth told him to quit. Roper blurted out that it "itched sumthin' fierce" and went on with his task until satisfied.

Cade and Bass were surprised by the low offer—no more than trail hands earned—but even more at the marshal talking money in front of Susannah. It wasn't done in front of most women. Bass pulled on his ear, unable to keep his eyes from showing keen interest and looked at Cade. Cade couldn't help wondering what Susannah thought and then fought back the jealousy of knowing she was in love with Bass.

"I think Dad should tell you that no one wants to wear a badge in Deer Creek." Susannah's expression was difficult to read. Was she trying to scare them off? Would she mention the rumors about her father being too old for the job?

Roper piped in with a coherent observation. "Uh-huh, Henry did. I liked Henry. He was nice to me."

"Henry Endore received a Christian burial and I spoke the word of the Lord over him," Seth said in a tone that suggested this corrected the horrible situation. "I used the twenty-third Psalm as my text. You know, 'The Lord is my shepherd, I shall not—' "

"That's not necessary, Seth." Susannah was embarrassed at her brother's insensitivity. "Deputy Endore was killed because he cared."

"I know that, Sis. I was trying to point out a comfort given. Not everyone killed is so fortunate."

Instead of waiting for either Cade or Bass to respond to her father's offer, Susannah rushed in with detail about their horses. As authoritative as any horseman, she explained the country was rough on horses even though it didn't look so. Ranchers needed savvy horses with lots of leg, she advised. A person could see across the land for miles but that didn't mean the space was flat and easy. In between there were hills, cutbacks, rocks and holes. Mean country on horses, she elaborated. Marshal Harding beamed at her observations. Cade nodded as he sipped his coffee, totally captivated. Bass sat, taking in her every nuance like it was something to eat.

Most of the ranches around tried to build remudas of eight or nine horses for each rider, Susannah continued and asked if the Bar 6 did that. Cade acknowledged they did. Curtly, she added that she was certain Elizabeth Rice didn't have nearly that many horses on her ranch. The lawman was smiling like it was a Fourth of July picnic, until she made that remark and then his face soured.

It made good sense for some ranchers not to raise their own horses but to buy what they wanted. She understood the Bar 6 kept that task for themselves, noting that the King ranch made considerable profit raising and selling horses. Cade smiled to himself; the whole Harding family was taken by the massive King ranch. Impishly, Bass asked if any of the horses could shoot and glanced at Marshal Harding. He grinned back but it was a smile that suggested he wasn't comfortable with the teasing of his daughter.

"I suppose if anyone could train a horse to do that, my father could," she said icily.

Cade tried to hide his glee at her response.

"Hey, I was just kiddin'," Bass said, his eyes pleading for her forgiveness.

She cocked her head to the side and smiled sarcastically. "You're forgiven. I guess I was getting a bit carried away. My father is an excellent peace officer and an excellent horse rancher—and he's done both without hiring any gunfighters."

"That's enough, Sissie." Emmett's face was tight. "Maybe we wouldn't be in this fix if I had."

Bass grinned and playfully pushed Marshal Harding on the arm and the old lawman grinned back. Roper didn't understand and pushed him on the other arm. Harding gave Roper a dirty look he also didn't understand. Susannah was weaving an elaborate tale of the area's current problem with stagecoach holdups when two sullen Mexican cooks brought steaming plates to their table.

Cade welcomed the distraction; he needed time to think. He couldn't accept the marshal's offer; he had responsibilities at the Branson ranch. Or did he? He had already declined Harding's offer earlier. Why did four ranchers have trouble with rustlers and no one else did? Was it simply an excuse for not being good cattlemen? He didn't know any of them well but never thought they were slackers—or foolish. If Harding had two extra men, why not leave them in town instead of hanging around a cow camp for rustlers that might not even exist? Or if they did, wouldn't come?

The waitress filled Cade's cup with fresh coffee and he thanked her, "*Gracias*," followed by a compliment in Spanish about the food itself.

Feeling strangely jealous, Susannah noted it was the woman's first smile since serving them. The woman completed her round of coffee filling and Susannah was aware she kept trying to catch Cade's attention. Smugly, Susannah was pleased to see he wasn't aware of her interest. She gazed at the unusual choker at his neck, having noticed it earlier. Had a woman given it to him? He hadn't been around her for some time now. A second wave of jealousy simmered for an instant before she ordered it away. Why did she care where he got it? she asked herself and let her gaze fall on Bass.

Seth immediately asked for his steak to be cooked more. Roper examined his and asked for the same. The waitress brought back the revised editions in a few minutes, annoyed by the extra effort required. With a dramatic cough, Seth suggested they say grace first and immediately proceeded with a wordy prayer. Bowing his head, Cade sneaked a look at Susannah and was happy to see she was looking back through half-closed eyes.

After waiting longer than he usually did, Marshal Harding growled, "Put an 'amen' to it, Seth. Damn, boy, you don't have to use up every churchy word you know at one setting."

". . . Thank you, Lord, for all you have given us. Bless this food for our use this day. And let us faithfully do your bidding. Amen."

"Amens" followed from Susannah and Cade. Bass took a drink of coffee.

"Let's eat," Marshal Harding added joyfully, "before it gets cold."

". . . a'fer it gits cold. Amen," Roper said, as if the phrase were a prayer by itself.

Quickly, the men ate heartily on large chunks of beef, steaming platefuls of beans and fried potato slices, plus a stack of hot tortillas, then downed the better part of an apple pie. Susannah ate slowly, savoring the closeness of the two young men. Cade couldn't remember enjoying a meal more in a long time. Most likely it was because of her. Their eyes would occasionally meet, dance together for a moment, then dart away for other things to look at.

Marshal Harding rocked back and forth in his chair as he ate, like an old man on a porch swing.

Roper watched the old lawman closely. No one talked while they ate, except Roper. He said he'd never seen a man wear such a fancy gun as Bass's before.

Marshal Harding started to reprimand him but Bass motioned for him to forget it. Then Roper wondered why there were so many Mexicans in town.

Quietly, Seth told him the town used to be all Spanish before Texas won their independence. Roper immediately asked why the Mexicans stayed.

"You want more pie?" the stout waitress said in a harsh monotone, without caring about what their answers might be.

"No, thanks, ma'am, two's my limit these fine days," Harding said with a wink, "but I'd have a mite more of that good coffee."

"A mite more o' that good coffee," Roper agreed. He obviously wished for more pie but couldn't ask for it since Harding didn't.

Seth advised the woman that the crust was crumbly and declined more pie. Susannah didn't care for either more dessert or more coffee. Cade and Bass both thought more coffee would be good. As an afterthought, Seth advised that he too wanted coffee. Slowly, the taciturn woman filled their cups without further comment, smiled widely at Cade, then left for the table with the army officers across the room.

"Well, boys, what do you think of my offer?" Harding couldn't contain himself any longer. "Maybe your pappy wouldn't miss you, Cade. He's got Dish an' John. Hell's bells, for that matter, you could work the roundup and wear a badge too." He avoided saying Cade's father wouldn't want him back, although he thought that would be the case. Such a statement might backfire.

"It's none of my business but why even have the law out there at the roundup?" Cade asked. "You said yourself that it might be for nothing. Why should we leave the town unprotected?"

Marshal Harding liked the reference to "we" but tried not to show it. He wanted to spit but there was nothing in his mouth to generate it. He pursed his lips and answered slowly, "That's a good question, Cade—and one of the reasons I want you wearing a badge. I guess I figured it would be good to show everyone that the law's on top of things. Even outside the town." He rubbed his mouth to wipe away the desire for tobacco.

Cade wondered if the real reason was to make a dramatic showing that he was worthy of continuing to be marshal.

Bass acknowledged the plan made sense to him. "I think it's a good way to go. Nothin' wrong with showin' your guns before you need to."

"Bass, what about your job singing at the Four Aces?" Cade suddenly asked.

Slightly annoyed at the question, Bass said, "Oh, Eliz . . . Missus Rice . . . won't care." His glance at Susannah was furtive. "She'll be glad to get rid o' me for awhile. Business is ugly in a saloon durin' roundup, ya know. Besides, anything that might help the town helps the saloon."

Any response was stopped by everyone's attention being pulled to the Mexican boy's large dog meandering into the restaurant, waving its tail and searching for something to eat. Bass chuckled and Cade smiled. Marshal Harding observed it could make a good cattle dog and Roper repeated the observation and slurped his sweet coffee. The young singer's hound stopped at the table with the soldiers and knelt on its hind legs two feet away. A dark-headed lieutenant with a full mustache and long sideburns kicked the dog hard in its chest and cursed loudly.

Staggered by the blow, the dog whimpered, then growled and the lieutenant's hand went to his flapped holster. A few steps away the Mexican boy yelled frantically for his dog to return. As the terrified boy reached the dog, apologizing in Spanish, the lieutenant's hand uncoiled from his holster and struck him across the face. Stumbling from the blow, the Mexican boy fell beside his dog, blood spurting from his mouth.

"Git your cur away from our table, Mex. You're lucky I didn't shoot it." His cruel laugh brought similar responses from the other soldiers.

Sitting next to him, a brown-bearded sergeant with spectacles announced loudly, "That's tellin' the dirty little Mex. Where's the owner of this filthy place anyway? We should git a free meal fer havin' to put up with that crap. I don't think we'll pay." Pleased with himself, he looked around the room like a rooster checking the barnyard for hens.

Cade was already on his feet before Susannah realized he had gone. Bass muttered, "Cade, that ain't nuthin' to paw an' beller about. It's just an ugly dog. Come on, we got business to tend to." He shook his head. "Well, that's Cade. You never know what he's gonna care about. Sorry, Emmett."

Susannah didn't reply. Her attention was already on Cade helping the boy to his feet. Dazed, the Mexican lad's eyes widened with fear as he gradually realized someone was holding him. Cade spoke quietly to him in Spanish and the youngster's eyes blinked first into recognition, then into an understanding that he was safe. Cade examined the boy's cheek and jaw and decided the blow's damage was limited to a cut lip and the inside of his cheek.

Behind them, the lieutenant growled, "Leave the Mex kid alone, mister. This is Army business." He folded his arms and chuckled, eyeing his two associates for approval.

Cade asked if the boy was all right and he nodded affirmatively, wiping the blood from his chin. Satisfied, Cade spun and stepped toward the table. A winter wind howled within him. He was cold yet fuming.

The third soldier, wearing a gold-buttoned shortcoat too small for him, whispered, "Easy, Lieutenant. That's the fella who jes' stomped the hell outta that big cowhand. He an' the other'n shot up them three."

A smirk on the lieutenant's face preceded his standing up two feet from Cade, his arms still folded. "What's your story, mister? Do you love Mex because you're part Mex—or maybe a half-bree—"

Cade's vicious backhanded slap slammed the lieutenant's face sideways and drove him backwards against his own chair. He lost his balance and crashed to the floor, thudding his chin against the chair as he fell.

"Doesn't feel very good, does it?" Cade said, staring at the officer sprawled on the floor. New pain shot through his own hand but he didn't want to acknowledge it.

Eyes tearing from pain, the dark-headed lieutenant felt his jaw and saw the red blood spurting from a split lip already turning purple. His face darkened and his bloody hand went to the holstered gun at his waist.

"You've already made one mistake today. That next one's a lot worse." Cade's eyes made the lieutenant move his hand slowly back toward his mouth and away from the holster. Turning in his chair, the chunky soldier held out a hand for the lieutenant to grab to help him stand.

"If he stands up, I'll put him back on the floor again," Cade said. "I don't like men who hit boys and dogs. How about you? I haven't heard an apology from him. He needs to say he's sorry to this boy."

The chunky soldier withdrew his hand like it had touched a hot griddle. Roper rushed past Cade to the downed lieutenant. The slow-witted man leaned over until his face was a foot from the bleeding officer's.

"Say, Yank, whatcha doin', hittin' boys an' dogs fer? What would yur muther say?"

Marshal Harding told him to return but Susannah immediately left her chair and escorted Roper back to his seat. She glanced at Cade who was watching her as she passed. He couldn't tell if she was horrified or just disappointed by his action. It didn't matter, he told himself. Some things a man can't let stand, regardless of the consequences. Besides, she was Bass's woman.

On the other side of the table, the spectacled sergeant announced piously, "Stay where you are, Lieutenant. You had it coming." He turned toward Cade. "Mister, that's a Federal officer you just struck."

"Yeah, I know. Saw a lot of them running away from us in Tennessee."

Chapter Ten

Clearing his throat nervously, the chunky soldier said in a tentative voice, "War's over, mister. We're all Americans now." He didn't look at Cade but noticed Bass standing at Emmett's table, his right hand resting on an ivory-handled gun butt in a studded holster.

"I take it your friend there was in charge of beating up on boys and dogs." Cade lifted an unused napkin from the soldiers' table. "Nothing to worry about, Bass. I saw the fella with the glasses unflap his holster. Guess he likes making mistakes too."

Wide-eyed, the spectacled sergeant's hands quickly eased away from his side to the top of the table and stayed there. Cade picked up the half-finished bottle of whiskey in the middle of their table, poured some into the napkin and handed the bottle back to the small-coated soldier who muttered, "Thank you, sir." Cade turned away to give the wetted napkin to the boy who was frozen in place by having someone fight for him.

He was surprised to see Susannah standing beside the young Mexican. She smiled and took the napkin and began gently dabbing the boy's face to remove the blood. Cade knelt beside the dog, patted its head and looked at the animal's rib cage. An abrasion from the kick was evident but it was definitely only a surface injury. A lick on his hand followed Cade's care.

"Don't get up, soldier. I said I want to hear an apology." Cade issued the challenge without turning around from examining the dog. "You didn't break any bones, so it can end here. If you're smart."

From the floor came the lieutenant's hesitant response. "I-I'm . . . sorry."

"I didn't hear you." Cade patted the dog.

After a soft "*Gracias,*" the boy guided his dog back to the lobby and reluctantly Susannah returned to her seat. A part of her wanted to stand beside this young man she'd been around since childhood but she wasn't sure he wanted her close. Cade Branson seemed different than the boy she had flirted with and kissed. Her father would have laughed at the incident—maybe even bought a bottle for the soldiers—if Cade hadn't done something. Bass would have done the same. She was certain of it and a bit saddened by the realization.

"I'm sorry." The lieutenant swallowed blood as he spoke again, loudly this time.

"For hitting a defenseless boy," Cade added in a low voice.

". . . f-for hitting . . . a d-defenseless boy."

". . . and for kicking a dog."

". . . and f-for . . . kicking a dog."

"Good, you can get up now."

The chunky soldier rose to help the lieutenant stand as Cade stepped to the soldiers' table. "As you leave—now—I want each of you to put a coin in that boy's hat." Cade looked directly at the lieutenant being held up by the soldier. "If I ever hear you bother him in any way, I'll find you and finish this. Do you understand, Lieutenant?"

The officer nodded without looking at Cade.

"I didn't hear you."

"I . . . understand."

Cade turned to the sergeant. "And you, I'm sure you want to apologize to everyone in the restaurant for your statement about not paying. I want to hear it—as loud as you were before. Wouldn't want these folks to think the Army's finest didn't know how to do the right thing."

The spectacled sergeant looked up at Cade; the soldier's forehead furrowed in concern about what this stranger might do next. He reached into his pocket, withdrew a small leather sack and emptied two coins on the table. "Easy, mister. We're going. We're going. And there's money on the table. See?"

"I didn't hear the apology."

The sergeant's magnified eyes were slits. He said loudly, "We're sorry . . . about saying we . . . weren't going to pay. This . . . is a good place to eat." But the spectacled sergeant couldn't resist adding under his breath, "We'll meet again, mister."

"Shut up, Ferguson. Just shut up," the chunky soldier said, struggling to keep the bloody lieutenant from losing his balance.

Cade returned to the table after satisfying himself they had left money for the boy. Bass grinned, slapped him on the back and muttered, "Your hands aren't going to be good for anything if you keep this up."

Cade mumbled an apology about not liking bullies and rubbed his knuckles gingerly.

Seth was visibly shaken. "Christians are supposed to turn the other cheek . . ."

"Hard to imagine many Christians makin' it through the day around here." Bass chuckled at the observation but Cade didn't.

"This is hardly the time, Seth," Susannah said. "Christians are supposed to care about those who can't help themselves."

"I'm quite familiar with what proper Christians are supposed to do."

"I'm sure you are, Seth. I admire your consistency. I find it interesting how some folks wear their religion like it was something to put on and take off whenever they feel like it," Cade said. "You know, Indians believe everything we do is an act of religion, everything is sacred. Since God is in everything, so every act of ours is, in effect, a prayer." He cocked his head toward Seth. "At least that's what my mother told me. Interesting thought, isn't it?"

"I-I can't imagine those heathens having anything to say of significance about God . . . and Christ," Seth blurted.

"No, I don't suppose you can."

Cade's voice was deceptively soft but he avoided looking at Susannah because his eyes would have given away his annoyance at the young man's self-inflated value of his own religiosity. Susannah stared at Cade as if she hadn't seen him before and she hoped he would look at her.

Shaking his head in admiration, Marshal Harding put down his coffee and pushed the cup away with his fingers. "Well, you'd be the first deputy of mine to take on the Army. Reckon I can make it forty apiece. Hell's teeth, the town council will just have to understand. I need you boys."

Bass looked up at Emmett and grinned. "I reckon you got yourself two deputies. What do you say, Cade?"

What he thought about saying was that he didn't care much about cattle and if he wanted to be around them, he would be riding with his brothers and his father. Bass had sold his gun before; Cade hadn't. He wasn't afraid—or was he? Bullets didn't care who they killed. Only a young fool thought otherwise. They were stepping into someone else's fight. To wear a tin badge. To get shot at—for cowhand wages. At least it would be better than being around his father.

What he really wanted to say was that he would work for free and fight anybody anywhere if it meant he would get to see Susannah often. A deep breath followed and he realized everyone at the table was looking at him and waiting for his response.

"What do you say, Cade? You in—or are you goin' back to your paw an' Dish an' see if they got some of that Christian forgiveness Seth likes to talk about." Bass looked like he wanted his friend to return to his family but couldn't bring himself to say so.

Cade was afraid to look at Susannah for fear of what he would see. Repulsion. She couldn't possibly want to be around a man who started fights everywhere he went. His eyes went first to Bass, then to Marshal Harding, who looked like he was going to burst.

"Yes, I have to go back. But if Paw won't take me, I'd be proud to be your deputy, Emmett," Cade answered, then added, "Might make things a bit awkward at the roundup, though."

A forced grin came to Bass's face and just behind it came a crimson ring around Cade's neck as he realized his friend might think the real reason he might join the marshal was to be close to Susannah, no matter how she might feel about him. Or Bass. Or Dish.

"That's fine, Cade. Fine as honey on your thumb," Marshal Harding said and the rest of the restaurant patrons turned in his direction at the loudness of the response. "I can almost feel those outlaws riding the other way." He looked up for the waitress, waved his arm and yelled, "Senorreeta, bring us a bottle of tequila. An' some cigars. We'll just forget I'm on duty for awhile. We need us a celebration."

"We need us a cell-o-bra-shun," Roper mimicked.

Bass chuckled. "Let's bring that boy back here—for some singin'."

"I'd like some fine singing. Aye, I would," Harding agreed.

Before Cade could respond, Bass was out of his chair and on his way to the lobby. He came back with his arm around the boy who was carrying his guitar and obviously puzzled. His eyes sought Cade and the young gunfighter smiled to reassure him. In Spanish, Cade told him what they wanted. Grinning, the boy asked if he should play the *Mujer Maldita* song. Cade bit his lower lip and shook his head.

"*Entiendo.*" The boy indicated his understanding that it would be inappropriate.

"How about *Turkey in the Straw?*" Bass asked enthusiastically. "Do you know that one?"

"No, señor, I do not." The boy's face was drawn with worry about his failure.

"Oh, well, how about—"

"*O Susannah.*" Cade couldn't resist. His eyes teased as Bass's face soured.

"Maybe some other time."

"How about letting the boy sing what he knows." It wasn't a question. With his right arm resting on the curved back of his chair, Cade sat sideways toward Susannah. In Spanish, he asked the boy's name, "*Cómo se llama?*"

"Miguel. Miguel Alvardo."

Cade introduced the boy to everyone at the table, as well as Bass still standing beside him, coveting the youngster's guitar. When Cade was finished, Miguel stared at him and said, "*Usted eres un gran guerrero.*"

With a grin that only went in to the right side of his face, Bass said, "Well, well, Cade you have an admirer. He just called you a great warrior."

Cade dismissed the compliment and asked Miguel if he would honor them with a song. Immediately, the boy sang a beautiful song about a Mexican woman who lost her love, then another ballad Cade had never heard before. From Susannah's soft smile, Cade knew she had heard it and liked the sweet-sounding tune. They clapped and the remaining patrons in the restaurant joined in the applause. To himself, Seth wondered if the reason was more out of fear of angering Cade Branson than an appreciation of the music.

"Let me sing one for yah, boy," Bass said, reaching for the guitar at the same time.

"*Puede el pedir prestada su guitarra?*" Cade asked if Bass could borrow his guitar. The boy nodded and released the instrument, keeping his eyes fixed on Cade. Bass's clear voice began to fill the room with the haunting lyrics of *Pretty Saro*.

" '*Down in some lone valley, in a lonesome place*
Where the wild birds do whistle,
And their notes do increase
Farewell pretty Saro,
I bid you adieu,
But I'll dream of pretty Saro
Wherever I go.' "

He strolled around the restaurant as he sang, smiling and nodding his response to the compliments. Cade knew his own face was crisp with jealousy as he watched Susannah concentrate on Bass's performance.

At the conclusion, accented with a full chording and the drop of Bass's head, she clapped and shouted, "More!" Seth followed her suggestion with his own applause and a shout for *Shall We Gather at the River*. Bass looked at Susannah and motioned for her to join him. She hesitated and shook her head. He waved again and Seth encouraged her, "Go on, Sis. Sing a hymn. That would be great." She frowned at him but stood amid encouragement from throughout the restaurant. Unsure of whether to urge her on or not, Cade said, "Do what you want, Susannah."

Standing next to Bass, Susannah whispered in his ear and he began strumming chords to *Grandfather's Clock*, a song rapidly becoming a favorite in Texas and throughout the land.

Her simple, sweet voice captured the room and applause followed her back to her seat. Cade stood and clapped his hands until they hurt worse than from his earlier fistfight in the saloon.

"Everybody join in," Bass shouted and began singing the lively *Turkey in the Straw*. He bounced around the room, stopping at each table to encourage participation.

Reluctantly, Cade sang along, knowing his voice was no match for his friend's.

That was followed by Bass's solo performance of *Yellow Rose of Texas* and finally a return to the table amid robust cheering from everyone in the room.

The Mexican woman presented the bottle of tequila, glasses and a handful of cigars on a tray and announced they were compliments of the owner. Bass returned the guitar to Miguel and he went on his way with more money jingling in his pocket from everyone at the Harding table, except Seth who said he thought such singing was "Satan's doing."

Bass told him that it most likely was and then added, "And that's mighty fine with me."

Susannah laughed the hardest and Cade was jealous but tried to hide it.

A half hour later, the group left the restaurant. A Texas sun pulled simmering heat waves from the earth creating blurred silhouettes out of people across the street. Overhead a hawk watched the town, sailing on unseen billows of heat. Bass promised to be at the Harding's tomorrow before noon; as usual, Harding was not spending the night at the jail. The marshal said he would swear him in at that time and they would head for the roundup from there. Harding's chest swelled when he talked about it.

Cade was going to Black Jack's and promised he would let Harding know what he was doing next but the old lawman absorbed the statement as if the young gunfighter would be joining him soon. Bass indicated he was heading back to the saloon to tell of his new job and to continue singing for the rest of the day and evening.

With a mischievous glint in her eye, Susannah said she hoped they could stay out of another fight until then. Cade tried to respond but no words could get past his feelings. There didn't seem to be anything he could do or say about it. All he could do was look.

Bass had no such problem; he laughed easily at her teasing, touched her arm and suggested Roper come along to keep them out of trouble. The old man immediately liked the idea but Susannah told him that he was needed at their ranch. Cade didn't think she liked Bass teasing Roper and he finally managed to tell the slow-minded man that they would take him along some other time. He wasn't certain Susannah liked that either.

"I have an extra Bible in the wagon if you would care to borrow it," Seth said stiffly. "They have several new ones in the general store too."

Bass grinned. "Thanks, anyway. I always let Cade deliver the word of God to anyone needin' it. Especially soldier boys."

"Thank you, Seth. That's very nice of you, but we're fine," Cade said, not sure if Susannah would have liked them to take Seth up on his offer or not.

"Say, I'll tell the general store you boys might be in for bullets or tobacco. Whatever. Put it on my tab," Emmett said cheerfully. "I have to go in there, anyway. Forgot to get some more rope."

"We dun fergot to git rope," Roper responded. "That's rope. Not Roper. We didn't fergot to git me."

Everyone laughed, including Cade. It seemed easier but he still couldn't think of anything worth saying to Susannah. She stared at him briefly and he nodded awkwardly, touching his hand to his hat brim. As they walked outside, Bass eased beside her, his hand seeking hers and squeezing it affectionately. She smiled at him and returned the intimacy. Cade was thankful for the Mexican boy's gleeful interruption, showing him how much money had been placed in his sombrero.

Marshal Harding stomped on ahead, eager to determine if their supplies were ready and to spread the word of his newly acquired firepower.

Excusing herself, Susannah turned around to find Cade beside the boy. Her eyes seeking his, she touched his arm. "Cade, I hope everything works out all right with you and your father—and Dish."

He smiled, embarrassed by her attention but pleased. "It

was nothing. Dish and Paw got ahead of their thinking. Bass would've done the same for me." He swallowed and found the courage to say, "I think most of the problem . . . is Dish's jealous . . . of you an' him."

Chapter Eleven

"And how about you, Cade Branson, how do you feel?"

Crimson dawning on his face, Cade opened his mouth as Bass joined them with a cheery question of his own. "What are my two favorite people doin'? Can you stay with us for awhile, honey, or do you have to be with your paw?"

"Oh, he thinks he needs me," she replied without taking her eyes from Cade. "I just wanted to thank Cade for helping you—and to ask him a question." Her mouth impishly curled at the corner.

"A question? About what?" Bass placed a hand on Cade's shoulder, then smiled. "No, he doesn't like to sing."

Cade forced a chuckle, his face fully layered in red. A twinge of jealousy slipped into Cade's mind and he pushed it away. This was his best friend. No woman should ever come between them. No woman.

"Susannah just wanted to know if I thought everything would be all right between my family and me." Cade's eyes reached out to her.

"Are you coming, Sissy?" Marshal Harding trumpeted from a half block away. "Leave those boys be. We've got things to tend to at the general store. Jail too. Got those lads with too much of the Devil's drink to let loose."

She shook her head. "Looks like I shouldn't be bothering you two. Guess I'll see you tomorrow at the ranch, Bass."

"You betcha, hon."

"I don't know about you, Cade. But I'd like to see you too."

"If the way was open, I'd be there fast." He surprised himself at the response. His emotions shoved out the words before he could consider them.

She bit her lower lip, mouthed a silent "yes" and scurried away to join the family. Bass assumed the conversation was about Cade hiring on with Harding and nodded his agreement to Cade's response. The two young men watched her without speaking. Before joining her father, she looked over her shoulder and smiled. At both of them.

"So you're headin' for Black Jack's," Bass said, patting Cade on the shoulder, breaking up his thoughts.

"Huh? Oh yeah, then I'll ride to our place. Just want to talk with him a little first."

"Think your paw an' Dish will let'cha come back?"

Cade looked at Bass, then at the hawk still working the hot sky. "Don't know, Bass. I just don't know."

"Thanks, Cade."

"For what?"

Bass glanced up at the same hawk and adjusted the studded gunbelt around his waist. "For standin' against your family. For me. Nobody's ever done anythin' like that. Ever. Not in this piss-ant town."

"Well, come tomorrow, you're going to be the law in this piss-ant town," Cade said. "Ever think that would happen?"

Bass threw back his head and roared.

Two couples strolled past them, stopping their conversation to eye the young gunfighters cautiously. The taller man whispered something to his wife after they were several strides away. She turned, spinning the light-blue parasol in her hands. After noting their holstered gunbelts, her admiring glance stayed longest on Bass. His smile was her reward and she returned it before returning her attention to walking.

Cade folded his arms, trying to keep his eyes from searching the sidewalk ahead for Susannah. His heart told him that he should've told her how he felt; his mind told him she had already gone inside the general store. "You would've done the same for me."

Bass looked over at his friend and his wide grin was as merry as Christmas morning. "When this gatherin's over, let's head for San Antonio. You an'me. All kinds of fun goin' on there. Cade, I've never seen a town so big. I bet there's over nine thousand people there!"

"Can't be that many, Bass. Austin isn't near that size," Cade responded, acknowledging to himself that Austin was the only large Texas town he'd ever visited. In fact, apart from the War, it was the only town he'd ever visited besides Deer Creek. Bass often told stories of visiting big cities like San Antonio and Galveston.

"Well, of course it's bigger, Cade. Used to be the Mex capitol—when them Spaniards had Texas, or most of it." Bass grinned and his eyes sparkled. "Why they've got ditches runnin' through the town, bringin' 'em water. An' they've even got a big theater where they bring in actors an' talkers an' such—all the way from New York and St. Louis. Hell's teeth, but who's counting?"

"I heard it was full of rustlers and cardsharks an' whores,"

Cade replied, absorbing his friend's use of one of the marshal's favorite curses.

"Yeah, probably is. Lots of saloons too. An' dancin'. An' there's hotels there. Lots of 'em but one in particular that's really something. Hotel Menger. Fancy like you can't believe. Oh, you'd love it, Cade. You talk about livin' right."

They walked together for a few minutes without talking. Finally, Cade said, "I'm for it. Nothing's keeping me here. But what about you and Susannah?"

Bass pursed his lips and frowned. "She'll wait. I love her. She loves me."

"Are you going to marry her?"

"I reckon to. When I got something to offer besides this gun an' that black horse. I'm puttin' a stake together. Gonna be somebody."

"I don't think she cares what you have, Bass."

"How would you know what a woman cares about?" Bass grinned. "Doesn't matter, anyway. I care. You can't ask a woman like her to marry you until you're ridin' fancy an' fine. That'll be me. An' soon." He looked at Cade who appeared lost in thought again. "There'll be a place for you, Cade. A good one. You wait an' see. A lot more'n deputy pay. Things are really gonna change around here when it's all said an' done. You never know. 'Nuff is 'nuff."

Cade studied his friend. Was Bass trying to tell him something? Or just blowing hot air to make himself feel important? Whenever they were together lately, Bass seemed distracted, but then the young singing gunfighter always spoke like he was two subjects ahead of himself. It was just his way of talking, that's all. A person couldn't choose his family but he could pick his friends. And he and Bass had been riding the same trail for a long time.

They had even enlisted in the Confederate army together, a month after Dish had. Neither were old enough to enlist but they went anyway. Cade's father insisted he and John stay behind to help with the ranch. John stayed. All three—Dish, Cade and Bass—rode with General Hood and had been lucky to survive the battle of Gettysburg as well as Hood's army getting torn up later in Tennessee.

Dish liked the regimentation of army life, Cade found himself in the exhilaration of fighting and Bass liked singing around the campfires and going on lone assignments as a sniper. Dish advanced to lieutenant; Cade chose to remain a private, although the gallant Hood always wanted him at his right when they charged. Bass never got promoted and said he didn't care to. Yet Cade knew his friend was a dangerous man. Then, and more so today. And rarely completely honest with anyone.

Bass wasn't being truthful now, Cade realized. He just didn't know about what. Had Bass actually stolen Branson beef? Not if it was supposed to have happened today. Definitely he was in the saloon all day, according to a lot of witnesses. But he was aware Bass had been out of town on the two days when the stagecoach had been robbed. No one else had noticed the coincidence. Certainly not Marshal Harding. Word was two Mexican bandits had done the holdups. Cade suspected Bass was involved but couldn't bring himself to question him about it. How else would he be building a "stake"? Certainly not from singing at the saloon.

Bass was his friend. His best friend. Bass would tell him what was on his mind when he was ready, if it was robbing stages, or whatever it was. Maybe he was involved in rustling too but Cade didn't think so. There was that time, though, when Bass was supposed to be ill but Cade couldn't find him in town. He assumed he was with Susannah.

They walked on together with no further explanation

from Bass about his cryptic statements, and no probing from Cade. A coolness crept between them and neither was comfortable with it nor understood how to stop it. Both were relieved to see a heavyset townsman approaching, swollen with drink and sharing a joke with himself. His giggling followed blurted phrases and hiccups.

"Shall we let Attorney Princeton pass?" Bass grinned. "Or shall we wait for him to find a Mex kid to bother?"

Cade answered by stepping to the side and waiting for the drunken lawyer to wobble closer. He couldn't remember ever seeing the man sober. From what he had heard, Hiram R. Princeton was actually quite good at his profession, in spite of a love of whiskey.

Thick of stomach and tongue but wearing a fine suit that had once fit a much smaller frame, the town's attorney saw the movement and said to an imaginary friend, "Well . . . hiccup . . . look there. A real gentleman . . . hiccup . . . I do thank you, sir, and my friend thanks you. Hiccup." He waved his arm toward an empty space; his coat sleeve wrinkled from having to extend far beyond its capacity to do so.

"You're both welcome, Mister Princeton," Cade replied and winked at Bass.

"Come around anytime." Bass stepped aside with an exaggerated bow to let the inebriated lawyer pass.

"See, I told you . . . hiccup . . . they were gentle . . . hiccup . . . men," Princeton said to the space beside him as he stutter-stepped forward.

With a hand over his mouth, Bass spun away to hold back the guffaw that wanted out. Cade sputtered and Bass burst out laughing. Cade couldn't hold back a response either and his explosion of laughter joined Bass's. The drunken man paused a few feet past them and turned his body partially around. His robust stomach bobbed against a vest that would soon be forced to give up its buttons.

"Did you like . . . hiccup . . . that joke? It is terribly funny . . . hiccup . . . heard it this morning." With that pronouncement, he waddled on, waving his arms and talking to himself.

At the third building, he stopped, weaving back and forth as if the earth below him was a see-saw. Somehow, he manged to find his key. After an agonizing process of connecting it with the keyhole, he finally disappeared into his office.

"Well, I hope he's not working on an important deed or something this afternoon," Bass said. "That boy ain't gonna know a whereas from a land grab."

Cade shook his head in agreement. Their momentary coolness was over. Bass said again that he was going to tell Elizabeth Rice about leaving the saloon to help Marshal Harding but would spend the rest of the day and evening entertaining her customers.

"What about after that? Emmett'll want you to stay on as his deputy. You know he doesn't really expect trouble during the roundup. He almost said so. He needs to look good to keep his job, Bass." Cade folded his arms in front of his chest. Straying sunlight found his Comanche choker and made it wink.

For an instant, Bass's face smoldered into darkness, then his eyes brightened. "Oh, we'll see how it goes with the roundup. Maybe I'll stay—if I can sleep in Susannah's room." His eyebrows danced. "What do you think your paw an' Dish will do when they see me wearin' a star?"

"Oh, Dish'll think it makes him look less of a man to have you there," Cade said. "But he won't do anything. Paw won't either."

Bass shook his head. "That'll be close to Dish's worst nightmare."

"Oh, I can think of worse."

"Yeah, like having to watch Susannah make love to me."

"Seems to me, rustlers are more likely to hit during the winter," Cade observed, pushing his hat back on his forehead and ignoring the remark about Susannah, "than to try something now with all those cowhands around."

"Could be. 'Cept rustlers don't like the cold. An' them cowhands can't shoot worth a damn. An' it's a lot easier to move cattle when they're already bunched instead of having to do all that work." Bass looped his thumbs over his gunbelt. "Or didn't you know, rustlers are lazy. 'Specially them Mexs."

"I don't understand, I guess," Cade said. "Seems funny, we sure haven't had any problems. Not that I know of, anyway." He cocked his head. "Except for today."

Rubbing the side of his neck, Bass looked away again. "What's wrong with helping that ol' man look good? An' gettin' paid for it, to boot."

"Now that sounds like a fella trying to impress his future father-in-law."

"Who's asking, my friend? Who's asking? That ol' man could do a lot worse than to have me as his son-in-law. Maybe I'll take over for him when he's ready to retire. 'Marshal Manko' has a nice ring to it." Bass's voice came like a song lyric.

Cade's eyes narrowed and, before they blinked, Bass thought he looked like an Indian warrior about to attack. The moment passed as Cade said, "Well, I suppose he could always hire Princeton to straighten you out."

Bass roared. Using one of Harding's expressions, he said, "Hell's teeth, why don't you go with me to the saloon an' have a little whiskey. I'm buyin'—an' I can guarantee one o' them gals'll take a shine to you an' take you upstairs. Make a new man outta you."

"No, thanks. I need to talk with Black Jack. I'll catch up with you. At the roundup, maybe. Or back here in town," Cade said.

"Sure. You'll recognize me. I'll be the handsome one with the badge."

"Watch out for those Mexican bullets—and angry cows. An' don't tell anybody you know how to rope."

"You should talk." Bass grinned. "Tell Black Jack howdy for me."

Walking purposefully toward them was a curly-headed cowboy in an old derby hat and cowhide vest. Wiping the back of his hand across his mouth, he stopped in front of Cade.

"You're Dish Branson's brother, ain't ya?" the derby-hatted cowboy said, smiling more from the impact of the recent whiskey he'd downed than the pleasure of seeing Cade.

"Yes, I am. Cade Branson."

The cowboy looked at Cade's extended hand before holding out his own. "Howdy, Cade. Jake Benson. I ride fer the Half-Moon 5. Bin meanin' to git with Dish. Thought he said he were comin' to town today. Well, anyhow . . . do ya want me to move them beeves o' yurn back to the main pasture? Took 'em up to that little waterin' hole like Dish asked. They wanted to stay at the crick, so I don' 'xactly know why ya had it dun. Yur money tho."

The cowboy wiped his mouth again with his hand. "An' I rode my black like Dish asked. Ain't the best cowhoss 'round but I rode 'im. Damn thing tried to throw me twice. That oughta cost ya more, I reckon." He thought for an instant. "An' I borried Pip's black hat too. Don' know why I had to wear that. Anyways, ya Bransons owe me twenty dollars."

Cade glanced over at Bass, who was shaking his head, then turned back to the cowboy. "You're going to have to ride out to our place. Dish didn't come in like he planned. You tell him you talked to me an' I said he should pay you forty."

"Forty? By Gawd, you're a good man, Cade."

Before Cade could say another word, the cowboy was scurrying toward a horse rack. Neither he nor Bass spoke until the cowboy was in the saddle and spurring his horse out of town.

"Well, now we know what happened," Cade said. "I can't believe Dish would do something like that."

"I can."

They shook hands and chuckled again about the drunken lawyer. Cade apologized for his brother's cruel deception and Bass told him not to worry about it, that seeing Dish react to his being Harding's deputy would be sweet revenge. Cade agreed and left for the livery.

Bass watched him walk down the street for a few seconds. Bass's shoulders rose and fell, then he walked slowly toward the saloon. A few strides later, he was smiling again and his stride quickened.

Susannah saw Cade go inside the livery. She hoped he would look her way but he didn't. Bass was nowhere in sight; she assumed he had returned to the Four Aces saloon. Wincing at the thought of him talking with Elizabeth Rice, she found herself drawn more to Cade than Bass. It surprised her. Afterall, she was all but promised to Bass.

Inside the store, Marshal Harding made a point of telling everyone that he had hired two gunfighters as deputies. It sounded like he had brought them to the area for that purpose and not that they were locals. His shoulders were as straight as he could make them and his voice was filled with bravado. Several townsmen noted the change to each other.

Neither Susannah nor Seth dared to ask what he thought the two men would accomplish at the roundup. Or really just Bass Manko. She smiled at the thought of having him close—without their having to sneak around. But her thoughts immediately ran off to find Cade and to hope he would come. He had reentered her mind today and wouldn't leave. She didn't want him to.

Quietly, Susannah told Seth it was smart for their father to make such an announcement, maybe more important than the actual hiring itself. This became a clear signal to outlaws to move on. She thought the news would travel fast and eventually reach the right people, whoever they were. Seth didn't seem particularly interested in her assessment. Instead, he preferred to thumb through a new leatherbound Bible, pausing whenever a customer drew near and dramatically reading aloud.

Embarrassed by her brother's theatrics, Susannah went to see how the loading of their wagon was going. Her thoughts swirled around Bass and Cade, mixed with her concerns about their safety. She never worried about her father's safety. Not any more. It was like nothing could ever hurt him. Maybe that was the only way she could deal with him being a lawman. Of course, so far no one knew how many outlaws were involved in the rustling or the stage holdups, or how they were organized. She had even heard whispers about a local gang behind it all. And even more whispers that her father was too old for the job. They hurt and she knew her father had heard them too.

Susannah couldn't remember her father ever mentioning such stories, either about a local gang or his being ineffective. As usual, his opinion was absolute; though publicly, he pronounced that the problem was as old as the Rio Grande and insisted the thievery was from Mexican outlaws coming and going freely across the border. But she couldn't push away this nagging sensation at the corner of her consciousness that there was something else going on in the region. Surely her father couldn't be wrong. Not about something as important as that. Surely.

Stepping outside the store, she smiled as the store clerk brought the last sack of beans to her father, standing impatiently by the wagon's open end. Nearby, Roper was examining the slightly bloodly right paw of the cattle dog who'd ridden in the wagon to town. The ugly black animal was her father's dog and didn't care much for anyone else. Several pink scars laced his broad back, mementos of past encounters with their horses. Susannah walked over and checked the wound herself. It was now a dab of dried blood.

"It's nothing serious, Roper. Looks like he scratched it on something."

"Are you sure, Miss Susannah? He be limpin'."

"I'm sure, Roper. He'll be fine."

From her second story saloon office, Elizabeth Bingham Rice watched the Hardings drive their loaded wagon out of town. Overcast and cool, even for autumn, the weather matched her mood. One of her bartenders reported the old lawman was bragging about two gunfighters coming to work for him. That news bothered her greatly. The events of the day had upset her more than she wanted to admit. Her navy bodice, gloves and hat lay across the back of an overstuffed, forest-green sofa, discarded in haste and frustration. Her bosom was covered only by the white chemise.

"Dammit. Where is Bass?"

Chapter Twelve

Elizabeth Rice's habit of talking aloud to herself was long acquired and took on a sense of theatrical performance at times, complete with exaggerated hand gestures and posturing. "What the hell was that son-of-a-bitch thinking . . . stealing Branson cattle? That's not part of the plan. The arrogant bastard!"

She chuckled at her language; the town's society mavens would be shocked. But they didn't accept her anyway. Never had. Soon, it wouldn't matter. She would control the whole region, as big a cattle baron as King was in his part of Texas. The first woman cattle baron. The only woman cattle baron. Oh, the wonder of it drove her daily.

She was only one ranch away from owning thousands of acres of superb cattle land and vast herds of cattle. Her fondest dream was nearly true. Four other ranches were already hers, in addition to the Circle R. Until the time was right for the unveiling of her absolute control, Absalum Sil, leader of her gang, appeared as the new owner of the

Richardson ranch. He also oversaw her other ranching acquisitions, with members of his gang acting as owners. Only two small ranches—the Half-Moon 5 and the River S—remained independent, besides the huge Branson operation. These lesser ranches would fall easily into her hands after the Bar 6—and virtual control of the valley—was hers. She even considered leaving them alone—for appearance's sake.

It wasn't easy building an empire, though; little things were always getting in the way of big objectives. This was a chess game against opponents who didn't realize there was even a game, or that they were in it, until it was too late. Emmett Harding was a senile fool and would never figure out what was happening until it was too late—or he was dead. Unless his hiring of gunfighters signaled something different. That bothered her, as did anything she didn't control.

In the beginning, Emmett Harding had been earmarked in her plan as a threat to be dealt with. She had sized up the old lawman as a savvy warrior who would not go anywhere, or do anything, he didn't want to. Initially, she decided to seduce him into ineffectiveness. She still recoiled from remembering his curt rejection of her advances. How could a silly old man think he was honestly attractive to her? And he certainly wasn't interested in bribes. He'd made that clear to her emissary.

It annoyed her now that she took so long to realize he was simply an old fool who wouldn't be a factor at all. In fact, she had even considered allowing him to stay on as marshal after she took control of the region, but that was only momentary. She would enjoy spitting on his dead face—and she wouldn't miss, like he usually did. She would handpick the new lawman from her outlaw band. Right after she replaced Sheriff Swisher.

" 'Be not afraid of greatness. Some men are born great, some achieve greatness, and some have greatness thrust upon them.' " Elizabeth smoothed her eyebrows as the passage from *Twelfth Night* eased from her lips. "Some women too." She accepted the truth that she would, indeed, be great. But the worry of the day wouldn't leave her.

Unable to turn away, she watched the wagon disappear from her view. "Did Marshal Harding hire new deputies to help him stop the rustling? If so, that's fine." Elizabeth nodded her head in concurrence. "But what if he's wise to me? Could that be? Surely not. That damn old rooster thinks he owns this barnyard and he barely can find his way around it." Elizabeth tried to laugh at her own joke but it came out a nervous giggle.

She must determine what he knew, if anything, and do so immediately. She wondered when the two gunfighters would arrive. "I wonder where they're from," she muttered. "Sil will know. Hell, he knows every gun from here to St. Louis." She shook her head in appreciation.

"Perhaps I should ride out myself to have a look-see at how the roundup is going. After all, I'm a ranch owner too. I could talk with him about it." She smiled at the reaction her appearance at the cow camp would bring.

"My, oh my, there'd be feverish cowboys that night." In self-admiration, she ran her hands over breasts covered only by the thin chemise, down her body to her waist and rested them on her hips.

She was beautiful and she knew it well. Her looks had given her opportunity; her mind had allowed her to make the most of it. If necessary, she might use her charms to turn the old lawman's new guns into hers. She purred and touched her nearly naked body again. She had already managed to keep Sheriff Swisher from investigating the cattle losses; he was easy to control with free access to the Gower House, her elegant whore palace, any time he was in town—and the promise of land when the region was fully in her control. She had no intention of keeping that promise.

After a few moments of smug satisfaction, she resettled her thoughts on the roundup strategy and the enjoyment of its successful outcome. In a few days, the Bransons would be dead and so would Harding. She licked her lips to savor the deliciousness of the whole thing. "Roundups are such wonderful things," she murmured.

Bass had assured her Cade Branson would never buck him and didn't care about his family's ranch anyway—that he would likely ride on after his family was killed. Cade's stand against his father and brothers indicated Bass was right. Yet, Cade would be a dangerous enemy, judging from his performance today. She hadn't thought much about him before, except to notice how handsome he was. Until today. Too bad. He would have to die with the other Bransons, she decided.

Where was Bass anyway? He left with Emmett Harding and Cade Branson.

She bit her lower lip and shut her eyes for a moment, then strolled to the long mirror above the bookcase in the corner. She wanted to see for herself what Bass would get to enjoy. She couldn't stay angry at him for long, no matter what he had done. For the first time, Elizabeth noticed her skirt carried spots of dried mud from her business outside the saloon. Annoyed at the discovery, she unsuccessfully attempted to brush it clean.

She continued to examine herself and saw that her undergarment was wrinkled as well. "Goddammit! I look like some damn daughter of Erin just off the boat. I'll have to change before I go out again."

The office was connected to a suite of other rooms which served as her living quarters. One room was exclusively taken over with her clothes. Winter velvets and fur wraps were already laid out for the approaching season. She liked living close to the center of town. Something about it kept her stimulated. At some point, though, she would purchase one of the great mansions in the city. For now, though, this was perfect.

"Of course, no matter how rich I become, or where I choose to live, those born of the right families will never accept me," she told herself. "Just like they didn't you, mother. Damn phony leeches."

A bolt of hatred crashed against her mind. The image in the mirror was evil rage. A vein throbbed its hostility across her forehead and her mouth twisted into unbalanced loathing. She swallowed and swallowed again, driving the disgraceful memories back into her soul.

Slowly, sensual thoughts reentered her mind, dancing toward Cade Branson. "You liked what you saw, didn't you? You have before too." She turned in profile to the mirror. "So did I. So did I." She spun around to let her dress fully extend and curtsied politely toward the mirror.

Only Bass Manko and Absalum Sil knew fully of her plans—or that she was behind the scheme. The outlaws in Sil's small band knew the objective but thought Sil had partnered with a mysterious Mexican bandit named Lear. They were told the Widow Rice knew nothing of what was going on. Sil also told them Bass would be eliminated as soon as the Bransons were killed, that his sole function was to keep an eye on the widow so she wouldn't get suspicious. The plan itself was simple, yet wonderfully bold. Leading them herself disguised as that Mexican bandit, she and Sil, Bass and the rest of her men had stolen cattle from the four small ranchers and harrassed them at nights until the targeted families had no choice but to sell.

Stolen beef was kept on her range in a box canyon and driven north at night to a ranch she had bought near the Red River. Of course, Emmett Harding never thought to look for cattle so close. Even if he did, Sil was as good as anyone in masking a trail. He was a cruel man, she knew, but effective. She could control him because he wanted her. She had promised him such affection, after they succeeded with the land grab. Getting those four additional ranches spread her control over nearly half the region—and gave her confidence to make the next move.

But her favorite part of the entire effort was disguising herself as Lear. She loved the name. Wearing a black wig and beard, and tan makeup, she dressed in flashy Mexican-styled clothes, a black sombrero and carried a long-barreled Smith & Wesson revolver with black handles. A black scarf masked her nose and mouth for effect. To minimize being identified by any gang member, she spoke only with Bass and Sil or, when necessary, grunted monosyllabic orders.

"Oh, Mother, you would be so proud of my performances. I know you would. No one in the gang knows I am a woman. Can you imagine that when you look like me?" She arched her back to emphasize her breasts.

Yet she could trust no one to help her think. That she had learned years ago—and was reminded of the harsh fact again by Bass's foolishness with the Bransons. She must be equally cautious with her emotions. This was no time to be impatient. Everything was going well, she told herself, but she couldn't relax. Like a caged animal, she began to pace the quiet room. Her full hair, now let down, bounced about her shoulders in rhythm with her bosom.

She didn't like change that she hadn't created. The saloon fight was unexpected; Bass hadn't asked for her approval to steal those cattle. She cursed again. A timid beam of sunlight found her eyes from its starting point between the closed window curtains. Angered by the mental interruption, she went back to the window.

From the thin line of separation between the curtains, she watched three Frenchmen talking as they entered her saloon below. She hated their arrogant ways, their pointed goatees and their white gloves.

"Why don't you go back to France, you fools," she muttered aloud and paused. "At least they will purchase the highest-priced cognac, won't they?" She nodded. "Yes, they will. And my best cigars." A leering smile crossed her face. "And my cheapest whores."

Her desire for perfection led her often to worrying about things that never happened nor were likely to happen. But within all details was the difference between success and failure. A love of the theater always seemed to give her the release she needed from the preoccupation of her all-consuming quest. As a young woman, she had even considered the theater as a profession but her other skills became too profitable to ignore. None of her employees understood her fascination for the stage but she didn't expect them to. They made snide remarks about her occasional recitations of passages from Shakespeare when they were sure she was out of earshot. She knew that too.

As a child, she had spent her days at a local theater in Akron, Ohio, watching the actors and actresses rehearse and then perform before applauding audiences. She was enthralled by it all. Her mother had been one of those actresses. The beautiful and gently naive woman died in an insane asylum for the poor when Elizabeth was fourteen, put there by an insidious disease that had stolen her mind. After that, Elizabeth went to her father, a lawyer who never acknowledged his daughter or her mother. Elizabeth had killed him with a knife while he mounted her in his bed. He was the first of eight men she had murdered along the way to San Antonio. Most died from poison—including her first husband, an old Ohioan rich with gold and land.

The same had happened to her rancher husband, Tobias Rice. Her third. Poor misguided fellow, but he owned one of the biggest ranches around. Actually owning the Circle R was the first step in her plan. Purchase of the saloon and the fancy brothel came next, after he was dead. The Trenchard ranch was her latest acquisition. Now she was fully ready to take the big step in her plan: the takeover of the Bar 6.

From the window, she saw several members of the touring Shakespearean troupe enjoying a stroll. Two men and a woman.

" 'Let every eye negotiate for itself, and trust no agent,' " she muttered a line from *Much Ado About Nothing* and smiled.

Every man paused to greet them, especially the actress, as they passed. The actress walked like a princess, swishing an emerald green skirt with a matching bodice and an overly wide-brimmed flowered hat. The planked sidewalk could have just as easily been a lighted stage as she drew attentive eyes to her. They were currently performing in town. Elizabeth had attended almost every night and tonight would be no exception.

For a few more minutes she watched, enjoying the way the young actress controlled the streets with her presence, but spending most of the time watching the taller of the two actors. He reminded her of an actor she had watched when she was growing up in Akron. She had had an enormous crush on him. As a girl nearing her teens, she thought he was the most beautiful thing she had ever seen and he had smelled heavenly.

"Steven Van Ost. Ah, you were a beauteous thing. Oh, what a fine smile. What strong arms."

Her mind returned to a cubby hole outside the Ohio actor's dressing room where she used to watch him undress. The tall actor walking the street outside was a fine substitute for that childhood fantasy and had been an excellent late evening's diversion. One she carefully kept from Bass Manko. But she enjoyed men. Always had. Using her body to get what she wanted came easily and early in life. Actual prostitution had lasted only a year or so, however, after she realized how to get more through marriage.

Abruptly, Elizabeth broke off her richly sensual chain of thought, yanked the curtains together so the sunlight couldn't distract her and decided to return to her desk. She always thought better there. Like a religious ritual, she paused at the wall containing her prized collection of framed theater program covers from San Antonio's ample schedule of performing arts as well as posters and covers gathered from her childhood. They were more than her pride and joy—they were her religion. Others prayed to crosses and crucifixes; she talked to theater program covers, and her mother who they represented.

They also served as "proof" of her innocent-sounding past. The town assumed she had served as a theater manager in the Midwest before coming to Texas at the beginning of the War. Deer Creek had been divided, Union and Confederate, so she had no problem blending in as a Northerner. She was already a rich woman when she met Tobias Rice and decided to seduce him into marrying her. The plan to become a cattle queen was only a vague daydream at the time. But the moment she mouthed the words, she knew it was her destiny. "Cattle Queen of Texas."

In the center was a framed poster of *King Lear*—her favorite—from a long-ago performance in Ohio. She touched the glass frame and, in a husky voice, declared, " 'Time shall unfold what plaited cunning hides.' "

Just below the framed program covers was a waist-high bookcase. Across its shiny walnut top were displayed a German porcelain figurine of a dancer, a French magenta vase with accents of gold, two Chinese hand-painted urns and a delicate wooden cricket cage, also from China. All were signs of wealth but held no real significance for her.

"Sing to me, my love," she purred at the tiny insect perched inside the cage. It was the only thing she owned that had been her mother's. The late actress believed strongly in the cricket's power to bring good fortune. Elizabeth didn't believe in the superstition, or any superstition for that matter. But the insect did provide a certain cheeriness to the room. Of course, Elizabeth had lost count of how many crickets had been in the cage. She had only killed four, however, out of unrelated rage.

She smiled and continued to the heavy walnut desk. It was empty, except for a leather-bound accounting ledger, an ash tray with a half-smoked cigar, a sheet with the most current whiskey inventory and a plate containing a cold pancake from this morning's breakfast. Elizabeth opened the accounting ledger and tried to go over entries from the Gower House but couldn't concentrate. Every few minutes, she stared at the ornate wall clock across the room and grew angrier over having to wait. Her left hand trembled and that angered her even more. She squeezed it hard with her right hand and the shivering quit.

She forced herself to go over the books. The Gower

House produced more income than her ranches or the saloon. The great mansion was always busy with rich visitors who would stay for days, usually in the company of a single lady. Everything a man ever wanted and more was there, she told herself. A long bar with every kind of whiskey imaginable. Gaming of all kinds—a roulette wheel, crap table, poker games. And women who knew how to take care of a man; she had selected each prostitute with care. There was a player piano on the main floor, a billiard room and a band in the ballroom. The mansion was decorated with velvet furniture coverings and heavy velvet drapes, brass railings and paintings of nudes. One was definitely of Elizabeth Rice herself in the Blue Room. She had posed for it two years ago.

The Gower House had been the perfect way to buy Sheriff Swisher's loyalty by simply giving the county lawman free rein of the place whenever he was in town. This was done solely through Sil's contact with the man—who thought Sil actually paid for all the lawman's enjoyment at the whore palace. Swisher knew nothing of her involvement. Still, she planned on replacing him with one of her own men when the time was right, or maybe Sil himself.

"Where the hell is Bass anyway? Does he think stealing their cattle was funny? Do I have to do everything around here?" Elizabeth slammed a fist on the desk in frustration. The sheet of paper fluttered to the floor but she didn't notice. She slammed the entry book closed.

The striking businesswoman had been in her office since the saloon fight, initially, just to wait for Bass Manko and his explanation. Then it became a time to brood. Depression wouldn't be far behind. It never was. She considered a pipe of tobacco mixed lightly with opium. This had proven effective in relieving the bouts of blackness that descended on her occasionally. She decided against smoking for now. Her mind needed to be free to think, even if the thoughts were murky.

She prided herself on her patience and self-control but that didn't include waiting when she shouldn't have to. Maybe Bass was spending time with Marshal Harding to find out something about his two new deputies. A thin smile timidly approached her mouth. Of course, that was it. That didn't excuse the cattle stealing but it was a step in the right direction. If that's what he was doing.

The knock on the office door was robust.

Elizabeth rose deliberately from her chair, grabbed her waistcoat and buttoned it in place. Another knock followed, supported by a cheery whisper, "It's Bass." She placed her right foot on the sofa and drew a double-barreled derringer from a special holster strapped above her fashionable buttoned shoe. It wasn't the only weapon she regularly carried. In her left shoe was a pearl-handled stilletto.

With the short gun in her hand, she checked the visitor through the tiny peephole in the heavy-framed door. Satisfied it was Bass, she slid the gun into her bodice pocket and pulled open the door.

Chapter Thirteen

Slamming the door behind him, Elizabeth screamed, "Where the hell have you been, you stupid idiot? And who the hell told you to steal Branson's cattle? What the hell were you thinking?"

Bass's face tightened and he took a half-step backward. For a split-second, instinct told him to reach for the gun at his hip. A natural reaction when attacked. Almost as quickly, his brain rejected the idea as foolish or worse and kept his hand from giving anything more than a reflexive jerk.

"Hey, hey, honey, you've got it all wrong. I didn't steal any Branson beef. No way. I think Dish was trying to get rid of me. The asshole doesn't like me. Can you believe someone not liking me?" His smile was as wide as his face and his eyes sparkled.

"Are you sure?" Elizabeth's eyes cut into his face but the anger within her was evaporating.

His devilish smile preceded the pushing of his hat off his head, letting it rest on his back by the leather tie-downs.

"Why do you think Cade was standin' there against his family? He saved my life, I reckon."

"I wondered why he was there."

"Well, little lady, are you gonna let me in—or should I find someone who wants me?"

Her voice changed to soft and inviting. "I've got some good Tennessee sipping whiskey. It's been a hard day for both of us. We'll drink a toast to us. Did anyone see you?"

"Of course not. I came in the back way, as usual. What did you expect? Me leading a parade to your door?"

Without waiting, she turned and walked past the sofa and went directly to a tall whiskey cabinet, adorned with inlaid carvings of English design. Bass followed like a happy puppy. She produced two glasses and a decanter of whiskey, poured two generous drinks and handed one to Bass.

Her hand trembled and she frowned. "Sorry, I twisted my wrist. It's still weak."

The handsome gunfighter accepted the glass and grinned. "Never thought I'd see the day Gilmore would be whipped, did you?" Bass raised the glass. "To the Cattle Queen of Texas."

"I'll drink to that."

Both drank in solemn silence. But Elizabeth bit the inside of her cheek to keep from chuckling at the solemnity. Holding his empty glass, Bass looked around for a place to set it down and decided on the bookcase next to the whiskey cabinet. He pushed his glass against the closest urn to get enough room.

"Goddammit, don't do that, you fool. Those damn things cost a fortune." She stepped over and grabbed the glass out of Bass's hand.

"Hey, I'm sorry. Hell's bells, didn't know it was somethin'. Looked kinda ugly to me."

Blinking her long eyelashes, Elizabeth looked up at him and smiled. "That's alright. Would you like another?"

"Sure. That's good stuff."

"Yes, it is. The best. And there'll be lots more of it once we take over."

He pulled her to him and their mouths found each other. He took her unfinished drink and laid it on the bookcase. Her freed arm surrounded him and they kissed deeply. They had been lovers for two years and involved in crime together for nearly that long.

It started on a lusty dare. They had robbed a stagecoach together, wearing masks, Mexican clothing and sombreros. Bass left behind his distinctive silver-studded gunbelt and she wrapped her bosom to hide that she was a woman. Taking off the wrap was his favorite part of their crimes, Bass always told her. Hiring him to sing in her saloon kept him close—and provided a convenient cover for his involvement in the ranch raids.

Only two stages were robbed before they were on to bigger things. Her desire to gain control of the region's cattle lands had come late one night. Lying in bed together, after passionate lovemaking, she blurted that she wanted to be a bigger cattleman than Richard King over in Brownsville. Uncontrollable laughter tightened into "why not" thinking. The basic plan was made right there and then. The foreman and cowhands were let go at her ranch and, against Bass's wishes, Absalum Sil and his outlaw band brought in. The first phase of the plan was completed rapidly.

There had been a few mishaps so far in the pursuit of her master plan. The most serious was the killing of Harding's young deputy who spotted them one night in the middle of a cattle-stealing raid and followed them. Bass had shot him. Another was purely the result of jealousy and more humorous than dangerous. Absalum Sil had given Elizabeth an unusual gold locket, hand-made, with a fine gold chain to wear around her neck. He said it was created for her in New Orleans. Not to be outdone, Bass held up a stagecoach on his own and stole a stunning silver and ruby necklace from a lady passenger. When he presented it to Elizabeth, she recognized the jewelry as belonging to the mayor's wife and told him to throw it away.

He thought about giving it to Susannah. Finally, he realized the threat it presented and tossed it into the high grass along the trail to town. It was found days later by some cowboys and eventually returned to the grateful woman. To soothe his wounded ego, Elizabeth told him that she wouldn't wear the necklace anymore. And hadn't, except when she knew he wouldn't be around or when she met with Sil.

A third problem turned out quite favorably in the reinforcement of their story of Mexican bandits being behind the rustling. One night, Beaumont Gray saw her riding in front of the gang. He was checking on his small herd gathered for protection not far from his ranch. Somehow, he escaped the gang's gunfire but sold out soon after, proclaiming to everyone that it was Mexicans who stole his beef.

Of course, there was the constant need to provide cover stories for her disappearances and for Bass's as well. Most difficult for Bass was to avoid his friend, Cade, becoming suspicious. Several times, he suggested to Elizabeth that they bring him into the gang but she refused and threatened to have him killed if Bass couldn't control him. Other than that, the violence against the small ranchers had gone smoothly with Mexican bandits getting the blame, or the ranchers themselves being accused of looking for excuses for poor management of their land.

"Oh, I thought you'd never get here," she breathed into his ear. "I need you." Quickly, their passion moved to her couch. As he eagerly removed her bodice, her derringer fell on the floor and he stopped with his hands surrounding her exposed breasts.

"Is that for me?" he grinned.

"A girl can't be too careful," she purred. "Especially around the devil when he's singing sweet songs."

"I'll remember that."

"In the meantime, what have you got for me?" Her hand went to the buttons at his groin.

An hour later, they lay exhausted; Elizabeth on the couch and Bass on the floor. Bass's pants, studded gunbelt and cuffs were huddled not far from him. His shirt was open but on. Her waistcoat and bodice were wadded up in the corner of the couch. Bracing himself on his elbows, Bass decided this was a good time to explain what had happened in the saloon.

"I didn't get a chance to tell you earlier about some . . ."

"You were busy with other things." She smiled sleepily and stretched her arms wide. "And you did them well."

"It's good news. Yeah, mighty fine. Harding's hired me as a deputy—to help see that the roundup goes without trouble." Bass's smile was irresistible.

"You're kidding."

"Nope. He thinks I'll be just the thing to keep rustlers away."

"Does he think there's a rustling problem?"

"Oh, hell no, he's just trying to keep his job. Make it look like he's really doing something. He's an old man graspin' at straws."

She laughed heartily and Bass joined in. Standing without making any attempt to cover herself, she walked over to the cabinet and poured another drink. Handing it to him, she motioned for him to sit on the sofa. She sipped on her drink as she dressed.

"What about your friend Cade Branson? That old fool want him too?"

"Oh, sure, but Cade's goin' back to his paw's ranch after he holes up for a day or two to let things settle. He's on his way to a friend of ours. An old buffalo hunter. Half-crazy coot who taught us both how to shoot—and drink." Bass took a long swallow, buttoned his shirt and pulled on his pants. "But you never can tell what Cade's gonna care about. He took a stand against a bunch of soldier boys who were makin' fun of a Mex kid during supper."

"What if he decides to care about Marshal Harding?"

"He won't. He'd rather be in San Antonio."

"And you? Can people tell what you're going to care about?"

"I'm lookin' at it."

Elizabeth's face was unreadable. "But if he goes back to his family, that means he'll be at the roundup. Can you deal with that?" Her eyes narrowed. "More to the point, can you deal with him?"

"I'm better with a gun than he is—and he knows it." Bass grinned and patted the handle of his gun now laying on the sofa. "I figure he'll stay at Black Jack's for a few days before he rides home. If his paw doesn't split a gut over it, he'll stay around there until the roundup's over. He hates Dish's guts, especially after the stunt he tried to pull. Hell's teeth, he doesn't like nursin' cows anyway."

Bass never tried to analyze his way through a situation, or plan for a long-term goal; he just reacted. When one was as good with a gun as Bass, maybe that was enough. Elizabeth swallowed the rest of her drink, still not responding to Bass's observations about his friend. The cheery song of the cricket blossomed within the silence.

"Well, I would've chosen a more romantic tune but what can you expect from a damn bug." His gaze sought hers for confirmation of his observation.

"My mother thought they were good luck."

He tried again, not yet comprehending her reaction. "I stepped on one this morning. Wasn't very lucky for him." His laugh was a bit forced as the whiskey began to spread to his brain.

"Perhaps that's why you're not worried about Cade Branson. Seems to me he could be quite a problem, if he decides to take Emmett up on his offer. What'll you do then?" She moved behind her chair. It was better to keep her distance from him when she wanted to think clearly. "Or what if he shows up at the roundup—with or without a badge?"

"If it comes to it, I can handle Cade." Bass finished his drink and looked for a place to set the glass. He decided on the floor in front of the sofa.

"Can you? That big clown Gilmore thought he could too."

Bass's smile returned. "You're comparing me to . . . him?"

Elizabeth Rice's smile was more of a disbelieving sneer. "What if that old fool Harding has stumbled onto us? What if hiring you is his way of keeping you close to him so he can watch you. He gets rid of you with a bullet in the back and then comes after me. What if he wants to be at the roundup because he's figured out what we're going to do? What do you think?"

Like red coals soaked in water, the handsome singer's face melted into gray. It had never occurred to him that Marshal Harding might be so cunning.

Slowly, his eyes regained their impishness. "Naw, couldn't

be. I was there. He's got it strong in his head that if there is any rustling, it's all Mexican. Thinks tellin' everybody he's got me an' Cade will keep them away. I tell you, he's an old man afraid of losing his job. Simple as that. He even wants me an' Cade to stay on, if we want to. No, that ol' man doesn't think anything—except you're something he'd like to get his hands on." Bass stood and finished buttoning his pants. "Did you two ever . . . you know." He saw his hat curled against the far end of the sofa and plopped it cock-eyed on his head.

"Of course not." Her face was total abhorrence of the idea, remembering Marshal Harding's rejection of her advances over two years ago, when she thought he might be helpful. "You think we can do this?" she said, running her fingers along the wood edging of the chair back to hide the trembling in her hands.

"Just like you planned, sweetheart. Just exactly."

"All right, here's what I want you to do," she gestured with her thumb and first finger touching. "First, make sure you know what Cade Branson's going to do—and where he's going to be. You don't want to be surprised. Second, make sure you stay in front of Harding. Always. I don't trust the old bastard, even if he is senile. Third, Sil's in charge during the roundup, not you. Got it? And fourth, stay away from that Harding girl."

"Sure."

"Which of the four did you agree to?"

"All of them, of course. That girl is nothin' to me. Never has been. You know that."

"That's not what I heard."

He laughed out loud and asked, "You want me to take care of the Trenchards after they leave?"

"No. That's Sil's job. He's going to handle it after the roundup."

"Sounds like he's gonna be a busy fella. You sure he's up to it?"

"Why don't you ask him?"

Without waiting for his reaction, she pulled away from the chair and walked slowly to the wall of her theater programs. She stared at each one, savoring some special memory.

" 'Our doubts are traitors, and make us lose the good we oft might win, by fearing to attempt.' " She muttered a line from *Measure For Measure*.

Bass bounced to his feet and eased across the room as she continued to mutter Shakespearean quotes to herself, seemingly lost in another time. As his arms wrapped around her, he kissed the musky softness of her neck and began to sing softly into her ear.

> *"Cattle Queen of Texas,*
> *Elizabeth she be*
> *I kiss her soft hand*
> *And hold her to me."*

It was part of a song he had made up for her. He only sang it when they were alone together. She spun into his body and kissed him sweetly.

"We'll make it, won't we?" Her eyes sought the truth from his.

"Of course we will."

"You'd better go and play some songs downstairs. Go out the back and come through the front." She lowered her eyes to her bosom. "You can come up later—and sing to me."

"Count on it."

They embraced and kissed goodbye. Casually, Bass picked up his gunbelt, swung it around his waist and buckled it in place. He drew the Colt, spun it in his hand and returned the gun to his holster in a single smooth motion.

"Get ready to be the Cattle Queen of Texas," he said, opening the door. He winked and closed it behind him.

She smiled at the door; Bass Manko always took away her concerns. Her shiver was a delicious reminder of their love-making. Behind her, the cricket's trilling interrupted her sensuous revisit. She picked up the derringer and threw it at the cage.

"Shut up, you stupid bug!"

The gun bounced off the wooden frame and landed on the floor. Immediately she forgot both the weapon and the cricket.

"I will be the Cattle Queen of Texas," she said, her eyes gleaming with intensity. "This is your last roundup, Bransons. Oh, 'twill be a lovely event."

Elizabeth's palm opened and her thumb touched her fingers, making an "o" with each as she mentally reviewed her ownership. Using her fingers in such an exaggerated way to list items as she talked was a long-standing habit. Her second husband, a merchant in Louisiana, always used his hands the same way when talking. Then eighteen, she admired the technique and adopted it as her own, after killing him for his money. That's when she met Sil and he had helped her. The hand movements gave her conversations a look of preciseness, she felt and helped to hide the shaking that popped up when she least expected it.

She repeated the ritual with her fingers, just for the joy of it. Five ranches were now hers, and hers alone. Her late husband's ranch was, of course, openly owned. Secret deeds held the true ownership of the others. There, on those special pieces of paper were the only mentions of her cattle company, KL Cattle Company. "KL" stood for King Lear.

Once the last big hurdle of getting the Branson ranch was climbed, she would stand alone as the power to be reckoned with in this part of Texas. Slowly, she would let her holdings become known. She had that transference all planned too. Everything would eventually be above board. And everyone would be in awe. Everyone would bow to the Cattle Queen of Texas.

Of course, the ranch sales had been stimulated by additional encouragement that no one knew about. Sil had threatened to kill the ranchers' families if they didn't sell. He and Bass ambushed the Richardsons on their way to California. That got Elizabeth's money back, from her purchase of the ranch. The key was waiting to do it so that news of their deaths never got back to Deer Creek. Any identifying information was destroyed as well. The other families were similarly disposed of and the sale money retrieved. Sil would also take care of getting her money back from the Trenchards on their way to St. Louis, after the roundup was over. The Trenchard family was leaving in a wagon later this week; Mrs. Trenchard had a brother in the Missouri city.

Each ranch now under her control was run by Sil or one of his henchmen. Absalum Sil was a competent cattleman and as cold as the Texas winter wind. Short and dressed like a farmer, he was easily underestimated. Elizabeth realized she could get along without Bass—although it would distress her personally—but she would not get far without Absalum Sil and his men. She also knew Bass thought it was the other way around.

Comforted by her review of the situation, she turned to more pressing matters. Her thumb and fingers clicked together, one at a time, reviewing her own next tasks. She had planned on having Emmett Harding ambushed one day on the way to town from his home. But since he had decided to be on hand at the roundup . . . his death there would be a bonus. She smiled as she recalled having started the rumor that he was no longer able to be an effective lawman because he hadn't found out who held up the stages or were stealing cattle. It had taken only three days to hear the rumor returned to her. Well embellished to the point that Harding was worried about his future.

At the right time, she would present a signed deed for the Branson ranch; a bribe to Attorney Princeton had secured Titus's signature from a will and she had carefully reproduced it. Absalum Sil was listed as a witness, as was Princeton himself and the outlaw who served as the Circle R foreman, Jordan Maher. None of the Branson sons would be around to cry foul, anyway. The region would be hers. Hers. Except for the piddling other two ranches.

"Ah, yes, it is a masterful plan," she told himself. " 'How poor are they that have not patience, nor boldness.' " Smiling, she raised her chin. "They will all rue the day they weren't nice to me—and you, mother."

Such was the vision that burned in her soul every day. Every single day. She would have the last laugh. She would be richer and more powerful than any of those bastards—the ones who looked down their noses at her mother, at all actors and actresses. She would have the grandest stage of all and they would be forced to applaud. All she had to do was keep following her plan.

"Elizabeth Bingham Rice. Cattle Queen. That has a nice ring to it." She smiled and said it again, "Elizabeth Bingham Rice. Cattle Queen."

She could be the next Richard King in the cattle business. Perhaps greater. It would only take putting her considerable mind to the task. She was a planner with much confidence in her abilities. Her skill at thinking strategically was exceptional; all of her late husbands had told her so, but she already knew the truth. More importantly, she was good at turning her plans into real, hard fact—and much gold.

"Ah, yes, much gold. And much power. I dedicate it all to you, mother."

Near the sofa, dirt from Bass's heels had dribbled on the floor. Compulsively, she went over, knelt and swept the crumbled pieces into her open palm with her other hand. She looked around for something to deposit them in and decided on her ashtray. After depositing the dirt, Elizabeth Rice shut her eyes and envisioned the shadows of greatness forming around her. This she did often. It was a powerful reinforcement for her mind. Her forefinger and thumb joined. "Cade Branson must die. It would be foolish to guess how he'll react." Her second finger and thumb connected. "Bass Manko must die."

She began to hum the song Bass wrote for her.

Chapter Fourteen

The Harding family's late afternoon ride from Deer Creek to their small horse ranch was mostly a quiet one, except for some unexpected chattiness every now and then by the marshal about Cade Branson and Bass Manko. Otherwise, the three Hardings were lost in their own thoughts. The old lawman was convinced the two young men would help rid the region of any outlaws. Absolutely convinced, it seemed to Susannah. How like him to offer them jobs so quickly, Susannah mused to herself.

Neither Susannah nor Seth dared to ask what he thought the two would be able to accomplish as his deputies. Actually only one, if Cade didn't come. She wasn't certain if no one would take the deputy job after Henry Endore was killed, or if her father hadn't asked anyone. He never said. Maybe Cade and Bass didn't understand what they were going up against. But secretly she was glad. It meant they would be around the ranch. She shouldn't feel that way but she did. She was strongly attracted to both young gunfighters, each for a different reason only she understood.

The creaking of their loaded wagon provided a rhythmic background to both daydreaming and talking. Cooler and cloudy wore the day. Rain wasn't far away, Harding observed as he spat toward the rear of the two horses pulling them. The brown stream wavered near their tails and dove to the ground. Weather was a subject he often expounded on, or cursed.

Roper rode the lawman's favorite sorrel, walking behind the wagon, often talking loudly to himself. Since the old lawman had let everyone out of the jail, there wasn't any reason for Roper to spend the night there. Seth rode his own bay gelding alongside the dimwitted jailer. He preferred the wagon but Susannah and their father sat in the plank seat. The marshal was handling the reins as he always did. In the back with the supplies, his dog slept. Large, black and mean to everyone except the marshal and, sometimes, Susannah.

After the creek crossing, six stray cows meandered up to the wagon and walked alongside for the better part of a mile. That was when Harding pointed out the silver-brown shape of a wolf entering the treeline to the northwest. Bunches of fat cattle were everywhere, like checkers in a new game. Here and there, a distant rider would wave and received a similar greeting from the passing group. Occasionally, Seth would make small talk about passing landmarks to try getting his father to continue his discussion of the gunfighters. But the son's subtle prodding didn't seem to have much effect on the timing of his father's conversation.

Whenever something occurred to the marshal he just barked it out, no matter who was talking or what the subject. Interrupting like that was another bad habit of his. But only his late wife had dared to dress him down about it. Not even Susannah tried.

Actually Seth wanted to share the encounter he had experienced in the general store with an old German with stringy white hair, just before leaving for the ranch. But the young Harding didn't think it was something he should bring up, at least not now. Moving stiffly, the old man had reeked of beer and had a voice that reminded Seth of a file against wood. His speech was littered with German words and phrases that sometimes made him difficult to understand. The old man had come up to Seth and asked if he knew Cade Branson and Bass Manko.

Seth didn't know why he was singled out but had answered that they had just been hired as his father's deputies. He started to explain that Cade Branson might not be coming but the old man blurted out a description of the gunfight in the saloon and said he had never seen any two men handle themselves so well with gun or fist. He thought they must be using false names and wondered if Seth knew Clay Hardin or King Fisher. The old man thought they might be those two, riding under false names.

Stunned, Seth had pretended to know more than he did. That's all the old man needed to ramble on. The young Harding listened breathlessly as the old-timer spun through a halting, garbled recital, of which Seth caught only isolated phrases. It was clear, however, that the German farmer liked them, whoever they really were. Seth had struggled not to act agitated at the report. He remembered now that he had felt like vomiting.

What kind of men had his father hired? Surely his father knew Cade Branson and Bass Manko were bad men. They weren't Fisher or Hardin, of course, and not outlaws, mind

you, but bad men to mess with. And definitely not among
the church-going, Bible-reading faithful. Seth could feel
the coldness within both, almost like a winter wind coming.
Would they be offended if he told them about the old man's
jabbering the next time they were together? Seth didn't
think so but wasn't sure he had the nerve. His father might
take Seth's recitation of the German farmer's observations
the wrong way if he told it now. He usually did about anything the young man said.

The young man didn't want to trigger another blow-up
by his father like he'd done a few months ago. Seth had
dared to share his suspicion that the rustling was real and
being controlled by somebody in the region, somebody who
seemed respectable. Marshal Harding's rejection of the idea
was hot, immediate and intense. Susannah had reminded
her father that Seth's concept might be worth investigating.
When she pressed for his reaction, he changed the subject.

Susannah's thoughts were also wrapped around the two
young men, particularly Cade Branson. He was good-
looking in a hard sort of way, wasn't he? She couldn't forget
the interest in his eyes, even though he tried to hide it. She
tried to think of something else. Her life was surrounded by
this majestic view of endless plains, flanked by rolling hills.
The hills in the distance were so free, so rugged.

And that brought her again to Cade Branson. Underneath his bold ways was a caring person, she thought. She
couldn't forget how immediate his response was to help the
young Mexican singer. No hesitation. No concern about
himself. None of the other men at the table had responded.
Not Bass. Not even her father. The realization of Cade's
gentle core drew her to him like nails were drawn to those
magnets she had seen at the general store. Anger spun
through her when privately she acknowledged the attrac-

tion. How dare he bother her so! Didn't he know she was in love with Bass Manko?

Her father she understood. And men like him as well. She could almost read his thoughts. Emmett Harding was a good man, or tried to be, as he saw goodness. Dependable. Stubborn. Yes, and narrow-minded at times but always fair. The two things he couldn't stand were liars and cowards. Men like her father would fight when pushed hard enough but not without giving ample warning first. The "rattlesnake code," some called it. His announcement in the general store was just that. And quite shrewd, she admitted to herself.

She knew her father always thought of his family's welfare first, even though he probably wouldn't admit it, saying his first responsibility was to the town. This was his strength—and his vulnerability. She understood that but she was positive that he didn't. She had to admit that she always thought of him as a lawman and a horse trainer, rarely as just a parent. She couldn't imagine him without a badge but knew the day was rapidly approaching. Would he be able to handle the rejection when it came? Did he ever think about such things?

If he were asked about losing his marshal's job, Emmett Harding would laugh at the stupidity of the question and go on with whatever he was doing. That would be the end of the matter too. No thoughtful reflection later. No stopping to even ask why the question came up. He wouldn't even explain to friends that he often stayed in town overnight without anyone knowing it.

Bass Manko she understood as well, when she was honest with herself. Charming and quite striking in appearance, many women would, and did, delight in his captivating attention—she had no doubt of that. Boyish, yet dangerous.

His eyes and smile could lead many a woman into things she never thought she would do. Would she marry him? Probably, she admitted to herself.

Dish Branson was in love with her too, or thought he was. He offered her a life that would be stable and secure. She knew she didn't love him. She had told him so several times. That didn't seem to matter. He kept returning to her with another marriage proposal. She would always say no.

But Cade Branson. Cade Branson. He was another matter. A mysterious thing to her. Simultaneously, she was pulled toward him and pushed away. A daydream took over. He touched her and the fire of that union built within her. Vivid pictures flashed through her mind of his holding her, driving heat throughout her body with his own. She shivered and wanted to hug herself. She frowned to cut off the emotion. She should not feel this way; she had never felt such a strong pull toward any man, not even Bass.

What kind of a life could a woman have with a man like Cade Branson? What a silly question to be thinking. He was a man of the gun. They could never have a life together. Never. A man like him was always drawing danger to him. Such a man could be killed at any time and most likely would be. If she were honest with herself, she would admit to fearing the soldiers in the restaurant would find him later in town. And he would be found in an alley. The thought of Cade Branson dying made her wince in her seat. She squeezed her eyes tightly to get that picture to go away. She could see his face with those penetrating eyes. But she couldn't imagine him dead and she didn't want to.

Thud! The wagon banged over a hole Marshal Harding hadn't seen. All contents rattled for an instant and then went silent again. Susannah looked back at the washout and wondered how her father had missed it. He didn't appear to want to explain or discuss the matter. So she returned to her thoughts.

She shuddered again. Cade Branson was a killer of men, she reaffirmed to herself, and would eventually meet a killer's fate. But so would Bass Manko—and he could never be true to one woman. She knew that, even though she loved being close to him. Who didn't? Even Cade Branson had stood against his family to help Bass.

Her father was a great lawman, Susannah decided, looking at his hard face as he concentrated on maneuvering a bend in the trail. He would have made a great anything he wanted to be, she mused. Even a great minister. It was probably where Seth got his inclination to preach but her father would never admit that. As if he could read her thoughts, her father patted her thigh gently, or as gently as he ever did anything. She wondered what he really thought of Bass, or Cade, or Dish. She wondered if he had ever realized she would marry some day and leave him.

Often he had told her and Seth that a man could "learn the insides of a man just by watching how he handles his hoss." It was obvious he was impressed when Cade took time to stable his horse. But her father had a way of defining people as being good or bad, strong or weak and then that was that, no matter what. He would treat everything he heard about them within the context of this structured opinion, even if it didn't come close to matching up with anyone else's, or the rest of the world's, for that matter. Susannah could remember him changing his mind only on one thing—the War. A good and noble cause. Until it took his two oldest sons.

Scuffling sounds drew her attention to the back of the wagon. Their dog was trying to find a more comfortable place to sleep. She glanced at his right paw, dotted still with dried blood. Nothing serious, she assured herself again. Just something he'd run across, or over, in his travels in town. Seeing the homely animal brought a wave of memories of her father telling her tale after tale of cattle dogs, how important they were, how to train them and particularly how great this beast was. He had always talked with her like she was a man, or a boy when she was younger. She would go with him whenever he was looking for company, just to be with him. It didn't matter where to her; she loved being with him.

Her late older brothers always seemed to have excuses, what she could remember of them. Seth occasionally went along but he never really caught his father's eye. Susannah felt sad about that. Every day she silently prayed the young man would suddenly become what their father could be proud of. But, even at a young age, he was drawn to preachers and church going. So, instead of Seth, she was exposed to thorough discussions about branding cattle, about Texas longhorns and Durham shorthorns, about curing buffalo grass into dry feed for winter, about short blue gramma grass and long blue stem grass, about remudas, roundups and river crossings, about every kind of horse imaginable, and what to look for when a colt got sick, about how to talk with them when putting on a blanket or a saddle for the first time. Never about being a lawman, though.

When she was alive, her mother would give Emmett Harding a chewing whenever she got wind of his man-talk to their daughter. Susannah suspected her mother didn't mind it at all—her mother knew almost as much about horses as her father did. But rather she did the nagging to remind him of their younger son's need of his counsel as well. Susannah loved such times together with her father. She could be close to him when no one else could. And she loved the land the way he did, truly a reverence beyond anyone's words. As he liked to say, he didn't have much time for "tellin' windies." Watching that powerful dog now made her emotions spill into a small tear at the corner of her eye. No, she wouldn't cry. Her father wouldn't understand.

Seeking attention, the dog brushed her hand. She gave him a gentle rubbing of his ears and a long scratching along his back. Her father called him "John Henry" and she did too. However, Susannah never noticed the animal actually responding to that name, or any other for that matter, when used by someone other than her father. The beast was unquestionably Emmett Harding's dog and spent most days sleeping in the middle of the marshal's office or an empty cell. The mere fact he had asked to be petted by her was a coup.

Easing the horses to a stop for a little rest, Harding shook his head slowly to ease the stiffness in his neck, then spat at the dirt. A scurrying ground squirrel missed the fury of the brown liquid by inches. He chuckled and thought about announcing that he was aiming for the animal. But no one else saw the accidental encounter. He was weary so he didn't claim any moral victory. The whole saloon incident had tired him. He didn't want to admit to himself that drinking tequila at the restaurant had something to do with it too. He drew a deep breath to pull the power of the land inside him. There was a lot to do in the next week, that was for sure, and he didn't have time to be tired. There was a lot he had kept bottled inside himself because it had to be. Soon, that would change.

Throughout the region, cowboys would be hard at work. Seasoned crews would push "tallowed" steers and "heavy cows"—those with calves—out of the brush, hills and ravines and into a holding ground near the river. These small herds would be moved to areas offering a break from winter winds and good grass. Places would be selected to hold cattle until they settled down for the winter or for driving to market in the spring. Those left behind would tend to stay due to the bountiful feed and water. They would also be perfect places for rustlers to quickly hit-and-run. Was there really a rustling problem? Would the threat of hiring two gunfighters keep the region safe? Would Cade Branson wear a star or just Bass Manko? When should he tell Susannah what he knew? Or Cade?

Thank goodness the flies were gone, or mostly so. Cowboys didn't need that aggravation on top of their work load. They would be checking the latest calf crop too. Orphan calves needed branding. Inevitably some wild stuff would end up in the pulled-together herd as well as other ranch brands. Both would need separation and that took time. Few cowboys rode armed, except for handguns. None were particularly good shots, especially with a handgun. Normally, revolvers were only carried for rattlesnakes and in case a cowboy was thrown and got caught in the stirrup of a runaway horse. The revolver was the last resort in stopping the animal.

The last two years Dish Branson had served as the wagon boss, leading the riders from the other ranches during roundups—spring and fall. It made sense for the ranches in the region to conduct their roundups at the same time so the cattle weren't worked more than once. Everyone seemed willing to cooperate in this way, including the newer ranch owners. Dish was accepted by the others, probably because of the size of his family's spread. Certainly not for his way of handling people.

After the roundup, most cowhands would be spread out

on various line camps for the whole winter. Remudas would be turned out for the same months too except for some of the top horses. Winter could bring more change if the rustling continued. He knew the ranchers who sold out were telling the truth. What he didn't know was why the county lawman had ignored their pleas for help.

Marshal Harding had already decided to leave it to Cade and Bass to choose how they would patrol the roundup herds. But he couldn't help wondering if they should split up or if they would be more effective together, even though they wouldn't be able to cover as much land. He smiled to himself that he assumed Cade was coming. He hoped they would stay on as deputies. That should satisfy the townspeople, at least for awhile. How would they take to any direct orders? As tough as he was, he rarely gave any. Any man who needed such wasn't worth having as a deputy. Henry Endore never needed any.

He had no doubts they would ride away if he pushed them in a direction they didn't want to go. But he considered himself a good judge of men and he knew they would also stand and fight for the town, even if their reputations were on the wild side. No matter that. These two gunfighters would be on his side. He had been wild once too, a long time ago before he met his Dorothy. There was a lot on his mind. He reminded his children often that a law-abiding town didn't just happen. Usually this was said in response to one of them suggesting he not work so hard or so long.

"Everything you do is religious. Indians reckon God is in everything, so everything you do is a prayer."

The beautiful statement surprised Susannah and Seth coming right in the middle of silence and coming from their father to boot. Marshal Harding had spoken as if he'd been talking all along. It was the repeat of a statement Cade had made at the restaurant. The lawman was silent again and popped the horses with the reins to get their attention back to the road. That was it, no more words on the subject.

Susannah had been amazed at Cade's observation. She found herself wanting more. Or was it simply the diversion of having someone, or something, different in her dull life? Certainly, though, Cade's statement was not what one would have expected from a gunfighter, one she had known all her life. Or did she know him?

Chapter Fifteen

As he rode, Cade Branson's mind sought refuge in his mother's memory. Scattered fragments of the past days were resting on the border between his conscious and unconscious mind. One fragment kept blossoming whenever he let go of the decision he faced and what might lay ahead. And that was Susannah Harding. Each time, he reminded himself that she was Bass Manko's girl and tried to return his mind to what he should do. Accept Harding's offer, return to the Bar 6 or head for San Antonio alone and start over.

He crossed a washed-out buffalo trail, scrambled up a steep bank and disappeared into the woods pushed against a steep, yellow bluff. His gray horse moved easily along a narrow pony path that wound through the trees and heavy underbrush. A familiar path to both. A sparrow flew across their path, chirping angrily at being disturbed. He stared wistfully at the fingers of sunlight grasping the branches. Loneliness was near once more. It wasn't too late to ride on.

No one would miss him. Except Bass—but he had Susannah to make everything right.

It was times like these that he felt like he was being followed. He wasn't afraid of the sensation, only fascinated by it. Maybe his mother was right. Maybe there was something that watched over him. A spirit guide, like those of Comanche warriors. There were also places he had seen that looked, and felt, like they were doorways to the other world, whatever that was. Haunted places. Black Jack Sante talked about them often.

Cade touched the choker at his neck. His fingers were stiff from the fight and his knuckles were puffy. They ached when he squeezed his hands into fists. The choker was, indeed, made by her uncle, but he was a Comanche, not a white man who had lived with the Indians. Inhaling deeply, Cade recalled his mother's last conversation with him. Whispered and hesitant it came, pushing back death until she could share it.

"C-Cade . . . d-do you know what that . . . means?" Martha Ann Branson winced at the pain engulfing her body. "I-I am going, Cade . . . t-to a better place. I-I will wait . . . for you. I w-will watch over . . . you. I-I love you."

"You can't go, Mother . . . please . . . don't . . . die. You can't . . ."

"Hush, my son. My warrior son. I must tell you . . . something . . . before I leave."

"All right, Mother." Tears welled in the eyes of the young Cade Branson and spilled down his cheeks.

"Your father . . . your real father . . . was a great Comanche war chief. T-That is his choker."

"What? I don't . . ."

"I l-loved him . . . more than life itself. Winter Kill was his name. A great war chief with the Water Horse band. Warriors *would follow him anywhere. H-His medicine was strong."* Her chest shuddered and she stopped. *The boy thought she had died but her eyes fluttered opened. She reached weakly for his hand. "Your father . . . h-he died in a fight against Rangers. He would not go to their reservation. I was with him . . . and you were in me." Martha Ann Branson squeezed shut her eyes. "I-I will see him. Soon. I can feel the touch of his hand . . . now." A single tear spun down her pale cheek.*

Young Cade reached out and wiped it away, his own face melting with wetness. "I don't understand . . ."

"Together . . . at some time ahead of us, Winter Kill and I will be reborn. All Comanche believe so. Oh, he would be so proud of you. Y-You remind me of him. He is close . . ."

Cade shook his head to stop the memory. His mother had told him the Rangers had returned her to Titus Branson, thinking the warriors had kidnapped her, instead of her running off to be with the great Comanche war chief. With her lover dead, she didn't resist and returned to the Branson ranch and the ever-cruel Titus. No one would listen to her claim her white husband had killed her father to get the family ranch.

Neighbors thought she had become mentally unbalanced by being with the Comanche. They thought she was being ungrateful when Titus could easily have not taken her back, after she had been with Indians. When she saw there was no way to bring Titus to justice, she chose to raise Cade and her other two sons as best she could. Titus didn't realize what had happened; he just thought Cade was born early.

Hearing that his real father was someone other than Titus came like one of Dish's fists to his stomach. His first reaction, after leaving his mother's side, was to vomit. How could she do this to him! How could this be? Gradually, though, he began to understand things that hadn't made sense to him before. Why he often acted differently than his brothers did. Why he felt pulled to the land and all that lived on it in a way his two brothers weren't. Why his mother had insisted on his learning the Comanche languge—and knew it herself when no one else in the family did. In some ways, he secretly felt superior to his brothers. And in some, lesser. He was a halfbreed and would not be welcome in either world if anyone ever knew.

Often, he wondered if there was a connection to his real father and why he became cold inside when battle drew near. His mind rejected the idea. It was silly to think that way.

He never talked about his mother's revelation to Titus, John or Dish. Not even to Bass. His mother had willed herself to stay alive long enough to tell him what she thought he needed to know of his real heritage. Of course, it wasn't enough. It never could be. He would never know his real father.

Her burial was done in the finest Comanche manner. He had insisted upon this and sought counsel from an old Comanche woman who had come to be their cook but was secretly his mother's friend—and her former sister-in-law. She was Winter Kill's sister, Wind-in-the-Valley. In broken English, she shared the truth with Cade. The old woman had taken over the funeral process without hesitation.

Titus and the two older sons didn't like the intrusion but no one wanted to buck Cade either; he seemed beyond consolation and close to violence. He simply told them to keep quiet and out of the way. Not even Dish had tried to intrude on his younger brother's grief. Surprisingly, Dish had actually supported the unorthodox burial, telling his father that he was saving money this way, not having to pay for a regular funeral. Neighbors were told the services were going to be private. Few cared, one way or the other. After the "kidnapping," Martha Ann Branson had kept to herself most of the time.

In traditional Comanche ritual, his mother's body was bathed and her knees pushed against her chest and her head bent forward toward the knees. A rope around the body held it in this closed position. Her pale face was painted fully red, and her eyes were sealed with red clay, a prayer from Mother Earth. She was dressed in her only Sunday dress and laid on an Indian blanket she had always taken care of. Cade learned it was their wedding blanket. After the blanket was folded around the body, rawhide thongs held it tighly in place. The body was placed in a sitting position on a horse.

Cade had chosen a gray horse, one of their best. It reminded him of winter. The old Comanche woman rode behind the body to keep it from sliding off and Cade walked beside them. No one knew where she was buried; Cade wouldn't let the others go with them. Dish thought it was in a cave in a canyon where she liked to ride. John thought the Comanches mostly placed their dead in trees or built scaffolds. Titus roared that he was glad she was gone and, in his drunkenness, rambled on about her running off with an Indian and putting a Comanche curse on him because she thought he had killed her father to get the Bar 6.

Cade had killed the gray horse so she would have a suitable mount in the hereafter, as suggested by the elder woman. After she left, he sat by the burial crevice, staring into a fire he built. A week passed. Wind-in-the-Valley became worried and came after him. He told her that it had snowed on him. Puzzled, she said there had been no such bad weather. Later, she told him that it was his late father's spirit guardian telling him that it would be near for him.

To honor his mother and real father, he took to riding only dappled gray horses with white manes and tails, like his current horse, January. It annoyed Dish, who thought the only horses worth having were brown or bay. John once suggested all three brothers should ride gray horses and make it a family tradition. Dish told John that was the silliest idea he had ever heard and that was the end of it.

At his urging, the older Comanche woman told Cade about his real father, and about the Comanches, especially about the time when even the moon was afraid of the tribe. He couldn't hear enough about the true warrior nomads who controlled Comancheria, of calling themselves "The People," of their every-day life, of raiding, hunting, making weapons, raising happy children, of living together with joy and pride, of praising *Taahpu*, who watched over them, the land and all things.

Evenings were spent learning about rituals, great feasts, buffalo hunts and dances of joy. He heard about the mystery of the medicine pipe, of the smoking ceremony to honor all powers in this world and the next, and how a man must use the pipe to have his words reach *Taahpu*. He learned of the spirit helper that stood alongside a warrior his whole life to guide and protect him. He understood that the Comanche warrior never cut his hair, wearing it to a very great length, because it strengthened his medicine. He thrilled to hear about the ghostlike manner of stealing guarded horses. Every man should be his own holy man, Wind-in-the-Valley advised, and should interpret for himself what the will of the Great Spirit was for him and his family. Tribal shamen only offered guidance, if asked.

The Comanche wasted nothing from a killed buffalo, except the skull, rump and spine. Even dried excrement was used as kindling. The buffalo's heart was left on the plains in spiritual tribute and to assure the continued growth of the buffalo herds. Wind-in-the-Valley thought that since the white man did not do this, that was the reason the buffalo left forever. Even the ravens quit coming to tell them where the buffalo had gone.

With sparkling eyes, she told him how Comanche children were taught to ride before they could even walk. That it wasn't enough for a Comanche boy to merely learn to ride, he must aspire to become a trick rider. At a full gallop, every lad could reach down and pick up an object from the ground. During battle, a warrior could actually lift a wounded companion onto his own horse and take him to safety. No comrade could ever be left to the enemy or all warriors lost honor.

Such was his favorite story about his father. Many times, she told him how Winter Kill, wounded himself, turned and rode back among a huge Kiowa war party to save Blue Bear, the biggest warrior in the village. As if the huge man was merely a child, Winter Kill yanked his badly wounded tribesman from the ground and away from the grasp of their enemies, all at break-neck speed.

His true father, he learned, was a wide-chested powerful man, a lodge leader with many followers, and a great war chief. He carried himself with unassuming dignity and was always concerned about others and their well-being. He had two warrior sons from an earlier wife and they died fighting with him at the Ranger fight. Cade was his only living legacy. Wind-in-the-Valley said Cade reminded her of Winter Kill in many ways. The war leader's spirit guide vision he'd had as a young man had come in the form of a horse and rider made of ice and snow that kept changing colors from gray to white to blue as it galloped toward him. The fearsome snow warrior struck down his enemies with a tomahawk of ice and finally disappeared into a blizzard. Gray, white and blue were the painted marks he wore into battle, along with a piece of solid ice rock tied to his waist; Winter Kill had found the magical stone laying among others on the lonely mesa where he had sought his vision.

Cade was most surprised to hear that fighting brought a change within Winter Kill. An cold intensity seeped through the warrior leader, turning his soul to winter. Everything was enlarged and in slow motion. Cade asked Wind-in-the-Valley to repeat what she had said to make certain he had heard it correctly. It sounded exactly like how he felt when he faced danger. It wasn't that he thought he couldn't be hurt or killed. Of course, he could. No one lived a charmed life; bullets didn't care who they struck or why. He had seen too many good men die in the War for no reason at all to believe he was invincible. That wasn't it. It was something else. It was something passed from his father.

One day, Wind-in-the-Valley had presented him with his father's sacred medicine bundle, a beaded buckskin sack filled with items for strength, wisdom and courage, and used to help Winter Kill consult with his spirit guardian, the powerful North Wind. She also gave him the small ice rock that Winter Kill had always carried into battle. The clear multi-edged stone was held by a buckskin thong with one long piece attached to a war belt. She had managed to take it after the losing fight before the white men overran the battleground. It was her thought that his war medicine had failed him because Winter Kill had eaten pork that morning—white man's pork taken in a raid. Cade kept the gifts in his saddlebags from that day forward, guarding their discovery from his family.

She also told him about the bitter destruction of their ways brought about by the white man's insatiable need for

land, about Winter Kill's refusal to go to the reservation—
and his last desperate fight for freedom. When Wind-in-
the-Valley passed on, Cade was almost as grief-stricken as
when his mother died. The last link to his heritage was
gone.

Maybe his father's spirit was beside him now. Maybe the
spirit of his mother was here too. Spirits both visible and invisible were said to reside near kinsmen sometimes. He
hadn't let himself feel this way for a long time. He wished
he could have met his father. Like a stone across water,
Cade's mind skipped to Titus Branson and his brothers. His
stepbrothers, really. He actually would like to see them
again. At least his brothers. Titus was a difficult man to be
around, and one he could not respect. His mother had told
him the whole story of the man's treachery to get her family's ranch. She made him promise never to avenge this
act—and, reluctantly, he had agreed.

The trail's stillness mixed with his own anxiety and made
him realize how much he missed what could have been true
brotherly closeness. But how could he ever forgive Dish for
wanting Susannah so badly that he was willing to see Bass
hang for something he didn't do? Dish's deception had cost
three men their lives.

How far would he go to get her, he asked himself but
couldn't bring himself to answer.

He reined in the gray and swung down. Trees bent toward
him to understand his coming. He stroked the sweating
horse's neck and pronounced they were going to take a
breather. From his saddlehorn, he lifted a canteen and
poured tepid water into his hat.

"Here, Jan, drink deep, my friend," Cade said, holding
the hat to the horse's mouth. He recalled the old woman
telling him that a Comanche warrior cared for his horse like

it was a pet, a loved one, and rode it like no other man on the plains. Cade added more water, which the horse gratefully accepted, took a swig from the canteen himself and slung the strap back over his saddlehorn.

One long sad inhaling of the wood's grayness returned him to his frustration. This wasn't his fight after all. He didn't owe Emmett Harding anything, even if he was Susannah's father. Why was the old lawman so insistent about hiring him and Bass as his deputies? Did he really think rustlers would attack during the roundup? Or was it just a move to make him look like he was still in control? Harding was just an old man who should retire before he was laughed out of Deer Creek. There was no way he was going to catch road agents or rustlers. Not anymore.

And what if rustlers did hit the Bar 6? Why should Cade care? The ranch would belong to Dish when Titus died— the vicious elder Branson had already announced it. John had held his disappointment that day while Dish was all smiles and back-slapping and assured his brothers they would always have a job—and a home.

A dark shape appeared at the lip of the clearing where he stood. A lone wolf. The beast was drawn by the smells of cattle, horses and man.

"*Samohpu*," he said as if talking to a friend. "There is no food here tonight, my brother. Only bullets. You must find field mice tonight. Go now but be on watch for me."

As if the animal understood, the shape faded into the woods.

Something Wind-in-the-Valley told him swam into his mind to answer his question about why he should help Marshal Harding. The idea was uninvited but came anyway. She had told him the greatest warriors—like his father— gave, when no one would ever find out. And the greatest warriors fought alone against many to protect a friend who didn't even know he was in trouble. No matter the cost. That was the way it should be. That was the way it would be for him. No matter the cost. Marshal Harding was a good man who needed his help. That was enough. He must go back.

After this was all over, though, he would ride with or without Bass to San Antonio. Go where no one knew him, to a place where he could start over. He would become a store clerk or something, with no gunfighter tag and no past. Maybe, eventually, he would find someone to share his new life. Maybe he would be lucky enough to find a woman as fine as Susannah. The idea of a place all his own was good. Maybe a general store. Maybe become a lawyer.

Or maybe he should go to the awful place where they kept the Comanche now. He knew enough of their language to be able to search for friends of his father and Wind-in-the-Valley. They could tell him more about this man who had loved his mother and was loved by her.

Returning to the saddle, a different question ambushed him: What was Bass holding back from him? It wasn't like his friend to do that. They always shared what was going on in their lives. In fact, some of the things Bass told him about being with Susannah, he wished Bass hadn't. The only thing he hadn't shared was the truth about his father. He couldn't bring himself to tell that—to anyone. He nudged the horse into a lope; they still had two miles to go. Leaving the woods, they skirted around the bluff and eased onto a deer path mostly hidden by brush and undergrowth.

Black Jack Sante pushed aside the bearskin that served as the door to his clumsily made shack. From the small corral to the west, his brown mule brayed an alarm. The skinny, morose man stood with a red umbrella held over his head. He never did like sunlight, even when it was filtered by the forest. His long, stringy hair was mostly gray; a single eagle feather was tied to a thick lock and lay against his head.

Another strand of hair was decorated with a series of glass beads. Squinting through thick eyeglasses, he watched the small silhouette grow larger as it emerged from the circle of boulders and yellow slabs of rock that skirted the bunched-up clearing where he lived. The former buffalo hunter lit a half-smoked cigar and smiled. He had taught Cade Branson well. Even when coming to an old friend's place, he rode carefully. This land rarely gave second chances to the careless.

Unconventional and aloof, he ate when he felt like it, slept the same way and was never comfortable around concentrations of people. If asked, he would say his best friend was himself—and his next best friend was a buffalo anywhere. He was known to have had at least six wives. No one had any idea of how many children, if any, he might have brought into the world. He simply didn't like most people but he liked this young man coming toward him now.

He scooted a bare foot along the packed-down dirt that served as a front porch. His buckskin leggings had a large hole in the left knee. Over a once-red undershirt, four necklaces of colored beads, all of different length, hung from his neck. Each necklace featured an eagle's claw. At his waist was a scarlet silk sash holding a bone-handled Kiowa scalp knife. Unseen, but just inside the door, was his Sharps .50 carbine. It was always loaded.

Maybe Cade would stay for supper, such as it was. Antelope stew was nothing like buffalo stew, but it was all he could shoot. Besides, corn liquor made everything taste better.

"*Aho*, Cade Branson." Black Jack greeted the young rider as Cade pulled his horse alongside the one-room building. His voice carried the hint of a New Orleans upbringing. A roof made of two laced-together buffalo hides flapped their own version of welcome.

"*Aho*, yourself," Cade said, starting to feel good about himself again.

"What brings you way out this way, boy? Has ol' Emmett been talkin' to you?"

Cade sat up straight in the saddle. "Matter of fact, he has. How'd you know that?"

"The spirits told me, sonny boy. He wants you to be his deputy." Black Jack responded.

"Me an' Bass. Bass said yes."

The former buffalo hunter clucked his tongue inside his mouth. "Bass said yes, huh?"

Without dismounting, Cade told him what had happened, including the saloon fight, Dish's treachery, the three men killed and Marshal Harding's offer. He didn't mention whipping Ed Gilmore or the confrontation with the soldiers over mistreating the Mexican boy.

"You got a hankerin' for that lawdog's daughter too?" Black Jack asked. Cade's response was slow coming and Black Jack grunted, "Thought so. Damn. She must be somethin'. Hard to believe anything like that could have come outta that ol' sonvabitch."

"Well, I rode out here to ask you what I should do."

The grizzled man pushed his eyeglasses back on his thin nose and grinned, showing brown teeth and black spaces. "I reckon you made that ride for nothin', sonny boy. You look like a man who already knows where he be heading." He cocked his head to the side and blew fat rings of smoke toward Cade.

Swinging down from his horse, Cade held out his hand. "Good to see you, ol' friend."

"You too," Black Jack said and slapped him hard on the arm with his free hand. "You timed it right. Got some antelope stew just about ready." He spun the umbrella in his fist. "Now don't go turnin' up your nose. I know it ain't buffalo meat. Nobody has to tell me that. Damn. But it goes down pretty good—with a little corn liquor. An' I just made a fresh batch."

"I'd like that," Cade said, chuckling. "Especially if you'll tell me how you knew the marshal was going to ask us."

Black Jack raised a thick gray eyebrow. "Sure. But I'm surprised at you, sonny boy. You've been standin' close to a king rattler—an' you've been readin' him to be a black snake."

Chapter Sixteen

Emmett Harding's sharp face took on a glow of satisfaction as they crossed under the weather-worn iron gateway to his small horse ranch. The ornate grillwork had belonged to his great-grandfather in Wales; the marshal and his wife had faithfully brought the big frame with them from Galveston. Silent and timeless kinship with the past abided in the proud sturdy gate. Susannah never tired of admiring the swirling designs in the iron curves and bends. Two lodgepoles formed the foundation for the overhead grillwork. Hanging down from the middle was an off-centered longhorn skull carrying a faded Double-H brand. Shadows of dusk gave the shape an evil appearance, Susannah thought, and hoped it wasn't an omen. The "H's" stood for Harding, of course, and his wife's maiden name, Hoisington.

A copper-tinged hawk left its comfortable perch on the gate and flew effortlessly away, complaining angrily about the disturbance. The sun was surrendering fast now. The world was no longer in its control. Streaks of rose and orange highlighted the horizon, providing the gate with an appropriately dramatic backdrop. Just beyond, a small pond proudly shimmered a reproduction of both the gate and the fiery sunset. As they moved past the entrance, Harding said Bass had told him that he couldn't be killed. He was too good, too fast, too smart. It was a disturbing statement and had obviously bothered the rancher. Susannah understood Bass was simply making a bold statement of his ability, probably to reassure her father of the soundness of his job offer.

In a harsh whisper, the lawman said he wished that were true of Tyrel, Jebediah and Dorothy. The names of his two dead sons and wife came like a song from his twisted mouth. Only once before could Susannah remember her father mentioning her older brothers by name. They were both killed at a place called Bull Run Creek. She didn't know where it was. Somewhere back east. She tried to find it on a map once, in the general store, but started crying and couldn't continue. It was the only time she had seen her father cry, except when her mother passed. And then Emmett Harding was black for a long, long time. That was the only time she remembered him taking off his badge and not wanting to be a lawman. Something was different about him after that, even after he resumed his duties. He became old, right in front of her eyes.

Behind the wagon, the urge hit Roper and the dim-witted jailer jumped awkwardly from his still moving horse, unbuttoned his fly and began to pee by the side of the fence. The well-trained bay stopped as soon as Roper's reins hit the earth. Susannah quickly turned her head and pretended not to have witnessed any part of the incident. Seth yelled something about "being mannerly," but Roper thought he was complaining about the marshal's horse.

Unaware of the situation, Harding stuffed a new chaw inside his brown mouth and stared across the horizon at a distant stone post, one of several marking the borders of the Bar 6's vast claimed range. One could also make out a small herd of cows with their frisky calves heading for water. He realized his daughter was staring at him. He smiled, choked back some tobacco juice and said, "Been wondering just how good those two are going to be. Can't make things any worse, I reckon. I sure do like the way they handle themselves, Sissy, I sure do. Going to make me look good, I reckon."

With that simple statement and no more, his thick-knuckled fingers, as dirty as they were leathery, gave the reins another snap and put the team into a smooth canter. Susannah smiled. She was wondering the same thing. His statement was as close as he would likely come to asking for her opinion. She accepted that and shrugged her shoulders slightly.

They pulled up in front of the small house with a worn porch across the front. A door was centered on the porch with two windows on either side. The porch was Harding's favorite relaxing place. There, he could feel a kinship with the wild spirits living within the hazy blue hills. Within aging cottonwoods was a freshly rebuilt stone cooling house for meat and milk. To the right of the main house, about a hundred feet away, was a small corral he used for training horses. A sturdy well took its stand a few yards from the corral. On the south side of the ranchyard was a second corral, much larger than the other. Ten horses were milling there.

Seth swung down, flipped the reins of his horse over the hitching post centered next to the porch and began unloading the supplies. After dismounting, Roper wandered off, in search of an owl announcing its pleasure over the coming night. Marshal Harding started to say something but Susannah thought he should let the dim-witted cowhand alone. It had been a big day, she said, for all of them. The lawman grabbed a large sack of flour and trounced inside the house.

He said nothing of how he felt entering the house, but it was both rewarding and sad. Evenly cut planked walls were accented with adobe and one lone wall of stone. A fireplace cut from the same rock was the center of attention in the main room. A small bed of orange coals from their morning fire greeted him with warmth. Although the evening was autumn crisp, the house was warm and comfortable. There was a majesty to the house, even though it was tiny, but an undefined sadness too. His Dorothy was no longer here to make it right. To make it home.

Harding paused for a moment to glance at a scarlet vase sitting on a lower shelf of a lopsided bookcase in the corner. A wedding gift from Dorothy's parents. Beside the vase was an eight-inch chunk of an old cottonwood tree. A crude Double H brand had been burned into the bark long ago. His first use of his special mark. His Dorothy had stood beside him when he did it. Aging shoulders rose and fell and he continued to the kitchen.

Susannah and Seth came behind him, each carrying a large box of foodstuffs and canned goods. Susannah recognized her father's hesitation for what it meant and blinked away a tear. The shadows of the room whispered of another strong presence living there in the main room, as well as their father's dominant personality. A woman's gentleness—a perkiness, a love of life—was expressed in simple ways throughout. A large colored rug covered much of the freshly swept planked floor. Bright yellow curtains set off each window, complete with real glass. She never passed through this room without whispering a greeting to her late mother. A gilt-edged glass bowl of wild flowers on a long table was her latest attempt to keep her mother's ways alive in their home.

Stumbling through the main room came Roper. In his arms was the other large sack of flour; he hurried with it into the kitchen, more because of the weight of his burden than for any other reason.

"Did you lose the owl?" Seth asked.

"Yeah. It didn't want findin'."

When the three Hardings and Roper returned to the main room, they saw a continuous line of flour that went all the way to the doorway. Obviously, Roper had torn his sack and left the trail. Seth was first to discover the mistake and he jerked to a stop, putting his hands to his face.

"Roper, what have you done?"

Susannah giggled and her reaction changed her father's from an expected howl to a guffaw. Seth was stunned at his father's response.

Roper stood without speaking, fascinated by the white line. His face was a puzzle. "Emmett, why'd ya put this hyar white line all across this room? Guess it's kinda purty. Is it, Miss Susannah?"

She put both hands to her mouth to keep from bursting out into laughter.

Harding shook his head. "Oh, Hell's teeth, we'll clean it up in the morning."

With that, he announced he was going to bed after he put away the horses and wagon. Roper made the same announcement, after commenting that he liked the new white line, and left immediately for his small room, one Susannah had fixed up for him years ago.

Seth wanted to talk but Susannah didn't; she wasn't in the mood for an hour or so of listening to him whine about their father not believing in him and her reassuring him that he did. Like so many other nights she'd known. Not tonight.

"Seth, you can put away the team. I'll take care of this flour," she said. "Dad, you look tired."

"Now, Sissie, your father isn't an invalid. I can put away the horses. In fact, I want to." He shifted the tobacco in his mouth but resisted spitting. Dorothy's influence remained true. "Besides, those poor animals would have to put up with Seth trying out his preaching." He chuckled.

Seth's back straightened. "I don't think preaching about God is anything to laugh about."

"Taking care of horses isn't either, boy. You help your sister."

That was that. Harding left to take care of the wagon and Susannah began cleaning up the floor with a broom and wooden dust pan. After a few half-hearted sweeps, Seth left for his room. A half hour later, Marshal Harding returned and she was nearly finished with the removal of the flour. Sadness in her father's firm face was evident but she knew it wouldn't do to say anything about her mother. Instead, she announced agreement that it had been a long day.

"Where's your brother? I told him to help. Cain't he do anything right?"

Without looking up, she said, "He just went to his room, Dad. I told him to go. He helped plenty. No need for two to finish this little bit."

He watched her for a moment. "Those two young guns."

She stopped sweeping to listen, unsure of what was coming next.

"Do you think I did right, hiring them? You know them. Didn't all three of you go to school together?"

It was rare for her father to question himself, at least out loud. She could only remember one other time. He had asked her about the flowers on her mother's grave and if they were pretty enough.

"Yes, Dad. I think they can help. If nothing less, the word should get around that you've got deputies to back you up." She paused and added, "I think Cade will come too. I don't think his father—or Dish for that matter—will let him back."

He nodded, acted like he was going to share something more, than said simply, "Good night, Sissy."

That was it. No further discussion. No more questions. He left for bed and Susannah was alone with her thoughts. After completing the cleanup, she went to her room, adjacent to her father's. But sleep didn't come fast. A full moon took command of the night sky and brought along some stars for companionship as she watched from her tiny window. Moonlight waltzed along a hand-carved walnut dresser, table and chair freighted all the way from Kansas City.

A small framed photograph of her mother and father on their wedding day adorned the dresser top. Emmett's youthful face stared at her from his seated position while her teenaged mother looked on from eternity, standing to his side, in the manner of the day. Something about the picture was both reassuring and disturbing to her. She couldn't put words to the feelings but they were always there when she looked at the image of yesterday.

Her clothes were uncharacteristically thrown in a corner, instead of folded neatly and returned to their proper storage or placed carefully on the chair for wear the next day. She could hear her father's rhythmic snoring in the next room. There was comfort in the sound. If he was comfortable, the whole world must be. Finally she drifted off with thoughts of Cade Branson and Bass Manko fighting over her.

A stray moonbeam patted her cheek and left.

In his room, Seth struggled with sleep. The young man spent most of the night wondering if his father would ever let him go to divinity school, and if his sister already knew the answer and didn't want to tell him. He patted the Bible on the small table next to his bed and recited, " 'He that increaseth knowledge increaseth sorrow.' " He mouthed "Ecclesiastes I" and smiled, but no sound emerged. Why couldn't his father understand that not everyone wanted to be a lawman or a cattleman? Why couldn't he see his son—his only remaining son—had been called to something more important? Why . . . ? His hand slipped off the Bible. He was asleep.

Two hours before sunup, he awoke, tried to go back to sleep and couldn't. Finally, he decided to impress his father by riding to the jail and opening up. He and Roper were to watch over the jail while the marshal was at the roundup. His father would be surprised and excited to see his son so dedicated. After pulling on his clothes, he slipped into the marshal's room. What was the sense of going early if his father wasn't aware of his dedication?

Seth stood by the old lawman's bed for several minutes, listening to the heavy snoring, hoping somehow his father would wake up on his own and be happy to see him ready to work. He rehearsed what he would say. On the scratched bed table, he saw his father's badge resting on the gunbelt where it always was placed. It bothered him that he was not offered a deputy's badge, even through the roundup. After all, he was serving in that capacity, wasn't he? He would ask Susannah what she thought. Through the window, he could see false dawn was flirting with the sky and decided he could wait no longer.

"Pa-Father, I'm . . . riding out . . . to the jail. Gonna open up . . . for you." He never could bring himself to say "Paw" like his other brothers had; "Father" was the only word that would come out, no matter how hard he tried. Harding didn't move. A buffalo snort was the only response. Seth tried again, this time pushing gently on the lawman's exposed right shoulder. "Father, it isn't dawn yet but I'm riding to town . . . to the jail." He liked that better; it gave a sense of timing to his statement.

Harding jumped up in bed, his head swiveling left, then right, trying to get a fix on where he was. "W-What? Where are they, boys? I can't get a bead . . ."

"F-Father, it's me. Seth. T-To the j-jail . . . I'm going. Dawn isn't here . . . yet. I-It's early."

Sitting up in bed, the lawman squinted his eyes, then rubbed them. "W-What in Hell's fury? Seth? Where are you going? This isn't Sunday, is it?"

"No, Father, it isn't. I'm just r-riding to town. I figured the town would like to see the marshal's office opened early." Proud of including a phrase his father would have used, Seth stepped backward from the bed and straightened his back.

Harding took a deep breath to remove the rest of the sleep in him. He shook his head and said, "Well, sure, Seth, that would be all right, I reckon. Now don't go laying a lot of Bible-thumping on any drunks wandering around town this time of the morn—or try to arrest them. Ya aren't a peace officer, you know. But you can tell anybody you see that I've got two new deputies. Don't tell them who, though, you hear?"

"Yes, I hear."

"Well, get along to it, then. You're wasting daylight. Probably should be there by now. Get yourself some breakfast at Lucy's. Charge it to the jail. Town'll be quiet. Roundup's startin' this morning. Be careful. I don't need to be worrying about you—with everything else going on."

"Do you want me to wear a gun?"

"Hell's teeth, no. You don't know how to use one anyway—and you're not a deputy. You're just a jailer."

Seth nodded and backed out of the door, uncertain that his idea had done what he intended. Why did the man always have to say the obvious? Why did he always have to assume the worst when it came to his son? It would be like his father to tell the mayor that he was training his son to be a jailer. How humiliating. With a deep breath, he turned and walked away. In minutes he had his horse saddled and was headed northwest. There was a black man in town he particularly liked to talk with. He worked for the blacksmith and read the Bible daily. Maybe he could walk over and talk with him after he opened the jail.

Marshal Harding heard the hoofbeats and cursed the noise. A glance at the window witnessed the first pink crack in the sullen sky and he knew it was time to get up. As quietly as he knew how, he dressed, pinned on his badge and pushed his feet into already-spurred boots. He touched his wrapped gunbelt but decided to leave it there for awhile.

Downstairs, he was surprised to see Susannah already dressed and preparing breakfast. She had awakened upon hearing Seth ride away. She seemed happy to be in the kitchen, preparing food for him. Theirs was a closeness that never needed many words. Or got many, at least from her father.

After three cups of hot coffee, matching helpings of fried eggs, salt pork and biscuits, he was ready to talk. In a calm, easy voice, he told her what he thought was going to happen in the next two days and what he wanted her to do. She listened silently, knowing this wasn't the time to show emotion of any kind. He was sharing something very important with her. Something he wasn't used to doing. With anyone. At least, not since his wife died. She bit her lower lip to hold back tears that willed their way to her eyes. She turned away so he wouldn't see her brush them quckly away.

Finishing his assessment and orders, he went outside to hurry the day. He wanted no further discussion of the matter—and expected none. Standing on the porch, he sucked in the dawn with a deep breath. The morning smelled good and new. An aromatic blend of dew, horses, hay and life. It was a great day to be a horseman. A great day to be alive. After shoving new tobacco into his mouth, he headed for the smaller of two split-rail corrals. His first spit missed the corral post he aimed at. So did the second.

He was torn about where he should go. Part of him urged that his place was in town, like his son. But he knew he must go to the roundup. If he didn't, nothing would happen as planned. He was sure of it. Even if the two young gunfighters didn't come as they promised, he would go to the roundup camp. He was certain they would show, or at least Bass Manko, but was anxious anyway. He kept telling himself it was way too early for them to arrive. About noon time, he kept telling himself. He decided to work with a young black filly he was keeping by herself in this corral. All the other horses were separated for selling; she wouldn't be a working animal. Or sold.

It was a worthwhile way to pass the time. The animal was already used to his gruff voice and hands. He decided the horse would feel a saddle for the first time. There was nothing he liked more than working with horses. Nothing.

When he was working with a new horse, time skipped over everything bad just to watch him with one of God's most beautiful creatures. Maybe this was what Cade Branson meant by every action was a prayer. Working with a good horse was holy, Harding thought, and wished his son understood that.

The black filly whinnied softly when he put the saddle blanket on her back; he comforted her with his voice as he placed it carefully. The blanket was old stuff to her by now. Some horses did need breaking but not this one, he muttered. She would make a good mount to keep for Susannah. Definitely a fine brood mare. No need to use a rope to lift her back leg off the ground either, to keep her from bucking. She was a gentle animal right from the start, and a smart one. A favorite of his already.

The glistening dark animal had only a small touch of white on her nose, like someone had walked by with a brush full of white wash and accidently touched it as they passed. Susannah had named her Rachael. The old lawman thought it was a bit come-uppity for a damn horse, but she wouldn't budge. When she wasn't around, he usually called the filly "Blackie." Nervously, the young horse watched as he brought the saddle toward her. But Harding's soothing words calmed the filly's instinct to run. As soon as the saddle hit her back, the horse flinched and crowhopped sideways.

Chapter Seventeen

Slowly Harding tightened the cinch but just enough so the saddle wouldn't fall off or slide underneath her easily. And not enough to overly frighten her. He talked and rubbed her trembling body with his leathery hands. His mind chewed hard on what he knew.

Working with the horse helped him think through the best way to utilize his two young deputies. The holding area for branding and sorting was moving almost every day so riders wouldn't have too far to bring the scattered herds. He didn't know what the other ranchers intended but he knew Titus Branson planned to winter about two thousand steers and dried-up cows in a rich valley pasture. Come spring, they would be trailed to a Kansas railhead. The rest of the herd would be allowed to find their favorite grazing places for the cold months ahead.

Every coulee, every wash, every line of timber and brush would be combed for cattle. Everyone's cattle. Riders from every ranch in the area would be pooled to help; food costs would be divided and shared as usual. It was hard work. Twelve- to fifteen-hour days. Would rustlers try to catch riders bringing small numbers from the many hidden places cattle could find? Or would they attack the holding area? No more than a handful of rangemen would be there at any given time. Cutting and branding were best done without too many involved. They wouldn't be watching for trouble. Too much to do. Maybe that would be the best place for rustlers to get the most cattle the easiest—and that would be the best place for his two deputies. If Cade came. "He has to come," Harding declared aloud and the black horse flinched.

The idea settled well in his mind. He liked simple, straight-forward things but this time he had played it differently. He had to. Of course, trouble might just wait until the roundup was over. But he expected a move during the roundup. No, he was certain of it. The key was to be good enough to anticipate it. Nagging at him was indecision about how much to share with his new deputies. Or deputy. Susannah now knew everything he did—or thought he did. She would do what he asked, he had no doubt about that. Sharing things with someone usually meant telling too many. He couldn't risk it. Not this time.

A dust cloud from a rider caught the old lawman's attention before the actual dark shape did. Not likely anyone from the roundup coming from that direction. Someone from town. Was Seth coming back? More likely it was Bass Manko. Had to be. The old man's shoulders rose and fell in disappointment, even as he told himself that Cade wouldn't be coming yet, regardless. Harding waved. Brown tobacco juice splattered against a corral rail. He had already forgotten the black filly; she would have to wait. The young horse paraded uneasily around the corral, testing the new weight on its back.

With only a passing, "You'll be fine, Blackie," he hurried toward the front of the house, his stiffened leg creating an awkward-looking, one-sided, up-and-down motion like he was walking on the side of a hill.

"Well, good morning, Bass. Hell's fire if it isn't good to see you, boy," Harding hollered as his gimpy stride brought him alongside the reined-up horse. He couldn't resist adding, "Don't suppose you know anything yet about what Cade's going to do?"

Bass grinned and held out his hand to complete the hearty greeting. He looked like he hadn't been to bed or wanted to. "Last time I saw Cade, he was ridin' hard for Black Jack's. That was yesterday."

Nodding his head, Harding pushed his enthusiasm, "Get yourself down and have some breakfast. I'll tell Sissy."

"Thanks, Emmett, but I ate in town. Thought we'd get a head start on things," Bass said, pushing up his hat from his forehead and forcing the leather tie-down to jump away from his shirt. A morning breeze sang to his sweating blond hair and tried to coax it into flight.

Harding responded with an approving nod. A slow-moving fly left from late summer annoyed the old rancher and he swatted it with his free hand, driving the insect to the ground. He spat at it and missed. As if assessing his poor aim, he stood quietly for a moment, spat a rich brown stream at nothing except the ground and grinned. "Reckon I do like a man who gets right at the tussle. Let me throw leather on my buckskin an' get my iron, then we'll get riding."

"That's a fine black you were working with." Bass waved toward the small corral. "Looks like she could be kin to mine."

Harding beamed, spat again and wiped his mouth with the back of his hand to remove stray spittle. "Aye, probably not as ornery as yours. She is a right pretty little thing, though. Not ready for cutting or brush-popping."

"Too nice a horse for that, anyway," Bass observed. "Would you mind if I left my guitar here at your place? Didn't figure them rustlers would take much to my singing." Bass motioned toward the instrument tied against his bedroll. "I've got all I need with me."

He patted the two silver-plated, ivory-handled Colts holstered at his hips in crossed silver-studded gunbelts. The second Colt rested on his left side with the gunbutt forward for a right-hand draw. His Winchester was in its saddle scabbard.

"Sure. You can leave it with Sissy."

"What can you leave with me? Good morning, Bass."

Susannah came through the door and rested her hands against the porch railing. Bass eyed her with interest and she enjoyed the attention. As she smiled, the dimples on her cheeks appeared even deeper than the last time he saw her. Brown hair was undone, embracing her shoulders, instead of in the usual tight bun. Her ranch shirt and Levis could just as easily have been a gown.

"Good mornin', Miss Harding." Bass rushed to add to his salutation, "You make the mornin' look mighty fine. Mighty fine."

"Why, thank you, Bass, that's very kind to say."

Savoring the compliment, she turned her attention to her father, tilting her head slightly to see him better as a shaft of light, coming from a crack in the porch roof, sought her face. "What is it you're going to leave with me, Dad?"

Bass jumped down from his horse. "My guitar. If that's al-

right with you." His move toward the bedroll assumed it
would be.

"Sure. Roper will enjoy playing it."

Bass's head spun toward her, a frown following. She
cocked her head to the side and he laughed long and hard.
"Oh, you got me there, lady. You sure got me good. Where is
Roper, anyway?"

"Oh, he's still sleeping. Mid-morning is his usual wake-up
time."

"Sounds like a great deal to me. Got another job like that
open?"

Bass slipped his reins around the hitching rack, carried
the guitar to the porch, singing a verse from *Female Highwayman*. Harding was studying Bass's horse and didn't see
Bass touch Susannah's arm as he left. She returned the intimacy with a sweet smile.

"Bass, if it's all right with you, I'd like to ride by the Trenchards and say goodbye before we head for the roundup."

"Sure. Sounds like a nice thing to do."

"Sissie, I'll take the buckskin," Harding said. "Don't
know when we'll be back. Two, three days, I reckon. Tell
Roper to head into town and help Seth with the office. You
know your brother left early to open up. Think he was trying to impress his ol' man."

She smiled. "Seth is a good son. Where's Cade?"

Bass was surprised at the question but covered it with his
toothy smile. "Cade's not comin'. He went to see . . . an old
friend."

"Well, good for him." Susannah replied, looking at her father, then at Bass. "You be careful, Dad. You have nothing
to prove. To anyone." Without waiting for his response, she
turned to go back into the house.

"Wait a minute, Sissy, got something to ask you." Harding was already lumbering toward the porch.

She stopped to wait for him and winked at Bass, who touched his hand to his hat. The lawman stepped onto the porch, his lined face grave. Susannah listened quietly as he spoke, nodding her approval occasionally.

Bass watched them, reminding himself that Harding might become his father-in-law, so he'd better be nice to the old man. *Susannah probably thinks that's why I'm doing this*, he smiled.

Finished with his one-sided conversation, Harding retraced his steps to Bass. He looked back over his shoulder and asked, "Sissy, you're sure you're going to be able to handle that?"

"Of course. I look forward to it."

"Aye, you be careful—and do just what I said."

"Of course, Father."

Bass greeted the old lawman's return with a smile and a question. "You gonna swear me in now?"

"Well, sure, Bass, let's get that done." Harding said, first reaching into his right pocket, then his left, to find the badge.

By the time Marshal Harding and his new deputy reached the roundup holding camp, assignments had long been made for the day. Outriders were gone. They were given circles of land to cover, overlapping earlier gatherings. It assured no land would be missed and, hopefully, no cattle. They were working Branson's land—Bar 6 range that the family actually owned, not just claimed for grazing rights.

The countryside was hilly, more so than elsewhere, providing a natural spoon of land and a perfect holding place of cattle. At least for a day or two, until they ate their way through the grass and the branding and sorting were finished. They would move to a new camp tomorrow, on to the Circle R range. Deep hollows hugged any shadows that came close and a creek snaked along the far ridges, trying to find a way out of the vast clearing unnoticed.

On both sides of its bank was a low wall of wild grape vines, downed timber and bunches of mostly dead cattails. Accompanying the maze was a dark line of birch, alder, and scrub oak, almost unbroken for miles. A few willow stood guard where the stream had once been deepest. Cattle were already in the holding area from the first gatherings of the morning. The roundup's lead drive men were a combination of riders from Branson's and Sil's ranches. They were the farthest out and would likely have the longest day.

From his position near the herd, Dish Branson saw the two riders coming before anyone else. Standing in his stirrups, he yelled his annoyance, "Did ya think we needed some music around the campfire? What the hell did you bring the saloon singer along for? I thought just you was comin'."

"Good morning, Dish, how are you this fine day?" Harding called back cheerily.

Dish yanked his horse away from the herd and galloped over to them. Harding and Bass eased their horses to wait. Reining the animal to a hard stop, he glared at the old lawman.

"Ain't sur why ya came anyway, Harding. This ain't Deer Creek, ya know," Dish snarled. "Ain't no drunks out hyar neither—'ceptin' them three River S boys that brought in their wagon last night." He shook his head contemptuously. "Jes' cuz that Widow Rice sweet-talked ya, don't mean ya have to be hyar. Ain't nuthin' gonna happen 'ceptin' a lot o' critturs is gonna git moved."

Harding leaned forward on the saddlehorn. "Deputy

Manko and I came out to see that this fine roundup goes nice and easy."

"Deputy Manko? Whadda ya mean?" Dish saw the badge on Bass's shirt and his face went white.

"I'm working for the marshal here, Dish," Bass said with a smile. "Oh, by the way, did that cowboy from the Half-Moon 5 ever come an' see you?"

"What? I don' know what yur chawin' 'bout, Manko," Dish blurted. "I got a roundup to run. Ya better git yurse'ves back to town." He returned his attention to the branding fire. "That's a Bar 6 calf. Cain't ya see his maw ov'r thar? Damn."

Without waiting for more words from Dish, Harding swung his horse wide and trotted over to the camp. Bass thought the animal reminded him of the lawman. Easygoing and slow. But likely a bit of a kicker first thing in the morning. He chuckled to himself.

"I don't think we'll see Titus here. He's too old for this. Too sickly," Harding growled and spat, slightly missing the neck of his buckskin but the horse didn't seem to mind.

Bass was amused. Titus was at least five years younger than the marshal, but he agreed to himself that the man wouldn't be here because of his condition.

Leaning against the chuckwagon, mostly in shadow, was Absalum Sil, watching them. Not much over five-two, Sil was thick-framed, hairless on his arms, chest and head, and wore filthy overalls, like some poor farmer. Bass thought Sil looked like a wild hog in his round face—one with slitted cat eyes. They rarely registered any emotion, except hate, impatience or arrogance. Bass was certain Sil didn't blink more than once or twice a day.

Without moving, Sil greeted them contemptuously. "Didn't expect to see no law out this way, Harding. Especially with a sing-song boy for a deputy."

Irritated by the statement, Harding pulled on his reins of his horse to keep it from grazing. He didn't like that when he was mounted. He held back his annoyance and answered Sil respectfully, "Sil, I brought Deputy Manko along so I'd have another good gun—if'n those rustlers come around."

"Whar's the first 'good gun'?"

"That would be me."

Sil chuckled. "You gonna spit at 'em?"

Harding chuckled and patted the neck of his horse. "Just might do that." He spat a solid stream of brown juice and Sil jumped away in time before it hit his boots.

Looking around, Bass realized work had come to a standstill. Every rider and every hand on the ground was watching them. He was embarrassed, being viewed in the same way as the old marshal. No one wanted them here. No one thought they could do anything anyway. He forced himself to remember this was part of the plan now.

Bass Manko sat rigidly on his black horse, avoiding Sil's intense glare. He told himself that he should have brought a note from Elizabeth explaining the situation. Sil seemed to respect orders from her. No one else. It angered him that she thought the little man was as important to this scheme as he was. When this was all over, he would kill Sil, he decided. If Sil ever turned his back.

"Long as you stay out of the way, you can stay. It's kinda boring, though. Just hard-working men," Sil responded.

Hard ridges rose and fell where his eyebrows should have been. The short man's hollow cheeks looked like he was constantly sucking them in. He turned toward one of the water barrels tied to the side of the wagon, grabbed the drinking cup attached by a piece of rope and ladled himself a drink. A short-barreled P. Webley & Son "Bulldog" revolver hanging from a lanyard around his neck clanged against the barrel.

Rising in his stirrups, Emmett growled to the busy men, "Boys, you just keep on with your duties. My deputy and I will keep an eye out. I'm not about to have you ranchers lose any more beef." He spat for emphasis and the cowhands returned to their work, shaking their heads and mumbling about the new arrivals.

Sil's men watched their boss for direction but most figured it was part of the roundup strategy.

After making a grand show of encircling the perimeter of the gathering area, Bass stopped to get a cup of coffee from the pot sitting at the edge of a dying campfire. Gradually, he took a position on the edge of the holding camp. His rifle lay ready across his saddle in front of him. Sipping the hot brew, he watched the herd swell with gathered strays. Harding nudged his buckskin toward the other direction and took a position under some cottonwoods where it was shady.

Well-trained men returned to separating cattle from the various ranches and branding the unmarked, while most of the riders came and went with animals of all sizes and brands. The day became long and boring for the young gunfighter. It was difficult to stay alert as the morning sun turned into noon. As he watched, Bass's mind wandered all over, returning most often to Susannah Harding and Elizabeth Rice. But he was irritated to find himself thinking about Cade Branson. What would his friend—his only friend—do when Dish and John were killed? Stay out of it, he continually told himself. Dish was an asshole and had never been nice to Cade. Never. But the thought was more a prayer than a statement of fact. *Sil will shoot you down, Cade,* the words hovered silently near his consciousness.

There weren't many men who intimidated Bass, but Absalum Sil did. And worse, Sil knew it. When this was over, Bass wanted to put a bullet in his brain. Elizabeth would know then who was the most important to her.

What passed as guilt skipped away to play; greed made a wonderful rationalizing platform. Dish Branson had everything. All Bass had was a guitar, guns, and a fast horse. But he had the promise of riches. Would he marry Susannah when it was all over—or Elizabeth? His loins responded with a vote for the saloon owner; his heart suggested Susannah would be the better wife; his mind told him he should concentrate on what was going on now, starting with assuring Sil that his being there was a good move. He knew the short outlaw didn't like surprises. He wasn't sure what the man did like. Those eyes were flowing with hate.

Although there was no threat of a Mexican rustling gang, Bass knew he must appear alert and looking for trouble. He nudged his black horse toward a sawed-off ridge, layered with earthen lines of red, yellow and brown. He reined to a stop beside a live oak that had no business being there. Shielding his eyes with his hand, he pretended to study a long fortress of cottonwood, live oak and heavy underbrush. Glimpses of riders and cattle darted among the trees. Impatience grew on him.

He tried humming an old trail song but that only served to reinforce his dislike for cattle. There was no way he was going to spend his life around them. Elizabeth had promised him the Four Aces saloon when this was finished. He could see himself finely dressed and strutting through the place.

To his left, from camp, came a rider. Bass knew it would be Sil before turning in that direction.

Chapter Eighteen

Absalum Sil's sorrel had the same approach to life that its rider did. A thoroughly vicious animal, the horse would kick and bite the other horses on the string so often that it had to be tied away from the others.

Wearing a short-brimmed glob of a hat and a stained undershirt beneath his overalls, Sil pulled alongside Bass. His revolver was shoved into the bib of his overalls to keep it from bouncing on his chest.

"What the hell are you doing here, Manko?" Sil's words slithered through clenched teeth. He faced away from camp so no one could hear.

Bass tried to act nonchalant, swallowing the twinge of fear Sil always brought. The young gunfighter explained the situation, trying hard to keep emotion from his voice. He didn't like Sil's haughty sneer as he talked. He suspected the pig-faced outlaw was jealous of his relationship with Elizabeth Rice. That thought helped keep him calm.

"Alright, you're here. Just remember who's in charge—

and don't get in the way. I don't know why you took that
stupid badge. It doesn't mean much out here. That's why we
bought off Swisher." Sil leaned forward in the saddle and
pointed toward the trees, in case anyone was watching them
from the holding area. "I'm going to let the Branson boys
get good an' tired before we hit them."

"Elizabeth thought my taking the badge was a good idea."

"She did?"

"Yeah. What do you want me to do?"

"Not one damn thing, Manko. You'll be here when it
happens," Sil replied. "You an' that fool for a lawman." Sil
snorted and Bass was certain it was the same sound a wild
boar made. "Where's that young Branson, the friend of
yours? He gonna pop up too?" He pointed at another tree.

"Oh, he rode off to see Black Jack Sante an' lick his
wounds." He imitated Sil's pointing gesture but avoided the
man's gaze. It was the gaze of a killer. A pure killer, one who
killed for the enjoyment of the process.

The corner of Sil's mouth twitched. "Yeah, I heard he
kept your miserable neck from swinging."

"Yeah, he did."

Bass restrained a smile. At least Sil would wonder. He ra-
tionalized to himself that the cruel outlaw leader was a good
man to have with him, not against him. A shiver found his
shoulders as he envisioned Cade confronting Sil. He was
glad Cade wasn't here. At least he wouldn't have to to deal
with that. Not now, at least. Bass shook his head, then swatted the air to hide the reaction, acting like a late horsefly
had bothered him.

Without further comment, Sil spun his sorrel toward the
rising dust that was the branding area and spurred it into a
fierce gallop. Bass chuckled but it came out a gurgle. He
coughed and tried to forget Sil.

Certainly Marshal Harding was right that the holding area offered the most opportunity for rustlers with the least resistance. None of the cowboys was even armed as they separated the animals into their correct ranch herds and pushed unbranded ones into areas where they could easily be roped, then pulled to the fire for branding. Dust was everywhere Bass looked, accented with swirling shapes of brown and black and the silhouettes of riders close behind swinging lariats. The day filled with the music of the roundup: creaking saddles, cursing men, whinnying horses, swirling ropes and bellowing cattle. He looked over at Harding on his horse clear across the opening. From here it was difficult to tell but Bass guessed the old lawman was dozing in the saddle.

Suddenly, commotion dragged him back to the herd. One of the maverick bulls wheeled around when he was roped and slammed into a horse and its River S rider—the short, red-suspendered cowboy with the handlebar mustache from the saloon. Both horse and rider were knocked to the ground. Riders rushed toward the bull, yelling and waving their lassos.

Awakening with a start, Harding kicked his horse toward the melee. The fallen rider was dazed and unable to find his feet as the infuriated beast whirled to attack again. His brown horse scrambled to stand again, a bloody mark along its sweating flank. The lawman's own lariat was above his head and on its way before the bull could fully turn to charge again. The loop settled over massive horns and Harding pulled it tight and swung his horse in the other direction, spurring it into a hard run to counter the bull's expected charge at the downed rider.

The jolt of the rope staggered the animal for an instant and made the enraged beast step sideways and away from its violent task. The old marshal kept spurring his horse to off-set the bull's regaining strength. Dish added his rope to the beast's head and another Bar 6 rider snaked a loop onto its back legs with a skillful throw. A fourth cowboy reached the downed man and helped the dazed rider onto his horse. In seconds, the brown fury was stopped in its tracks with three ropes pulling in three different directions.

"We'll take 'er from hyar Marshal. Come an' take his string fer 'im." Dish hollered, obviously impressed by the old man's quick response. "Do be thankin' yah fer jumpin' in like ya did. Reckon yah dun saved ol' Willy from gittin' nasty hurt."

"Looks like you're still quite the hand, Marshal." A slightly-built Bar 6 cowboy rode up beside Harding and took the taut rope from him. "Didn't figure you for a roper."

"If I can get that close." Harding grinned.

Shaking his head in appreciation, the cowboy said, "Know what you mean."

"Turn that big sonvabitch loose out in the grass some-whars!"

"No, we gotta brand 'im first. That's that same he-cow that dun got away from us last spring, remember?" Dish commanded.

Directions, observations and compliments swirled about. A calf sauntered toward Harding as if trying to decide if he was his mother or not. Halfway there, the calf stopped, studied the shape for a moment and turned away.

"Drag his ass over by the fire. Easy now. He'll cut yah in two if'n yah give 'im a chance."

"Whose brand yah gonna put on 'em?"

Dish though a moment. "River S. Willy earned it."

"Ya wanna dehorn the bastird?"

"I'd like to shoot 'im. Naw, he earned them horns. Jes'

burn 'im an' git him outta hyar. Sonny, yah git them ropes off after he's burned, alright?"

"Hell no, it ain't alright. The sonvabitch'll kill me."

"Well, I ain't lettin' 'im drag off three good ropes. What do yah wanna do?"

Harding swung down. "Grab hold of my horse, son. He's ground broke but I'm not interested in knowing how much." He handed the reins to the nearest rider and walked toward the fire. The acrid smell of hot iron on the beast's side reached him. "You boys back off and I'll take the strings off."

Dish frowned and spit his concern, "Jesus, Marshal, he's a killer. I wouldn't if'n—"

Harding pointed at the heeling rope. "Just keep those ropes tight. I'm going to take off the head ropes first. He'll stand. You watch and see." Two quick flips removed the lariats around the bull's horns and the animal snorted its understanding of the freedom it meant.

"When I pull off this heeling rope, let him have a way to go," Harding shouted and waved his hand in the direction the animal was headed. He motioned for the rider with the rope on its back legs to let the restraint slacken and the lawman loosened the loop and let it fall to the ground. Instead of backing up, however, he stayed close to the bull's back legs, motionless, his hands at his sides.

"Better git outta thar now, Marshal. He'll ram yah."

"Shut up, Butter," Dish commanded. "The marshal knows what he's doin'. Can't yah see?"

The big bull shook its head, then its body to remove the vestiges of the last minutes of entrapment and branding, then, as if nothing had happened, trotted calmly toward the open edge of the herd and headed toward a foothill known only to him. For a minute longer, silence controlled everything, then a loud "yahoo" broke into the tenseness.

Smiling, Dish rode over to Harding and held out his hand; the glove had been removed as a symbol of sincerity. "Wouldn't have believed it, if'n I had'una seen it. You dun busted more'n your share of cows, Marshal Harding."

Other riders followed on foot and on horseback, some touching Harding's shoulder before returning to work. Even some of Sil's outlaws were impressed. Quickly, though, every man was back to their tasks.

Another Bar 6 cowboy rode over to advise Dish that Willy, the downed rider, was going to be all right. Just some bruised ribs. He added that the same bull had killed a rider just last spring.

Nodding, Dish announced loudly that the chuck wagon had hot coffee and beans going for the noon meal. Supper was expected to be "son-of-bitch stew," a hearty mixture of calf's liver, brains, heart, lean beef, onions and sweetbreads, swimming in a hot sauce. It was announced with enthusiasm as one of the men's favorite meals.

The cowboy smiled and galloped away to rejoin the cutting riders.

Bass watched it all, amused at seeing the old lawman suddenly respected, simply because he could rope and understood bulls. *Maybe Elizabeth should hire Marshal Harding as a cowhand after she took control of the Branson ranch*, he laughed to himself. *Mighty fine. Mighty fine.* Certainly the old fool didn't have a clue about what was going to happen. A handful of well-placed bullets would change everything. His gaze took in Sil drinking coffee near the campfire. The outlaw leader apparently hadn't paid any attention to the ruckus.

It was nearly dusk when the last group of outriders came in. Five men rode slowly into camp after a long day of gathering, pushing a hundred double-wintered steers, a few cows and some unbranded calves. Mostly Bar 6 and Circle R animals with several other brands mixed in. The night camp set close to the highest ridge, which ran like a black fence over the rolling hills of grass. It was the changing hour when sunlight becomes gray dust and the sun itself attempts one last charge at the horizon, bringing gold and red. Grass danced to welcome the victorious evening's cooling breezes. The day had been hot; nightfall's relief would be welcome and so would a good meal. The gathered beeves moved rhythmically along an extended belt of sparse grass, headed for the main herd with the experienced urging of its riders.

Sitting on a large rock near the freshly enhanced campfire, Marshal Harding kneaded the throbbing muscles of his upper leg. His rheumatism was trying hard to tell him that he shouldn't be doing this kind of work anymore. In defiance of his physical ailments, he spat tobacco juice at a smaller rock a few feet to his left. He missed and the brown liquid splattered into the dirt a foot to the right. The fire reflected off the badge on his vest. Around the campfire sat tired men. All smelled the efforts of a good chuck wagon cook at work, and the fragrance of the stew had them eager to chow down.

Weariness showed in the incoming riders' faces. Three were Bar 6 men, including John; two were Sil's. Their saddle equipment included double ropes that had seen plentiful use during the long day. Just as evident were strapped-on handguns and Winchesters in their saddle boots. Talk about rustlers had been a primary topic but not the only one. Horses, ropes, gloves, women and everything they had to do to get the main herds ready for winter after this roundup was finished were thoroughly discussed. The same topics would be explored tomorrow. And the next day.

Tomorrow, Dish wanted some of the men to work the

creek bend just to the south of here for more steers. He knew there had to be several hundred down there, plus some unbranded calves still with their mothers. He wanted all the young ones stamped with the Bar 6 before they separated. Unless they belonged elsewhere, of course.

An ever-playful man of indeterminate age, Willy sat down alongside the tired lawman to defend himself about the morning's battle with the bull. His ribs were definitely sore and he talked between gasps for breath. Tired riders sitting close by laughed at his animated version of the event, as he alternated between waving his arms and grabbing his painful ribs.

Then like the two were connected, the talk moved on to cowhorses and even Harding joined in. "Hell's teeth, I want a hard-haided son-of-a-bitch, a horse that'll bust through every good goddamn thing, by God, to get a cow moving his way. A good cowhorse has got to hate steers, by God. Got to."

"Yeah, I want my pony to love rocks. I want 'im sure footed, an' faster goin' down one o' them slides than flat out on a prairie," another rider added.

"Had me a little bucksin onst that was the best I ever did rid," Willy said. "Runty li'l rascal that'd jerk down any he-cow 'round. Didn't matter how much bigger'n it that he-cow 'twere neither. Jes' snap an' he were down."

Techniques for staying dry on a swimming horse somehow came out of Willy's thoughts next. And then he switched to the brown horse of Poco's that had went lame that afternoon; it was that cowboy's favorite roping horse too. Harding had seen him walk back to camp leading the hurt animal, instead of riding in and taking a chance on aggravating the injury. He liked that. It reminded him of something Cade Branson would do.

Talk slid over to wild Indians. Someone said that warriors liked to whip their horses into a second wind before going into a battle. The horse became more aggressive, more in tune with the fight, one cowboy philosophized. Another thought that was the best way to make a cowhorse work in a roundup.

Willy said that he'd heard a warrior going into battle would tie a rope around his waist and then to his horse. That way if he got knocked off, the animal would drag him away from danger. That thought triggered some discussion about whether or not it would be better to be dragged away or not.

Harding thought it said a lot about the cowhand that he never mentioned being hurt.

"Hey, the camp! I'm a tired hombre looking for some hot coffee."

The call came from the hazy gray beyond the campfire and its growing group of waiting riders. Three men reached for their rifles laying beside them.

Emmett Harding shuffled to his feet and hollered, "Come on in, Cade—and glad to have you."

Bass Manko stood in the shadows of the chuck wagon with a tin plate in his hand. He had been talking with two of Sil's men. The look on his face was that of a man who had just been shot.

"What's the matter, Bass?" the taller outlaw asked. "Ain't that the youngest Branson?"

"Yeah, that's him."

"Thought you said he were with some broken-down buffalo hunter," the outlaw glanced at his shorter friend for support of the statement.

"Who wants to know?" Bass snapped. His face went through a string of emotions faster than a man could fan a pistol.

"Sil won't be takin' well to him a'comin' hyar."

"That's Sil's problem," Bass said and walked toward the campfire.

Harding greeted Cade like he hadn't seen him in years. When the old marshal finally took a breath, Cade asked simply, "Is that deputy's job still open?"

"Aye, sure as we be surrounded by beef, son." Harding enthused and reached into his right-hand pocket, then his left and withdrew a badge. "Never can remember where I put those things. Brought it along—hoping." He held out the star and said, "Hold up your right hand."

Cade smiled and lifted his hand.

"Do you swear to do your best?"

"I do."

"You're sworn in." With a grin so wide it must've hurt his face, Harding handed the badge to Cade. "Put it on, boy, put it on." He shook his head and added, "You know, that star has a way of changing a man."

"Black Jack told me what you think is happening."

"Well, that rascal. He should be more careful what he goes around whistling about." Harding's grin remained in place. "Even a blind hog finds an acorn now and then."

"Are we going to take 'em now? I'll tell Dish an' Bass."

Harding's grin disappeared. "Hold on a mite, son. Lordy, I've got myself a warrior for sure."

He didn't know how to read the look on Cade's face. His voice lowered. "Right now, all we've got is a hunch. If we start up now, those snakes are going to slide back under the rocks and we're going to look silly. Sorry I be to say it, but we've got to let them move first."

"Those are my brothers you're talking about."

"You have to trust me, son."

"I do."

"Good. Don't tell anybody anything—not Dish, not John and not Bass." Harding put a sun-weathered hand on Cade's shoulder. "We're going to get them, son. They think they're smarter than everybody. Especially this old goat."

"What the hell's this hyar all about?" Dish stood ten feet away, holding the reins of his horse in both hands in front of him. "Ya gittin' hard up fer deputies, Marshal?"

Cade and Harding turned toward Dish. Cade pinned the badge on his shirt, grinned and said, "He is at that, Dish."

"Not hardly." Harding spat and stepped away to allow the two brothers an opportunity to talk.

Limping slightly, he wandered back to where Willy and the other cowboys were continuing their discussion about Indians and horses. Spitting to a flat rock and clipping its edge Harding said, "You boys ever hear how Comanche warriors love their horses damn near more than their womenfolk?"

Dish watched the lawman before turning his attention to Cade. "Ya didn't come to he'p with the gatherin', I take it."

"Don't you remember? Paw ran me off."

Dish shook his head. "Come on now, Cade. Ya ain't gonna beat me o'ver the haid wi' that, are ya?"

"Did you pay that cowhand?"

Dish continued shaking his head, chuckling as he did. "Yeah, yeah, paid the sonvabitch forty dollars too." He stopped, swallowed and said, "Kin ya forgive me, Cade? I . . . ah, I guess I figgered if Bass weren't around, Susannah would, ya know . . . I jes' weren't thinkin' straight, that's all." He held out his right hand, taking the reins in his left. "Don't figger ya'd want to shake it, but . . ."

"You're my brother, Dish." Cade accepted the handshake. "It's Bass you should ask for forgiveness."

"I bin workin' up to that. Honest. Cain't quite git thar yet but I will. I promise." Dish grinned sheepishly. "Thanks, li'l brother. Ya kin be best man at my weddin'."

Cade smiled. Black Jack had told him to give his brother another chance. It seemed strange, at that time, that the former buffalo hunter hadn't come to Bass's defense, except to say no man deserved to hang for something he didn't do.

"Where's John?" Cade broke the awkward silence.

"Oh, he's over helpin' Toolie with the cookin'. He'll be mighty glad to see ya. Bin a'frettin' an' a'stewin' about you—an' us. Ya know John."

Cade started to respond when Dish saw Bass clearing the shadows. "Well, thar he is. Deputy Manko, I figgered they'd have you singin' to our beeves by now."

"Good evenin', Deputy Branson, what brings you here? Thought you were gonna see Black Jack."

Pushing his hat back on his forehead, Cade said, "He says howdy."

"Probably said '*Aho*.' That's not what I meant."

Uncomfortable, Dish looked over at the cook working at a well-used Dutch oven. John was hovering nearby. "Hey, Toolie, that stew ready? We got us some hungry hands." He grabbed Cade by the arm. "Let's git us a plate. You're gonna take to this hyar stew. It's real fine. Real fine. Ah, you too Bass."

"I'll talk with you later, Cade," Bass said.

Bass watched them walk away. You shouldn't have come, Cade. I told you that, he thought as a grin slowly slipped onto his face.

Chapter Nineteen

From her window, Elizabeth Rice watched Attorney Princeton walk into the bank as planned. Late afternoon sunshine patted the buildings with yellow. It was a perfect day. A perfect day. Earlier, Bass Manko had left for the fool marshal's ranch, assuring her that they would be playing cattle-watcher, just like she hoped. Only the addle-headed jailer was around. Oh, and she had seen Harding's son ride in—to help him clean up the marshal's office, she assumed.

Princeton was carrying all the available cash she could round up from the saloon, the whore house and sold cattle. A suitable amount was necessary to make the "payment" for the purchase of the Bar 6 appear large enough. Of course, her desk still contained several hundred dollars in gold and certificates. It didn't matter that she intended to have the major investment back in a few hours, plus the rest of the bank's deposits. She just never wanted to be without money—that sensation was deeply embedded from childhood. Her mother would be proud.

Acting as Titus Branson's attorney, Princeton was to make the deposit in his name. He would announce the money was for the purchase of the Bar 6, that the ill rancher had decided to get out while he could do so. Elizabeth would be declared the new owner. It was a nice touch. She allowed her mind the luxury of skipping ahead to the time when all the Bransons were dead and gone. Glorious it would be. After the Branson brothers were killed she intended to ride out to see Titus Branson and comfort him on his loss. A little poison in an offered drink would finish it once and for all.

Who should she get to ramrod the whole valley's cattle operation as all her ranches were consolidated into one great holding? Absalum Sil? Of course not. His usefulness would be shortlived after all this was over. She already knew how she'd administer the poison too. Just like it was with her late husband.

The Bar 6 herd was two times that of all the other valley herds combined, including her Circle R cattle. God, what a prize!

She would need a top-notch cowman to coordinate everything and make it grow richer. What about the Bar 6's own foreman? No, that was Dish himself, she smiled. As soon as the old rancher and his sons were dead, she would activate the KL Cattle Company for real. The King Lear Cattle Company—the name of an empire!

Her mind silently savored lines from one of the Earl of Kent's speeches from the play. Her thoughts wandered to another day, another kind of stage, another kind of performance. Transfixed, she stared at the window for minutes after Princeton disappeared into the bank. She then turned her attention to preparing for her next role. The attorney served a useful purpose, she concluded to herself. It wasn't his fault that he wasn't brilliant like she was. Few were given such a gift. Men like Shakespeare and women like her mother—and now her, the Cattle Queen of Texas, were rare.

The creation of the bank robber was similar to many roles she had performed before. Each had its own special touches, of course, but the approach was identical. Hers was a gift in the art and discipline of becoming someone else. That was what she learned from her mother.

Immediately, she began completing the task of transforming herself into Bass Manko. The disguise was Sil's idea. She had been reluctant about it at first, but became convinced this was a stronger approach than her dressing as her Mexican rustler. She was already dressed in Mexican pants that flared over her boots with large-roweled spurs. Her upper body was naked. She admitted to herself that playing a role, any role, gave her more satisfaction than anything. Even lovemaking. The process was slow and ceremonial.

Grease paint began to tan her exposed skin. Frequently, she checked the mirror for hard-to-get corners on her ears and neck. Her eyes weren't nearly as wide as his, but there was nothing she could do about that. She counted on bank patrons, and any other witnesses, seeing what they thought they saw. It always worked.

After tightly wrapping her bosom with bands of cloth, she put on a blue shirt, adding black studded cuffs. Sil had secured the cuffs and gunbelt. They weren't exactly like Bass's but close enough. A long cattleman's coat streaked with permanent dirt helped cover her bound bosom and hide her hips. She chuckled to herself about Bass enjoying taking off the tie-down. Her boots carried platform layers in the holes and soles to make her two inches taller. Walking fast was a little awkward but it actually served to give her character more swagger, like the young gunfighter. A black, wide-brimmed hat lay on the sofa. Ignoring the hat, she belted on the black gunbelt, lined with silver studs. The gun wasn't like Bass's; it was the long-barreled revolver she carried on the rustling raids. As she dressed, she practiced the speech pattern she would use to imitate Bass's distinctive voice. Then came a blond wig. It was a woman's but Bass's hair was shoulder-length. Perfect.

Studying herself in the mirror, she placed the hat on her head, then pulled the kerchief tied around her face up over her nose. She admired her new self, smiled and recited a passage from *Othello II*, " 'When devils will the blackest sins put on, they do suggest at first with heavenly shows.' " Her shrill laughter bounced off the dreary wall. She would wait until just before stepping into the bank to mask herself. No one would think anything about the young singer walking in town. The only people who knew Harding had made him a deputy were out at the roundup camp.

"Who wants to know? Mighty fine." She mimicked the gunfighter's jerky way of talking. An unexpected twinge of lust went through her. She would have to find a new lover.

She looked again in the mirror. Maybe just a bit more grease paint on the sides of her nose. Her hand clipped the top of a bottle of perfume sending it rolling across her dressing table. Flowery fluid spew in all directions, splatters hitting her long coat and pants. She cursed loudly and began wiping at the stains with a towel, but the spots were immediate and steadfast. After several mirror examinations, she decided the marks didn't hurt anything. They looked like the kind of discoloration Bass might have picked up during the day. And the smell of perfume would fit him as well. When didn't he smell like some woman had been close to him? She chuckled at this and decided it was providential.

Satisfied, she prepared herself for her performance by reviewing the details she must handle well. Her thumb touched each finger of her right hand as she recounted her list. Her plan was simple. After she held up the bank she would walk across the street and slip behind the saloon. There were already signs in back of a horse being tied there for awhile. It would appear Bass had escaped from town that way. She had made the trail this morning, returning the horse to the livery before noon. An enjoyable morning for a ride, she had told the livery manager. He had been interested only in watching her bosom bounce as she rode.

She would go up the back way into her room unnoticed and quickly hide the money and change clothes. If someone did see her, they would think it was Bass. She could say that he came into her room, threatened her and left out the window. Good. She liked having angles covered several ways. Thorough preparation always paid off.

If anyone tried to come after her from the bank, Princeton was to stop him by urging the man to wait and let the law handle it. Any delay would be enough for her to escape. The lawyer would turn over the bank statement showing a large deposit in Titus Branson's account—proof of her purchase of the ranch in any court, even though no money was any longer there. Of course, in addition to the large bonus promised, Princeton would be given a case of whiskey as a gift for his part. It would look like he drank himself to death.

It was a wonderful plan. She would not only get her own money back but everyone else's in town. Sil was supposed to bring Bass to town as if they caught him trying to get away. She strongly suspected Sil would kill him instead.

Ready, she walked in character to the door of her room

and slowly opened it. The hallway was empty. Efficiently, she stepped outside, locked the door and proceeded along the gaslamp-lit corridor and down a back stairway that would let her leave the building without passing through the saloon.

Crossing the street was a challenge with the hustling traffic. Once on the other side she was only a short block from the bank. The sights and sounds of the town drew her momentarily out of character. Tonight she would go to the theater, she promised herself. To celebrate. Maybe find a young man to continue the celebration.

"Hey singer! Wait!"

The call came from behind her. Panic shot through her body. Steeling herself for the worst, Elizabeth turned slowly to face the greeter. Her hand found comfort in gripping the revolver on her hip. It was no one she knew. A man in a three-piece suit with a big cigar and a bigger grin below thin eyebrows.

"Remember me? I'm the one that wanted to hear *I'll Take You Home Again, Kathleen* in the Four Aces," the stranger said, extending his hand. "That song always brings me luck. Don't know why, it just does."

Elizabeth shook his hand heartily while her other hand pinched the bridge of her nose as if to keep from sneezing, giving her a natural way to avoid the man's eyes and cover her face.

"Sure, sure, how ya been? Your luck still holdin'?" Elizabeth responded in an imitation of Bass's manner of speaking, fighting back every tingle of fear. "Sorry, but I'm fightin' a cold. Nasty stuff."

"Boy, I know how that goes," the businessman responded. She smelled whiskey on his breath and was glad of it. "Here, I got lucky after you sang that. Always do. Wanted to give you a little something—for the luck—but you were already gone." He held out several folded certificates.

"That's mighty kind o' you." She accepted the money and tried her best to imitate Bass's easy, confident manner. "Sorry, but I gotta run. Meetin' a fella in the bank."

"Sure. I just wanted to say thanks. Again."

"Mighty fine." She spun away and continued walking. She held her breath, waiting for the man to realize he hadn't been talking to Bass Manko.

"See you around. Maybe you'll sing it again."

She jumped at the sound, then realized it had worked. She waved her arm nonchalantly and headed for the bank.

Morning found tired men already on their feet drinking coffee and cursing the day. Dish wanted to check the remaining Bar 6 land for strays. Cade suggested the three brothers do that work and let the rest of the roundup crew move on to the Circle R. Sil immediately liked the idea and said he was certain some cattle had worked their way down into a long line of draws where it was hard to see. Buffalo grass was thick but so were the trees and brush. The steepness of the draws made getting them out difficult. He thought they would find more unbranded calves and their mothers but thought it made sense for the rest of the roundup to move on.

Dish agreed with Sil's assessment and quickly gave assignments to the teams of riders and told Toolie to find a new camp for the night. Marshal Harding asked if he could join the three brothers, telling Bass to ride on ahead with Toolie. For once, Bass seemed eager to accept an order and rode out with the wagon.

For the three Bransons and Harding, the rest of the morning scampered along like a young dog chasing a rabbit.

Their mid-day meal was a can of tomatoes each and some
jerky, washed down with tepid water. They switched to
fresh horses brought along for the afternoon and were back
in the saddle too soon for everyone, except Dish.

By early afternoon, they had finished. But this herd had
come hard on both horses and men. Each cow and steer had
been driven from a hiding place deep within a world of wiry
brambles, trees and thick bushes.

Making the reluctant animals stay in the open was almost
as tiring as getting them there in the first place. Their
horses were drenched in sweat, matching their riders. No
one argued—or cheered—when Dish finally pronounced
they should head for the new camp with their recovered
herd. Relief from the hard work simpered into trail-weary
silence, broken only by the bawling of the seventy-four
head of cattle moving in front of them.

Rolling his stiffened shoulders, Cade Branson squinted
against the afternoon sun. A deep breath briefly drew in
new energy. He was too tired to think of anything, except
eating. Soon they would reach the new roundup camp, hot
coffee and a good supper, and be free from these cattle.
They only served to remind him why he didn't want to be a
rancher. That was for Dish and John. He tried to stay alert.
It had to be coming. Harding said it was. But when.

What if the old man had guessed wrong? Maybe Sil
planned on taking over the roundup camp first. His mind
rejected that idea as more trouble for Sil than it was worth.
He was beginning to agree with Harding that it was prema-
ture to tell his brothers about a possible attack. Other than
Sil being a disagreeable sort, there was no indication of a
planned insurrection. Maybe the rumors about Harding being too old were right after all. Cade tried to focus on the

trail and the reluctant herd in front of them. Unwanted thoughts were shoved into the shadows of his mind.

Like a song, the hooves of horses and cattle made soft pushing sounds in the trail-beaten dust, interrupted by loud clacks on the sun-baked red clay, then back to soft patters as the ground changed back and forth underneath them. Immediately ahead of them was a ten-foot-high knoll, adorned with red rock, buffalo grass and a forlorn bush with three scraggily branches. Behind the raised mound was open land, eventually cut off by a treeline. To their right, trees had taken command, creating a thick wall along the well-established trail.

A cold shiver jolted Cade's exhaustion into strained attention. On top of the knoll was an instant of movement, then it was gone. Had he imagined it? Everything had become too quiet on the curving trail ahead. Sounds that should have been all around were strangely absent. It would be there.

Ambush.

Cade's weariness vanished into a heightening sense of danger. Or was he just seeing things because he was tired and anticipating Sil would make a move like Harding said he would?

He studied the knoll ahead, like a man thumbing through a book for one particular sentence that didn't belong. If a knowing man concentrated enough, he could make out movements where there weren't any to most people. But not this time. Whatever movement had been there was gone. Now there was only a feeling. Cade studied the trail snaking out in front of them for answers that could mean life or death but saw nothing to reassure or confirm. Maybe it was a deer or even a cougar. No, his mind told him it had been a man.

Did Dish or the old lawman see the movement? Or John? He glanced at Dish, riding next to him. The middle Branson appeared to be oblivious to the tenseness Cade felt. His older brother was an easy-to-read story of fatigue, humming to himself and lost in the rhythm of his horse's walk, accented by the jingle of bits, spurs and the creak of his saddle. His long coat was streaked with dust and tattooed with dried rain spots from the morning's light rain. Cade couldn't help but chuckle. Dish loved roundups as much as Cade hated them.

John appeared to be fussing about something to himself. Probably worried about whether Toolie would set up the cooking right without him to help, Cade guessed. Then he glanced at the older man riding ahead of him. He liked this gray-haired lawman. Always had. Fear of him as a child had grown into great respect. Especially now. Harding had anticipated this attack on the Bransons. That's why he had come to the roundup—and why he wanted Bass and him as deputies. Cade had a hunch the old man thought he wouldn't be able to get him there any other way except as a deputy. Or be comfortable enough to take him into his confidence.

Black Jack Sante had told Cade what Harding suspected, that Absalum Sil and Elizabeth Rice were trying to take over the region's cattle business, that the new ranch ownership was only a front for them, that the next step was to eliminate the Bransons. However, the hermit didn't know how or why his marshal friend had come to those conclusions. Just that he had—and that he was considering asking the two young gunfighters to join him as his deputies.

Harding's face was taut from a hard day cutting cattle from the heavy brush, riding with them like he was twenty years younger and saying nothing about it. His right leg dangled free of its stirrup to ease the throbbing in his stiffened knee.

"What are you gonna do now, Cade Branson?" Cade asked himself quietly.

How silly to ask such a question out loud at a time like this. Besides, he knew the answer before the query formed in his mouth. There weren't too many options. He had expected an ambush—but as the day went on, that threat had disappeared behind hard work.

One option would be to ride back the way they came and find another trail. That was the safest move but it just didn't sit right. It would mean moving these cattle back through the trees, losing some of them again for certain and Dish wouldn't go for that, no matter what was going on. And there was, of course, some risk of being shot in the back. If a man's going to die, he should be facing his enemy.

Another option would be to ride past at a gallop, firing as they went, letting the cattle bolt in front of them. But if they didn't get all of the ambushers with their initial shots their backs would quickly be fat targets with no immediate cover.

Or they could pull up right here and dig in across the knoll, maybe in the treeline to their right. That would invite being picked off after nightfall, or even before, since their adversaries owned the higher ground. He didn't know how many were against the four of them either.

Three really. John wasn't armed and didn't want to be. He had made that quite clear and Cade had almost told him what they were likely to run into. Maybe he was just being too jumpy for his own good, Cade told himself. Maybe it was nothing but his imagination behind that knoll. Maybe it was nothing more than a tumbleweed moving across. If so, Dish would have something to laugh about for weeks.

He would deal with that possibility later. Reaching over, Cade touched Dish on the shoulder to get his attention. As soon as Dish turned his head toward him, Cade whispered, "Ambush ahead. I'm going to surprise them if I can."

Dish's eyes widened as he returned to the reality of the trail and left his empty daydreaming. Cade motioned for him to keep riding down the trail and to advise Harding to do the same. Dish frowned but finally nudged his tired mount into a faster walk to pull up alongside the marshal.

Harding immediately yanked his Winchester from its saddle sheath at the same time as he glanced back at Cade, who nodded. Holding the weapon in one hand, the lawman reached into his dirty shirt pocket. Tanned fingers wrapped around a tobacco square, squeezing it momentarily out of new tension. He bit off a chunk with relish. Grinning like a wolf, he turned to Dish and Cade with the tobacco pushing out his cheek and offered the remaining chaw.

Neither wanted any and Harding muttered to Dish that he wouldn't say anything to John until they got closer. The oldest Branson brother was riding to Harding's far right, herding their string of four tired morning horses and receiving more than his share of the dust.

Dish didn't argue; his face was white and his eyes bright. A hesitancy in his motions went unnoticed, then he pulled his rifle from its leather and cocked it.

Chapter Twenty

After declining the tobacco, Cade patted the neck of his tired gray to calm the well-muscled horse. This wasn't January, but he knew a mustang could be trusted to warn his rider every time. An icy sensation was growing within him.

Winter flowed into his soul.

He had felt this same coldness before his first real fight with his brother—and throughout the War and every battle since. It was more like an inner quiet, an automatic controlling of his senses so they worked at another dimension. Like some unseen force took over his body and directed it. Wind-in-the-Valley said the feeling was the power of Winter Kill—and his spirit helper. She said he should consider the medicine as quite sacred and vulnerable to leaving him if he mistreated it.

Regardless of where the feeling came from, there was something about this kind of moment that made Cade feel strangely alive, almost reincarnated. And when he was closest to death, Cade Branson was a dangerous man.

Where the trail wound around the knoll would be where the ambushers were waiting, he thought. Yes, someone was there, or several someones. Cade still couldn't see anything; he just knew it. Sil's men had either tracked them or figured out this was the logical trail into camp since it was the only one free of trees and brush.

Whoever was waiting wasn't looking at them now anyway, Cade decided. The ambushers would be hunkered down to make certain they had surprise in their favor. When the riders came around the knoll behind their small herd, they would open up on them at close range. Rustlers would be blamed. It was a good plan.

The four riders were only fifty feet from the rocky incline and the trail's bend around it. Dish and Harding stared straight ahead, except when the old man spit long streams of tobacco juice. They rode more slowly now, as if steeling themselves for the coming assault. Harding's hands tightly gripped the cocked rifle laying across his saddle. He spat into the dust and kneed his horse into a brief trot to bring him alongside the oldest Branson brother.

John's eyes widened as Harding finally whispered the news. When John started to say something, Harding hushed him into silence. The old lawman handed him the pistol from his belt holster. John stared at the gun in his hand for a long time as they rode close together, looked up and pushed it into his waistband. His mouth was set hard.

Harding smiled and whispered, "Aye, you're going to do fine. They not be Welsh warriors."

John's face became puzzled. "I pray so."

"There's a good lad."

Dish's narrowed eyes burned into the knoll to see what was waiting for them on the other side. His rifle lay across his thighs on the saddle. His face was hard; he hadn't questioned his youngest brother's hunches. Whether to reinforce the impression of their being unaware of the ambush or to push back the advancing fear, Dish burst into an off-key version of his favorite song, "O Susannah, don't you cry for me. I'm g'wan to Alabama with my banjo on my knee . . ."

It was time to change the situation, Cade decided. Time to attack. Sudden movement might tip off whoever was hiding and into firing before he was ready but Cade thought the risk was worth it. He reached back into his saddlebag and pulled out a spare pistol. A spin of the cylinder assured him of its loaded condition. After tying the reins together and slipping them over the saddlehorn, he leapt smoothly from his gray and gave him a pat on the rump to encourage a continued trot.

He bolted up the blind side of the knoll. In four swift strides he was near the top but still below it and out of sight of the waiting outlaws. The ambushers were hunkered down unseen on the other side. Dropping to his knees, he listened. A piece of red clay was stuck to his pistol barrel halfway up the gun. Another clay sliver had attached itself to his coat sleeve. That broke his concentration for an instant.

"Nice goin'," he said to himself, flicking the mud aside with his fingers. He switched the weapon to this left hand and drew his holstered pistol with his right.

At his position, the knoll stretched slightly away from him. It was little more than an uneven mixture of jagged rock, red clay and underbrush, plus the lone struggling tree. Twenty feet away, on the other side of the hill, were men waiting to kill him and his brothers. Anger was replacing the coldness within him.

He couldn't see anything beyond the top edge of the

knoll. He didn't want to push his luck by peering over it but was confident their unknown adversaries would be slightly below him when he stepped over the edge, and that they would be looking the other way, toward the trail and the approaching swell of horses and cattle. He assumed they hadn't discovered one of those horses had no rider or they would have reacted by now.

Cade's face was without expression, except for the warrior's song in his eyes. Someone was going to be sorry—very sorry. Pent-up frustration and anger from his family's ill-conceived desire to hang Bass was clamoring to come out. It was one thing to forgive Dish; another to forget. He listened one last time to pin down as best he could if there were just three men. No, there were four. He was positive now. He concentrated on his unseen enemies, waiting for the right moment to face them. If all four turned on him at once, he would die. He pushed that thought away and heard himself whisper the warrior's bold cry, "*Hokay hey*, today is a good day to die."

". . . of course, I can hear 'em comin' . . . keep your damn head down, or they'll git wise to us."

"Oh hell, they's barely awake. That ol lawdaig's prob'ly sleepin' in the saddle by now."

"I'm not worried about Harding. It's Dish I want first—an' his little brother. That Cade Branson's mean with a gun. He's yours, Luke. I'll take Dish."

"He'll never know what hit him."

"It'll take more'n one slug."

"I got more'n one."

"What 'bout John Branson?"

"He isn't worth a bullet. Nothin' like his ol' man. We'll get him last. Lennie, you go for the marshal—an' Pete, both of us'll hit Dish."

"Ah, Mister Sil?"

"Yeah?"

"I'd rather shoot at Dish than at a lawman if it's all right with you."

"Oh hell, Pete take Harding. Lennie, shoot . . . at something."

Their words dropped off as the sounds of cattle grew louder. Sil patted the fat gunny sack beside him in anticipation. Below, the riders were just yards away from rounding the knoll and into gunfire. Waiting any longer would make them an easy target. Cade could hear a boot drag against rock. Four rifle hammers cocked almost in unison. A muffled cough punctuated the still air, followed by an urgent plea to be quiet.

Cade frowned at the fragments of conversation he gathered. One of the ambushers was Absalum Sil himself. Had to be. There weren't many voices like that around. Sil's plan was a good one, Cade thought. Time to let him know it wasn't good enough. Sucking in a long, deep breath and letting its calmness slowly slide between clenched teeth, Cade slipped over the ridge like a late afternoon shadow.

There was no sound to his movement at all. Below him were four men staring intently at the bend, their backs to him. Besides Sil, he recognized two from the roundup.

"Afternoon, boys. Move and you die." Cade's voice was gravelly with courage, cocking the revolvers in his hands as he spoke.

All three of Sil's men turned upward with whitened shock filling their faces. Their eyes were telling them something that couldn't be. Cade Branson was on the trail below, riding to his death. He simply couldn't be here. The youngest outlaw, no more than seventeen, with a pockmarked face and a scrawny mustache, glanced back at the trail as if to verify what he knew should be true.

Sil didn't move. It almost seemed to Cade that the hog-faced outlaw expected him. Sil locked himself into an awkward-looking squatting position. His worn overalls hung at his waist and his fat hands gripped a rifle but it was pointed in the direction of the trail. His revolver dangled from its lanyard around his neck. He could have been a statue. A homely statue. Sil didn't look at Cade, slitted cat eyes mere lines on his round face, staring into the dusk.

The lean outlaw with long yellow hair spun his rifle toward Cade. The youngest Branson ripped the man's chest with two quick shots and the man flipped backwards down the abrupt slope. Two rifle bullets trailed his descent, coming from Dish or Harding or both. One shot thumped into the hurdling body, the other spat against the rock.

Stepping to his right, Cade fired the pistol in his right hand at the second outlaw who was also moving to his right. The man's rifle fired at the same instant and missed. Cade's bullet drove through the ambusher's shoulder. Cade fired again with his left pistol and lead ripped into the man's stomach. His rifle dropped in pained reaction to the impact.

Kneeling, the young outlaw was painted in shock and fear. He held his rifle stiffly, like he had fogotten it was there. He looked down at the gun and his mind slowly registered its importance. Terrified, he jerked in panic and threw the gun away like it was scalding hot. His hands moved slowly into the air.

Cade's attention was split between the wounded man and Sil.

"W-Wait . . . please . . . wait . . . I'm hurt, I'm hurt," shouted the bleeding outlaw. "P-Please . . . I'm . . . h-hurt. P-Please."

Cade stepped closer to Sil and aimed both pistols at the outlaw's head. Out of the corner of his eye, he saw the youngest outlaw begin to shake. The teenager was about to vomit, his body heaving. Cade decided the young man was too scared to try pulling the holstered revolver at his waist.

Sil's face was a dark ruddy red. His eyes of narrrowed hate were locked onto the treeline on the far side of the trail. He hadn't moved from his earlier position. His guns remained as they were.

"Drop the gun, Sil. Now." Cade went over to the fuming outlaw leader. "It's all over. Unless you think you're fast enough. Try it. I'd like to see it."

The hog-faced outlaw leader finally looked up at him. Sil's knuckles were white from holding the rifle. "I don't know what you're talking about, Branson. Me an' my men were chasing rustlers when all of a sudden you jumped us."

"The Winchester, Sil."

With a snort, the outlaw leader dropped the rifle.

"Now the pistol. Pull that rope over your head and throw it."

Sil lifted the lanyard past his hat and flipped the gun casually toward the front of the knoll.

"That's a real interesting story," Cade said. "That what you told Trenchard . . . and Gray . . . and Donnell . . . and Richardson when you stole their cattle and ran them off? That what you said after you murdered Henry Endore?"

"I don't know what you're talking about. I'm just a poor rancher. I came here to raise cattle."

Cade responded to movement to his left. "Don't move. Don't move a hair. I don't care much for anyone who tries to kill me an' my brothers. I'd just as soon shoot you now an' save me the trouble of taking you to town for hanging. What's in that sack?"

"Just some Mex hats. Found 'em when we were trailin' the rustlers."

"Sure you did, Sil. Try this—you were going to leave them on this knoll to make it look like Mexican bandits ambushed us. Clever, Sil."

"That's bullshit."

"Oh God, Mister, uh, oh, please," the wounded man cried, "please . . . I didn't . . ."

"You didn't think you'd be where you are now, that's what. You thought you'd be laughing over four dead men, didn't you?"

An eyelash blink later came the savage thunder of a rifle shot and the wounded bandit half-stood for an instant. Wildly, he grabbed at loose rocks nearby as if they could steady the numbing within him, then crumpled and rolled down the open slope of the knoll. His body thudded against his unmoving partner. The echo of the gunfire followed, like a playful puppy.

Cade looked down the open slope of the knoll and saw Dish with a smoking rifle, coming up the slope.

Dish waved and levered the smoldering shell from his gun. "How ya doin' up thar, bro? Don't kill all o' 'em, leave some fer me."

Cade was stunned. Did Dish think he was in trouble? Probably he couldn't see well from that angle. Cade knew his brother thought he was saving his life. He gave a crisp salute in appreciation and returned his attention to Sil and the trembling outlaw, then looked for Harding and John.

Harding's head and rifle barrel were barely clearing a downed tree and the bobbing hat had to belong to John. Behind them were the horses they were riding. Cade assumed his oldest brother had the assignment of holding the reins. Their cattle hadn't gone as far as he thought they would. It looked like most were grazing. Their four tired morning horses were mixed in with them, enjoying the same grass.

"Sil, you an' your young friend here better lay flat—or you'll end up the same way. My family doesn't care much for your kind of snake," Cade said. The young outlaw slammed himself against the ground and squeezed shut his eyes. He fought back the vomit that wanted out.

Sil didn't move.

"Be thinking about what you're going to tell me about this," Cade said to the sickened teenager. "If it's truth, you might live. I know this wasn't your idea."

"Keep your mouth shut, Lennie. He's just jawing."

"If you do, Lennie," Cade said, "you'll hang right alongside Mr. Sil here."

Shoving the pistol in his left hand into his waistband, he walked over to the terrified outlaw. Without another word to Lennie, Cade yanked the young man's belt gun free from its holster and tossed the revolver toward the far side of the knoll's surface. It thumped and skidded to a stop next to a clump of buffalo grass. With his outstretched right hand—still holding a pistol—Cade motioned for the others to join him.

Dish was clearing the ridge, eager for someone to shoot at.

Cade's gaze quickly took in the rest of the knoll's surface and beyond. In a sparse wooded area, not far from the knoll, he noticed the outlaws' horses were tied. This was the only open trail to the new roundup camp so it wouldn't have been hard to guess their route. But one of them might have followed the cattle gathering to make certain. He remembered now feeling like he was being watched earlier this morning. A strange sensation. Along the back of his neck. It wasn't the first time in his life he had felt that way. The last time was during the War. Just before a Union raid hit their extended line.

The slope was steeper than it first appeared and Dish dug

his heels into the soft earth to keep his balance as he climbed, reaching the top first. The old lawman's bowlegged strides were not suited for an uphill climb. He took three steps forward and staggered to keep his balance. Swinging his arms in the air with his right hand holding his rifle, he took one step sideways, cursed that he should have ridden, and spat before resuming his advance.

"Do them bastirds dun got anythan' to eat?" Dish's first comment was flippant. His expression changed when he saw Sil. "What the hell? Well, lookee hyar. Sil, ya hog-faced sonvabitch, I shoulda know'd. Ya hard up fer beef, farm boy?"

"Marshal Harding figured it out, Dish. Sil—and Missus Rice—were going to kill all of us and take over the Bar 6. They wanted the whole region. They already own the Richardson and Gray ranches. Donnell too. And the Lazy T. She already had the Circle R. That leaves us the Half-Moon 5 and the River S. They stole the cattle and ran off those folks."

Dish's eyes narrowed. "How come ya jes' now come to be tellin' me this?"

"We had to wait for them to try it, Dish. Else it was just guessing."

"Ya weren't worried 'bout yur big brother takin' a bullet?"

"I knew you could handle anything."

Dish grinned. Quick strides placed him over Sil; the nose of his rifle slid along the outlaw leader's back and nudged his hat forward over his face. "Is that straight talk, Sil? Did'cha think ya was gonna kill all o' us an' git the Bar 6? Did ya think ya were that good? Hell, no farmer's gonna beat me."

"I didn't do nothing of the kind. Your brother is out of his head. I tried to tell him we were hit by rustlers an' we're trackin' them when he jumped us." Sil spoke without looking at Dish. Only the slight trembling at the corner of his mouth revealed any sign of emotion. His face was bloated with withheld anger.

Dish studied the overall-wearing man without saying a word. His rifle barrel rested on Sil's back. Cade took a step closer and told him more what he had learned from Black Jack Sante and from Harding himself about the land-grabbing scheme. Shaking his head, Dish said "Goodbye, Sil."

"No. He's going back to town—to stand trial," Cade said.

"Ya playin' lawman on me now too?"

"Maybe I am. But that's the way it's going to be, Dish."

Anger flashed across Dish's face, disappearing like lightning in the sky. "Thar are times, li'l brother, when ya push me too—"

"You know I'm right, Dish."

"I wouldn't be goin' that fur with it." Dish saw the odd-shaped sack. "What'cha got thar, Sil? Sumthin' to eat?"

Cade responded. "Take a look. It's sombreros. They were going to leave them here so Mexican rustlers would be blamed."

Lifting the sack, Dish let the hats tumble onto the ground.

"Ya figgerin' on killin' our paw too, Sil? He's a sick ol' man but he ain't ready to check out yet. Ya man 'nuff to face that ol' rooster—or did ya figger on shootin' him in the back like ya dun tried with us?" Dish kicked Sil hard in the stomach.

Sil groaned and doubled over.

"Didn't think much o' us Branson boys, did ya, Sil?" Dish snorted and kicked him again. "Reckon ya dun underrated my li'l brother, didn't ya?"

"That's enough, Dish," Cade said but it wasn't harsh.

"Yeah, yur ri't. He ain't fer shootin'. He ain't nothin' but a dirty-ass hog." Dish spun and walked away.

Cade turned toward Harding lumbering toward him; John was parallel to Harding with a dozen feet separating them. John's strides were becoming more and more hesitant.

Reaching the squatting Sil and the two Bransons, Harding spat and glanced down the hill at the two dead ambushers. After a second spit that didn't have much in it, he shook his head, panting his initial response, "Well, looky here. Absalum Sil, you're under arrest for the murder of the Richardson family—and attempted murder of all of us—and a few other things I'll put words to later when you're in my jail. Aye, and the murder of my fine deputy, Henry Endore."

"Go to hell, Harding. You haven't got a thing on me."

"Oh now, we'll see about that." Harding's face pushed into a hard frown, turning every wrinkle into a fixed deep line. He nudged the weathered hat back on his forehead, showing exactly where the sun didn't have a chance to reach. "Your girlfriend, the Widow Rice, likes to wear a pretty locket. You know where it came from. So do I."

All three Branson men turned to pay attention to Harding. To a red-faced Sil, the old lawman explained that he and the Richardsons went back a long way. The locket Sil had given Rice was a special piece of jewelry Emil Richardson had made for his wife on their wedding day.

"I'd know it anywhere, Sil. Never seen another like it. Emily Richardson loved that necklace," Harding continued. "I knew they wouldn't sell out like that—or leave without saying goodbye. Sent a few wires along the way they were supposed to be traveling. A Ranger west of here a week found them. Dead. All of them. You made it look like Indians had done it." Harding's chest rose and fell as the thought of the family dying reached him once more.

"You've been out in the sun too long, Harding. I don't even know what you're talking about. If Missus Rice has that kind of necklace, she'll have to tell you where it came from. Not me."

Harding smiled. It was a cruel smile that surprised even Cade. For the first time, he noticed the lawman's rifle was pointed casually at Sil's head.

"Your lady friend has already told me where the necklace came from." Harding's face was pulled tight with anguish as he revisited the knowledge of his friends being killed. "She's real proud of it. Thinks you had it made for her in New Orleans. Said you gave it to her as a 'new neighbor' gift when you bought the Richardson's place."

"So Elizabeth Rice is a liar. That's not my problem."

Cade stepped beside Harding whose fingers were gripping the gun like it was his only connection to the world.

"I'm sorry about the Richardsons. I didn't know them well, Emmett." Cade's voice was soft. Without looking at Harding, he eased Harding's rifle barrel away from Sil's head.

Something deep inside Harding hurled itself into his throat and he swallowed it back.

"Aye, good folks they be. Good friends. The kind you can't replace. Like a fine spring morn." Harding rubbed his mouth. "Hell's teeth, why didn't they tell me they were getting pushed? I could've done something. Something."

"What about the others?"

"Sorry I am to say, it doesn't look like any of them made it out of Texas."

Sil's face clicked into a sneer. A flash of movement followed. Harding's rifle barrel popped against Sil's jaw, spewing blood and teeth.

"Don't, Marshal," Cade said. "Your friends, they wouldn't like that. He isn't worth it."

Harding stared at Cade, his wrinkled face cracking from sorrow. "L-Let me kill the bastard. Just turn away."

"I can't. You made me a lawman—like you. And you can't either."

For the first time, Sil was afraid. His thick frame shivered.

Harding took a deep breath that shook his body but calmed him down. "You're a lucky man, Sil." He took another long breath. "What do you say we find out what this young lad's got to say for himself?"

"Wait, Marshal. What about the Trenchards? Aren't they leaving soon? Can we . . ."

Harding forced a thin smile. "Right now, those fine folks are enjoying the hospitality of my ranch. I rode over and told them before Bass and I headed for the roundup. They're safe, I reckon."

"Good for you, Emmett."

"Wish I could've been smart enough to save my . . ." Harding clenched his teeth and looked away.

Dish pushed hard on the young outlaw's shoulder, knocking him off-balance. "This fool don't know anythan'. He cain't even puke ri't. I say we string 'im up and git on to camp. I'm damn tired. Gittin' hungry too. Not much to that can o' tomatoes." He turned to John. "How far'd them beeves git to?"

"Not far. They were more interested in that grass than bullets." John tried to smile at his joke. "I long-tied our saddle horses. They're grazing too."

No one responded to his report. Instead, the three men stepped toward the shaking young outlaw lying on the ground with his face in the dirt, not daring to look up. Cade reached him first. The barrel of his pistol pushed under the boy's chin and lifted his face toward them. "You've got one chance to save yourself from a hanging, boy. Was this Sil's idea? Tell us what you know."

Chapter Twenty-One

The young outlaw's face was layered in fear as he carefully rose to a squatting position. His gaze initially locked onto Cade for approval as he moved. But a frightened glance slid toward Dish, who shook his head angrily. The young outlaw's eyes darted away. "I-I don't know . . . nothin'." His voice broke awkwardly from a man's to a boy's abruptly, like a strange hiccup. But talking seemed to help his flighty stomach and he straighted his back.

"See? I told ya this clown didn't know nuthin'," Dish said. "Lemme shoot the fool an' let's git on with it."

He sought Harding's approval of his observation but the old lawman was adding to his chaw and paying attention only to biting off the right amount from the remaining square. The process allowed him to regain his composure after confronting Sil.

"No, I want him to talk." Cade stared at his brother. "You already shot the other one before he could tell what this is all about."

"Would ya rather I dun let 'im shoot ya?"

"He didn't have a gun, Dish. He was wounded and had given up."

"Oh, sorry. Couldn't tell from whar I was a'standin'. Guess I could'a asked first. Polite-like. Thought the bastird was a'gonna shoot my li'l brother."

"I know you did. Give the kid one more chance. If he's not smart enough to take it, he's yours."

Chewing vigorously on the new tobacco, Harding spat a satisfying brown line toward Sil. The outlaw leader glared at the marshal as the brown stream splattered in front of where he sat, holding his arms close to his battered stomach.

Harding grinned. Rested from his climb and rejuvenated by more tobacco and the release of pent-up frustration about the Richardson family, Harding growled his way toward the young outlaw. "I agree with Dish. Sonny boy here isn't worth the trouble." He pulled his hat low over his eyes. "I'm going to get a rope. We can hang the bastard over there." He waved toward the trees in the distance.

"Keep your mouth shut, Lennie," Sil snorted.

"Last chance, Lennie." Cade's voice was a dull knife scraping on a piece of oak. "We've already got Sil for murder. He's going to hang no matter what you do. You have a choice."

"P-Please . . . d-don't. I-I'll tell ya what I know." The teenage outlaw's hands were shaking. His face was whirling from pale white to darkened red and back again. "W-We were s-supposed to k-kill Dish . . . an' you . . . an' all of you. I-It . . . were Sil's doin'. H-He gave the orders. H-Honest, I ain't lyin'." His battle to keep from vomiting was fully resumed and he swallowed three times quickly, stopping the surging bile, at least for the moment.

"Absalum Sil? Your boss? He ordered you to kill us, why?" Cade asked, seeking affirmation; his eyes cut into the young man's waning courage.

The outlaw gulped down the bile inching up his throat. "Y-Yes, sir. H-He an' that fancy Rice widow. They's after all the ranches 'round here. We weren't supposed to know she were in it—but Luke did. He saw her change once from . . . that fancy Mex disguise she was always wearin'. She led them raids on them folks. Most o' 'em anyways. Luke said she were really somethin' to look at, naked an' all. He said it were real funny to see her . . . bosoms . . . while she were still wearin' that beard o' hers." He gulped again but knew he was losing control of his stomach. "Got four of them ranches already. Sil's men what run 'em. Ain't that somethin'? Luke said it was real funny cuz none o' us are good cowmen." He tried to smile, then abruptly turned away from Cade and regurgitated.

Wiping his mouth with the back of his hand, he returned to talking. Vomit nestled in the corners. "They got a deed fer the Bar 6. Already signed purty-like—with your paw's writin', I hear tell. Ain't seen it myself, mind you, but that's what Luke told me. Said there's gonna be proof o' him gittin' paid too. Somethin' about the bank . . . bein' robbed . . . today, maybe." He tried to laugh but Cade's stare drove the sound back inside him. "I . . . ah, I don't know . . . about that. Luke didn't tell me." He wiped his mouth again. "That's Luke. Down there."

The boy-man coughed away his nervousness, forcing the creeping back into his throat. He eyed Cade suspiciously and finally spoke his concern. "Don't know why you're askin' me all this. You're in too."

"What do you mean, Lennie?" Cade leaned forward, his words coaxing response.

"I, ah, you an' Manko," Lennie's face registered the realization of what he was saying. "Luke told me."

"What did he tell you?"

"Luke said Bass, well, ya know he was in it from the git-go."

Dish's chin lifted. A wry expression rolled across his face.

Cade looked at Harding and the old lawman shrugged his surprise.

"Bass . . . Bass Manko, he's involved in this?" Cade asked.

"Well, sure, ya know that. Luke said you an' Bass were closer than brothers."

Cade glanced at Dish, then at John. "Yes, Bass and I are good friends, that's true but what's that got to do with Sil and Missus Rice?"

The teenaged outlaw stared at Cade, trying to decide if he was teasing him or not. Finally, he asked, "You don't know what I'm talkin' about, do ya? I told Luke you didn't—an' he gave me crap about it. Luke said Bass shot that deputy when he came up on us when we was movin' cows off of Richardson's land. Wait 'til I . . ."

After a fearsome spit in the direction of the knoll's edge, Harding strode closer to the boy outlaw. The old man's brow was furrowed with sudden dislike for what he was hearing.

"Sonny boy, are you saying Bass Manko murdered my deputy?" Harding's voice cracked on the last word.

Lennie's laugh was answer enough, but the young outlaw reinforced the emotion with an explanation about how a disguised Elizabeth—along with Bass and Sil—led the attacks on the small ranches. He said the men in the gang were told to call the mysterious Mexican bandit "Lear." He didn't think anybody but Luke knew it was really her. He described her disguise in detail and wanted to share what Luke told him about her body in the same way but Harding told him that wasn't necessary.

While he spoke, Lennie eyed Cade exclusively and finally blurted, "Did you really whip that Big Ed Gilmore with your fists?"

Dish responded first. "Yeah, he did—an' he's whipped me, too. So don't be lyin' to us, kid, or he'll pound your sorry ass into the ground."

Lennie's eyes broadened into white circles. He looked down at his groin and knew what the wet spot meant. He couldn't keep the shiver from running across his back.

"I'm tellin' ya the truth. Honest. I don't wanna hang. I stole some cows. An'-An' I helped drive 'em to the canyon. Sure enough, I did. But I never drove 'em north to the Red River ranch. I never shot nobody neither. You can ask Luke . . ."

"I believe you, boy," Marshal Harding interrupted. "If you tell us where the stolen cattle are held and sign a confession like you've just told us, I guarantee you can ride away. Free and clear."

"Yessir, I will. Just show—"

Bam! From the trees a heavy rifle roared. Its snarling echo rammed against everything it touched.

Marshal Harding, Cade and Dish dove for the ground. The teenage outlaw leapfrogged into a flat position and squeezed his eyes shut. John spun awkwardly toward the deadly pronouncement. Sil's head bristled with a black hole. The rifle in his hands shook, as if it were afraid. He gurgled and fell face forward, jerked three times and was still. Fierce afternoon sun made their shadows shiver and draw closer to each man as reality sank in. No one spoke.

Dish saw the gun first, beneath Sil's unmoving body. "Damn! Whar the hell did that come from?" Dish said, studying the far trees, his own Winchester searching for a target as he spoke.

Cade was already standing again. "Oh, that'll be Black Jack."

"Black Jack? Sante? What's that ol' drunk doin' in them trees?"

"His idea. Thought we might need a little backup. Looks like we did."

Rubbing his hands together like he was washing them, Harding was the next to speak. "Sure wished you could've let an old man in on that sort of thing. Damn near had a conniption fit. Hell's teeth, that gun is loud. I reckon Black Jack scared those buffalo to death just with the sound." He walked over to the dead Sil and pulled the Winchester free of the body.

Cade waved toward the treeline and yelled, "Thanks, Black Jack. Come on in."

A moment later, a shadow with an umbrella over his head appeared riding a mule and waved back.

Harding wasted no time writing out what the outlaw kid had confessed to. Completing his task, he took the crumpled paper to Lennie, along with a stubby pencil. The young outlaw remained prone with his eyes shut.

"Get up, sonny boy. It's all over. At least, it is for your boss." Harding grabbed his shirt and pulled.

Lennie leaned on his elbows and stared at the unmoving Sil. "I-Is he dead?"

"He is," Harding growled. "You don't have to be afraid of him any longer. Read this and sign it."

"Will it keep me from hangin'?"

"You have my word—but I want to know where all those cattle went. Then you can ride free. I want you gone from this valley and I don't want you ever to come back."

"Yessir." Lennie swallowed. "I don't know whar all them cattle is. I reckon they sold lots o' 'em. Had to pay all o' us, ya know. Made over sixty dollars a month, most months. You can't make that ridin' fer no brand."

"No, you can't, Lennie but you'll live longer to spend what you make." Harding's countenance was stern.

"Yessir, I reckon so. We always took 'em first to a box canyon—on Circle R land. I was surprised how hard it was to find . . . the first time I went thar. Only heard about the place up near the Red." He blinked away fear and stared again at Cade. "Never went myself. Honest. Jordan an' Luke an' some of the boys—Velera, he went most times—they took small bunches north ever' now an' then. Moved 'em at night, leastwise 'til they got free o' here. Sold most, I think, to Comancheros an' whoever had . . . gold."

"Who knows where this Red River ranch is?" Harding asked.

"Ah, Lu . . . ah, Jordan . . . Jordan Maher does, fer sure."

"He's the foreman for the Circle R?"

"Yessir, that's him. I reckon Velera would know too. Ah, Decker, he would. Others too. Jes' not me."

Standing again, Dish's mouth twitched and came open. He winced, shook his head and finally said, "I knew thar was somethin' about Manko that didn't add up. Sorry, li'l brother, but I did." He paused for Cade to react but the youngest Branson was staring at the cattle down below. "Sure didn't figger on that Rice woman bein' in on somethin' like this. Reckon she's a mite more than jes' purty to look at." He smiled and dropped his rifle to his side.

Finally John spoke, staring down at the dead Sil. "Wonder how they planned on getting rid of Paw—after they killed us? Sounds like they've got a fake deed with his signature on it."

"Hell, Paw'll dun be dead by winter, John. March at the latest." Dish was still staring at Cade.

"I know that, Dish. I asked how they got his signature. He hasn't signed anything like that."

"Princeton," Cade spoke without turning from the cattle.

"What?" Dish stared at Cade.

"Did the attorney, Princeton, prepare the will?"

"Wal, sure nuff. It's all full o' wharas's an' wharfer's an' sech. Legal as she be." He paused. "The Bar 6 goes to me."

"We know that, Dish." John's voice was steady.

"Princeton's going to wish he hadn't done that." Cade drew his Colt, ejected empty shells from his pistol and reloaded it. Reholstering the gun, he did the same with the second and returned it to his belt.

The others watched him without speaking. Only the faint murmur of their cattle broke into the silence.

Dish remembered his own rifle and shoved new cartridges into the loading chamber. His face was drawn tight. Knotted veins danced along his forehead. Harding spat on the blood circle dawning under Sil's body and was pleased, for once, with his aim.

Standing at the far edge of the knoll, John picked up Sil's pistol and held the gun with both hands in front of him, more like he was using it as a compass rather than a weapon. The attached lanyard dangled from the handle as if alive. He stared in the direction of the unseen roundup camp, imitating Cade's reflective stance.

"Actually, faking our father's signature on a deed wouldn't be hard to do, if he's dead when they show it." John said. "Who's going to dispute it? We'd be dead. I'm sure that deed has witnesses—and they'd testify that Paw sold the ranch to them. Simple as that." He continued to stare at the gold-lit land flattered by the attention of the afternoon sun.

Walking back toward them, John observed that this plan

was truly brilliant. He stopped several feet from the others and looked away again.

"There's a piece still missing," he said. He didn't wait for anyone to ask what it was. "To keep everything looking right, there has to be some kind of proof that father was paid for this sale. That would end any possibility of foul play. Then, of course, they would have to find a way to get that money back. If they've somehow done that . . . it's perfect." He began walking again.

Cade looked at his oldest brother as if he hadn't seen him before. The man's insight was unsettling. Almost like he had been thinking about such a strategy himself.

Dish's eyes were bright, almost childlike. He swung his arms in a wide circle as if cranking up the words to respond but none came. He was annoyed by John's interference and tried to stare him down, but John was looking only at Marshal Harding. Cupping the outlaw pistol in his hands like it was some kind of fragile vase John stopped near the young outlaw who was handing the signed confession back to Harding. Shifting the outlaw gun to his left hand, John withdrew the Marshal's pistol from his waistband and returned it to the old lawman.

As he handed him the weapon John said, "Yesterday, Marshal, I heard two men at the water barrel—they were riders for that new owner of the Trenchard place. I forget his name." John held up his forefinger for emphasis. "They were arguing about who would run our ranch after it was taken. None of these men saw me. I was on the other side of the wagon, looking for another rope. I, ah, lost mine. In the brush. They didn't know I was there. It didn't make any sense to me. Until now. I thought they were just passing the time, you know." He examined the revolver in his hand, rubbing the barrel with his thumb.

"Damn, John, sur wish ya'd a'tolt me that a'fer." Dish shook his head. "Nobody tells me nothin' 'round hyar." If he was impressed with his brother's thoughtful observations, it didn't show. He rubbed his mouth to rid the next thought before it came.

"Marshal, the kid said something about the bank—and John said they would need proof of . . . Titus . . . being paid," Cade studied the old lawman. "What do you think?"

Harding worked up a ball of tobacco juice and sent it flying behind him. He saw Black Jack getting closer and held up his hand as an indication the answer would have to wait.

"*Aho*, you black-hearted son of a bitch. Still ridin' that damn mule, I see," Harding belted a warm greeting.

Black Jack reined his mule behind a clump of dried grass, over a foot high even with its lifeless strands half-bent. A ring of rock separated the rest of the land from the ambush ridge itself. On his side of the almost level land it was reborn as grass and sweet earth. He cradled his Sharps carbine in his right arm and held the red umbrella over him with his left. A slight breeze caught the ends of his scarlet sash and the eagle feather in his long gray hair and sent them waltzing.

Chapter Twenty-Two

The skinny buffalo hunter squinted through his thick glasses. "Thought you boys were jawin' too much and not payin' attention to what's-his-name—that farmer. He sure looked like he knew what to do with that 'Chester."

"We do thank you, Black Jack," Cade responded. "I'd like you to meet my brothers, Dish and John."

"Well now, *Aho*, Dish . . . John. Reckon I heard a mite 'bout you two."

Dish laughed heartily. "Yeah, I bet you have."

"It's good to meet you, sir," John said.

"Black Jack'll do." He laid his rifle across the saddle and scratched himself under his arm, holding the umbrella. His pinkish undershirt had sweated through. Several times. His bead necklaces jingled as he rubbed. "What's next, boys?"

"Well, let's wire for the Rangers. We must do something to stop these heathens." John's words came with an urgency.

"What the hell good'll that do?" Dish said.

"We could wire the Rangers, son. That we could." Harding responded, barely hiding his sarcasm. "That won't change the problem, though." He straightened his back and adjusted his shoulders. "No, son, there's a better answer. You get rid of Sil—and the lady—an' the problem goes away. Two can play this game. One's already gone."

"I didn't fight Comanch' an' Kiowa an' Mex an' ever' other damn thang to give up to no pig-faced farmer an' sum fancy lady," Dish snarled his defiance. "Or sum liquored-up mouthpiece." He glanced at Cade. "Or no saloon singin' sonvabitch."

Cade wanted to challenge his statement, but not his comment about Bass; none of them had ever fought any Comanche—or any other Indians; but he held the thought.

John bit his lower lip, hesitated and finally said what had been hovering in his mind since the ambush. "Maybe the prudent thing to do would be to leave. Go home."

Dish's face was a snarl. "That's runnin'. I ain't runnin'."

Harding scuffed the ground with his boot, drawing a thin line in the edgy surface. He looked up, his eyes bearing down hard on Dish. "John's right. We need a plan to get into camp without Sil's men shooting at us before we're ready."

"I didn't say that exactly." John raised his chin, showing no signs of backing down. He realized his hands still gripped the outlaw's gun. Like it was scalding hot, he separated his hands from the gun in an exaggerated retreat and watched it thud on the ground.

"That thar's a good way to git a bullet in yur leg," Dish advised.

"Not if you've been taught since you were knee-high to nothing that you never carried a bullet in that chamber." John's response was surprisingly hostile.

Ignoring his older brother's show of courage, Dish said,

"Well, boys, what's next? Sil's men are waitin' fer them to come back an' celebrate us bein' daid."

"They'll kill our men." John's plaintive comment matched his eyes. "Maybe we should go ask Paw what to do."

"Paw? What the hell are ya talkin' about, John? He'll be full liquored by now. Wouldn't ev'n know who ya was. If'n he did, he'd figger it were yur fault. Damn, don't ya know that?"

Harding folded the signed confession and placed it carefully within his inside coat pocket. "Remember, we don't have anything on Sil's men. Nothing. Not even a drunk and disorderly charge. We'll also need one of them to tell us where the Red River place is. We'll get the Rangers to shut that down."

"You saying they can go free?" Dish challenged.

"Yes, if they'll do it peaceful like. I want them out of the valley. Gone. Tonight." Harding paused. "All except one of them to give us the directions and . . ."

"Bass Manko." Dish's response was quick and eager.

"That's the one. He'll have to stand trial for murdering my Henry. The boy here told us that, clear and true. Right, sonny boy?"

"B-Bass Manko, well, yeah."

John walked over to Cade. "Cade, are you all right with that?"

Dish stared at him as did Harding. No one spoke for three long seconds. Waiting.

"I say we ride for camp. Take the herd with us. One of us dresses like Sil. Rides up front," Cade finally declared. "They'll be lookin' for four riders. We'll give 'em four. Maybe we can get close enough to surprise them and keep this thing from getting bad."

He glanced at Black Jack and the strange man only

smiled his appreciation for Cade's strategy and swung down from his mule.

"What about our men, Cade?" John asked.

"They'll have to be surprised too. We can't risk anything else."

"I-I could ride in first, tell them that Dish an' you an' the marshal were killed—and ask for our men to come with me to help with the bodies." His voice weakened as the expressed thought became real in his mind.

"How 'bout that, Cade? Won't that work?" Dish asked.

Harding spat. "Once they know you boys are done, likely they'll shoot John where he stands—and your boys would be next." The stern Welsh manner was prominent in his observation.

Folding his arms over his chest, John suggested he tell Sil's men that everyone had been wounded and needed help so Bar 6 men would come back with him. Cade pointed out Sil's men would want to know whether the ambushers were hurt or dead. Whatever he said would be the wrong answer in terms of how they would react.

"We'll do it Cade's way. But what about Manko?" Dish's face was taut.

"Bass is mine." Cade's visage matched his brother's.

"I ain't dressin' like no farmer." Dish jerked his head sideways to look again at Sil.

"I will." Cade headed for the dead man.

With Black Jack's help, Cade took Sil's hat and overalls. At first, he balked at wearing the red undershirt but finally decided it was necessary for the disguise. Even the buffalo hunter had difficulty dealing with the rancid smell as he yanked the shirt from the dead man.

"Lordy, Lordy, that there is worse'n a sun-baked dead buffalo," Black Jack declared, holding the shirt by a corner.

"I've got to wear it. Give it to me." Cade swallowed and accepted the foul clothing. He gagged and shook his head. His nostrils burned with the acrid odor.

Black Jack laughed and so did Dish. Without any comment, John removed the long coat and hat from the dead outlaw and put them on. When they got to the bottom of the knoll, Dish saw the curled body of the tall outlaw and decided to wear his hat. Black Jack agreed to circle wide around the camp and provide unexpected support from the opposite side if it was needed. Harding would do the same. The fourth rider, they decided, would be young Lennie, who was warned the first bullet would be for him if something went wrong.

A bawling cow interrupted the walk to their horses, making each man reach for his gun. Even John grabbed for the outlaw weapon now in his waistband.

Realizing what it was, Dish pointed at the swollen udder, a sign of a lost calf. "When we gits to camp, better see she gits milked a'fur lettin' her go. Maybe thar'll be a calf in need o' a mother." He realized the significance of his statement and shook his head. "Wal, if'n we gits to camp." He waved his hand at the cow and it quickly turned back to the shadows that were the rest of the herd.

"Yeah, her calf's dead," John said. "I saw it back in the brush. Tried to milk her but she didn't like the idea. I thought a little walking would do her good." He looked at Dish, then at Cade. "We're not going to get out of this, are we? I've been praying but I—"

"Don't count us out yet, John," Cade interrupted, his voice soft and calming. "But we're going to need you. Can you shoot if it comes to that?"

"I won't let you down—or Dish."

"Thanks, John. Maybe we can do this without gunfire."

Cade folded his clothes, squeezed his hat into his saddle-bag and tied his long coat to the back of the saddle. He placed his rolled gunbelt and holster in the leather bag but shoved his pistol into the overalls pocket. Only his choker and the eagle feather on his hat were handled carefully. They were placed in the other bag where Winter Kill's medicine bundle was stored. He returned the badge to Harding for safe keeping.

The old lawman wasn't sure what he should make of the returned star but took it without comment.

Dish thought they should ride the outlaw's horses and let their mounts go with the herd and the other horses. Cade agreed. They asked Lennie to tell them which one Sil rode. The ill-tempered sorrel was easy to pick out anyway and John didn't think Cade should try to ride it. Dish figured he had to if they had any chance of getting close.

Cade agreed.

"Watch 'im, tho, Cade. Damn thang'll try to throw ya."

"Thanks."

He swung into the saddle and sat there, waiting. The sorrel's belly heaved once, twice, and Cade felt the animal bunch itself to explode. He drove his spurs into its flanks and surprised the horse. A crowhop followed, then another. Each time, Cade spurred it. Each time the next jump was less intense. Finally, Sil's horse lowered its head and began to walk.

"Wal, I do believe ya made yur point," Dish observed.

John quickly added, "Be careful, Cade. He's no good."

"Fits, doesn't it?" Cade patted the sorrel's neck in spite of his dislike for the horse.

Five minutes later they were headed out. A rich texture of gold, violet and rose crawled across the dusking sky as they rode toward the roundup camp.

Harding clapped his leathery hand across the back of his neck to rid himself of a pesky horsefly. The old lawman sucked long at the rawhide air. It didn't help. He stared at Cade Branson as if in a trance. Finally he raised his stiffened leg to relieve the ache and spat defiantly. But he avoided anyone's eyes. His own were filmy as they searched for something on the hillside.

"I should've known early on that something was wrong. I did, sort of. No more than last spring. Sissy said it first. At the breakfast table. I knew she was right. I just didn't want to be bothered. Too much to do." His breath came in stutter-steps. "I told myself I was seeing snakes where there were only sticks. Worried, maybe, the gossip was right, that I was too old to do lawing anymore." He rubbed his chin like it itched fiercely. "That's when I started staying in town some nights. Prowling around quiet-like—and watching to see what the cat dragged home."

"You were watching Missus Rice." Cade's statement was more of a question.

"Yes. But all I had was that necklace—and the fact she left town on nights when there was rustling in the valley."

"You're leaving something out."

Harding looked down and rubbed the butt of his Winchester resting in its saddle sheath. "Aye, I saw Bass leave too."

"But . . . why?"

"Why did I make him a deputy?" Harding looked around for something to spit at. He choose a jagged bush, spraying only a drooping branch. "Two reasons, I reckon. First, I thought it was the best way to get you interested. Second, even if you didn't come, I wanted him close." He inhaled slowly and spat again, not aiming at anything. "Didn't know he had been the one who killed Henry. I wouldn't have given him the star if I did. No matter what."

Cade's eyes widened. "The Trenchards? When you told them, was . . ."

"Now you're underrating an old lawdog, son," Harding said. "Bass stayed outside. The Trenchards have a fine looking daughter, you know. She was interested in talking to him."

Their conversation slid into silence as they passed a familiar rock formation, shaped like an Indian peering into the future, some said. Dish never could see anything resembling any person in the rock structure. Cade remembered to himself Wind-in-the-Valley telling him it was a sign that stone was the most ancient of people and the wisest, if a man ever listened.

Dish motioned for John to swing wide to keep the cattle from spreading out too far. "Ya gotta keep 'em tight, John. This hyar bunch'll break fer it, if'n we don't."

Cade nodded. They were headed into trouble and his brother was worried about cattle.

"No offense, son, but has anybody ever said you move just like an Indian? All silk and smooth." Harding studied the young man as he spoke. "Damn glad you're on my side."

"Well, thanks, I guess," Cade said. "Say, you never did answer me about the bank. You think there's going to be a holdup there? No one's in town to stop them."

"Roper's there. Seth went in too. Not one thing we can do about it from here, if they choose this time for mischief elsewhere." Harding acted as if he wanted to say more.

"Yeah, I guess so."

"Hell's teeth, if you don't look just like Sil," Harding changed the subject. "Dammit all, I suppose we're going to miss supper. Had my mouth all set for some more of Toolie's stew," he teased and wiped the back of his hand across his mouth. "You should've tasted the cooking my Dorothy could put up. Boy, I'll tell you, it was enough to raise a fellow up to swearing he'd never sin again. My son would like that, come to think of it."

Cade laughed.

Harding chuckled at his own statement, then pulled out the remaining square of tobacco and bit into it. He offered the rest to Cade.

"No, thanks," Cade replied and added quickly, "Don't be too hard on Seth. He'll be a good man. A good minister, if that's what he chooses. He just needs some living."

Harding cocked his head to the side. "Oh, I know. He's like his mother. Just like her. All full of phrasing—and the good Book. Told her once that those Bible stories were full of fighting, killing and lusting around and she didn't speak to me for almost a week. Damn, if she didn't." He chuckled. "Wish she were here, Cade. Her and my two other . . . sons. Now they were fighting men, like you. Lord a'mercy. That awful War took them from me."

"I'm sure you do miss . . . all of them. She sounds like a great woman—an' they must've—"

"No man'll ever have better than a woman who stands beside him." He turned away, coughed and spat.

Chapter Twenty-Three

Sweet silence gradually overtook them as the sun finally surrendered. After each man chewed on thoughts only he understood, Cade said the Comanche thought silence was a virtue, a sign of being close to God. Harding seemed fascinated by the thought, saying it over to himself as if preparing to share it with others at the right time.

Cade guessed the first to hear it would be Susannah. He wanted to tell the old man more but found himself increasingly focused on keeping Sil's horse from bolting; the animal smelled camp. The big sorrel shook its head and yanked on the reins, and kept gathering itself to run. Cade steadied the animal with his legs and low, easy words. And constant restraint with the reins.

Harding shuffled his boots in the stirrups and began telling Cade about seeing Elizabeth Rice. He said she could make a man forget to think about much else. She tried to make him think she was interested in him awhile back. Smiling, he said he was no prize and began to wonder about the late Tobias Rice. He wasn't much better looking, or younger, than the lawman was. Harding's drawled conclusion was that the woman was actually capable of murder—or anything else—to get what she wanted.

When he saw her wearing the Richardson locket, he knew immediately something wrong had happened to his friends. She had volunteered the source of the gift, just as he had told Sil. That led him to check into Absalum Sil's back trail in New Orleans. A warrant for his arrest for murder and larceny was waiting for him. So was one for an Elizabeth Franklin, whose description matched that of Widow Rice.

Cade knew the old man wanted to talk more but he was getting anxious. "We'd better get ready. Camp is just beyond that ridge. I'll take Lennie with me and get out front."

"Right, son."

Dark clouds sashayed across the murky purple sky, prodded by a wind that showed signs of bravado. Dusk sounds were comforting, mixed with those of the cattle, assuring the riders everything was in its right place and nothing harmful was near. Soon the campfire glow appeared as if it were magic. But its flickering gold didn't yield the usual friendly feeling. Only a gnawing sensation of trouble drawing closer.

"Spread out best you can," Cade whispered as he pulled the brim of his hat lower on his forehead and nudged his horse forward. He shook his head to ward off the odor from Sil's shirt. "Lennie, get up here with me."

Harding nodded, realized Cade might not be able to see his visual agreement in the creeping darkness and said, "We'll be ready. Ride with God, son. Keep the wind in your fist."

"Better take off your badge, Marshal. The fire might reflect off it."

"Sure. I'll tend to that right now."

Sil's horse snorted, stomped its hooves and pulled on the reins. Cade wanted to jab his spurs into the cantankerous animal but decided against it. Instead, he yanked back on the reins to make certain the horse understood who was in control. The horse jigged, then began to walk nicely. Cade rode alongside the young outlaw and told him what he was to do. Together, they trotted around Dish, toward the front of the herd.

"I'll have my gun at yur haid, Lennie boy," Dish warned as they passed. "Don't do anythin' stupid." He licked his chapped and split lips. A lonely wisp of firelight slashed across his rugged face and lantern jaw, making him look even more like his father than usual.

Lennie nodded and shivered. The young man's boot slipped from a stirrup and he barely caught himself. Embarrassment popped through the veneer of confidence and paraded across his face. He didn't know whether or not to joke about it but saw Cade wasn't watching him and Dish couldn't see that clearly in the darkness. At least he hadn't dropped the reins.

"What if they don't . . . give up?" Lennie asked, raising his chin defiantly.

"We'll be outnumbered. You'll be dead." Cade levered his Winchester into readiness and laid it across the saddle in front of him. His fingers caressed the trigger.

Night sounds disappeared into an eerie tension as they neared the fire. A strange yet familiar chill rolled up Cade's back and settled in his head. He was calm; everything in him was still. He took a deep breath, drawing in the velvet cool air. He wiped each hand on Sil's overalls, as if to help him pierce the darkness ahead. Moonlight washed stingily across the herd as he moved to the front with Lennie only a stride behind. Ahead, dark shapes were appearing near the campfire's yellow blossom. Cade was thirty feet away and closing.

"Here comes Sil an' the boys now. How'd ya do, Boss? Did ya find them Mex bastirds? I see ya got the herd they stole." A choked-off snicker followed as a lanky shadow stepped forward to meet them.

Cade recognized the smirking speaker as Jordan Maher, acting as the Circle R foreman. Cade inhaled and nearly gagged. His back jolted to relieve his body of the stench. Winter wind swept through his soul and he could see the camp well. Bass Manko was nowhere in sight. He held up his hand with his thumb folded against it to indicate the four men Sil went after. He moved the hand to his mouth and whispered, "Lennie, say we got all of them."

Lennie glanced at Cade, then at Maher. "Y-Yeah we got . . . all of them."

A threat of concern tiptoed into Cade's mind. Where was Bass? He hadn't resolved the accusation of his involvement yet, but he didn't like the idea of him getting an edge either. Could he take Bass with a gun? Probably neither of them would live. He concentrated on Maher, who was moving closer.

"What's next, Boss? Like we planned?"

A pumpkin-faced man with leather cuffs jumped from the darkness. "Hey, that's not Sil, that's—"

"Cade Branson." Cade reined the sorrel, raised his Winchester and pointed it at both men. "Sil's dead. So are the other two. Lennie here has signed a confession. The land grab's over, boys. You can ride out—or you can die. Right here, right now."

"There's only three o' ya, Branson." The pumpkin-faced man's gaze settled on Cade.

"Try again."

"I got the fat'un, Cade." Black Jack's hearty announcement bristled through the night. The old buffalo hunter was settled next to the horse remuda.

"I've got Maher—and the fellow behind him with the long gun." Marshal Harding's distinctive Welsh voice seemed to float unconnected to anything or any place. The stumpy outlaw standing three feet behind Maher dropped his rifle and raised his hands.

Cade guessed the lawman was behind the grove of trees west of the campfire but wasn't certain. He spoke quietly to Sil's horse and hoped the animal would stand. What it would do if shooting started was anybody's guess.

From the left side of the herd Dish yelled, "Bar 6, git yur iron. You too, Half-Moon 5 an' River S. Ev'rbody else is ag'in us. I'll 'splain later. Go! Nobody else better move—I kin see ri't good an' I'd like to do sum shootin'."

Shadows jumped. Jingling spurs signaled a rush toward bedrolls or the chuck wagon for weapons. Somewhere in the gray, near the wagon, Toolie's shotgun boomed into the air and his broken German followed, "Oooch mein lieber Gott! Ich haben ein . . . more barrel, who wants this?"

From every corner of camp, Bar 6 cowboys returned, running with rifles and handguns. Half-Moon 5 and River S riders joined them. They stood in a semi-circle behind the gathered outlaws. Slowly, Sil's men raised their hands. Jordan Maher looked around and did the same.

The pumpkin-faced outlaw's right hand slid behind his back.

Wham!

Black Jack's Sharps carbine tore into the night.

The outlaw was slammed forward like he was hit from the back with a sledge hammer. His revolver flipped into the air, then thudded against a log. Out of control, his body slid and bounced on the ground. He raised a wavering hand toward Maher and opened his mouth to speak. Only blood came. His face and hand shuddered to the earth.

From the horse string, Black Jack snarled, "Sorry, Cade, that's the second fella today that's tried sneakin' 'round. I don't like it, jes' don't like it."

Cade swung his rifle back and forth along the gray men standing still. "Do what I say and you'll make it through this night. The next one who tries something dooms all of you. Got it? Now unbuckle your gunbelts." He watched the outlaws quickly comply with his order. "Decker, I know you carry a gun in your boot." He looked around the campfire as it painted gold on strained faces. "Valera, the knife too."

From the trees, Harding commanded, "Jimmy Pierson, don't make me guess where you keep that derringer, laddie."

Glaring at the young outlaw, Dish rode alongside Cade. Dish's beady eyes sought one particular target. "Where's Bass?" he yelled. "Where's Bass Manko?"

"I ain't seed him . . . since a'fer you rode in. No sir, I ain't," Maher answered, looking around as he spoke.

"He's tellin' it straight." The bruised-ribbed Willy stepped into the light of the campfire and waved his arms in support, wincing slightly as he did.

Pistol shots snarled in the night. The sickening sound of bullets striking flesh followed. Then came Black Jack's choke-filled curse and the roar of his Sharps again. A galloping horse disappeared into the night.

Cade was stunned.

"Goddammit, that were Manko," Dish snarled. "He dun shot Black Jack."

The white blaring in Cade's mind told him Bass had shot Black Jack and escaped. So it was all true. His best friend was a murderer and a thief. He needed to think. He must think. His mother told him that his real father considered this the mark of a great man. The ability to think under pressure—and act accordingly. Think, then act boldly.

"This would be a bad time to try something." The words oozed from his mouth without help. "No, I'd like that. One of you try something. Please."

But he would have to wait until Sil's gang was completely under control, no matter how badly he wanted to see his old mentor. Fury was climbing alongside his other feelings. A breeze hastened to his face and was gentle and cooling. If anyone moved, the man would not see the sunrise. This he vowed aloud. A dark part of him truly wished for such an encounter and he tightened his grip on his weapon. Patience.

"Somebody try something. Come on." Cade's soft words belied the cold storm building within him. "Who wants to fight me? No guns. Just fists. You and me. All alone. Come on, isn't there one of you yellow bastards who's a man?"

The only response was from Willy. "They all dun know'd ya whipped Big Ed Gilmore, Cade."

It was Dish who finally calmed him. "Easy, li'l brother. No one's gonna fi't ya. None o' these bastirds got that kinda guts. This hyar's over. You go on an' see how ol' Black Jack be. We got 'em covered." He looked away from Cade and eased his horse closer to Sil's surrendered men. "Ya see, boys, yur real close to dyin'. Real close." He shook his head. "Marshal, ar' all these peckerhaids free to ride or is thar sum ya want fer other thangs an' sech?"

"I want all of them out of this valley—by sunrise. Any one of them left on this range will be run down and shot like the dog he is." Harding's voice was coming from a different location now. It sounded like he spat into a pile of dead branches.

"Señor Branson, what about our clothes, our theengs—at ze Circle R?" The question came from a stout Mexican called Valera.

"Ya git a hoss from the string. That an' yur life."

"*Sí*."

"An' don't cross Bar 6 land when ya git."

Harding's command added a further restriction. "Valera, you and Jordan will stay behind with us. You're going to show us where that box canyon is—and the ranch at the Red."

Gold from the campfire struck the closest side of Jordan Maher's face as it slid into surprise.

"We know all about them so don't insult us with some lame-dog tale," Harding barked. "And if the rest of you know what's good for you, you won't ride north either. We will assume you're headed for that Red River ranch—and you won't get there, or anywhere. Got that, boys?"

Cade spurred Sil's horse without thinking about the consequences. The animal crowhopped, then spurted toward the shadowy line of horses.

Seeing the downed Black Jack beside a cottonwood ten feet from the closest tied horse, he reined hard and the sorrel dropped its rear end and skidded its back hooves in the dirt to stop. He jumped down while the horse was still moving. Cade dropped his rifle and hurried to the body, leaving the reins to supply a ground tie or let the animal run. He didn't care. Next to the tree was a crumbling skull of a buffalo, half buried in the earth. He was struck by the coincidence.

"Black Jack? Black Jack? Are you . . . ?" Kneeling beside him, Cade cradled the old buffalo hunter's head in his arms.

Sante's eyes rolled open under blood-smeared spectacles. His bloody right hand trembled toward Cade. The young gunfighter saw his shirt was mostly dark from fresh blood. It was hard to tell where his shirt ended and his crimson sash began. Bass's aim was good. Too good.

"T-This t-time . . . I ain't ridin' no more. Reckon I-I'll scout . . . on ahead fer ya, Cade. You remind me . . . of your father . . . Winter Kill. He were somethin'. I were with them Rangers that . . . kilt him an' his warriors. He went down fightin' like ten. I kept meanin' to tell ya . . . You ride proud, ya hear? Bin mighty nice . . . knowin' . . ."

His eyes shut and Black Jack was still. Cade stared at the unseeing eyes. Questions welled up from his soul. Why hadn't Black Jack told him that before? How did he know? Had he talked with Cade's mother when the Rangers brought her back?

It seemed like an hour before Dish came to tell him that all of Sil's men had ridden away, except for Valera and Jordan Maher. Solemnly, Cade said he would bury Black Jack here and place the buffalo skull on his grave, then go after Bass Manko. Gently, Cade removed one of Black Jack's bead necklaces and put it on himself. He fingered the eagle's claw and shut his eyes for a moment.

John offered to bury the body so Cade could pursue Bass with the marshal and immediately went to the chuck wagon to get a shovel. Cade spoke quietly to the unmoving Black Jack in Comanche. He stepped over to the skull, pulled the earth away from it with his fingers and yanked it free. Only the horns and eye-socket structure remained. A garland of black dirt surrounded the base as he placed it alongside Black Jack. He knelt beside the dead man and removed the eagle feather from the buffalo hunter's hair and tied it to the skull in tribute. John returned and Cade asked him to place the skull over the grave. Solemnly, he said he would return to talk with Black Jack's spirit. John wasn't certain what to say and could only mutter that he would do as Cade asked.

After watching his younger brother in silence, Dish left and ordered several riders to help move the small herd to the larger gathering. Since all of the nighthawks on duty were either Bar 6 or Half-Moon 5 riders, he didn't worry about changing them but ordered a sweep of the camp to make sure none of Sil's men were still around.

Marshal Harding spoke quietly to the young outlaw and Lennie kicked his horse and rode away into the darkness without looking back. Responding to the questions, the old lawman began telling curious Bar 6 hands and the other rangemen what had happened. One asked what would become of the three ranches owned by Sil and Rice; Harding said that would be up to the judge. Another asked if Widow Rice would be hanged and Harding said she would if she were convicted. So would Bass Manko, he added.

Cade switched to his own clothes and gunbelt from his saddlebags, returning his pistol to its holster. He withdrew his hat, stroked the eagle feather to return it to shape and jammed the hat on his head. He said something quietly to himself as he retied the choker around his neck. Sil's clothes were tossed into the fire. He stood near the renewed flames letting their heat take away the remaining smell from his body. But they couldn't remove the ache of Black Jack Sante being killed by his best friend.

Harding insisted he put the deputy badge back on. His quiet words with Jordan Maher produced an accurate description of where both the hidden canyon was and the Red River half-way ranch. Rice had renamed it the "KL" but the outlaw didn't know what that stood for.

Dish decided to keep the outlaw's high-crowned hat; he liked the way it fit. Unable to make up his mind about what he should do, John laid the outlaw's coat and hat in the chuck wagon for later determination.

After January was saddled, Cade and Harding rode away from the roundup camp, headed for town. Bass Manko's tracks went in that direction and the old lawman thought they needed to see if everything was all right in Deer Creek. Dish wanted to go with them but knew his place was with the men and their cattle. As he said, they had a roundup to finish. John wasn't certain whether he should stay or go along but Cade told him to stay. Dish also volunteered to keep the now-bound Valera and Jordan Maher until they could check out the canyon. Harding said neither man was to be allowed to leave until he returned.

Marshal Harding and Deputy Branson rode hard, not trying to track Bass in the darkness. Both thought he would head for town—and Elizabeth Rice. Night was fully in charge when Harding and Cade saw a rider pushing his horse hard toward them.

"Who's that coming?" Cade asked. "Is that Seth?"

"Yes, I believe it is," Harding agreed. "He went to town to help Roper in the office."

"Well, he isn't coming to put on a prayer meeting."

"Don't be too sure about that."

Seth tried to rein his lathered horse but the frantic animal wouldn't stop.

"Turn him in a circle, Seth," Harding urged. "Not too tight or he'll fall down. Real easy now. He's liking the running. Give him time, lad. Give him time."

The two men watched as the young Harding gradually slowed the horse into a circular walk. Seth's eyes were wide and his clothes were wrinkled and dirty, sweat seeping from under his cockeyed hat.

Finally, he blurted, "S-She tried to hold up the bank.

S-She was dressed like B-Bass Manko. Missus Rice." He stared at Cade as he spoke.

"When did this happen, Seth?" Harding asked, spitting straight at the ground beside him and strafing his own horse's right front leg.

"Ah, yesterday. Late afternoon, it was."

Harding looked at Cade, shrugged and said, "Tell us what happened."

Seth was eager to talk about the unbelievable situation happening so suddenly. He had even thought of a perfect Bible quotation to share, mentioning the idea twice without either Cade or Harding asking to hear it. In an excited voice, he told about Susannah unexpectedly coming to town and going directly to the bank president. When Elizabeth Rice came in the door, every man in the bank held a gun. Susannah too. She was wearing a deputy's badge. He was disappointed his father felt it was necessary to have her involved and not him.

Afterward, she had shared Harding's hunch and her orders from their father to warn the bank.

Harding nodded. "There is lovely when plans work the way they're supposed to."

Pounding the air for emphasis, Seth declared, "I knew that Rice woman was evil. I knew it. Hearing she had theater posters in her house was the last straw. Those things belong to the devil. So does her saloon and her house of . . . of bad women. She's evil." His face glowed with righteousness.

Harding spat, barely missing Seth's boots. "Could be, son. Could be. What do you think, Cade?"

Without waiting for Cade's response, he explained Elizabeth Rice's strategy. Obviously, the trick was to show evidence of the Bar 6 being sold before the deaths of the Bransons—without there being any financial exchange actually occuring. And, of course, without any agreement from Titus Branson himself. The last part was simple: forge his signature on a deed and keep it secret until the right moment. The money part was harder. A well-timed bank robbery seemed the right tactic. Especially when the town marshal was gone.

So Hiram Princeton, acting as Titus Branson's attorney, would deposit money in Titus Branson's name that represented payment for his ranch. Princeton would tell the banker about the reason for the large deposit. Rice or someone working for her would follow and rob the bank, removing those funds and any other on hand. Only the record of the funds being deposited would remain. He didn't know how she would do it, or if it would actually be her, but he knew it would happen.

Cade was jolted by the declaration of Susannah's involvement and the lawman's expectation. "You told Susannah that you expected the bank to be robbed? And you sent her to warn everyone. Why didn't you tell me?"

Chapter Twenty-Four

Marshal Harding grinned. His apology rolled out in typical Welsh fashion. "There is sorry I am that I didn't."

"That's it?"

"Well, if truth be told, I was afraid you would worry about my Sissy and I needed you thinking straight."

"What do you mean?"

"Now, son, old I may be but I'm not dead. Are you going to tell me you don't have feelings for my daughter?" Harding cocked his head to the side.

"Well, yes . . . but there's . . . Bass—an' my brother Dish."

"Do you think she would be caring for a man like Bass? You think Susannah should have a say about which Branson she wants to be with?"

"Dish will own the Bar 6 after . . . Paw dies."

"Aye, he will at that. Do you be saying my daughter will choose owning things over being with the man she wants?"

Cade swallowed, unsure of what to say. In the corner of

his mind, the fact that he was a halfbreed waited for an opening to come out.

Seth could hold back his quote no longer. " 'All they that take the sword shall perish with the sword.' "

"Well, sometimes—and a lot of folks who never pick up a sword get cut up by those swinging it everywhere they go," Harding snorted. "That's the problem with preachers. They spout stuff that's thick with words and thin on muscle. Most of them don't sing so well either. Unless they're Welsh."

"Oh, I don't agree at all, father." Seth was as indignant as he ever was with his father. "Preacher Reese was absolutely thrilling last Sunday."

Cade wanted to hear more about Susannah and her feelings but sensed Seth wasn't yet to the end of his story. "So, Missus Rice is in jail, right?"

Harding smiled victoriously.

"W-Well, no, that's why I w-was coming to g-get you."

"What? What do you mean? Good Lord, tell us. Is Sissy all right?" Harding's eyes narrowed and tore into his son.

From deep within his stomach, fear came thudding against Cade's throat.

Seth looked down at his saddlehorn, rubbing it furiously.

"Seth, is she?" Cade's stare was even more urgent than Harding's.

Finally, Seth said Bass Manko had surprised he and Roper in the jail, clubbed the old man with his revolver and both rode out of town before anyone knew. Susannah wasn't there at the time; she was talking with the mayor, explaining the situation and the marshal's strategy.

Cade's relief was audible; Harding, only his eyes changed.

"How did Bass get in the jail? Wasn't it locked?" Harding asked, his gaze returning to formidable.

"No, it wasn't. You never lock it so I-I didn't either. B-Bass just burst in . . . before we . . . knew he was there. R-Roper went for the shotgun. He had it on your desk. Bass hit him over the head . . . with his gun barrel." Seth paused and looked away. "I-I'm afraid blood went all over your papers."

"Damn my papers, son, how bad be Roper hurt?" Harding's face was a wrinkled worry.

"I-I don't know. Susannah and the doctor were with him when I left." Seth said. "Bass and the widow . . . got away."

"Let's ride, Cade."

"Wait for me, Father."

Cade and Harding popped their horses and darkness swallowed them quickly. Seth wheeled his horse awkwardly around and slapped the reins against its flank. A lumbering lope followed, then the horse gradually took the bit again and flattened into a run.

After an hour of hard riding, Cade yelled they must let their horses stop and rest or they wouldn't make it to town.

Reluctantly, Harding agreed and pulled up on the prairie with no thought of where they were or what was just over the next rise. The old lawman eased down from his tired horse, more quiet than usual. He rolled his shoulders to eliminate their ache and tried to walk off the growing pain in his knee.

Cade reminded him of a small creekbed twenty yards to the west and suggested they lead their horses there and let them water.

"They be too hot to drink," Harding observed and squatted on the ground, holding the reins. "We'll stay here until they cool down. They'll smell it soon enough."

Nodding agreement, Cade knelt on one knee. One question galloped through his mind as fast as their horses had been running: How did Harding know the bank robbery was going to happen? The question followed him like a hungry calf after its mother.

Seth limped toward the two men, leading his horse.

"What's the matter, Seth?"

"Oh, I banged my knee against the desk when I left."

Harding shifted the chaw to his other cheek and observed dryly, "Read a little of that fine Gospel over it and that will make it go away."

Seth wasn't certain whether his father was kidding or not. "It's just sore." Seth stood on one leg and shook the other before continuing. His walk immediately improved and he headed toward them.

"Things not always be what they seem," Harding began without prompting. "Hiram Princeton, for example. A man too fond of intoxicating drink, for sure. But a man whose friendship with Emil Richardson goes far beyond any monetary reward such as Mrs. Rice might entice him with."

"Princeton told you what was going to happen."

"Right you are, right you are. Amazing isn't it, how smart an old lawman becomes when he has good help."

A half hour later, they skirted across a line of lumpy hills south of Deer Creek. A Texas sun pulled itself slowly from the earth, creating blurred silhouettes against the cold horizon. Overhead an owl watched them, sailing on unseen billows of crisp autumn air. Morning found the three riders returning to a town yawning to life. Weariness had overtaken their zeal of an hour ago. Marshal Harding was dozing in the saddle, Seth was humming a hymn and Cade Branson was remembering the good times with Bass Manko and trying not to think about what he must face—and what he must do.

Through the maze of yesterdays, Susannah kept walking

into his mind. Could he ever tell her of his heritage? Could he handle the rejection once she knew? She deserved to know, he told himself. Did she really care about him as the old lawman indicated, or was it a father's wishful thinking? What would the marshal think, knowing he was a half-breed?

What would his mother say if she was alive? How would Susannah take the news about Elizabeth Rice—and Bass Manko? His mind pounded with each thrust of his horse's hooves.

He knew two things for certain. First, that he loved her more than anything he could ever imagine. And second, he was immensely proud of her; she had stopped the bank holdup and the removal of the financial setup to control the Bar 6. Marshal Harding had trusted her with an important part of his plan to stop the land grab. A dangerous part.

Looking back at it, the old lawman felt he had no one else he could trust. If he had told the bank president earlier, the story would have spread across town in hours and his secondary trap would have failed. Cade now understood why the marshal had to go to the roundup. Only then would the outlaws' strategy begin. Harding had gambled with the lives of the Branson boys and made no apologies for it. That was the Welsh in him—or was it the way of a savvy lawman everyone had underrated?

A sawmill was the first structure to greet them, then came the familiar rooftops of two-story buildings that pushed against the sky. The echoing clang of a blacksmith signaled their entrance onto the main street. A string of freight wagons were getting an early start at hauling cotton bales.

An inebriated businessman having difficulty with his horse and buggy passed them without realizing they were near. There was an unspoken urgency in town that comes with the advent of autumn and the realization winter isn't far behind. They passed a livery, busy with harnesses and buggies being readied, followed by rows of false-fronted buildings on both sides of the street. The streets and planked sidewalks were empty. Signs in retail establishments offered an array of services and products but no one was around to notice.

As they rode beside the closed general store, someone stepped out of the marshal's office farther down the street, holding a cup of coffee.

It was Susannah Harding.

Cade would know her anywhere. His heart jumped. She stood taking in the morning's crispness, letting the white steam of the coffee embrace her. Long brown hair lay undone and hatless upon her shoulders. A long coat covered her shape yet didn't. Her thoughts were somewhere else until something pulled her gaze toward the end of town. The badge pinned to her shirt twinkled a welcome. She turned toward the three riders, raising her hand over her eyes to help clarify her vision. Certain of her hunch, she raised a hand over her head and waved.

"Marshal, ah . . . Sus—ah—your daughter is outside your office. She sees us," Cade said. An eagerness lit his voice.

"Well, good. I imagine she's right happy to see her father again." Harding tried to hide a smile.

"I'm sure she is."

"You ride on ahead. I'm still a bit creaky this morning."

"Yes sir." Cade kicked his gray horse into a lope and the tired animal responded immediately. He didn't hear Harding's appreciative chuckle.

"Why is Cade riding ahead of us, Father?" Seth asked from his position to the left of Harding.

"Oh, that boy is always in a hurry, it seems."

"I think he wants to see Susannah."

"Oh, really?"

Cade swung his horse into the railing and leaped down, leaving the reins ground-tied. In three strides he was holding her in his arms.

"Oh, Cade, I was so worried. If something ever happened to you I don't know what I would do."

Her body pressed against his and all the weariness of the night vanished. He held her to him as he had wanted to do for so long. They were the only two people in the world for a few precious moments. He kissed her cheek and she kissed his. Their mouths found each other.

"Don't you go staring, Seth," Harding said as he pulled his horse into the railing.

"Shameless," Seth said haughtily.

"That it is, son, that it is." Harding spat toward the street, missed and hit the sidewalk, splattering brown juice across its planked edges.

He swung from the saddle and couldn't remember feeling so tired. It seemed like weeks since he had left his home. The black filly he was training was a fading dream. But he had been right. He wasn't too old for this business at all. Even if no one ever said it, he knew.

"Hey, you two, get yourselves inside. You're going to embarrass your father, Sissy."

Susannah pulled slightly away from Cade, glanced at Harding and laughed. She turned back to Cade and found his mouth again. She discovered Black Jack's bead necklace as her fingers explored his neck and face.

"Where did this come from?"

"It belonged . . . to Black Jack Sante." He swallowed. "Bass killed him."

Her forehead furrowed with sadness. "I-I'm sorry, Cade. Father has told me about him—and that he was a friend."

"Black Jack was more . . . like a father."

She held him tight to her.

"You make that star look mighty good."

"I wasn't sure what you were looking at," she teased. "Do you want me to wear it . . . on my wedding dress?"

He laughed. "Sure, why not?" This time what he felt came easily. "I love you."

"Oh . . . I wasn't sure you would ever say it. I love you, Cade Branson."

Minutes later, they were inside the marshal's office. They were greeted by a unique aroma of tobacco, whiskey, coffee and the smoky odor of an oil lamp. The office was small but clean. All of the cells were unlocked and empty. The north wall contained a large oil painting of horses in springtime and a presentation of the U. S. Constitution.

On the opposite wall was a rack containing four rifles and two shotguns. Three wall pegs held two gunbelts, one with a long-barreled horse pistol and the other, a Colt six-shooter. One peg was empty. A coat rack in the corner was draped with a long overcoat.

Susannah hurried to turn up a gas lamp. The brighter light seemed to pull her back again to the day's events. She explained that Roper was doing well; he was resting in a hotel room and the last time she was in there he was asking for coffee with a lot of sugar. That brought relieved laughter. His head was badly cut where Bass had clubbed him but the doctor said it would heal. She also reported the bank's money was safe and Bass and Elizabeth Rice were headed west. The mayor had talked about getting together a posse but decided it was best to let the marshal and his deputy

take charge when they came. Her gaze couldn't stray from
Cade's face, even as she talked.

His eyes sought hers. "Your father told me what you did.
That was really something. You are one brave lady."

"And?" Her eyes sparkled.

"And a beautiful one."

"That's more like it. You're getting good at this."

From the second desk drawer, Harding found a whiskey
bottle and poured three glasses. Seth declined before he
even started. Cade stood beside the desk piled high with papers and now streaked with dried blood, holding Susannah's
hand. Ignoring a little spilled whiskey surrounding a dead
fly, Harding handed a filled glass to Susannah, another to
Cade and took a deep swallow of his own.

"To Roper."

"To Roper," all three added.

As they silently enjoyed the whiskey, Cade studied Susannah. There was so much he wanted to tell her. A sudden
lump in his throat came as he realized he must tell her that
he was a halfbreed. Would that change everything? How
would Emmett Harding feel about his daughter marrying a
halfbreed? He squeezed his eyes to drive away the certain
rejection. Enjoy this now, he told himself.

She sipped on her whiskey and sought his eyes. She
couldn't remember feeling happier, in spite of Roper being
hurt. In her heart, she knew Bass Manko was not a good
man. Yet, his charm was hard for any woman to resist. She
was surprised at her own reaction when she acknowledged
he had chosen Elizabeth Rice over her. It was one of relief.
Now she could have Cade. She knew there was no way he
would have expressed his feelings toward her as long as he
thought his best friend liked her.

"I'm sorry about Bass," she murmured, her eyes touching his lips.

Cade's mouth was a thin line. "Yeah, I know you . . . liked him a lot."

"No. I . . . liked you a lot—but you wouldn't let me close."

Harding put down his empty glass on the desk and walked over to the wall rack of rifles and shotguns. He lifted a double-barreled shotgun from its resting place, cracked it open and checked the loads. Satisfied, he closed it and returned to his desk.

"Where'd I put those shells? Oh, yes, here they be." He opened a shallow drawer, grabbed a handful of shotgun shells and shoved them in his coat pocket. "I hate to break up this fine party but I've got to get on the trail of those two. Tell Roper I'll see him when I get back."

"But, Dad, you haven't eaten . . . and you haven't slept either. You can't go." Susannah looked at Cade. "The town's money is safe—and they're out of your jurisdiction."

"That hasn't made much difference so far," Cade said.

"Hell's teeth, it doesn't now. They murdered my friends. That's all the jurisdiction I need." Harding's tired eyes stared at the desk.

"Susannah's right, Emmett. You stay here. I'll bring Bass and Missus Rice back," Cade put his arm on Harding's shoulder. "I know where he'll go. San Antonio."

Harding's glare signaled he didn't agree. The old lawman gathered tobacco juice in his mouth and loosed it toward the spitoon next to the desk. He missed.

"Are you saying I'm too old for this?"

"You know I'm not."

"Susannah said they headed west."

"They'll turn south."

Susannah's face was wild with worry. "Look, the mayor talked about getting a posse together. Why don't you—"

"That's an invitation for good men to get killed." Harding reopened the drawer and took more shells.

"And what are you two?" Susannah's face turned dark. Her eyes flared with anger. And fear.

Seth wanted to say something about the wonders of heaven and to ask his father if he had prayed for forgiveness of his sins but couldn't bring himself to make such a bold stand.

Without further discussion, they decided. Both Cade and Marshal Harding would go after Bass Manko and Elizabeth Rice. Susannah knew there was no use in protesting. She bit her lip to keep it from trembling and avoided looking at either her father or Cade. The two men would grab some supplies from the general store and take two horses each. Both of the mounts they came in on were worn but both wanted them for later.

"Seth, you go wake Jennings and get supplies for us. Don't forget tobacco. I'll get two more horses from the livery," Harding said. "And you two, say your goodbyes."

Cade's neck reddened but it didn't stop him from kissing Susannah as Harding closed the door.

"I just found you, Cade Branson. I expect you to come back to me," she whispered into his ear.

"Nothing will keep me away, Susannah Harding," he said and untied the choker from his neck. "Take this—as my promise. It was my father's. His name was Winter Kill. He was a Comanche war chief."

She stared at the gift, then at Cade. "Your father . . . isn't Titus?"

"No, he's not. It's a long story and I don't have time to tell you all about it now—but I wanted you to know," Cade said, his eyes searching hers for truth. "I-I love you, Susannah. I want to marry you—but you need to know who I am. I am the son of Winter Kill. I am a halfbreed, Susannah. You would not want to marry a halfbreed."

"Cade Branson, I should slap you in the face," Susannah blurted. "You think my feelings for you would change because of that? How dare you."

"B-But I . . . Dish will get the ranch. I don't have anything."

"You have me. Do you need anything else?" Susannah took a half step back and put her hands on her hips.

"If I have . . . you, I have everything." Cade choked as he spoke. "I loved you from the first time I saw you come to school. You had on a light-blue dress. With blue ribbons in your hair."

"Is that why you took one of them?" Her smile followed.

"Yes." He grinned. "I still have it."

Minutes flew in each other's arms.

Outside, the lawman finished strapping the shotgun alongside his Winchester sheath on the tall bay from the livery. Seth brought their packed saddlebags and refilled canteens. Harding told his son to ride out to the roundup and tell Dish what had happened.

Joining them, Cade was initially bothered to see Harding had brought a black horse for him but quietly decided there was some magic in that it was a match for Bass's.

Susannah stepped through the doorway, holding tight the emotions that wanted to translate into tears.

"I name you deputy in charge while I'm gone, Sissy," Harding growled. "Tell the mayor I said so."

She nodded but tears could no longer be held back. He cheeks streaked with hot strings of worry.

The old lawman spurred his bay horse into a lope, trailing his earlier horse. Cade swung the black horse to follow. January, his gray, followed at an easy lope.

Susannah watched them leave and whispered, "Come back to me, son of Winter Kill."

Chapter Twenty-Five

"Looks like you're right about them heading for the big city, Cade. And wasting no time getting there." Marshal Harding pointed at the scuffled tracks curling south five miles from Deer Creek.

"If they keep up that pace, they won't be riding." Cade glanced back at the sleepy town and knew everything he wanted was there. Susannah Harding was there.

The marshal and his deputy spurred the livery horses into a gallop, leading their own horses behind them. The two tired lawmen kept a steady pace matching the fast escape of Elizabeth Rice and Bass Manko. Land quickly became blurs of green, gray and violet. Waving buffalo grass was held in place by the distant ribbon of hills running parallel to the trail. Three hours out of town, the fugitives' hard-running horses slowed to a walk when their riders evidently decided pursuit was unlikely.

Discovery of the apparent slow-down served as a stopping place for Marshal Harding and Cade to relieve themselves, take a drink from their canteens and switch saddles to their own horses. Hardtack and corn dodgers became a mid-day meal while riding. Lost sleep from the night before came in spurts the same way, with one rider awake at all times. Continuous, monotonous riding was broken by a regular rotation of their horses while making certain the outlaws didn't turn off unexpectedly.

As the day wore on, Harding explained more of what he knew about the now-broken plot to take control of the ranches. Cade was impressed with the lawman's analytical skills. He nurtured the thought that Harding used the expectation of his going home at night to allow him to follow up on his suspicions with no one the wiser. He realized the marshal used the gossip about his being too old to lull Rice and Sil into mistakes.

Neither Elizabeth Rice, nor Bass Manko, nor Absalum Sil thought he was smart enough to figure out what they were doing. His explanations were free of egotistism and he was actually quite critical of his not realizing Bass had murdered his deputy. He said Black Jack had warned him in a cryptic sort of way about Bass before he suspected his involvement.

When it was his turn to talk, Cade found himself sharing what he knew about the Comanche way of life, especially the unique bond that existed between a warrior and his spiritual guardian. To an attentive Harding, he explained how this connection was revealed in a mystical vision. Throughout the warrior's life, his spirit guardian would speak to the warrior, understand what he needed and help guide his destiny. But it was a help not to be taken carelessly or it could leave as mysteriously as it came.

He talked easily about how the Comanche saw stone as a life-force, part of the universe around them, seen and unseen—that stone offered wisdom if man would only ask and listen. He spoke of the wonders of a medicine pipe and how it provided a man with the opportunity to connect with the Great Spirit. And the belief that man is a part of the great circle of life, not the center of it. Reluctantly, he began to tell about Wind-in-the-Valley working at the ranch and sharing these special things with him. As if his soul was nudging him ever closer to the truth, he spoke of his mother teaching him the Comanche language, as well as Spanish.

Whether weariness broke down his reluctance, or love spilling out of his heart and into words, or just his own innate tendency to attack a problem head-on, Cade told the old lawman of his true heritage. They were easing their horses through a narrow ravine surrounded by thickets of plum bushes and fat grapevines when Cade felt the truth swell within him and demand relief, regardless of the consequences.

"Marshal, you need to know something. First, I love your daughter. More than anything. You also need to know that I am a halfbreed. My father was not Titus Branson; it was a Comanche warchief. His name was Winter Kill. My mother loved him very much."

Suddenly wind snaked through the ravine, gathering cold as it came. A slice of the moving air slapped Cade's face. It was so much colder than the rest of the breezes that he couldn't help wondering if this was his father's spirit guardian reassuring him that he was doing the right thing. Or was it trying to warn him?

Brushing aside an aggressive branch, he continued, "Susannah knows this. I just told her. When we get back I want to marry her—but I won't do so if you don't give me permission." He swallowed. "I will understand if you don't. Learn-

ing this truth was . . . was difficult at first, for me, so I know
how it must hit others."

An almost invisible shrug of the older man's shoulders
followed. He spoke slowly, deliberately, as if each word were
loaded, cocked and fired from a gun. "Thank you, Cade. I
know that took great courage." He spat to the side of the
trail as they climbed out of the ravine and reentered level
ground. "Reckon it's time for me to share something too. I
know about your father—your real father."

Another heavy stream of tobacco juice punctuated his
statement. He glanced over at Cade. No sign of any emotion showed itself in the young man's tanned face. He was
riding quietly, looking straight into Harding's eyes. His
steady gaze made Harding uncomfortable. The old lawman
had never experienced a man's eyes burning through him
like that before, like a knife opening up a side of beef to find
the vitals inside.

Looking away, he pointed at the white marks on a collection of flat rocks just ahead. Horseshoe prints extended to
the south, continuing signs of their quarry heading toward
San Antonio and, by the distance between tracks, still
walking their horses.

Right now, though, that seemed unimportant.

The old lawman stared up at the autumn sun gradually
losing command of the sky. "A year back it was, I suspect.
Maybe longer. Time doesn't stay in place for me anymore.
Doesn't matter. Anyway, I was visiting Black Jack." He lowered his gaze to see if Cade would react but the young gunfighter was staring straight ahead. Harding's gaze took in the
necklace of beads around Cade's neck. "After we got
through talking about the rustling and the like, I told him
three young men were spending time around my daughter
and I was worried about what kind of men they might be."

He spat, wiped the excess from his mouth with the back of his hand. "Hell's teeth, I don't like Titus Branson. Don't like him at all. You know that. No offense, but I was worried about his two sons. If one be the lucky man, what kind of a husband would he make? Would the son be the father? I was just as worried about the one she seemed most attracted to, Bass Manko. I knew where he came from—and I knew what he was up to. Or thought I did."

Cade shook his head in disbelief. "Black Jack. That rascal. He told you. I should've guessed. Damn, did he tell the whole world?"

"No, son, he didn't. You know that. He only told me because he knew it would help me," Harding said. "He rated your father—your real father—mighty high. Said he was as close to a lord of the prairie as there ever was. Aye, those were Black Jack's very words, 'lord of the prairie.'"

"I didn't know he knew . . . until he told me when he was dying." It was Cade's turn to glance skyward. "I should've told him myself."

Harding nodded his understanding. "I only wish he could've been around to see the wedding. He would've been busting his buttons and twirling that umbrella like some winter wind had hit it."

Cade's smile split his face. From deep within came a wild yell. A rebel yell that roared across the prairie and could be heard echoing its way back to Deer Creek.

Harding chuckled. "Now, of course, my little Sissy has to agree. But I know her pretty well. I figure she's had her sights on you for some time. You just didn't know it. That's women for you."

"I only want her to be happy."

"I know she will be, son."

They rode into nightfall, both talking at the same time,

about everything from children to understanding women to good horses. Dusk was heavy upon them when Harding suggested they stop and camp for the night. A hot meal and coffee would be welcomed and their horses were leg-weary. The old marshal guessed they would reach San Antonio by mid-morning and the only thing they would gain by going on was to be so sleepy they wouldn't be much good. It was his only reference to confronting Bass Manko.

Cade readily agreed. The two men worked the tiring horses around a low barren ridge, then pushed up a narrow cut to a new plateau sitting alongside a winding, string-like creek that couldn't make up its mind which direction it should go. Overhead, one star was already encouraging its brethen to join him alongside a brazen full moon taking over the darkening sky. On the other side of the creek, a proud wild bull started up a slope then turned to look back, furious that he had been bothered.

With a casual gesture, Harding pointed to a dim path leading through the slope ahead of them. Graying light was making the loose rock cutbacks tricky as they climbed the side of the slope, even for Cade's January. Harding's horse stumbled crossing a narrow cut and nearly fell. He slid surprisingly smoothly out of the saddle to check its banged foreleg.

"Well, it's a long way from his heart," Harding said and rubbed a handful of dirt over the scrape. It didn't surprise Cade that the old lawman didn't swear at the animal when it failed him. He was an easy man to misread, Cade decided, but his true nature came out when he was around horses.

Cade motioned toward an open space among a collection of cottonwoods as a suitable camp. Harding liked the idea and decided to lead his horse instead of remounting. They slipped into the shadows and felt their weariness grow as the realization they were ending the day came over them. Cade would have preferred an area where he could have seen anyone coming more easily but this was far safer than camping anywhere near the trail. He noticed the old lawman looked years older in the fading light, or was it the strain of the day?

After watering them at the stream, the horses were picketed where the grass was ample enough to keep them content and quiet through the night. Both men liked the fact that the animals couldn't be seen from the trail either.

Cade made a small fire, close to a tree. What smoke there was would dissipate as it rose through the branches.

Harding watched his preparation and was impressed. "I like a man who's careful."

"They're the ones that get to brag around the campfire."

"You don't think they'd doubleback on us, do you?"

"No, but that's reason enough to plan for it."

Supper was quick but hot. A small pot delivered black coffee and a worn skillet heated slices of jerky and warmed sliced potatoes and a lone onion. The night itself was growing cooler but the thick stand of trees protected them from most of the wind. Still, both men wrapped themselves in their long coats and blankets as they sat and ate by the dying campfire.

The lawman made an observation about a fire making a man feel good, besides making him feel warm.

Cade agreed, but added it wasn't smart for a man to sit looking into a fire. If trouble came he wouldn't be able to adjust his eyes back to the darkness quickly enough.

Harding said it sounded like something Black Jack would say.

Cade acknowledged that's where he first heard it.

Harding studied the shadowy countenance of his young friend for a few moments, as if trying to decide something.

The old lawman scratched his unshaven, craggy face. He was tired—deep tired.

Cade was unaware of Harding's concern, concentrating on a cup of coffee. As soon as he swallowed the last sip, he laid it beside his tin plate and utensils. He would clean them in the morning.

"I'm sorry about Bass." Harding was stretched out now, not far from sleep. "I know he was a friend."

"He was my *best* friend," Cade responded. "It's hard to believe all this, Emmett. Really hard. You know, he saved my life once."

"Tell me about it." Harding rubbed his hands together to get some warmth and to get rid of the nervousness tearing at him.

Cade snapped a small stick in half and tossed the two pieces into the night. A tenseness passed over Cade's face and disappeared. He explained that Bass had coldcocked a man about to knife him while he was brawling with another man. The fight had started when the man made snide remarks about Dish. Harding silently savored the fact of a brother defending his brother even when they weren't close.

Cade wanted to tell the old lawman that he wasn't certain he could arrest Bass. Or face him in a fight. He just couldn't. Down deep, he wasn't certain whether or not part of the reason was fear. Bass Manko was better with a gun than he was. Better than anybody that he knew. Finishing the tale, the lithely-built gunfighter looked at Harding, his eyes narrowed.

The lawman was going to ask something but there was a slight rustle, barely heard, down in the blackness of the heavy trees that brought him alert. Did Cade think there was something out there? Harding stared at the trees but couldn't see or hear anything. Before Harding realized what was happening, Cade was yanking off his spurs.

"What are you doing that for? Getting ready for bed?" Harding asked, his voice brimming with an undefined concern.

"I'll be right back."

"You want me to go with you?"

"No. Stay here."

"You think there's something out there?" Harding reached for the rifle laying beside him. Next to it was his double-barreled shotgun and his shoulder-holstered Colt.

"Something's out there," Cade said and slipped into the trees. In seconds, he took a position on the far edge of the trail.

Harding figured Cade could listen better and possibly see movement. Separation was a smart tactic as well, the lawman thought. He was a little unnerved by the young man's swift movements in response to a sound Harding wasn't sure he had heard at all. Most likely, it was just wind.

Looking up at him, Cade motioned he was going into the darkness and circle their position to see what was there. Harding gripped the rifle in his hands. He tried to shift his stiffened right knee for comfort without making any noise. But his spurs jingled as loud as church bells in the night air. He cocked his Winchester and the rhythmic "click-click" was, at least, reassuing.

If there was someone out there, they would have to come from the direction Cade went, wouldn't they. Harding wondered to himself.

Absentmindedly, he swallowed his chaw, almost choking as it went down. He gagged on the tobacco's bitterness, squeezing his eyes tightly to keep the tears from following the awful taste. That was embarrassing. Now he was sweating in spite of the night's coolness.

Harding was amazed at the muted silence of their surroundings. He looked over at their tied horses and jerked back. Nocturnal whispers had totally disappeared, leaving only the low song of the horses grazing. Even more surprising, he couldn't even hear Cade moving through the trees. It was as if the young man had never been there.

A thought born of Cade's real father made him shiver. Silly, Harding said to himself, Cade's just a damn fine tracker. He learned that from Black Jack.

"I'm coming out. It's alright."

A minute later, Cade appeared at the edge of the trail. Harding had heard nothing, even when he knew the man was moving toward him.

"What was it, Cade?"

"A he-cat's out there. Smelled our horses." Cade reentered their small encampment in swift strides.

"Where is that son-of-a-devil cat now?" Harding asked, examining the trees for movement.

"He left."

"Well, I suppose if he isn't bothering our horses he can do anything he wants."

"That's what I told him."

Harding stared at Cade. "You didn't learn all that from Black Jack."

"No, I guess not. Just always had an understanding with animals."

"That's the Comanche running through your veins, son."

"Yeah. Probably so."

"Your father would be proud of you."

"I would give a lot to have known him."

"Look in a mirror, son. He's there."

Chapter Twenty-Six

Somewhere outside of San Antonio, the trail of Rice and Manko blended with many headed into the largest city in Texas. The two Deer Creek lawmen rode on, heading into the heart of the prosperous commercial district. San Antonio had definitely rebounded quickly after the War. It had become a fascinating blend of dormered Spanish mansions, adobe tenements from a grand yesteryear and obviously newer structures of wood and brick, northern in style and texture.

Four-story hotels, general stores, saloons, grocery stories offering Eastern delicacies and theaters crowded against distinctive Roman Catholic cathedrals and old missions. An unpredictable San Antonio river wandered through the town, bringing forth cottonwood and cypress trees and past the Mission San Antonio del Valero that had been the site of the first memorable battle for Texas independence from Mexico and now served as a U. S. Army quartermaster depot.

Everywhere they looked, people were busy with their tasks. Aristocratic ranchers and rich merchants mixed with cotton farmers and townspeople, mostly German immigrants and Mexican peasants. Many buildings throughout the city housed officers, troops and supplies. In the distance, the clock tower of the old *cabildo*—town hall building—caught Cade's eye. He was fascinated by its size and couldn't help wondering what Bass thought of it.

This morning, his mind was even more rebellious about the idea of confronting his friend. Maybe there was a reason for Bass's actions that he didn't understand. Maybe he was simply in love with Elizabeth Rice and felt compelled to help her. Cade understood that thought. If Susannah was put in jail, he would do everything and anything to free her. He knew he would. That must be the same with Bass. But why did he run from the roundup camp? Why did he kill Black Jack? The old buffalo hunter was Bass's friend too.

They passed the tiny Chapel of the Miracles and Harding's observation snapped Cade away from his second-guessing.

"That's where folks go to have a miracle happen to them. A sweet idea, isn't it, Cade?" Harding said and quickly added, "You know the crucifix in there came all the way from Spain. Spain? Can you believe that?"

Cade didn't answer. He was intrigued by the network of ditches—*acequias*—meandering through the town. He'd never seen anything like this but remembered Bass talking about it. The ditches carried precious water to irrigate fine residential gardens. They were built long ago by the Franciscan priests who established the missions. He inhaled and shook his head to remove the stench; the ditches also served as a crude sewer system. He told Harding they reminded him of Sil's shirt. Both men laughed.

"That smell reminds me of something else. 'Tis the fine odor of Sheriff Swisher," Harding observed. "When we get back, I plan to tell him that I know he was paid off by Rice and Sil. I'll give him a week to clear out."

"How do you know that?"

"Don't really. But I'll bet 'tis so. Once I tell him I know, he'll tell me."

"You're an old fox."

"'Tis better than being just old." Harding's mouth twisted into a jack-o-lantern smile. "I think my new deputy should run for county sheriff."

"I like being your deputy."

They passed a small, stone-walled, one-story house with a crisp-looking fence encircling the yard. Next to it was a Roman Catholic parish with a big, free-standing bell that called everyone to service—or warned the town of Indian raids, when that used to be a problem. A woman watched from the porch of the stone house. Cade wasn't certain but he sensed someone was watching from one of the windows. Could Bass be hiding there? He thought his friend and Elizabeth Rice would enjoy themselves in that fine hotel he talked about, not some flea-bitten room. Still, planning on Bass doing what he was supposed to do could be dangerous.

Feeling ornery, he waved vigorously in the window's direction. The woman on the porch hesitated and waved back. Jerky motion behind the white curtains in the window followed. Cade chuckled and told Harding what he had done.

"Well, if it was Manko, he'll be worrying about when we'll come to visit." Harding spat and part of it struck the leg of his livery horse.

They rode on into the guts of the bustling town, past stores offering every manner of goods and wares, a wagon-

maker, blacksmith, two liveries, sawmill, hotels, a grain supply store, more saloons than Cade could keep track of, several cathedrals and a great hall that Harding advised had
the biggest ballroom in the world. Every time they passed a
saloon, he pressed to listen to hear a certain voice singing.
So far, he had heard only pianos and a small band.

"What's that place, Emmett?" Cade pointed toward a distinctive bulding where several businessmen were entering.
After a quick spit, Harding said it was the Casino Club, re-
stricted to well-heeled ethnic Germans and U. S. Army officers. It was a center of performing arts and operas and a
place where German was openly spoken—and a lot fancier
and more exclusive than a similar establishment in Deer
Creek.

"Not a place we're likely to be invited to. Neither would
Bass or Missus Rice." Harding grinned. "Unless she can disguise herself as a German businessman."

"I wouldn't put it past her."

Cade envisioned the striking woman and was more and
more convinced that his friend was simply under her spell.
Bass Manko was no murderer. He couldn't be. They had
grown up together. They were blood brothers from a ceremony they had made up. The blood was real, though.

"The sporting district is just southwest of here," Harding
observed with little passion. "You think Bass would go
there? Every kind of whore imaginable. And some are in
fine casinos. Even mansions. Billiards, too." When he realized what he had said, red crept from under his collar and up
his neck.

"I think they'll go to a hotel. A fine one. They won't expect anyone to follow them," Cade said. "What's the best
one?"

"Well, for them I suppose it will be the Hotel Menger. On

the other end of town. Quite the place for rich men—and women too, I suppose." He spat into the street and watched the brown blossom scatter. "What if they aren't there, Cade? Or anywhere around here?"

At that moment, Cade knew he hoped that was the case, that he wouldn't have to face Bass or arrest him—or worse. "Well, I guess he's gotten away then. Or they have."

"Damn, hope they're here."

They moved out of the way of a string of freight wagons loaded with cotton bales and other produce as the coach drivers maneuvered their horses through the crowded street. A squad of arrogant Union soldiers rode past, eying their badges with considerable interest. Two Irish immigrants crossed directly in front of them, talking and waving their arms in energetic conversation and barely cognizant of the two lawmen. On the porch of a hotel, two old men sat in rocking chairs, commenting on the world as they saw it from their privileged position. New management had evidently recently taken over the hotel's operation. A freshly painted "Latshaw Hotel" barely covered the faded "Blue Lodging" signing underneath.

Cade nodded a greeting to the man with a full gray beard wearing faded Confederate pants and kepi cap. Turning toward Harding, he observed that the place was definitely not the kind Bass would be attracted to.

The bearded former Confederate waved back and nudged his companion in thick glasses and a checkered shirt that had seen better days. "Do ya know who them fellers is?"

"Who?" The second oldtimer pushed his glasses against the bridge of his nose and studied the far side of the street.

"Thar, Jimmy. Them lawmen. Right thar, passin' ri't in front o' us. Damn, Jimmy, can't ya see nuthin'?"

"Oh . . . them. Nope, never seed 'em a'fer. Who are they? Ain't Rangers."

"Hell, how would I know, Jimmy? Ya reckon they's lookin' fer somebody?"

They began talking as old men do, about past fights and gunfighters. The former Confederate finally returned to the subject of the passing riders.

"Jimmy, some men jes' look plain dangerous an' they ain't . . . an' some don' look dangerous at all but they is . . . an' then thar's a few that's both. They dun look dangerous—an' I reckon they is, sur as hell."

"Could be, could be. I reckon we gonna see us a war, yessir, a war it be. Too bad tho, t'was a ri't good place to live, weren't it?"

"A mite quiet, Jimmy. A mite quiet."

"Sure as hell ain't gonna be no longer."

In the middle of town, Harding and Cade pulled up in front of the nondescript building with "Marshal" hand-painted over the doorway. They dismounted and tied their horses to the rack. Cade felt strange to be in a big city. It was strange and exciting, yet foreboding when he thought about why they were there.

"Right down the street . . . there, that's the Hotel Menger. I hear it's one fine place." Harding pointed in the direction of a four-story building with a dark blue awning over its massive door. "I'm going to tell the marshal why we're here. Maybe he'll lend us a hand. We've got no jurisdiction here but I'm sure he'll be obliging. You want to go with me? Then we'll head for the hotel." He spat a glorious brown stream that barely missed the hitching rack post.

"No, you go on. Ah, I'll stay here."

As soon as the old lawman entered the San Antonio marshal's office, Cade walked away from the tie rack and went into the lobby of the Hotel Menger.

A gas lamp split the entryway into ragged spaces of dark

and gold. The carpeting was richly patterned and heavy
drapes adorned the front windows. A red-haired clerk with
a narrow mustache, heavily waxed, was behind the lobby
desk.

"I'm looking for two old friends. Checked in yesterday, I
think. He's yellow-haired—and she's quite a looker. He can
sing up a storm. You might want to hire him for your saloon."

"Yeah, sure, they're in twenty-three. Well, she's not there
now. Saw her go out earlier. That's one good-looking lady.
Guess he's sleepin' in. Probably worn out, if you know what
I mean." He winked and glanced up the stairs like a deer
drinking at a stream. "Oh yeah, I hear he's singing tonight
at the Painted Stallion." He arched his eyebrows as high as
they would go.

"Thanks. I'll go see if he's interested in getting something
to eat."

Cade said nothing more and moved up the stairs. He
knocked hard on the door with a painted "23" and said,
"Bass, this is Cade. I want to talk. No shooting. You have
my word."

Silence, then a raspy, familiar voice.

"What the hell are you doing here, Cade? Go away. I'm
tryin' to get some sleep. I'm singing tonight. Big night."

"No, Bass, this can't wait. We can do this easy or we can
do it hard but I'm coming in to see you," Cade returned the
challenge.

"Are you here as my friend, or are you wearing Harding's
star?"

"I'm in town as a deputy for Deer Creek—but I'm here as
your friend."

"That's a long way from meaning anything, Cade."

Movement was followed by silence. It seemed longer

than the minute it was. Then came a short rattle at the lock. The door swung open. Inside, it was dark. No further sound was heard. Nothing moved within the room. A chuckle crossed the tense space, followed by Bass singing.

" 'Well I had myself a dream the other night,
When everything was still.
I dreamed that I saw my girl Susannah,
She was coming around the hill.
Now, the buckwheat cake was in her mouth,
A tear was in her eye . . .' "

He stopped suddenly. "Cade, either come in or go home where you belong. I don't like being jerked around by some lawdog away from his roost. Especially by someone who used to be my friend. I'll make an exception this one time—for you."

Cade took a shallow breath when he wanted more, inhaling to gather in all the courage loose in the hallway. He stepped into the terrifying void. As he entered, he moved instinctively to his right, against the wall. He didn't remember drawing his pistol but it was cocked in his right hand.

"Hell's teeth, Deputy Branson, you've got one ugly way of sayin' 'Good Afternoon,' " Bass said. A toothy grin followed. His blond hair brushed against his bare shoulders as he spoke. He sat cross-legged on the bed without boots. His revolver was pointed at Cade's stomach. His shirt was on a nearby chair that also held twin silver-studded gunbelts with empty holsters.

In the far corner were saddlebags, a canteen, a trail-stained duster and his black hat. No signs of a woman were anywhere in the room. As Cade's eyes became comfortable with the dark confinement, he could see a bottle of Irish whiskey and another pearl-handled pistol laying on a night table beside the headboard.

"I reckon it was a bit showy," replied Cade, grinning. "Where's Missus Rice?"

"Missus Rice? Oh, you mean Elizabeth. She got herself all purtied up and went shopping. You know women—well, maybe you don't."

Cade holstered his pistol and Bass responded by laying his weapon on the bed. There was a look in his friend's eyes that wasn't totally sane, Cade thought. He'd seen that look before. Without hesitation, Bass began reminiscing about their childhood days together.

Soon Cade couldn't resist and joined in, laughing as he did. Their talk was easy with no mention of the killings, robberies and land grab scheme that separated them.

Scratching his hair, Bass looked down at the floor and said, "Susannah Harding, now that was some fine-lookin' gal, wasn't she? I remember you trying to peek down her blouse a time or two, when you didn't think I was watching. Nothin' like Elizabeth, mind you, but what woman is?" He glanced up at Cade. "Did you know she was waiting in the bank—with a gun? And a goddamn badge? Ugly stuff, Cade. Everybody else had a gun too. Who would'a thought that ol' lawdog Harding was that savvy."

"Yeah, I heard," Cade said. "I also heard Missus Rice was dressed to make it look like you were holding up the bank."

Bass ignored Cade's remark. "Guess with me out of the way Dish is a lucky man. How about you? Some sweet-smelling lady gonna tie you down one of these days?"

"Not many women want to get hitched to a man with a gun," Cade said and the words bit hard coming out.

"Well, what brings you here, lawman? Got a feeling it wasn't to chat about old times," Bass said, glanced at the closet, blinked and returned his gaze to Cade.

"Wish it were but there isn't time," Cade said in a flat, but firm, voice. "I came to give you a chance to get out of here, out of town—before Marshal Harding and the local law come."

"Why would you be doing that, Cade?"

"Bass, I should be arresting you right now for murder— but I can't. I'll tell the marshal you were already gone when I got here."

"That's mighty nice of you. All right. How about one quick drink for old time's sake." Bass smiled and turned toward the table. His hand moved casually toward the whiskey bottle but grabbed the pistol on the table instead. Behind him, he heard the ominous cock of Cade's redrawn pistol.

"No, thanks," Cade said. "Either way."

Bass laughed and lifted his hand away from the pistol and poured himself a drink. "You've got sand, Cade, but you always did. I could've killed you when you came through that door."

"You could've tried."

The nearly empty room seemed smaller than when he first entered. Wobbly shadows watched from every corner. Cade sensed Bass considered reaching again for his gun. A flicker in his eyes. A wildness Cade had seen before, long ago. Bass's inclination passed as quickly as it came.

"You forget I saved your bacon, back when we were always fightin' somebody, anybody," Bass said.

"No, I'll never forget that, Bass. That's why I came to ask you to leave—as an old friend, instead of the peace officer I'm supposed to be."

"We were more than friends, Cade, we were blood brothers, remember?"

"Of course I remember."

"You want me to tell you I'm innocent of all that stuff you rattled off?"

"No. I know you aren't. Friends don't lie to friends. I know you killed Henry Endore—and Black Jack. I know about the plot to take over the ranches. I guess, though, I don't know you."

Bass studied Cade as he swallowed his drink. "Reckon this'll make you a big man around Deer Creek, won't it? Cade Branson made Bass Manko cut and run."

"More likely the town council will question why I didn't do my duty and shoot you when I had the chance," Cade responded. A small grin at the corner of his mouth followed the thought. "My only excuse is you weren't here—or weren't you listening?"

Bass started to say something, paused and chuckled. So did Cade, out of habit more than anything else. The outlaw spotted the bottle of Irish whiskey again. Leaning over to pick it up, his back turned to Cade. Was that an accident or was he testing him, Cade wondered.

Without turning around, Bass said, "You know, I almost told you what we were doing."

"What did you think I'd do?"

"Join us. Hell's teeth, we would've owned the whole damn state before we were through, Cade." He stood up and turned toward Cade. "Can you imagine that? We'd have been kings."

"Come on, Bass, they'll be coming soon. There isn't much time."

"So where do you want me to go? I haven't had supper yet an' Elizabeth's got our money. Her money. But I grabbed it from her desk before I, ah, helped her leave town." He chuckled and licked his lower lip with his tongue. "Say, how's Roper? I didn't mean to hurt him—but the damn fool was gonna try to shoot me."

"Susannah said Roper will be fine. We didn't see him for ourselves."

"Had to get right after us, huh? Should'a known you'd come."

"You and I talked about coming to San Antonio—after the roundup, remember?"

"Oh yeah," Bass said. "Did I ever tell you about the last time I was here in this hotel? Same room too. Me an' a black-haired gal. Whoa, could she make a man feel good!"

Cade said nothing, stepping back to look out down the hallway. Satisfied it was empty, he returned to the room. "We'll go out that back stairway. You can stay out of sight until you get to the livery. Hopefully, no one will be waiting." He reached into his pocket and withdrew some folded certificates. "Here, this'll pay for the stabling or a new horse. You'd better head for the border."

"You think of everything, don't you?"

"No. I didn't think you would become an outlaw."

The room shrank with tension.

It was Bass who broke the crawling closeness of the room by walking to the lone window. A faded purple curtain of indeterminable material was pulled aside to view the dusk-laden street below. His gaze took in the marshal's office down the street. There were no signs of activity.

"Just wish I could say goodbye to Elizabeth before I go. I love her, you know. What about letting her go with me?"

"No. She's got to stay and stand trial for murder and a lot of other things. I'm only interested in your leaving here," Cade said, growing impatient. "Besides, she isn't here— and you don't have time to wait for her. Get your boots on."

"You're a cold man, Cade Branson. I should've remembered that. How'd ya know I was here?"

Cade breathed deeply to relieve the emotions slugging at his insides and answered, "You told me it was a place you liked. It was worth a try. I was going to check the saloons next—for somebody singing pretty."

Bass chuckled, "Should'a figured. Mighty fine, it's good to see you, Cade. I'm sorry it came out this way. I really am, Cade. I didn't figure on seeing you again." He glanced at the gunbelts. "Can I go carryin'?"

"Yes, I guess so."

"You know I'm better than you with a gun."

"You've said that."

"Hey, but who's asking? I thank you, Cade. I really do. You're a good friend."

"I was. The next time I see you, we'll settle things about Black Jack."

"You wouldn't like the outcome, Cade—and you know it."

Cade shook his head and stepped outside into the hallway. His hurried glance both ways assured him no one was yet coming. Bass joined him with his gunbelts in his left hand. Holstered revolvers dangled from his fist, bouncing together as they walked. Neither man spoke as they went down the darkened corridor toward a back stairway that led to an alley doorway. Bass was a stride ahead. Even the gas lamp seemed uncertain and flickered timidly.

"There's a mean draft in here somewhere," Cade said as a cold streak slid across his cheek.

"Who's asking? I don't feel nothin'."

Twenty feet from the stairway, Cade heard footsteps coming up the steps. In one motion, Bass spun toward him, drawing a pistol from the gunbelts in his arms and threw them toward Cade.

"No, Bass!" Cade cried out, too late to stop the madness. His own gun was already in his hand.

Orange and blue flame exploded from Bass's gun and the bullet caught Cade's side as he threw himself down, firing as he dove.

Hurriedly, Bass fired twice more. Dust popped from Cade's shirt with their impact.

From the floor, Cade emptied his gun into him, his shots coming so rapidly they were one long bellow.

Bass hit the hallway wall and slid toward the floor, ending in a grotesque sitting position with his head resting on his bloody chest. Slowly, his head rose with blood gushing from his mouth. "I-I'm s-sorry . . . Cade. You w-were my only . . . f-friend."

His eyes slid upward and his head dropped again to his chest.

Cade pushed himself to one knee, unaware of the widening crimson blossom on his own shirt, the shock of his wounds not yet to his brain. He spun to meet the footsteps behind him.

From the stairway came a horrendous shriek. Wild-eyed and livid, Elizabeth Rice ran at the unseeing Bass. Her porcelain face was painted with the fear and the strain of being on the run. Her crimson dress struggled to cover her bosom where one button had been forgotten after a hurried tryst with a businessman she had met the day before. They were discussing the purchase of a whore house she had admired.

Elizabeth's face was cracking with hatred. She tried to inhale but no air would join her. She crumpled to the ground in a choking sob and pulled Bass Manko's unseeing face to hers.

Cade looked away, feeling weak. His eyes weren't focusing well. Gathering himself, he stumbled, then stood, losing his balance again and almost falling. He staggered over to Bass; his fingers closed the lids of unseeing eyes.

"Y-You were my only real brother."

The hallway began to swim as he turned and staggered away. He was unaware of the roar of a shotgun from the top of the back stairs. Behind him, Elizabeth's gun bucked skyward and fired, raining down pieces of the ceiling as she slammed backwards against the wall. Her gun flew into the air with a life of its own.

"M-Mother . . . w-where are you?" Elizabeth's curse was more like a wounded animal wimpering than a human crying. Her face was the same color as her dress. She gave a great heaving sob and dropped her head to her chest.

At the top of the stairs, Marshal Harding dropped his smoking shotgun and hurried toward Cade. The young gunfighter was down, his face and body against the hallway carpet. The fibers under him were transforming into dark red. An empty pistol lay beside him.

"You can't leave me, son. Cade! Cade! Look at me. Susannah's waiting for you."

Cade's eyes fluttered open. His hand reached for Harding's and squeezed it weakly. "I-I was g-going to let him go. I couldn't . . ."

"I know, son. Rest easy now. It's all over." Harding opened Cade's bloody shirt to examine the wounds. None had hit vital areas that he saw but Cade had lost a lot of blood.

"E-Emmett . . . is it snowing?"

"Oh my God, hang on, son. Hang on!" His concern echoed down the hallway.

Cade closed his eyes and tried to smile. "I'll make it, Marshal. My father . . . just reminded me . . . that I'm a Comanche warrior. I'm the son . . . of Winter Kill, you know."

Harding smiled. "Aye, an' you be tellin' him you're going to be the next county sheriff too. After you marry my Sissy."

SONS OF THUNDER
COTTON SMITH

No one in the small Texas town of Clark Springs knows that their minister's real name is Rule Cordell, or that he used to be one of the most notorious outlaws the Confederacy had ever seen. He's been trying very hard to put his days as a pistol-fighter behind him, but that's getting harder to do lately. When his friends and neighbors are threatened with losing their family spreads to a cunning carpetbagger, Rule realizes it's time for his preacher's collar to be replaced by a pair of .44s. But he won't be able to do it alone. If he's going to rid the town of this ruthless evil, he'll need to call on a very special group of warriors—the Sons of Thunder!
